2050

EXODUS

BOOK 2

BY
PHIL M. WILLIAMS

Printed in the United States of America.
First Printing, 2020.

Phil W Books.
www.PhilWBooks.com

ISBN: 978-1-943894-57-4

Cover design by Tugboat Design

TABLE OF CONTENTS

A NOTE FROM PHIL

Dear Reader,

   If you're interested in receiving my novel *Against the Grain* for free and/or reading many of my other titles for free or discounted, go to the following link: http://www.PhilWBooks.com.

   You're probably thinking, *What's the catch?* There is no catch.

Sincerely,
Phil M. Williams

1

DEREK'S DEPARTURE

Derek woke abruptly, crying out to the dead in his dream. His heart pounded, as he tried to orient himself in the dim light. He touched the trunk of the coconut tree next to him, remembering how he swam to this little islet to escape the Netas.

Derek stood from the sand, brushing off his fatigues and his T-shirt. He stepped onto the beach, instantly struck by the bright beauty of the moon and stars. His boots and socks were on the beach, drying, obscured by a large piece of driftwood. He slipped on his socks and laced up his boots. Derek knew he couldn't stay in San Juan. He needed to take refuge in the jungle.

Needing energy for the journey, he walked back to the coconut grove. Using his knife, he cut open a few more coconuts, drinking the milk and eating some of the meat. He stopped by the mango tree too, gorging himself on ripe mangoes, not knowing when he'd eat again.

He walked south, temporarily back toward San Juan, palm trees rustling in the breeze. His knife was attached to the scabbard on his belt, and he carried the scuba mask and snorkel. The islet was narrow and only four hundred yards from tip to toe. At the south end, old concrete pillars marked what was left of the bridge that once connected the islet to the mainland. Derek put on his mask and snorkel and dove into the dark water. He swam the one hundred yards back to San Juan.

Once ashore, he walked west along the beach at a brisk pace, his boots and socks sloshing with each step. The beach didn't provide much cover, but he cared more about speed than stealth. From his scavenging trips, he'd learned that the few hours before daybreak were the best times to travel. The early risers weren't up yet, and those who hunted and scavenged at night were finally asleep.

Derek walked alongside what was left of an upscale neighborhood, the houses long since flooded and blown away, where only the sturdiest of concrete homes remained. Beyond the waterfront neighborhood, he passed a commercial district with massive rusty fuel tanks, the precious juice probably siphoned long ago. After about a mile walk, he came to the mouth of a river. Caiman eyes glistened in the moonlight, but they were tucked into the river, away from the ocean. *They must not like the salt water.*

The river's mouth was only fifty yards across. Derek put on his mask again, took a deep breath, and dove into the water. He swam freestyle, as fast as he could, trying to stay close to the ocean, his heart pounding in anticipation of a caiman attack. When he emerged, he ran for a few minutes, eager to vacate their territory.

A putrid smell cut through the sea air, slowing his run to a walk. It was a vicious cocktail that smelled like a mixture of feces, rotten eggs, rotting cabbage, and mothballs. A body lay on the beach up ahead. Derek approached cautiously. It was bloated, the flesh alive with maggots. He lifted his wet T-shirt, covered his mouth and nose and took a wide berth around the dead body. Derek recognized the blue prison uniform and now he recognized the beach. It was the same beach he'd been dropped on two weeks ago.

That can't be right. Derek thought for a moment. It felt like he'd been on the island for years, but it had only been two weeks. Up ahead were more bloated bodies in blue uniforms. *They must've been killed by the Aryans during the roundup.* Derek remembered that nearly every week IPC—Island Prison Corrections—left fresh meat on the beach.

The Aryans had collected their slaves, but the Race Wars, Sunday's gladiator games, were canceled because of the hurricane. Or at least that's what Derek had presumed.

From the river, he walked two miles on the beach, still heading west, the island still asleep. From there, he crossed a small stretch of jungle and walked another two miles on the beach. The farther he walked, the fewer remnants of civilization he saw. Now when he looked away from the ocean, all he saw was dense jungle. Daybreak was coming.

I need to get off this beach. I'm exposed. Derek looked at the jungle. *But what or who will I find in there?*

2

JACOB AND THE FIRST ESCAPED CON

As far as anyone knew, Summer was the first person to ever escape from one of the US island prisons. A few men had escaped the Chinese island prison in the South Pacific, but that was an inside job. A handful of Chinese naval officers had been involved, paid off by the prisoners' wealthy families. The officers were subsequently sentenced to life on the South Pacific island prison, and every rescued prisoner was found and returned.

But Summer had done it without insider help. Her group of inmates had built a DIY submarine, and she'd piloted it immediately after a hurricane, while the naval blockade was out of the area. At least, that's what she'd told them when she'd washed up on the beach. According to her, the submarine was at the bottom of the ocean. She'd had to break the plexiglass to escape the cockpit, causing the sub to fill with seawater and the added weight pulled the pontoons and the sub into the oceanic depths.

Cesar and the men of Project Freedom had taken Summer to their earth-sheltered bunker. When she'd been introduced to Jacob, she'd stared at him, as if she knew him, but Jacob had never met Summer before. She'd been given a room, access to a shower, fresh clothes, and an MRE of spaghetti and meatballs. After Summer's meal

4

and shower, they had planned to interview her, but she'd fallen asleep in her room, obviously exhausted. Everyone had been chomping at the bit to question her, especially Rebecca, but nobody had the heart to wake her after her ordeal.

The next morning, Jacob, Rebecca, Cesar, the two mercenaries, and a few of Cesar's men sat around a table, eating breakfast. Most ate cereal in reconstituted milk. When Summer walked into the mess hall, all conversations stopped. Summer wore clean fatigues and a T-shirt that was too big. Her wavy brown hair was cut above her ears and uneven. Despite the clothes and the haircut, her beauty was undeniable. She had sea-blue eyes, with a round symmetrical face and beautiful ivory skin, despite being a bit sunburned.

"Good morning. Are you hungry?" Cesar asked with a smile.

She smiled back sheepishly, and nodded.

"We have cereal."

"That would be great. Thank you, Cesar."

Cesar instructed one of his men to bring her breakfast. He pulled out a chair next to him and said, "Please, sit."

Summer sat next to Cesar and across from Rebecca and Jacob at the table.

Cesar made eye contact with Summer and said, "After breakfast, I'd like to interview you about yesterday's events and your time on the island. Would that be okay?"

Summer nodded again. "That would be fine." One of Cesar's men placed Summer's cereal and a glass of water in front of her.

"We also have coffee, if you prefer."

"No, thank you. I'm not sure I can take the caffeine."

As Summer ate her cereal, Rebecca asked, "Did you know anyone on the island named Derek Reeves?"

Summer swallowed and replied, "I knew a Derek, but I didn't know his last name."

"He's average height. Dark wavy hair. A beard. Tan skin."

"That's a lot of men on the island." Summer paused for an instant.

"The one I knew supposedly killed some Chinese banker for killing his girlfriend."

Rebecca's eyes bulged. "That's him!"

"That can't be," Jacob said, shaking his head.

"We came in on the same prison ship," Summer said. "I met him on the beach—"

"This should probably wait until Cesar's had a chance to interview her."

Rebecca glared at her husband. "Don't interrupt her. She knew Derek. This is why we're here."

"It's Cesar's show, not ours." Jacob looked across the table at Cesar for back up, but he was stone-faced.

"Not for the money we're paying him. You think I don't know about your metal suitcase?"

Jacob pursed his lips but didn't respond.

Rebecca addressed Cesar. "Do you mind if I talk to Summer?"

"By all means, Mrs. Roth," Cesar replied.

Jacob gritted his teeth and clenched his fists under the table.

"I'm sorry. Please continue," Rebecca said to Summer.

"I met him on the beach," Summer said. "He was roommates on the boat with my fiancé."

"Your fiancé was on the prison ship too?"

Summer swallowed hard. "I'd rather not talk about him."

Rebecca nodded. "I understand."

"Derek and I were taken by the Aryans. They gather up all the new prisoners and sell them like slaves. I was lucky. I was purchased by a group called 1776. They were really good people."

Rebecca arched her eyebrows. "*Were*?"

"They're all dead now." Summer looked down.

"I'm sorry for your loss," Cesar interjected.

"I'm so sorry," Rebecca echoed.

Summer raised her gaze back to Rebecca. "Was Derek your brother?"

"Ex-husband."

"We ended up in the same group."

"You said everyone in the group is dead." Rebecca's voice trembled.

"When I left, myself and Derek and Fred were the only ones left."

Rebecca breathed a sigh of relief. "So, he's alive?"

"I don't know. Derek and Fred helped launch me in the submarine. I thought Fred was gonna pilot the sub, but …" Summer shook her head. "He wanted to stay with his family." She took a deep breath. "I thought Derek and I could fit together in the sub, but it was too small, and Fred wasn't sure there would be enough power with the extra weight. So, I left, but before I did, the Netas were shooting at us. I don't know what happened to Fred and Derek, but I think they might've been killed by the Netas."

Rebecca leaned forward, like a dog eager for a treat. "But you don't know for sure?"

Summer shook her head again. "I don't."

"Who are the Netas?" Jacob asked.

"They're a Puerto Rican gang who never evacuated. When the hurricanes came, they looted the island. They took all the leftover military stuff."

"We have drone footage of Derek dead. Would you look at it?" Rebecca asked.

"Sure," Summer replied.

Jacob coughed, nearly choking on his cereal. He cleared his throat and said, "Don't you think she's been through enough?"

"I'd like to help."

"It's not necessary. The drone footage is definitive proof." Jacob gestured to the escaped convict. "Summer herself said that he was likely killed by the Netas."

Rebecca shook her head. "Summer said he *might've* been killed by the Netas. And this drone footage doesn't add up. Derek was alive yesterday morning, the same time that the drone supposedly found him dead. What are the chances?"

Jacob replied, "What are the chances that we find the first person *ever* to escape the island prison *and* that she knew Derek?"

3

SUMMER AND THE ROTHS

Summer sat across from Cesar at his desk. He was clean-shaven, his face boyish, his dark hair parted to the side, yet he had a presence that his employees responded to.

"What is it that you do here?" Summer asked, her hands folded in her lap.

"We're in the import-export business, and we do a bit of location and recovery," Cesar replied, his hands steepled on the desktop.

"What do you mean by *location and recovery*?"

"We help families of island prisoners find their loved ones."

"That's why the Roths are here."

"Precisely," Cesar said. "We rescued you, didn't we?"

Summer nodded. "I'm very grateful."

"I'm sure you are, and I'm sure you can't pay us back."

Summer swallowed, her stomach tumbling. "No."

"There is a way." Cesar smiled. "First, I'd like for you to tell me about the flash drive."

"You went through my stuff?"

"Forgive me. This is a secure facility, and we don't know you." Cesar leaned forward, his elbows now on the desktop. "Do you know what's on the flash drive?"

"You didn't look at it?"

"My men simply checked for anything that could be dangerous. A flash drive is only dangerous if you open it."

"It's footage from the island. It supposedly proves that the US government is sending activists there. I'm supposed to take it to Panama."

"Ah, Silver City."

Summer's eyes widened. "How did you know?"

"Silver City has the largest agorist community in the world. It's a poorly kept secret."

"Can you help me get there?" Summer asked, excitement in her voice.

Cesar pressed his lips together, silent for a few seconds. "If you can help me, I can help you."

Summer's expression darkened. "I can't give you the flash drive."

"Of course not. But I'd like to watch it and possibly make a copy, if it's something I might find useful."

"What would you need it for?"

"Information is power, but proof of the information is *more* powerful." Cesar opened his laptop and turned the screen toward Summer. He walked around his desk, next to Summer, and held out his hand. "The flash drive."

Summer hesitated, wondering if she should trust him. Then she removed the flash drive from her pocket and placed it in Cesar's open palm. He inserted the flash drive into his laptop and sat in the plastic chair next to Summer. They watched Roger Kroenig, the former congressman, with the Spanish fort at his back.

He looked so young compared to the man Summer had met after his six-year incarceration on Psycho Island. His hair was brown at the time this video was made, and his face hadn't been ravaged with wrinkles and sun damage. The stress of Psycho Island unnaturally sped the aging process.

Tears formed at the corners of her eyes as Roger told his story about how he was snatched from his home in the middle of the night and declared an unlawful enemy combatant, a UEC. From there, he was quickly given the Antisocial Personality Test, declared a sociopath, and shipped to the island, all with the efficiency of Amazon Prime delivery.

Other activists gave their full names, sent messages of love to their wives and children, and told their arrest and sentencing stories, which were all nearly identical to Roger's.

Summer had to look away when they showed footage of the gladiator games run by the Aryans. There was also video of gang warfare and the Netas with their weapons and military vehicles. The video showed dead bodies and brutality and pure unadulterated evil. Roger had stated the facts in the interviews. However, he'd videoed the brutality because he wanted the world to see, but, more important, he wanted the world to *feel*. Ever the brilliant politician, even incarcerated on an island hellhole, Roger knew that appealing to human emotions was the most powerful form of persuasion.

At the end of the video, Cesar said straight-faced, "Do you mind if I make a copy?"

Summer was in a trance, reliving her own personal hell.

"Ms. Fitzgerald? Are you okay?"

Summer blinked, a tear spilling down her face. She wiped her eyes with her thumb and index finger. "I'm fine."

"Do you mind if I make a copy?"

"Go ahead."

Cesar copied the video and handed the flash drive back to Summer.

"Is that it?" Summer asked, replacing the flash drive in her pocket.

"One more thing. The footage that Mrs. Roth asked you to watch of Derek Reeves …"

"What about it?"

"I want you to tell her that it *is* Derek, and it looks authentic."

Summer crossed her arms over her chest and glowered at Cesar. "It's not authentic, is it?"

"The Roths need closure. If you can help me give that to them, I'm sure we can send you to Panama with some new clothes and money in your pocket."

* * *

Summer sat in the command center, watching footage of another tropical wasteland. Rebecca and Jacob stood behind her, watching over her shoulder. Cesar sat next to her at the metal desk.

She saw thin men and women wearing rags, even a few children. She saw men with machetes and shotguns. But she also saw people farming and hunting and trading. And she didn't recognize anything that looked familiar. If Derek was shot and killed by the Netas, the killing likely would've occurred in front of the old Spanish fort. The dead man did, indeed, look like Derek, but his body was nowhere near the fort. In fact, it was in a place she'd never seen before.

At the end of the video, Cesar said, "What do you think, Ms. Fitzgerald?"

Summer turned in her chair, looking up at Rebecca. "May I talk to you alone?"

"I won't allow it," Jacob said, crossing his arms over his chest.

"It's not your choice," Rebecca replied through gritted teeth.

"I'm *paying* for this operation."

"I don't give a shit. I'll speak to whomever I damn well please."

Summer had wondered about the Roths. Jacob had to be wealthy. He was short and thin, with a small paunch. He looked to be about fifty. And Rebecca looked like the prototypical trophy wife. *Why does she care so much about Derek, her ex-husband?*

Summer stood from her seat. "We can talk in my room, if you want?"

"That's a great idea," Rebecca replied.

The two ladies left the command center, leaving the men speechless. Summer's little room was only a few doors down from the command center. Rebecca entered the room and shut the door behind them. Rebecca was naturally pretty, with high cheekbones and bright brown eyes. She was likely improved with a perfect thin nose, pouty collagen lips, and perky breast implants. If it wasn't for Summer's work as a nurse, she might not have noticed the improvements. They were very well-done.

"What did you see?" Rebecca asked.

"I need to get to Panama," Summer said. "If I tell you what I saw, can you help me?"

"Yes. Of course."

"Cesar asked me to tell you that it's Derek in the video."

Rebecca cocked her head in confusion. "Why would he do that?" Then her eyes widened. "Unless … this is all bullshit."

4

DEREK AND WELCOME TO THE JUNGLE

The jungle canopy was thick, only allowing sporadic sunlight to filter through. Derek followed a small game trail, hoping to find an abandoned home, secluded from the psychopaths who occupied the island prison. The jungle smelled sweet and rotten at the same time, the humidity thick and stifling. It was slow going as Derek ducked under thick vines and stepped over fallen logs and limbs.

A twig snapped, stopping Derek in his tracks. Birds chirped and sang. Tiny creatures scurried on the leaf litter. He slapped his neck, killing a mosquito gorging on his blood. Then he heard the rustling of branches. Something or *someone* large moved down the trail. Then footsteps. Heavy footsteps. Coming from both directions on the game trail. Derek stepped off the trail, looking for a place to hide, but it was too late.

Shouting in Spanish pierced the air. Birds flew from their perches. Derek ran through the thick jungle, dodging tree roots, vines, and branches, not seeing more than ten feet in front of him. More footfalls were behind him, crashing through the jungle. More shouting in Spanish.

Derek increased his speed, his adrenaline pumping. He glanced back for a split-second. That's when he crashed through the jungle edge, the sun suddenly bright overhead, Derek's momentum carrying him into a fast-moving river. He was turned and flipped in the white-water as he was carried downstream. Derek gasped for breath, whenever his head popped above the water. He was twisted and turned again, his head crashing into a rock. Everything went black.

5

JACOB AND SMUGGLERS AND CON MEN

"What did you expect? They're smugglers and con men," Jacob said, standing in their bunker bedroom.

"I expected you to make sure they did their job," Rebecca said. "You're skeptical about everything, but you were perfectly happy to believe their bullshit because you don't give a shit about Derek."

Jacob threw up his hands in frustration. "Of course I don't give a shit about Derek! He's *your* ex-husband. Why *should* I care?"

"Because *I* care. Because *Lindsey* cares. Or are you too damn selfish to see past your own insecurities?"

"Insecurities?" Jacob sneered at his wife. "This doesn't have anything to do with insecurities. This has to do with time and money. We're wasting valuable time and money on him. Time and money that I'm not devoting to you and Lindsey and Ethan and David."

Rebecca spoke softer now. "What kind of example are we setting if we don't help him?"

Jacob blew out a heavy breath. "What do you want me to do?"

"Summer knows how to rescue him. I want you to sit down with Summer and hear her out. Then I want you to work with Cesar to come up with a plan."

Jacob drew back, his forehead creased. "He lied. You still want to work with him?"

"He's the only person I know with a base close to Puerto Rico and a submarine. What other choice do we have?" She held out her hands.

"I don't know."

"You're one of the most powerful men in the world. I'm sure you can keep him honest. Be the hero, Jacob. For me." Rebecca placed her hand over her chest.

6

SUMMER AND THE REAL RESCUE

"I assure you, Mrs. Roth, the video is no fake," Cesar said. "It's possible that the facial recognition software falsely identified the person as Derek. It's also possible that Derek is, in fact, the man in the video."

Summer, Cesar, the Roths, and the two mercenaries sat at a round table in Cesar's office.

Rebeca narrowed her eyes at Cesar. "Based on Summer's eyewitness account, I think we should assume that it was a false identification."

"As you wish, Mrs. Roth," Cesar replied.

"We have the only person ever to escape from the island right here." Rebecca gestured to Summer. "This is a huge advantage. She knows where Derek is and how to rescue him."

"We're listening," Jacob said, eyeing Summer.

"When there's a hurricane, the naval blockade moves out until the weather clears," Summer said. "When this happens, you can pilot a submarine to the island, rescue Derek, and make it back before the blockade returns. You can't use boats or planes because they'll be caught on satellite and destroyed by the drones. After a hurricane, the drones return much faster than the blockade."

"We're already aware of this fact, and I'm afraid it's not that simple," Cesar said. "You're assuming Derek is exactly where you think he'll be. You're assuming that it won't take long to locate him. Even if he's alive, he's probably moved on from San Juan. Your group is dead. Why would he stay where gangs are hunting him? If I were him, I'd hide in the jungle."

Rebecca surveyed the group, her expression serious. "Then we go and find him."

"We will," Rob said, reassuring Rebecca. He was one of two mercenaries—former SEALs providing security for the Roths. "Once a hurricane clears out the navy, we can go to the island and launch drones with facial recognition software. We can program them to start where Summer last saw Derek and work outward in concentric circles. We'll need small stealth drones to avoid detection, and we'll have to launch these from Puerto Rico. They don't have the range to make it from here. Once the drones find Derek, we'll go there on foot, rescue him, and bring him back to the sub. Then we have to hope we have another hurricane so we can get back." He turned to Cesar and asked, "Is your submarine diesel electric?"

"Hydrogen fuel cell," Cesar replied.

"Good. With AIP, we can stay submerged for weeks."

"Up to two months."

Billy, the other former SEAL on the Roths' payroll, let out a low whistle. "*Whew-wee*. You boys are big-time."

"What's AIP?" Jacob asked.

"Air-independent propulsion," Rob replied, stroking his blond beard. "Otherwise we could only stay submerged for a few days, but, with a big-enough fuel cell, we don't have to worry about surfacing and becoming a target for the drones."

"What are you thinkin' for comms?" Billy asked Rob.

"A local encrypted Wi-Fi mesh network. I have a source for the communications equipment and the drones, but we'll need to move quickly. Hurricane season is almost over."

"Man." Billy slapped the table with his palms. "This is dangerous work. Ain't gonna be cheap. Sounds like we need to renegotiate."

"Cesar didn't seem to have any problems with his drones being shot down to find Derek the first time. Why do we need stealth drones?" Rebecca asked, glowering at Cesar.

"Rebecca." Jacob shook his head at his wife.

"Unless," Rebecca said, leaning closer to Cesar, "your drones were never in any danger since they were never in Puerto Rico to begin with."

Billy cackled and said, "*Whew-wee*. The lady makes a helluva point."

"He's right," Cesar said, nodding to Billy. "This mission won't be cheap."

7

NAOMI AND BACK TO LIFE

Naomi's left eye fluttered and opened, the light causing her to shut it again. Something covered her other eye. She opened her left eye again, disoriented. She lay in a hospital bed, hooked to IVs. Bandages covered her chest. Her back ached as she lightly touched the bandage on her head and over her right eye and the right side of her face. Her head throbbed just behind her right eye socket. Her chest and cheek burned. The shades were drawn, light filtering in at the edges. Vernon slept on the couch against the wall, his button-down rumpled, his shirttails out, and his tie on the floor with his shoes.

"Vernon?" Naomi said, her voice raspy. "Vernon?"

He stirred and sat up, gazing at Naomi in the dim light. "You're awake. I'll call the doctor." Vernon ran from the room in his stocking feet, leaving Naomi alone.

A minute later, the overhead lights turned on, not bright, yet forcing Naomi to close her eye again. She adjusted to the increased light and saw a nurse, with Vernon standing in the background.

"How are you feeling, Naomi?" the female nurse asked.

"What happened?" Naomi asked.

"You were in an accident." The nurse checked her IV and looked over her bandages and vital signs.

"I'm in a lot of pain."

The nurse placed a controller attached to the IV in Naomi's hand. "This button will add more painkillers to your IV. Don't go crazy with it, but go ahead and press it twice."

Naomi pressed the button twice.

A white-haired doctor entered the room and said, "Good morning, Mrs. Sutton. How are you feeling?"

"My back hurts. I have a massive headache behind my right eye socket. My chest burns and my right cheek too. What happened to me?"

"You were in an accident two days ago. Your car exploded, throwing you back against your home. That's why your back aches. They're just contusions though. I expect the back pain to dissipate in a week or two. You were also hit with shrapnel from the blast, and you were burned on your chest and the right side of your face."

"How bad is it?"

"You've sustained second-degree burns. The good news is, these burns will heal in two to three weeks, but the bad news is, they'll hurt in the meantime, and you'll likely have some scarring, but plastic surgeons can minimize the scarring with laser cosmetic surgery." The doctor cleared his throat. "Unfortunately, a piece of metal from the blast hit your right eye, and we had to enucleate your eye."

Naomi felt nauseated. "What do you mean by *enucleate*?"

"We had to remove your eye. We may have to do an additional minor surgery so we can fit you with a glass eye. They can match it perfectly with your left eye."

Then it all came back to her. The fight she'd had with Alan. He knew she'd been having an affair with Vernon. He'd left in a huff that morning, vowing to take the car by himself. She'd chased after him, but he'd beat her to the car. Then the explosion. She looked to Vernon, her eye wide open. "Where's Alan?"

Vernon dipped his head and said, "He's dead."

21

8

DEREK AND BO

Derek woke, his eyes fluttering and his head pounding. He lay on a bed of straw. Overhead was a thatch roof. Derek touched his aching head. It was partially covered with a very large leaf, tied on with lashing. He groaned and tried to sit up, but a wave of nausea forced him back down. His eyes darted around, searching his surroundings. He was in a circular mud-brick hut. Bamboo shelving held various fruits and herbs and plastic bottles and containers. Pots and pans and knives hung from rusty nails. A single opening in the shape of a door let in the only light. The opening was covered with mosquito netting. Footsteps approached. A man entered the hut with a basketful of mangoes. He wore raggedy shorts, a T-shirt, no shoes, and a sheathed knife hanging from his neck. The man set the basket on a bamboo shelf. Derek tried to sit up again.

The man knelt next to Derek and placed a hand on his chest. "Hold on, hoss. Lay back down. You ain't ready for that."

Derek lay back down. "Who are you?"

"I'm the man who fished you outta that river. Name's Bo. Now, who are *you*?"

"Derek."

Bo was short and thin but with sinewy muscles. He had a gray-

and-brown beard and a bald head. Derek figured he was around forty.

"How the hell did you end up in the river?" Bo asked.

"I was bein' chased, and I fell in."

Bo nodded but said nothing.

Derek touched the leaf on his head. "What's this?"

"The leaf ain't worth a shit. That's just to hold the meds I got under-neath. I put aloe and cannabis with spiderwebs holdin' it in place, then the leaf to protect it all. The cannabis is for the swellin', and the spider-webs are antibacterial."

"Thank you. I owe you my life."

Bo nodded again, then rose to his feet and grabbed a water bottle from a shelf. He handed the bottle to Derek. "You must be thirsty."

"Thanks," Derek said, taking the bottle. He opened the cap, lifted his head, and gulped the water.

Bo grabbed the plastic chair, turned it to face Derek, and sat. "Where are you from?"

"Virginia. The Shenandoah Valley."

"What *gang* are you from?"

"I was originally taken by the Aryans, but I escaped. Went to a group called 1776. They were a bunch of antigovernment activists. We were holed up in an old Spanish fort along the ocean."

Bo narrowed his beady eyes for an instant, then said, "I believe you." He chuckled. "Which is good because I was plannin' on killin' you if you lied."

Derek's eyes bulged; then he eyed the knives hanging from the wall.

"Relax. I ain't gonna do nothin' to you. Lucky you don't have any gang tats. I woulda let you drown. I figured, no gang tats and a man on his own, he might be all right. I could always kill you later, if you gimme any trouble."

"I should get goin'. I don't wanna overstay my welcome." Derek tried to sit up again, his head swirling, but Bo guided him back down again.

"Prob'ly gotta concussion," Bo said. "You gotta headache? Dizzy? Sick to your stomach?"

"Yeah," Derek replied, wincing.

"You should wait till tomorrow. See how you feel."

9

JACOB AND FORTY MILLION FED COINS

"We have to make a decision," Rebecca said, standing next to the bed, her hands on her hips.

Jacob and Rebecca had argued last night, not coming to a conclusion, but agreeing to sleep on the matter.

Jacob sat up in bed, rubbing his eyes. "It's forty million Fed Coins, Rebecca. It would bankrupt us. You can forget about my early retirement. We'd be back to square one. And there's no guarantee that we'll rescue him. There's a good chance he's already dead. I think we should cut our losses and go home."

Rebecca scowled at that. "Summer saw him alive. We're the only ones who can save his life. How much is Derek's life worth?"

Jacob whipped the covers off his body and stood from the bed, facing Rebecca. "You're sacrificing our family for your ex-husband."

"That's not true. I understand that it'll deplete our savings, but, if we save, we can make it back in a few years."

"*We?*" Jacob arched his eyebrows.

"Don't be like that. I know you're the one with all the money but don't treat me like I'm some gold digger who's spending your money."

"You're asking me to do something that no other man would do."

"I know. But this is exactly why I married you. Why I love you.

You're different than other men. You're better." Rebecca reached out and took his hand. "Please. If you want me to go back to work …"

Jacob shook his head. "Based on what you used to make? You'd have to work ten lifetimes."

Rebecca hung her head, tears brewing. "I know."

Jacob exhaled a tired breath. "I can't believe I'm doing this."

10

SUMMER AND FINDING DEREK

They stood in the command center of the Project Freedom bunker complex, huddled around a map of Puerto Rico. Summer pointed out the Spanish fort on the northwestern point of Old San Juan. She pointed out the approximate area where Derek and Fred helped her launch the submarine.

"This is the last place you saw Derek?" Cesar asked.

"Yes," Summer replied.

"You said the Netas were coming on the beach here." Rob, the blond mercenary, pointed to the beach along the oceanside of the fort.

"Yes."

"Then you heard gunshots as you drove from the bay?"

"Yes."

"You also said that Fred wanted to be with his family."

Summer nodded, remembering the mechanic holding his dead baby.

"And he asked for the scuba mask and snorkel that was in the sub."

"Yes."

"I think Fred sacrificed himself for Derek," Rob said. "Think about it. His wife and child had just died. He could've taken the submarine himself, but he declined, saying he was *staying with his family*. Then he takes the scuba mask and snorkel. I think he gave the snorkel and mask to Derek and told him to swim across the bay. Then Fred went to the beach, and the Netas shot him. But I think Derek swam here." Rob pointed to the islet across the bay from the fort and Old San Juan. "This is where I would go. He can't return to Old San Juan. Swimming is the only escape, and that islet is the shortest swim to land. It's only a quarter mile swim, and, with the snorkel, Derek could've stayed submerged. The Netas might not've seen him."

"Where do you think he went after that?" Rebecca asked.

"I think he went to the jungle, outside of the city. Let me explain why. This islet, the Isla de Cabras, probably floods fairly often." Rob pointed to the islet, then the bridge on the map, connecting the islet to mainland San Juan. "And this bridge is long gone from the hurricanes, so you'd have to swim from the mainland to get here. This islet probably isn't occupied for those reasons. But Derek couldn't stay here very long because there's no fresh water. I think he'd swim back to the mainland here. If it were me, I'd do this really early, while the island was still mostly asleep. Then he probably walked along the beach to get out of the city." Rob traced his finger along the San Juan beachhead. "It's only about three miles, and he's out of the city. Maybe he walks a few more miles, but maybe people are waking up then, so he hides in the jungle. From there, I bet he looked for someplace to settle in the jungle, away from people."

"It's an island of psychopaths, and he just saw all his friends get killed," said Billy, the other mercenary. "I'd hightail it to the jungle too."

"I think we park the sub here." Rob pointed to a tiny island, just outside of San Juan. "On the backside to stay away from the surf. This island never had a bridge. It was uninhabited before, so I know it's uninhabited now. It'll be a good place to launch the drones. It's less than three miles as the crow flies to the Isla de Cabras, so, if Derek's still there, we'll find him. But, if he went this way to the jungle, we're in the ballpark of where he probably entered. We need to move quickly.

Hurricane season is almost over, and the longer we wait, the more likely that he's farther away or even dead."

Rebecca looked away.

"Rob and I put together an itemized list of what we need," Billy said. "We have suppliers who likely have these items on hand, but we need to get everything shipped immediately. Shippin' is gonna be pricey. The good thing is the stealth drones are small. We can have the drones and the communication equipment airlifted to Jamaica. Then the ship that brought us here can deliver the goods from there. Absolute best-case scenario, three days. But we need to place the orders and make the arrangements right now."

"We can contact our base in Venezuela with the ham radio," Cesar said. "Our base can contact anyone in the States."

"Is your submarine nearby?" Rob asked, looking at Cesar.

"I'll have a submarine here in two days."

"I haven't seen a dock."

"We have a dock a few miles from here. We only use it when we have large shipments. It's much safer to take small shipments from the beach."

Rob pointed to Jacob. "You need to move some funds if you're serious. If we're gonna risk our lives, we expect to be compensated."

Jacob cleared his throat, his expression dour. "Of course. I'll relay a message to my attorney. He can initiate the bank wires."

* * *

After the meeting, the men went to the communications office to make arrangements.

In the hallway outside the command center, Rebecca reached out and squeezed Summer's hand for a beat. "Thank you for helping us."

Summer nodded, flashing a small smile. "Thank you for arranging my trip to Panama."

Rebecca had asked if the ship bringing the drones could take

Summer to Panama. Jacob had agreed, meaning he would pay the ship captain to make the extra trip.

"I have some extra clothes you can take," Rebecca said. "I think we're about the same size."

Rebecca was about two inches taller at five six, but both were equally thin, although Summer was a little more muscular and athletic.

Summer looked down at her oversize fatigues. "That would be great. These aren't exactly flattering or comfortable."

"How about some breakfast?" Rebecca asked.

"Sure. Hopefully, they have some of that cereal I had yesterday."

Rebecca twisted her nose in disgust. "The milk's reconstituted."

Summer deadpanned, "Two days ago, I would've killed for reconstituted milk."

The two women went to the mess hall and made their breakfast. They sat across from each other at a long table, eating their cereal. Cesar's men had already eaten, so it was just the two of them.

"This is so good," Summer said, her mouth full.

Rebecca smiled tightly.

The conversation was sparse as they ate. Summer moaned in ecstasy as she consumed the sugary cereal. Rebecca ate reluctantly in comparison. Summer drank the remaining milk from her bowl. She set down the bowl and wiped the corner of her mouth.

"What was he like on the island?" Rebecca asked.

"Derek?" Summer replied.

Rebecca nodded. "Were you two friends?"

"Not exactly."

Rebecca furrowed her brows. "Enemies?"

"Not exactly." Summer pursed her lips.

"Then what?"

"He killed my fiancé."

"My God." Rebecca covered her mouth with her hand. "Why …"

"The Aryans forced them to fight. I'd rather not go into details. It's still raw."

"I understand. I'm so sorry."

Summer sighed, wiping the corners of her eyes with her index finger. "Derek also saved my life."

11

NAOMI'S REFLECTION

"The FBI's investigating," Vernon said, sitting next to Naomi and her hospital bed.

Naomi pressed the remote, raising the head of the bed, her back aching as she sat upright. "But they don't have any leads."

"Not that I know of." Vernon leaned back in his chair.

Naomi clenched her jaw. "The Roths did this. You know it, and I know it, and, if we know it, the FBI definitely knows it."

"We can't prove it."

"First they ignored me because I wasn't relevant. When I became relevant, they tried to buy me. When I refused, they tried to kill me."

Vernon nodded, his face solemn. "Maybe." Dark stubble covered Vernon's face. His dark eyes were bloodshot.

"One way or another, I *will* expose them, and I *will* bring them to justice." Naomi balled her hands into fists.

Vernon opened her fist and held her hand. "Don't worry. We'll make them pay. But you need to heal first."

Naomi took a deep breath.

Vernon changed the subject. "I called Blake and your mother. Alan's mother too."

Naomi had been sedated for two days and had only been awake

for five hours that Wednesday. Preoccupied with her injuries and thoughts of revenge, she hadn't even thought of her piece-of-shit son or her mother. Certainly not Alan's mother. "And?" Naomi asked.

"I called them Monday as soon as I heard. Yesterday too. Blake hasn't responded. Your mother is … out of it. I tried to explain the situation, but she's having a hard time processing."

Naomi sighed. "Maybe that's for the best."

Vernon nodded again. "I'm sorry."

"What about Francine?" Naomi was referring to Alan's mother.

"She wants to handle Alan's funeral arrangements."

Naomi frowned, the movement causing her facial burns to bark in pain. She waited an instant for the pain to subside, then said, "Does that mean she plans to pay for it?"

"I got the impression that she wants to *control* the arrangements. It is one less thing for you to worry about."

"What did you tell her?"

"I said that I'd have to ask you when you woke up."

Naomi let out a ragged breath. "She can handle the arrangements, but she has to run anything major by me first. I want him to be cremated. That's not up for discussion. Alan did *not* want to be pumped with chemicals and put on display. And the funeral date will have to depend on my recovery."

"I'll let her know."

A nurse entered the hospital room.

Vernon let go of Naomi's hand and leaned back in his chair.

"Good afternoon, Mrs. Sutton. How are you feeling?" the nurse asked.

"The painkillers helped," Naomi said.

"That's good. I need to change your bandages and clean your burns. It's painful, so I'll give you a mild sedative, and I'll increase your pain meds."

Naomi nodded, putting on a brave face, but her heart thumped in her chest, and her eye was wide open.

The nurse inserted medication into Naomi's IV. "You may feel drowsy in a few minutes. I'll be right back."

A few minutes later, the nurse returned with a stainless-steel cart. On top of the cart were ointments, saline, and a hemostat. She grabbed a towel from the bottom shelf of the cart. Naomi's eye was hooded; her body numb. The nurse gently placed a towel behind her head and another one around her neck. She removed the wrapping around her head. Then she applied a saline solution to the bandages that covered her right eye and cheek. The excess liquid was soaked up by the towels. The bandage was nonstick gauze, held loosely with medical tape, the tape only touching healthy skin. The nurse removed the bandages with her hemostat. Despite the meds, Naomi's left eye watered, and she groaned in pain.

Once the bandages were off, Naomi glanced at Vernon.

His face twisted in horror.

"Mirror," Naomi said.

"Excuse me?" the nurse asked.

"I want a mirror."

The nurse's eyes widened, betraying her bedside manner for a split second. "It's better to wait until you've had more time to heal."

"I agree," Vernon said, not looking directly at Naomi.

"*Now*," Naomi said.

The nurse left the room for a minute, returning with a hand mirror. She held the mirror up to Naomi's face. The right side of Naomi's face was a monstrous reddish-pink blister. The brown pigment of her healthy skin clashed with the red, a clear line delineated on her face. But the vacant eye socket was the most horrific. A red gash extended a few inches to the left and the right of the swollen red socket, marking the piece of shrapnel from the blast.

Vernon staggered from the room.

12

DEREK AND THE DREAM

Derek had stayed in Bo's hut for the past two days, recovering from a head wound and a severe concussion, spending most of that time sleeping. Bo had brought him water, iguana meat, and mangoes, but Derek had been nauseated, only eating small amounts of food. Derek had sensed that Bo was annoyed with the situation, given Bo's body language and short answers to Derek's questions.

On the morning of the third day, Derek felt well enough to rise, his legs wobbly, but his head clear. He grabbed a plastic cup and exited the hut, moving aside the mosquito netting as he did so.

A dormant firepit was about fifteen feet from the entrance to the hut, a metal grate over the pit for cooking. Bo called it a Dakota firepit. It was an underground firepit with a secondary hole connected by a tunnel for oxygen. It produced much less smoke than a typical firepit, which was important for stealth.

A pile of materials lay next to a tree nearby: cut wooden and bamboo poles, an old tarp, mosquito netting, and half-dried vegetation. No sign of Bo. Derek walked a few steps to the water filters. Bo had three bamboo tripods. A bamboo cannister hung from each of these tripods. They were filed with multiple layers of sand, gravel, and charcoal. Another smaller bamboo cannister hung underneath.

Bo added river water to the top. The dirty water migrated through the filter and exited clean as a whistle. The second cannister collected the clean water. Bo had said that he was afraid to drink directly from the river because of the many dead bodies that he'd seen in it. Derek tilted one of the clean water cannisters into his cup. He drank the water.

As Derek drank, he studied the filter system, thinking he could duplicate it. He knew he'd have to make his own camp soon. *I don't know how long I can survive in the jungle alone.*

Footsteps approached from the west. Derek watched Bo return with a machete in one hand and a bundle of vines in the other. He dumped the bundle of vines with the wood and bamboo poles and approached Derek, still holding his machete.

"Feelin' better?" Bo asked.

"Yeah. Thanks," Derek replied. "I know I was supposed to leave yesterday. I think I'm okay to go now. I know you prob'ly want your space back."

Bo nodded. "A man needs space. With you in there, the hut's tighter than a bull's butt in fly time."

"I really appreciate everything you did for me. I owe you my life. If you need any help from me before I go, I'd be happy to give you a hand. I can hunt and butcher animals. I know plants. I can forage."

"You can start by buildin' your own damn house. I got all the materials for a decent sleep shelter." Bo pointed at the tree with the pile of supplies gathered there. "It ain't gonna be a mansion, but it'll keep you dry and off the ground."

"You want me to stay?" Derek asked with raised eyebrows. "I figured you were itchin' to get me outta here."

"I just want you outta my fuckin' house."

They laughed in synchronicity.

Derek spent the rest of the day working on the shelter. Bo checked on him periodically to give him instructions. In the afternoon, Bo helped Derek finish, knowing that they were running out of daylight.

Ultimately, it was a very simple structure. Four main posts. A raised platform that would be Derek's bed. A sloped roof covered with a tarp and held down with bamboo and vines used as lashing. The mosquito netting was lashed in place to cover the bed.

"Not bad, huh?" Bo said, admiring the structure, his hands on his hips.

Derek nodded. "Better than sleepin' outside with the mosquitoes and snakes."

* * *

Despite his new digs, they ate dinner in Bo's hut. More iguana meat and mangoes. They faced each other, sitting on mismatched lawn chairs.

Derek swallowed some iguana meat. "The meat's pretty good. Tastes like chicken. You'll have to show me how to catch 'em."

"A little gamey for my taste, but they're easy as hell to catch," Bo replied, chewing the reptilian flesh. "I'll show you tomorrow."

Derek nodded and swallowed some mango. "You said something yesterday about stealin' from the gangs. I couldn't tell if you were jokin' or not."

Bo spoke with his mouth full. "Ain't no joke. I do some stealin'." Bo swallowed his food. "Not because I need to, but because I like to fuck with the gangs. It's the adrenaline rush. I always was an adrenaline junkie."

"What did you do before?"

"I was in the military."

"How did you end up here?"

Bo narrowed his eyes at Derek and said, "How did *you* end up here?"

"I killed the CEO of the Bank of China."

Bo deadpanned, "The only good banker is a dead banker."

"He killed my girlfriend."

"Well then, sounds like you killed two birds with one stone."

"I've heard that before." Derek paused for a moment and asked again, "What about you? How did you end up here?"

Bo didn't answer right away, finishing the last of his iguana meat. "I was in Venezuela, trainin' the rebels. They were shitbirds. Undisciplined. Lazy. Three of 'em were only lookin' to rape and pillage. I told the brass, but they didn't give a shit. A woman came to us, cryin', her clothes ripped. The third one in three nights. These three shitbirds were takin' liberties with the locals. I took care of the problem. Then the brass took care of me. I was shipped back to the States. Dishonorable discharge. I moved back home to Mississippi, but I couldn't find work. Then a buddy hooked me up with a job in North Carolina. My daddy used to be a crop duster. He taught me to fly. I had my pilot's license, so I was flyin' tourists over what was left of the Outer Banks after the floods. Disaster tourism. People are so fucked up."

Derek swallowed his food. "It's like how people used to rubberneck at accidents. We don't have that problem anymore because the computer's drivin' most of 'em."

"Yep. That's what it was like. I was gettin' paid to show 'em the wreckage. While I was doin' that, I was still pissed about what had happened. The army was all I knew. I started talkin' about what was goin' on in Venezuela. At first, I just told passengers, people at bars. Then I posted some shit online. Not too long after, SWAT showed up to my trailer and took me away. I was shipped here faster than a hot knife through butter. When I got here, those fuckin' Aryans tried to catch me at the beach landin', but I got away. Swam out to sea and they lost track of me. Then I made it to the jungle. I learned a lot about jungle livin' in Venezuela, so it was natural for me."

Derek nodded. "I knew a guy who served in Venezuela. He got involved with 1776. He was in the games with me. Got killed. The Aryans stabbed him before the fight because they wanted a white guy to win."

"What was his name?" Bo took a bite of mango.

"Jordan. I never got his last name. Said he was with Army Special Forces."

Bo swallowed and wiped his mouth with the back of his hand. "I was Delta. We were part of SF, but I don't remember a Jordan. We were all spread out though. I tell you what. Those fuckin' games the Aryans run? That there is a helluva good time to steal."

"Have you ever stolen from the Netas?" Derek asked.

"Once, but they have pretty tight security," Bo replied.

"You think we could steal one of their planes? You were a pilot."

Bo cocked his head, studying Derek's face. "You tryin' to escape?"

"You never thought about it?"

"I used to dream about it, but that's all it is. A dream."

13

JACOB AND NEWS FROM RAMESH

Jacob sat in front of the ham radio, in the Project Freedom communications room, waiting for Rebecca to leave. They'd just finished talking to Lindsey, relayed through the ham radio. Everything was fine with her and the boys. They'd double-checked with Jeeves to make sure. A part of Rebecca seemed sad that the bot was a competent caregiver, as if her own competence as a mother was somehow diminished. As soon as she left, Jacob had Cesar's man in Venezuela call Ramesh, the CFO of Housing Trust, and Jacob's right-hand man.

Once Ramesh was on the line, Jacob pressed the button on the wired walkie-talkie and said, "I have good news and bad news. I'm not resigning, but I may be here another month." He let go of the button.

Cesar's guy in Venezuela was on an encrypted cell phone with Ramesh on Speaker, so Ramesh could hear and could respond to Jacob through the ham radio, and Jacob could do the same.

Ramesh replied, "I'm glad you reconsidered your resignation. We have a shareholders meeting next week. I had hoped you'd be present."

Jacob pressed the button. "I definitely won't be back by next week. How is the share price?"

Ramesh replied, "We're down another 14 percent this week. I don't think we'll maintain our GSE status. A full government takeover is coming. It's just a matter of how and when. Could be next month or two years from now. When that happens, a lot of people will lose their jobs."

"I'm aware of that. I'll be back as soon as I can. I'll call you next Wednesday."

"One more thing. Naomi Sutton was nearly killed in a car bombing. Her husband died. She survived, but she was badly burned and lost an eye. I'm only telling you this because some conspiracy theorists are saying that your family was behind the hit. One in particular, a person who calls himself or herself Braveheart, has been especially popular. He or she operates an encrypted vlog called The Underground."

"Thank you, Ramesh. That'll be all," Jacob replied. He hung the walkie talkie back on the ham radio and stared at the desktop in a trance. Jacob thought about his family. *Were they involved?* He knew they weren't above murder for hire, but he didn't know. He didn't want to know. He thought about that video of him attempting to bribe Naomi Sutton with campaign donations. *The FBI claimed that no copies exist. They can't know for sure? If that video were to surface* ... Jacob winced. *The optics would be very bad.* Jacob thought about another major problem. *Sutton might have a real shot at the presidency now. Especially after surviving an assassination attempt. She'll have public sympathy. If she wins, she'll want revenge.*

14

SUMMER AND THE *DORADO*

Everybody had hoped the ship would arrive quickly. Rob and Billy had estimated three days, best-case scenario. It had arrived on Saturday afternoon, right on time. Since Summer didn't have anything, Rebecca had been kind enough to fill one of her own suitcases with clothing and toiletries for Summer.

Now Summer stood barefoot on the beach, with her shoes in her hand, her pants rolled up, and the suitcase next to her. She watched the anchored ship just offshore. The Roths, Cesar, his men, and the mercenaries were there too. The ship was a ninety-footer, formerly used for long-distance recreational fishing, and named *Dorado*, after the tasty fish.

According to Rebecca, who had spoken with the captain on her initial trip to the US Virgin Islands, they no longer fished because fish were scarce and diesel was too expensive for recreational fishing to far-off lands in search of the last dregs of ocean life. The captain couldn't make ends meet with recreational fishing, so he'd started doing dangerous and illegal work, such as smuggling, because the profit margins were much higher.

The men on the ship lowered an inflatable boat into the water with two small cranes. Then a dozen boxes. Once loaded, the inflatable boat motored toward the beach. As the boat slid onto the shore, the man steering the boat raised the propeller and cut the engine. Cesar's men grabbed the boxes and stacked them on the beach for inventory. Jacob and the mercenaries, Rob and Billy, looked through the supplies, making sure everything was accounted for.

"I guess this is it," Summer said to Rebecca.

Rebecca surprised Summer with a hug. "Good luck."

"Thanks. You too." They disengaged, and Summer gestured toward the boat and her suitcase. "Thank you so much for everything. Please tell your husband I said thank you too."

Rebecca smiled. "I will."

Summer picked up the suitcase, walked through the loose sand to the hardpack, and the beached inflatable boat. A two-foot wave crashed ashore, the water moving up the beach, wetting Summer's feet and ankles before retreating to the sea.

A Latino man took her bag and placed it in the boat. In accented English, he said, "Welcome aboard."

As the inflatable boat motored toward the ship, she thought about the irony that she'd been sent to the island because of a video featuring Jacob Roth, and she'd just been rescued, in part, by the very same man.

15

NAOMI WILL CHANGE THE WORLD

Naomi: Your father's funeral is next Saturday. Do you want me to send a car to pick you up? Let me know.

Naomi's hospital bed was adjusted so she was almost in a sitting position. She looked at the string of unanswered texts to Blake. She'd been in the hospital for five days. Alan had been dead for five days. And Blake didn't give a shit. *Why am I surprised?*

When Vernon had called to notify Blake about Alan's death, he hadn't returned his voice messages either. Finally, Vernon had delivered the bad news via text. Naomi might've been worried that she hadn't heard from Blake, but she knew Secret Service agents went to New York to provide protection immediately after the assassination attempt. Also, Vernon said that he'd gotten a text response and was sure Blake was alive and well. Naomi had wanted to see the text, but Vernon had said that it was better if she didn't. In the end, Naomi had demanded to see it, and Vernon acquiesced. The text had read:

Blake: *How you gonna get hard fuckin that burnt bitch?*

In that moment, Naomi had wished Blake had been killed by a Roth hitman.

Naomi tapped on her phone, navigating from her text messages to the internet. She typed her name into the search bar and checked the related headlines.

Naomi Sutton and the Deep State: Did she make a deal with the devil?

Many Conspiracies, No Legitimate Leads

Who Did It?

Will She Run?

Naomi tapped the link for *Many Conspiracies, No Legitimate Leads*. The article chided the conspiracy theorists as immature-tinfoil-ha t-wearing-man-children living in their mothers' basements. The conclusion was that they should leave the investigation to the professionals at the FBI. The most popular conspiracy was that the central bankers and the military industrial complex had ordered the assassination for two reasons. First, Naomi made political promises to cut military funding, and she's opposed to the Federal Reserve, preferring the money supply to be created and managed by the US Treasury. Second, her campaign was gaining traction and relevancy.

Naomi placed her phone on the overbed table, the remnants of her lunch still cluttering the surface. Her burns and her empty eye socket were still covered in bandages.

A knock came at her hospital room door. Vernon stepped into the room wearing a tailored suit and a sly smile. After sleeping in his own bed, he was back to his beautiful self: radiant brown skin with just a hint of redbone, manicured beard, fresh fade, broad shoulders, and a face that was a perfect mix of pretty and manly.

"I have good news," Vernon said, sitting in the chair next to the bed.

Naomi forced a smile, not wanting to spoil Vernon's positivity.

"Latest polls have you neck and neck with Corrinne. The only reason you're not ahead is because some people think you might drop out of the race. Once you're back on your feet, it's over for Corrinne." Vernon was referencing the upcoming Democratic primary.

"That's great," Naomi replied without enthusiasm.

"This *is* great news." Vernon narrowed his eyes at Naomi. "Are you having second thoughts about running?"

"No. Of course not."

"Good. Because this is your time to change the world."

16

DEREK MAKES PEACE

Derek followed Bo downhill, through the jungle, along a tight game trail. Bo cut vines and vegetation with his machete. Derek carried a sturdy bamboo pole with a rope attached and a slipknot at the end. The *whoosh* of falling water became louder. They came to a rocky ledge, ten feet above the riverbank, just downstream from a waterfall. Whitewater fell from thirty feet above, drowning out the sounds of the chirping todies and the high-pitched peeps of the coqui frogs. The waterfall formed a wide pool in the rocky riverbed, the water slowing dramatically. Just beyond the pool, the river narrowed, and the water continued downslope.

Bo pointed to the riverbank below. Iguanas sunned themselves on the rocks, unaware of Derek and Bo, none of them looking up. Bo took the bamboo pole and lowered the slipknot. He found a fat iguana, hooked the slipknot around his neck, and yanked on the pole. The iguana thrashed, but Bo pulled the ten-pound iguana up to the ledge. The dragon-like creature hissed and flailed. Bo put his boot on the animal's back, grabbed his knife, and sliced the carotid artery on both sides of the animal's neck.

As the reptile bled on the ledge, Bo said, "If you wanna survive, you gotta take in more calories than you burn. These iguanas are easy to catch and give us an unlimited food source." The reptile tensed with the death throes, then went limp. Bo undid the slipknot from the dead iguana and handed the pole to Derek. "Give it a shot."

The iguanas had scattered after one of their buddies had been taken, but they had a short memory and were soon back to their favorite sunbathing spots. Derek lowered the slipknot. He placed the rope around an iguana's neck, but the animal jumped through before Derek cinched the knot.

"Gotta be quicker," Bo said, chuckling.

Derek waited for a few minutes, letting the iguanas relax. He tried again, this time snagging a large one. Like Bo, Derek stepped on the reptile's back and sliced its carotid artery with his knife. As a hunter and a farmer, Derek had experience butchering animals. Chickens, turkeys, pigs, deer, groundhogs, rabbits, and even snakes.

"How many do you wanna catch?" Derek asked.

"That's plenty for now. It's tough to dry meat during the rainy season."

Derek glanced up at the waterfall, a little rainbow forming in the mist. "Beautiful."

Bo nodded. "Yep. You're lucky you didn't go over them falls. I snagged you upriver, not too far from here."

Derek beamed at the scene: the blue sky, the dense green jungle along the riverbanks, the sun reflecting off the water, and the rainbow in the mist of the waterfall. "I'm lucky to be alive."

17

JACOB TAKES STOCK

Jacob glanced at Summer on the inflatable boat, motoring toward the ship, ultimately toward civilization. She cost him forty million Fed Coins and at least one month of his life. *I wish she'd drowned in that fucking submarine.* He turned back to the cargo, trying to disguise his disgust.

Rob and Billy took inventory, making sure the drones and communications equipment that they'd ordered were accounted for. The biggest item was a wireless buoy covered in flexible solar tiles. Inside this special buoy were solid state lithium ion batteries and the Wi-Fi mesh network with a one-hundred-mile booster that would form the communication network between Puerto Rico, aka Psycho Island, and the Project Freedom base in the US Virgin Islands.

Rob opened a cardboard box to check one of the flat-black drones. Billy held up a wetsuit, checking to see if it would fit his muscular frame.

Jacob took his own mental inventory: *fifty bat-size drones, communications equipment, scuba gear, two mercenaries, one submarine rental, the use of Project Freedom's base and support staff. All for forty million Fed Coins. By far the worst investment I've ever made. And for what? All to give the appearance that I'm the person Rebecca thinks I am. Is it worth it? Would she do the same for me?* Jacob thought back to the beginning, when their love had been so all-consuming, when they couldn't keep their hands off each other. *What happened to us?*

Billy clapped Jacob on the back, waking him from his thoughts. "Now we need a hurricane."

18

SUMMER AND THE DROP-OFF

It took almost two days to motor from the US Virgin Islands to Puerto de Carti, Panama. Early Monday morning, the captain of the *Dorado* dropped anchor in the Caribbean on the Atlantic side of Panama. The captain didn't want to pay docking fees to offload one passenger and one suitcase. Summer thanked the captain and his men. They'd fed and housed her on their vessel and had treated her with respect. Of course, they'd been paid for their efforts.

Summer sat in the inflatable raft with her suitcase, the bright sun on her face, and the wind whipping through her short hair. Two men from the *Dorado* navigated the boat toward the beach. They motored past a small submerged island, the stunted palm trees sitting in a foot of seawater at high tide. The sailor lifted the propeller and cut the engine as the boat landed on the white sand beach. Blue water lapped the shore with small waves. Driftwood and seaweed littered the sand. It didn't look much different than Psycho Island.

As soon as Summer exited the inflatable boat, her two escorts turned the boat back toward the sea. "Wait," Summer said.

The men turned to look at her.

"Where am I supposed to go?"

In accented English, one of the men said, "*Señor* Roth say, man be here for you."

"When?"

The two men shrugged their shoulders and left Summer on the beach.

Summer stood on the empty beach, her suitcase in hand, scanning her surroundings. At the docks, one-quarter mile north of her, men loaded two large sailboats with goods. A road led inland from the docks. To the south, all she saw was beach and jungle. Summer walked on the beach, toward the docks and the road.

A shirtless man emerged from the jungle with a goofy grin. Summer's stomach lurched; her heart rate spiked. She increased her pace, but he jogged in front of her, blocking her path.

"*Hola*," he said. "*Necessitas ayuda?*"

Summer shook her head, her hands shaking. "Excuse me." She tried to walk around the man, but he moved, still blocking her path.

"You no Spanish?"

"My friends are coming."

"I carry you bag." The man grabbed Summer's suitcase, but she wouldn't let go.

"No," Summer said with a death grip on her suitcase. "Leave me alone!"

But the man wouldn't let go. "I carry you bag."

Summer thought about the flash drive in the front pocket of her shorts. She let go of the suitcase, and the man grinned again. She kicked off her flip-flops and sprinted down the beach. Summer didn't hear footsteps behind her. After one hundred yards or so, she glanced back. The man rifled through her possessions.

Another Panamanian man emerged from the jungle, this one well-built, wearing fatigues and a T-shirt. Adrenaline coursed through her veins, and she ran faster. He ran behind her on the beach, yelling, "*Señora. Señora* Fitzgerald."

Summer stopped in her tracks at the mention of her name. She turned toward the man.

He jogged toward her, closing the gap. "I take you to Silver City." He touched his chest. "I am Roberto."

Summer put her hand to her chest, and her shoulders slumped in relief. "Thank you."

Roberto turned and pointed to the man still rifling through Summer's suitcase. "That for you?"

She nodded.

"I be back," he said.

Roberto ran back for her bag, scaring the thief in the process. Roberto knelt in the sand, repacking Summer's suitcase. She approached, kneeling and helping the Panamanian man. Roberto and Summer walked a short distance through a jungle trail, to the roadside and an SUV. Roberto loaded Summer's suitcase into his Toyota four-by-four. They drove south on a narrow asphalt road filled with hairpin turns, the jungle crowding the roadsides. After about twenty miles, they turned onto the Pan American Highway. Roberto stepped on the accelerator, the SUV zipping down the highway at 100 kilometers per hour.

"How far is it to Silver City?" Summer asked.

"Three hundred kilometers to Yaviza," Roberto replied. "Then you take boat in Rio Tuira. Maybe sixty kilometers more. You make it before night."

"Have you been to Silver City?"

"Many times." Roberto beamed, showing a silver tooth. "Very beautiful."

19

NAOMI AND STILL MRS. SUTTON?

"You can go home tomorrow as planned," the doctor said. "We'll provide home care for another week to ten days. A nurse will check on you once a day to change your dressings and to make sure you don't have any infections."

Naomi sat in her hospital gown, her bed propping her upright. Her right cheek and eye were still bandaged, but she no longer wore an IV. "Thank you, Doctor."

"You're welcome, Mrs. Sutton." The doctor smiled and left Naomi's hospital room.

Mrs. Sutton. I certainly don't feel like Mrs. Sutton. *Do I go back to my maiden name? I'm sure Diane would say a name change is terrible for branding.* Diane was Naomi's head of marketing.

Vernon knocked on the open hospital room door. He smiled and approached Naomi, holding a box of doughnuts and a cup of coffee. "I brought you breakfast." He placed the coffee and doughnuts on the overbed table.

Naomi smirked at the box of sugary-filled treats. "You trying to kill me?"

"It's a slow death but a good one." Vernon opened the box and grabbed a chocolate-glazed doughnut. He sat in the chair next to the hospital bed.

Naomi bit into a cream-filled doughnut, the sugar coursing through her veins.

Vernon wiped his hands with a napkin. "Tomorrow's the big day, right?"

She nodded, chewing her doughnut.

"I could drop by after work until you're back on your feet."

Naomi swallowed, remembering Vernon's reaction to her hideous face. "That's not necessary. A nurse will be by once a day for the next week or so."

He cocked his head in confusion. "You sure?"

"I'm sure."

"Did you still want me to take you to the funeral on Saturday?"

"I'm thinking about not attending."

Vernon sucked air through his teeth. "I don't think that's a good idea. The press will definitely be there. President Warner might even attend."

Naomi shook her head. "I'm not ready to be in the public eye. I'm afraid, Vernon. What if they try again?"

Vernon leaned forward, grasping Naomi's hand. "They won't, but, if they do, we'll be ready. We'll have the best security for you."

Naomi nodded, her head bowed. "Do you think I'm ugly?"

"What are you talking about?"

"I saw the way you looked at me without my bandages."

Vernon's mouth turned down. "It's not like that. It breaks my heart to see you in pain."

Naomi looked into Vernon's dark eyes. "You haven't kissed me since …"

Vernon glanced to the open door and whispered, "What would happen if a nurse saw us?"

"I don't care."

"It's not just that. You've been in a lot of pain. I didn't wanna hurt you."

"My lips are perfectly fine." Naomi looked away, tears welling in her eye.

Vernon stood from his chair, cupped her chin, and gently turned her to face him again. He leaned over and pressed his lips to hers. They separated, and Vernon glanced at the open door again. "We really should wait until you get home. Imagine what the press would do to us."

Naomi sighed. "You're right. I know you're right."

"One thing at a time. Let's focus on getting you home and settled."

"I'm serious about not being ready to be in public. This funeral …"

"One thing at a time." Vernon sat back in his seat and held her hand. "No need to worry about it right now. It's five days away."

Naomi pursed her lips. "Francine did this on purpose. She wanted to make it difficult for me to attend." Alan's mother had scheduled the funeral without Naomi's permission.

"We can always postpone it."

"People have purchased plane tickets and made arrangements. To be honest, I don't know if I'll ever be ready."

"The sooner the public sees you and your bandages, the better. They need to be reminded of what happened to you."

20

"I need help with something," Bo said.

They'd just finished breakfast, with plans to venture a little farther from camp to forage for fruits and herbs.

Derek followed Bo into the jungle, only fifty yards from their camp. They came to a pile of brush and debris. Bo started to move the brush; Derek helped.

"What's this?" Derek asked.

"A weapons' cache," Bo replied. "I didn't know if I could trust you, so I hid my guns out here."

Under the brush pile was a mound of leaves. They uncovered the leaves to find a mound of soil. They took turns digging to uncover an airtight plastic foot locker. Inside was an M4 rifle with a sling, a 9mm pistol with a holster, a cleaning kit, and boxes and bags of ammunition.

"I prefer the M6, but this is the best rifle I've found," Bo said. "You can use the handgun in the meantime, but we'll keep our eyes open for another rifle."

Derek gestured to the cache. "This for hunting?"

Bo wagged his head. "Too much noise. It would alert others to our position. It's protection for when we're far from camp."

"You ever have anyone come to your camp?"

"Not since I've been here. We're pretty secluded. The jungle's thick all around us."

* * *

Derek cleared the narrow game trail with a machete. He wore his fatigues and boots, the handgun holstered on his hip, and a pack strapped to his back. Bo was behind him, also carrying a backpack, his rifle slung across his chest. Once they made it to the river, they switched spots, Bo now in front. They walked north along the river-bank. According to Bo, the farther north they went along the river, the more likely they were to encounter other humans. Bo had instructed Derek on basic hand signals and told him that it was important to keep noise to a minimum. Two miles from camp, they stopped at a grove of hibiscus with beautiful pink and white flowers.

"Vitamin C," Derek whispered.

Bo nodded.

They filled half of Derek's backpack with hibiscus flowers, then moved farther north, still maintaining good noise discipline. They stopped at a wild mamey tree, the branches heavy with fruit. They filled Bo's backpack with the large brown-skinned fruits. They went north again, then east into a clearing. Massive grasses—twice as tall as a man—waved in the breeze. They cut stalks of wild sugar cane with the machete and packed the remaining space in Derek's backpack. They heard Spanish voices in the distance. They slipped back into the jungle, not wanting to be seen.

* * *

An hour later, back at camp, Bo made tea from the hibiscus leaves. Derek cut the ends of the mamey fruits and peeled the sandpaper-like skin to reveal a beautiful salmon-colored flesh. He removed the pit and diced the fruit into chunks. Once he had two full bowls, he handed one to Bo and sat on a lawn chair. The fruit tasted like vanilla and nutmeg mixed with apricot and banana.

"Not bad," Derek said. "I've never had mamey."

"I had it in Venezuela," Bo said. "That tree's the only one around here that I know of. We have the mango grove real close, but I get sick of mangoes."

"My daughter loves mangoes."

"How old is she?"

"Seventeen." Derek took a bite of the fruit, savoring the sweetness. He swallowed and asked, "You got any kids?"

"Not that I know of." Bo touched the side of a ceramic mug. "It ain't too hot." He handed a mug to Derek. "I hate drinkin' pipin'-hot tea in this heat."

Derek took the mug. "You ever married?"

Bo chuckled to himself. "That's one helluva story." He took a deep breath and said, "I was eighteen, just graduated from high school, had no idea what I was gonna do with my life. I had this girlfriend, Lori. Short little blonde thing. Had me wrapped around her finger. Thought I was in love. She chose me over this rich kid, Boone. He was a few years older than us. In college. Always had an eye for Lori. Lori's daddy worked for Boone's daddy at Tenix Holdings in Biloxi."

"What do they do?"

"Finance and real estate."

Derek nodded.

"Anyway, I got her pregnant. I thought her daddy was gonna kill me. Her parents wanted her to get an abortion, but I begged Lori not to do it. Maybe I was young and stupid, but I wanted that child. She said she'd keep the baby, but I had to get a job. Jobs were scarce, even then. I used to work with my daddy, crop dustin', but drones took over that business. I couldn't find a job, so I joined the army. Told her that, once I got out of basic, we could get married, and we could be together. When I went away to basic, she was five months pregnant. The first month in basic, we didn't have time to do nothin'. After about five weeks, we had a little time to email or videocall. I tried callin' her, but she didn't pick up. I wrote her an email, tellin' her what was goin' on, but I never heard back. Every chance I got, I tried to call her. I sent emails. Texts. But nothin'. Then after basic, I had a short leave before AIT."

"How long were you in basic trainin'?" Derek asked.

"Twelve weeks. So, I hadn't talked to her for twelve weeks. I went home and went to her parents' house, but she wasn't there. Her dad sat me down and told me that she was with Boone. I asked him about the baby. She had an abortion. Our baby was six months old when she decided to ..." Bo paused for a moment. "Mississippi didn't allow abortions that late. Her parents sent her to New York. I went to Boone's parents' house to confront her. Nobody answered the door. I was yellin' and carryin' on like a damn fool. They called the cops on me. The cops cut me a break, let me off, but said if I bothered Lori or Boone again, they'd arrest me."

"What did you do?"

"Reported early for AIT. I was supposed to be a mechanic. I changed my MOS. I became a grunt, and the army became my family." Bo swallowed, his Adam's apple bobbing up and down.

"I'm sorry, Bo."

"That was a long time ago. Water under the bridge. I bet she's happy with her choice though." Bo drank some of the hibiscus tea. "You got an old lady?"

Derek didn't respond right away, thinking about April. "My girl-friend was murdered. That's why I'm here. Remember?"

Bo winced. "Shit, I'm a dumbass. I wasn't thinkin'."

Derek shrugged. "I was married for eight years."

"Oh yeah? What happened?"

"She traded up."

Bo grunted his understanding.

"After everything, I never stopped ..." Derek blew out a breath. "None of that matters anymore."

"Ain't that the fuckin' truth."

21

JACOB AND THE DRILLS

On Saturday afternoon, they'd received the gear, and they'd unboxed and prepped the drones and the communications equipment. On Sunday morning, Cesar's submarine had arrived in Sandy Bay, and the men had finalized their planning and prep work for Monday's live drills.

Jacob stood on the beach with Rebecca, watching the bay and a single buoy, the bright blue water smooth as glass. Billy was on the beach too, tapping on a bulky tablet. Cesar's men stood around, rifles at the low ready, providing security, so the mercenaries could work unencumbered.

"Watch this." Billy gestured to the water as if he was introducing a magic trick. "Behold the power of the CRACUNS."

Ten bat-sized drones broke the surface of the water, one after the other, floating in the still water. Their little propellers buzzed and the drones lifted from the water, tilted toward the beach, and zipped over-head looking for the face they'd used for the training exercise.

Billy beamed, looking to Jacob and Rebecca. "Pretty cool, huh?"

Rebecca smiled back politely. "The drones are called CRACUNS?"

"Yep. Stands for corrosion resistant aerial covert unmanned nautical system. *Whew-wee.* That's a mouthful."

Jacob looked into the ocean. The special buoy bobbed in the bay. Rob was underwater, attaching the buoy to the sea floor. A submarine was anchored underwater, just beyond the buoy. Rob surfaced in his scuba gear and swam toward the beach. Once he was in knee-deep water, he took off his flippers and his mask. Rob approached Billy.

"How's it going?" Rob asked.

"Everything's workin' fine," Billy replied.

Rob nodded. "Good." He unzipped the top half of his wetsuit.

Rebecca's gaze was locked on Rob's muscular upper body. Jacob clenched his jaw.

"The buoy's in place," Rob said. "Let's make sure we can communicate with Project Freedom through the Wi-Fi mesh network."

22

SUMMER'S JOURNEY

Roberto and Summer had driven south about two hundred miles—three-hundred-plus kilometers—on the Pan American Highway until they reached Yaviza, the end of the line. On the outskirts of town, Summer noted all the small farms dotting the landscape, many farmers using electric tractors. Roberto drove them across the river bridge, the water below bustling with small watercrafts: fishing boats, sailboats, and cargo boats transporting bananas on the Chucunaque, a tributary leading to the Rio Tuira.

As they drove closer to town, the houses were small but well-built concrete structures. The town was livelier than Summer had imagined, with shops, markets, electric vehicles, and even a baseball stadium. Roberto parked near a riverfront dock.

"It's beautiful here," Summer said.

Roberto beamed. "*Mucho* money from Silver City."

Roberto led Summer to the docks. Most of the people spoke rapid Spanish, but some spoke English, and others in tribal garb spoke another language that she'd never heard before. The docks were home to boats and men who made their living on the water. She and Roberto stopped at a cargo boat, where men loaded green bananas and mangoes.

A short, stout man smiled and said, "Roberto."

"Alvaro," Roberto said, returning his smile. The men hugged briefly. Roberto gestured to Summer and said, "*Mi amiga*, Summer."

Alvaro looked to be middle-aged, with salt-and-pepper hair that covered his ears. He turned his attention to Summer and said, "*Mucho gusto.*"

Summer cocked her head in confusion.

"Ah. *No español. Lo siento.* Nice to meet you." Alvaro's English was accented and slightly better than Roberto's.

Summer and Alvaro shook hands.

* * *

Summer and Alvaro chatted as he piloted his small cargo boat downriver toward Silver City.

"Roberto said you go to Silver City every day," Summer said.

"*Jes.* There's big money in Silver City. Good trading. You're American, no?"

"Yes."

"Why are you here all alone?"

Summer forced a smile. "Long story."

Alvaro smiled back. "I like long stories."

"I think my father lives in Silver City. I'm here to find him."

Alvaro creased his forehead. "Is he missing?"

Summer pursed her lips and said, "Kind of."

"I understand. Lots of people in Silver City don't want to be found."

"Do you live in Yaviza?"

"My whole life. Used to be all the young people moved to Panama City, but now we have jobs. Everyone stays home and buys a house in Yaviza."

* * *

Four hours later, they arrived at the lively port of Silver City. It was a mix of modern and old-world. Lots of sailboats but also many modern cargo ships. According to Alvaro, Silver City also had an ocean port for larger vessels. Also according to Alvaro, Silver City occupied about thirty square kilometers of the peninsula between the Tuira River and the Gulf of San Miguel, although much of the area was maintained as a wildlife refuge.

Alvaro insisted on taking Summer to the immigration office. Alvaro said this was the best place for Summer to find her father.

"Immigration? I thought Silver City was a free place?"

"Depends on where you want to live in Silver City. Some places, anyone can live. Other places, the community has immigration rules and security, all paid by the residents. If your papa lives in a place with immigration, they can contact him. If he's in one of the other communities, we will have to go there and look."

Summer frowned and said, "I don't have any money to pay you."

"No need. I've been paid," Alvaro replied.

As they exited the cargo ship, Alvaro's men unloaded big boxes of bananas and mangoes. Alvaro tapped on his phone, summoning an autonomous taxi. The electric taxi drove them through the heart of Silver City, her small suitcase on the seat between her and Alvaro.

Summer peered through the window, surveying the city. It was unlike any city she'd ever seen. In fact, it didn't look much like a city at all. It was more of an ecofriendly town. She expected the buildings to be covered in solar roof tiles but very few were. Most of the buildings did have large rainwater tanks, many of them covered and protected with vining plants.

Many more bicycles and electric motorcycles were here than were cars. Buildings were tight together, no taller than five stories, and painted bright tropical colors. Green spaces occupied as much space as the streets and the buildings, with large communal gardens. Businesses were mixed with residences. Restaurants, a pharmacy, various markets, and even small factories were interspersed among the homes. The sidewalks were just as busy with foot traffic as the streets were with vehicle traffic.

Based on the style of dress, the people could've been from any southern city in the United States. The people were mostly fit and healthy. Many of the young people were enhanced, too perfect to be natural born.

"What do you think?" Alvaro asked.

"It's amazing," Summer said. "Where does the power come from? Very few people have solar roof tiles."

"A thorium plant provides the power. Much cheaper than solar."

"Most people in the US have never even heard of this place."

Alvaro chuckled. "That's what your government wants. They're embarrassed that Americans come here for freedom. If you go to Googleplex Earth, they still have a picture from eleven years ago, right before they started building."

"What about people who live here and take pictures and videos and post them on the internet?"

"The US spends *mucho* money with viruses to stop that information. Most people here wanna be left alone anyway. If you know what to look for, you might find some things."

The immigration building was at the edge of the city, a tiny one-story concrete building. Definitely one of the city's ugliest structures. Alvaro asked the autonomous taxi to wait, as he accompanied Summer inside. She gave the middle-aged woman at the counter her father's name.

She typed on her computer and frowned. "I'm sorry, miss. I don't have any record of a Patrick Fitzgerald."

"That means he's not here?" Summer asked.

"That means, either he's not in any of the selective immigration communities or he's elected to be anonymous."

"Can you tell if he's elected to be anonymous?"

She shook her head. "I don't have the clearance to see that information, and, even if I did, I can't give out that information without permission from the person."

"What about a message?" Alvaro asked. "Can you call someone with clearance? Then they can give the message?"

The woman hesitated for a moment. "I suppose I could do that. What's the message?" The woman picked up a notepad and a pen.

"Tell him that Summer's here," Summer replied, thinking that anyone could say his daughter is here. *He might think it's a trap of some kind.* "Also, tell him that I'd love some beef and Irish Stout stew." It was an old family recipe that only Patrick and Summer would know.

"Beef and Irish Stout stew," the woman repeated, as she scribbled on the pad. She tapped her cell phone and walked away from the counter for privacy.

Summer watched the woman like a hawk, leaning over the counter to listen to the call, but all she heard was the woman murmuring into the phone.

After a few minutes, the woman returned. "My boss left a message for him."

"So, he's here?"

The woman winced, realizing her mistake. "I'm sorry. I can't confirm or deny his whereabouts."

Summer sighed and turned to Alvaro. "I guess I'll wait here."

"Then I'll wait with you."

"That's not necessary."

"It is."

They went outside, and Alvaro sent the taxi on its way. They sat on a bench that doubled as a bus stop, still within view of the immigration office. Summer's suitcase was at her feet.

* * *

After thirty minutes of people watching, Alvaro asked, "You hungry?"

"I don't have any money. Remember?"

"My treat. There's a market three blocks down that way." Alvaro pointed toward the city. "I'll go get some food." Alvaro stood from the bench. "What do you want?"

"Whatever you're having."

Alvaro placed his hand on Summer's shoulder and squeezed. "Don't worry. He'll be here."

Summer smiled tightly.

"Be right back."

Summer watched as Alvaro walked down the street, then turned her attention to the sparse foot traffic and the electric vehicles. A few people said hello and good afternoon as they walked by. Across the street, two green parrots fluttered around each other before disappearing into a large mango tree.

Summer wondered what she'd do if her father didn't show. *He's here. He has to be.* An electric pickup truck zipped into the immigration office parking lot, the brakes chirping as the vehicle ground to a halt. A man ran inside, but, from her vantage point, the pickup shielded the man. Summer stood from the bench, grabbed her suitcase, and hurried toward the building for a better look.

As she approached, her father exited the immigration office, only a few steps away. He froze, his eyes widening as he recognized her. She let her suitcase drop, took three quick steps, and hugged her father, squeezing him tight. In this parking lot, in her father's arms, the dam broke. She cried tears of joy and relief. In many ways, her escape from Psycho Island was still so surreal. But there, reunited with her father? It was real. *I made it.*

23

NAOMI AND THE OFFER

Naomi sat, propped upright in her hospital bed. It was her last evening in the hospital. She tapped on her tablet, checking the news. Vernon sat in the chair next to the bed doing the same.

Thorium to Power California Desalination Plants

What do Googleplex, Next Generation Robotics, and China have in common?

Naomi Sutton Disfigured (Exclusive Pictures!)

Naomi tapped the link to the last article with a shaky finger. *Did someone from the hospital take my picture?* It was a gossip rag, with obviously altered pictures. Naomi breathed a sigh of relief and tapped the link for *What do Googleplex, Next Generation Robotics, and China have in common?* Apparently, they were all buying silver mines around the world to secure their supply of the vital metal that just so happened to be the best conductor of electricity.

Vernon's cell phone buzzed. "Yes, Nina?"

At the mention of Naomi's receptionist, she checked the clock on her tablet. It was 5:49 p.m. Nina went home at six.

"She's on the line now?" Vernon paused for a moment. "I'll ask her." Vernon removed his phone from his ear and looked to Naomi. "Corrinne's on the line with Nina. She wants to talk to you."

Naomi hesitated, thinking.

"She must be feeling the heat," Vernon said.

Naomi raised one side of her mouth in contempt. "I'll talk to her."

"You sure?"

"Yes."

Vernon put his phone back to his ear. "Go ahead and put her through."

A few seconds after Vernon hung up, Naomi's phone chimed on the overbed table. Naomi swiped right and said, "Hello, Corrinne."

"Hello, Naomi. I'm calling to extend my deepest condolences for your loss and to wish you a speedy recovery. If you need anything, please let me know."

Naomi rolled her eye. "Now that you've checked all the etiquette boxes, you can tell me why you're really calling."

Vernon put his fist to his mouth, stifling a laugh.

An awkward silence followed. Corrinne cleared her throat. "I assure you my sentiments are sincere."

"And I'm sincerely hanging up if you don't get to the point."

Another awkward silence came. "I know, with your injuries, you'd rather not be in the limelight, but you are still a very valuable member of the party, and I'd love for you to be my VP."

"I have an offer for *you*." Naomi paused for effect. "How would you like to be *my* VP?"

"You won't win." Corrinne didn't sound convinced.

"Watch me." Naomi disconnected the call.

24

"How long have you been here?" Derek asked Bo, two empty plastic plates in his lap.

The sun was nearly gone, their jungle camp bathed in a dim orange glow. Derek and Bo sat around the Dakota firepit, cooking their iguana meat.

"Three years maybe."

"You don't know?"

"I used to count the days. Then I just counted the wet and dry seasons. Now I don't count anything."

"This is my twentieth day on the island."

Bo arched his eyebrows. "Shit. I didn't realize you were that green."

"Feels like a lifetime."

"It's like that at first. Eventually, you settle into a routine, and, before you know it, years have gone by."

Derek shook his head. "That's what I'm afraid of."

Bo moved the skillet of cooked iguana meat off the flame. "What other choice do we have? These are the cards we were dealt. Live or die."

"Or we could figure out how to get outta here. The group I was with built a submarine. I helped launch it. That woman's prob'ly free as a bird now. It can be done."

Lightning struck in the distance. Bo looked up at the dark clouds moving in from the east. "Rain's comin'."

Derek frowned at Bo's obvious attempt to change the subject. "We can't live like this forever."

"Nothin's forever." Bo held out his hand. "Gimme those plates."

Derek handed them to Bo. "You're right. We could die tomorrow."

Bo stabbed the iguana meat with sharpened bamboo shoots and set the meat on the plates. "You don't know if that woman made it. All you know is you launched a submarine. That's it." Bo handed a plate to Derek.

Derek took the plate with an appreciative nod. "She might've."

Bo scowled, skeptical. "You know how to build a submarine?"

Derek sighed and said, "No."

"You know where to get the parts?"

"No."

"Neither do I. You got your head in the clouds. I'm assumin' it took years for your old group to build that sub. How many people were scavengin' materials and buildin' that thing?"

Derek exhaled heavily. "Quite a few."

"The problem is, you still got hope. As soon as you let go of hope, you can learn to accept that we're never leavin' this island." Bo took a bite of his meat.

Derek held out his hands, palms up. "What about the planes? We don't have to find any parts. We just have to steal one." Derek stabbed his meat with a bamboo shoot and took a bite.

Bo swallowed, shaking his head. "We've talked about this. Even if we could steal a plane, the drones would destroy us."

"During a hurricane, the naval blockade and the drones leave. What if we waited for a hurricane and stole the plane then?"

"Those little Cessnas don't do too well in hurricane-force winds."

"What if we waited for the perfect time? As soon as the hurricane slows down enough for us to fly? Dependin' on how quickly the hurricane moves, we might have a small window."

Bo pointed his bamboo shoot utensil at Derek. "I tell you what. We'll go check their base. See if it's possible."

"That's great."

"Don't be gettin' your hopes up. I ain't sayin' yes."

Derek grinned at Bo. "You're not sayin' no either."

25

JACOB, INTO THE DEPTHS

For the second straight day, the mercenaries drilled in Sandy Bay. Jacob and Rebecca watched from the beach, the morning sun warming their skin. Cesar's men dotted the beach, providing security. The submarine was on the bottom of the bay with Rob, Billy, and three of Cesar's men inside. Rebecca pointed to the surf. Rob and Billy emerged in their scuba gear, holding a DPD, a diver propulsion device. The DPD looked like a man-size silver bullet, with handles on top and a protected propeller in the rear. Cesar's men used DPDs to smuggle goods from their submarine into rivers and tributaries along the Gulf Coast and the East Coast of the United States.

Rob and Billy carried the DPD from the surf onto the beach. They ran into the jungle, stashing their equipment along the edge, behind thick vines. They didn't acknowledge Jacob or Rebecca. This was a timed trial run, so they wore their game faces. They removed their scuba tanks and masks. Rob opened the watertight compartment on the DPD, removing boots, fatigues, and their rifles. They changed out of their wetsuits and crept deeper into the jungle.

* * *

Forty minutes later, Rob and Billy returned with one of Cesar's men, the one who had been designated to play Derek. They outfitted "Derek" with scuba gear and gave him some basic instructions. Then the mercenaries changed into their own scuba gear. The three men ran into the surf with the DPD. Just like that, they were gone, into the depths.

I doubt it will be that easy.

26

SUMMER SETTLES IN

Sunlight filtered through the blinds. The smell of coffee and bacon wafted into Summer's nostrils. She opened her eyes. The rotating ceiling fan cooled her face. She sat up in the queen-size bed, feeling refreshed and rejuvenated. Summer padded to the bathroom, peed, washed her hands, and brushed her teeth. She went to the kitchen, stretching her arms overhead.

"Hey, sleepyhead," Patrick said, turning from the sizzling bacon on the stovetop.

Summer smiled at her father. "Good morning. Need any help?"

"You could set the table and pour some drinks. The coffee's ready, but I also have juice in the fridge. The water is very clean. It's filtered from the rainwater tank."

Summer grabbed two plates and glasses from the cupboard, remembering where they were from last night's dinner. She set the table and added silverware. She opened the fridge and grabbed a large glass bottle of fruit juice, unsure of the contents. "Do you make your own juice?" Summer asked, holding up the bottle.

Patrick removed the eggs from the stovetop and glanced at Summer. "A guy from Yaviza sells fresh juice at the market. He makes whatever's in season. Then we take him back the empty bottles for a discount.

I think that's pineapple guava."

They sat down at the kitchen table and ate breakfast. The night before Summer had told her father her harrowing story. She'd cried when speaking about being arrested and giving birth to baby Byron while in custody. She'd cried again when she'd told him about Connor dying in that dilapidated baseball stadium. She'd detailed her time with 1776 and the video she'd been given and her impossible escape in the one-man submarine.

Most important, she'd told Patrick that she wanted to find Byron. Her father had said that he would do everything in his power to help her, but kidnapping a child from the United States as current fugitives would be a dangerous and complicated operation. They would need help to be successful.

Patrick had come clean about his vlog, The Underground, and his alter ego, Braveheart. Patrick had told Summer about the tip-off that he'd received from 1776 that the FBI had figured out his identity and had planned to arrest him. He'd expressed his regrets for leaving Summer without a goodbye, but he hadn't wanted to put Summer or himself at risk by sharing knowledge of his whereabouts.

"That was so good," Summer said, wiping her mouth with a cloth napkin.

Patrick beamed. "Glad you liked it."

"I'm a little worried about this immigration meeting tomorrow. What if they decide not to let me stay?"

"This community follows the nonaggression principle. People who have a violent criminal record might not be allowed here, but that doesn't mean they can't stay in Silver City, just that they can't live in this community."

Summer shook her head. "But I was sent to Psycho Island. As far as anyone knows, I'm a psychopath and not to be trusted. I can't imagine they want me here."

"The board knows about the test and how it's used to eliminate antigovernment activists. They'll understand. Remember, Steven

Parker Jr.'s on the board. He's a friend of mine and a good man. There's a reason Roger wanted you to give the video to him."

"I just wanna get rid of the damn thing. I don't want any more secret videos."

* * *

After breakfast, Patrick gave Summer a tour of Silver City. They drove in his little electric pickup through Patrick's neighborhood. Many houses were concrete and stucco, built on concrete pillars or stilts, without basements. The heavy rains in the wet season made basements impossible. Many homes were brightly colored with Spanish-style courtyards and balconies. The roofs were mostly terra-cotta.

The neighborhood was more jungle than suburban neighborhood, only small areas cleared around the houses, and separated from their neighbors by thick jungle. Some residents cultivated a lawn on their cleared lots, but most elected to cultivate gardens and fruit trees. Patrick's house was one of the smallest in the neighborhood—a two-bedroom home on concrete pillars, with a kitchen garden and some tropical fruit trees. The houses in the neighborhood were well-built and functional but also beautiful. One house stood out above the rest.

Summer pointed to the massive mansion with a five-car garage, pool, courtyard, and acres of manicured grass. "Who lives there?"

"Truman Bradshaw, but he's only here part-time," Patrick replied.

"Where have I heard his name before? Isn't he that rich guy with the nuclear company?"

"He's the CEO of Thorium Unlimited. He's one of the richest, most powerful men in the world. He financed Silver City. Roger Kroenig negotiated with the Panamanian government to sell a thirty-square kilometer area of the Darién, and Truman funded the project and the development. His thorium nuke plant gives us nearly unlimited clean electricity for pennies a kilowatt."

Summer raised her eyebrows. "He did all that for people to have a free place to live?"

"I don't think it was totally altruistic. He wanted to live free, but, unless you go to a very underdeveloped area with a tough climate—like Zomia in Asia—you'll run into government interference. Besides, he's made his money back and then some."

Leaving the community, they stopped at the front gate, the metal bar lowered, blocking their path. A metal sign was affixed to the tiny building next to the gate. It read Freetown. The robotic guard scanned Patrick's face, and the metal bar raised. The robot had the size and stature of a human being and was made from titanium and aluminum. A hump on its back was filled with solid state lithium ion batteries. An M6 automatic rifle was strapped to its chest. Patrick drove past the gate, waving at the robot. The robot waved back.

"What's with the robot security? Is there a lot of crime here?" Summer asked.

"Actually, very little," Patrick replied. "People here are more concerned about the Panamanians reneging on their deal or the US military shutting us down. A lot of residents have guns for precisely that purpose. We have a strong militia too."

They drove through Silver City. Summer had been there yesterday, but Patrick wanted to show her some of his favorite places. He pointed out his favorite restaurant, The Blue Iguana. He showed her The Natural Food Market, where he did most of his shopping, and a little movie theater called The Silver Screen.

"How many people live here?" Summer asked, as they cruised through Silver City.

"Around ten thousand," Patrick replied. "We gain about thirty new residents a week, although that's just an estimate. It's hard to say exactly because many people don't report their residency."

"What do you use for money? Yesterday, Alvaro used his phone to make purchases, but I don't know what he was using for money."

"That's up to the buyer and the seller. Most people use Silver

Coin—the local cryptocurrency that's 100 percent backed by silver. Some people still pay with physical coins. Gold, silver, copper, platinum, and palladium. Some even barter. But very few local vendors take Fed Coins or any other government-sponsored banker cryptos."

Just outside of town, they drove past a concrete building protected by concrete fencing and robotic guards similar to the one in Patrick's neighborhood. Patrick pointed to the building. "That's one of the silver vaults for Silver Coin. An independent audit is conducted every month to make sure they have the silver they say they do."

"I could use some silver," Summer said. "What's the job market like?"

"Silver City's growing. A hospital's not too far from here. They're always looking for medical professionals. We should check it out."

Summer nodded and said, "I'd like that."

Patrick glanced at his daughter with a grin. "You're gonna do great here."

27

NAOMI'S SECURITY TEAM

Naomi and Vernon rode in his autonomous Lexus from the hospital toward her home in Georgetown. They were tailed by a black SUV. After the assassination attempt, Naomi had been assigned a Secret Service detail. They were a ten-man rotating security detail, with at least two men assigned to Naomi at all times. Everywhere Naomi went, the Secret Service agents were sure to follow.

Vernon's Lexus parked in front of Naomi's town house, in the exact same spot where her Toyota had exploded. Naomi was in a trance, remembering the last thing she'd said to Alan. *Would you please wait?* Then the blast had blown him to bits and had slammed her against the front door of her home, taking her eye and her beauty.

The Secret Service agents parked nearby. They jogged to the Lexus, scanning for threats, handguns under their suit jackets. One of the agents opened the rear passenger door.

Naomi stepped from the Lexus. "Thank you."

"You're welcome," the agent said with a nod.

Naomi glanced at the concrete curbing, still charred from the blast. She felt sick to her stomach.

Vernon walked around the Lexus, joining Naomi. He asked, "Are you all right?"

"I'm fine," Naomi replied.

Vernon and Naomi approached her town house. He opened the front door. A robotic dog stood ten feet away, scanning their faces, a semiautomatic rifle attached to its back and pointed in their direction. The doglike robot was two feet tall and about sixty pounds. It had a long neck, with a grasping apparatus for opening doors and retrieving items.

"Jesus Christ," Naomi said, her hand to her chest.

The dog lowered the rifle into a compartment on its back, concealing the weapon. "Welcome home, Naomi," the robot said, then loped back to its charging station.

Vernon shut the door. "I told you about the guard dog. It already has our faces in the facial recognition software."

Naomi cocked her head, her eyebrows arched high. "What if it didn't?"

"The Secret Service detail set the parameters. There's one verbal warning, but, if the intruder continues inside, it'll shoot to kill. If the intruder has a weapon, there's no warning. The dog's hooked into the cameras, so, even when it's charging, it knows when someone's trying to enter the house."

Naomi broke eye contact. "Do you think they'll try to kill me again?"

Vernon thought for a moment. "I don't know. But, if they do, we'll be ready."

28

DEREK RETURNS TO THE NETAS

Their journey had started yesterday, and it had brought back painful memories of Derek's time with the Aryans and 1776. Derek and Bo had hiked through the jungle to the edge of San Juan. They'd waited on the edge of the city for nightfall. Once protected by the cover of darkness, they'd stealthily jogged through the city to the old army base occupied by the Netas.

At this point, they were exhausted but still had work to do—plus the sun would soon rise—so they'd camped in the jungle that was once the base golf course. Here they'd dug an open grave, then slept most of that day and night.

Now it was very early the next day. By the moon's position in the sky, Bo estimated it was around 2:00 a.m., but they were well rested after sleeping away the previous day. As they hiked through Neta territory, navigating the jungle by moonlight and compass, Derek was second-guessing his idea to steal a plane from the Netas. He didn't realize how far Bo's camp was from San Juan and the Netas. They'd walked at least ten dangerous miles just to get there, which meant they'd have to walk ten miles back.

They found the solar farm and entered through the hole in the fence that Derek had cut with bolt cutters just ten days earlier. They walked under the ground-mounted solar panels. A small concrete building guarding the solar farm was twenty yards to their left, next to a gate. A light was on, one guard visible.

Derek's stomach fluttered with nerves as they crept to the building. The guard sat at a metal desk, his head propped with his arm, his eyes closed. Bo entered the building. Before the guard realized what was happening, Bo had the man in a tight choke hold. Derek was detached as he watched the man gasp and struggle. It took several minutes for the man to die. Only when the man went through the death throes did Bo let go.

They took the guard's electronic keycard and his rifle. Then they carried the man back to their temporary camp in the jungle, only a few hundred meters from the solar farm. They stripped the man, dumped him in the hole they had dug earlier, and used their foldable shovels to cover his body with soil. Derek dressed in the dead man's fatigues and hat. They'd figured, with the rainy season, it would only take a week or so for the aggressive vines to cover the gravesite.

Derek and Bo cut through the now-unguarded solar farm; then they walked around the hill that protected the bunker complex. They hid near the front corner. Two roads led inside the bunker, both roads guarded by a gate and two concrete guard houses approximately thirty yards from the bunker. Lights were on, and silhouettes were visible. Men with rifles. The front of the earth-sheltered complex was windowless and concrete, with two massive garage doors for vehicles and two people-size doors. Lights illuminated the front.

Bo whispered, "Those doors aren't wide enough for a plane."

"You sure?" Derek whispered back.

"Positive."

"They have to keep 'em here. If they left 'em out, they'd be destroyed by hurricanes."

Bo shrugged. "Maybe there's another bunker someplace."

"It's possible, but I don't think so."

"Did you see any planes when you were here before?"

"Not in that garage." Derek pointed to the near garage door.

"Maybe all their planes were shot down?"

"Maybe. Shit." Derek blew out a breath. "What do you wanna do?"

"It's up to you, hoss. This is your show."

"We're here. I have a keycard. I might as well check that other garage."

Bo gave a thumbs-up.

Derek walked into the light of the earth-sheltered bunker, the rifle they'd stolen slung across his chest. He didn't creep or sneak. He moved purposely, as if he belonged. Derek thought that, if someone saw him wearing the army fatigues of the Netas, they would think he was one of them. Derek's heart pounded as he pressed the keycard to the scanner, and the door unlocked.

He stepped into the garage. Emergency LEDs provided very dim lights near the exits, but it was enough light to make out the silhouettes of the planes. Six battery-powered Cessnas. Bo was right. The wing span would've been too large, but the wings were all neatly folded back. This was a common retrofit for plane enthusiasts who wanted to save hangar space. Derek thought about looking through the garage, maybe scavenging some useful items, but he didn't think it was worth the risk. Plus, if they planned to come back and steal one of these planes, it was important that the Netas didn't suspect that they'd already had a break-in.

Derek slipped back outside and walked to Bo.

"What was in there?" Bo asked.

Derek grinned. "The planes have foldable wings."

29

JACOB AND RICH OR POOR

"The shareholder meeting didn't go well," Ramesh said through the ham radio. "They were upset that you were unavailable. A few of our largest shareholders are threatening to sell."

Jacob sat in front of the ham radio, in the Project Freedom communications room. He pressed the button on the wired walkie-talkie and replied, "If they sell, where does that leave us?" He let go of the button.

"That much closer to a full government takeover. If that happens, we may not have jobs."

Jacob winced. "It's unlikely, but I'll try to secure additional funding. I'll call when I have news."

"Please let me know as soon as you do."

"Will do." Jacob disconnected the call. He thought about his savings going up in smoke trying to rescue Rebecca's ex, and, at the same time, he might lose his job as CEO. His stomach turned, bile rising into his esophagus. Jacob swallowed, his throat burning with the hot vomit. He hung his head, resting for a few minutes. Then he called Cesar's man in Venezuela on the ham radio and asked to relay another call to the States. This one was to Jacob's brother, Eric.

"I'm surprised you're still down there," Eric said through the ham radio.

"I may be here another month," Jacob replied.

"A month? It shouldn't take that long to prove to Rebecca that her ex is likely dead."

Jacob let out a tired breath. "It's a long story. I'm calling because I need emergency funding. Housing Trust is facing a full government takeover."

"I doubt I can help."

"Will you at least look into it? We can discount equity shares."

"Give me a couple of days. We'll talk on Friday."

"Thanks, Eric."

"Sure." Eric disconnected the call.

Jacob left the communications room and walked to the mess hall. A handful of Cesar's men and Billy ate a lunch of assorted MREs. Cesar's men chattered in Spanish, and Billy ate by himself. Jacob grabbed a bottle of filtered water and sat across from Billy.

"You not gonna eat?" Billy asked, lifting his chin toward Jacob.

"I'm not hungry," Jacob replied.

"This one ain't too bad." Billy took a bite of spaghetti.

"Have you seen my wife?"

Billy spoke with his mouth full. "She went for a swim. Don't worry. Rob's watchin' her six."

A wave of concern flashed over Jacob's face. He thought about the way Rebecca had looked at Rob in his wetsuit yesterday. "I need to go down to the beach."

Billy gave a thumbs-up and shoveled the last bits of spaghetti down his gullet. Billy threw the empty MRE package into the trash can and escorted Jacob to the beach. As they exited the jungle, Jacob saw Rebecca in her red bikini, standing a bit too close to Rob, all smiles as they bantered. She flipped her hair off her shoulders. As Jacob and Billy approached, Rebecca took a step back, grabbed her towel from the sand, and covered her nearly naked body.

Jacob glared at his wife. "This isn't a beach vacation."

Rebecca glared right back. "You've made that abundantly clear."

Rob and Billy walked away, giving the "lovebirds" their privacy.

"What are you doing?" Jacob asked through gritted teeth.

"I'm trying to make the best of a bad situation."

"By flirting with Rob?"

Rebecca blushed scarlet. "I wasn't flirting."

"I see the way you look at him."

"We were just talking."

Jacob pointed at Rebecca, his finger jabbing the air between them. "I waste our savings on your ex-husband, and you have the audacity to disrespect me. To top it off, I just found out that I may not have a job by the time this is over."

Rebecca's eyes widened. "What happened?"

"We're on the brink of a government takeover."

"We'll figure it out."

Jacob slumped his shoulders. "When I'm broke, you can run away with Rob."

She frowned. "Don't be ridiculous. I love you. Rich or poor. Sickness and health. Remember that?"

Jacob nodded. "I remember."

Rebecca moved into his personal space and kissed him, slow and soft.

Jacob reciprocated, wrapping his arms around her.

Then she whispered into his ear, "Don't you forget it."

30

SUMMER'S IMMIGRATION HEARING

Summer was in the community center of Freetown to determine her residency status. It was a closed-door meeting in a small room, only Patrick in the audience. She sat on a wooden chair, facing a long table and a panel of five men, each with a name placard and a tablet in front of them. It was a big night, so she wore a nice sundress that Rebecca had given her. Moments before they'd started the meeting, Patrick had looked nervous, which was why Summer was nervous now. *Will they accept me as a permanent resident?*

"Are you familiar with our bylaws?" Steven Parker Jr. asked.

Steven was a wrinkled old man, short and frail, with a bulbous nose and thinning white hair.

Summer forced a tight smile. "My father told me about the nonaggression principle. And he said I'd need an RRA policy to handle any possible disputes." A Rights and Responsibility Assurance policy. Assurance agencies acted as private mediators, insurers, and investigators in the event of disputes and criminal activity. Assurance rates were commensurate with the risk of the policy holder. Most Silver City communities required a policy for residency, and most businesses required a policy for purchases and employment. According to Patrick, 99 percent of Silver City residents carried an assurance policy.

"Do you have any questions about that?"

"No."

"If you decide to acquire property here, you'll be subject to dues to pay for security and upkeep of the roads and the community center. Myself and the rest of the council are elected for two-year terms. We're all unpaid volunteers."

Summer nodded. "I understand."

The old man glanced at his tablet. "It says here that you already have a job at the hospital."

"I'm a nurse—"

"I can't hear you, Ms. Fitzgerald," Steven said, leaning in her direction.

Summer cleared her throat. "I'm a nurse. I went to the hospital yesterday. I start Saturday."

"Good for you, young lady." The old man grinned, easing Summer's anxiety.

Truman Bradshaw interrupted. "I'm more interested in why you were arrested. And how on earth did you manage to escape US Penal Colony East?"

Truman Bradshaw was tall and thin with dark wavy hair. He had a long thin nose and face, almost horselike, but he wasn't unattractive. Summer knew the billionaire CEO of Thorium Unlimited was around fifty, but he looked closer to forty.

Patrick had been shocked that he was participating on Summer's immigration board. He rarely attended council meetings, even though he was President of the Freetown Council. Usually, he delegated his duties to his VP Steven Parker Jr.

According to Patrick, Truman was also the Mayor of Silver City, which didn't mean a whole lot, as the city was "governed" by the free market. Patrick had heard through the grapevine that, when Truman found out about Summer escaping from Psycho Island, he had been intrigued enough to attend the immigration hearing.

Summer said, "A friend of mine, Mark Benson, his sister worked for Jacob Roth. Mark talked his sister into putting a surveillance camera and a mike into Jacob Roth's office. Mark was convinced that the Roths were evil masterminds, and he was bound and determined to expose them. Anyway, she videoed a meeting between Jacob Roth and Naomi Sutton. During the meeting, Roth tried to bribe Sutton. Mark gave me the video, and I hid it for him."

"That's why you were arrested?" Truman asked.

"As far as I know."

Truman nodded to himself. "How did they find the video?"

"They never found it, but they knew about my involvement. The FBI was surveilling Mark, and he must've said something about the video. They arrested Mark, but he wouldn't talk. They'd also arrested our friend Javier for posting antigovernment content on social media, and he told the FBI about my involvement."

"Then you failed the Antisocial Personality Test." Truman stated this as a fact.

Summer looked down and said, "Yes."

"When were you sent to US Penal Colony East?"

Summer raised her gaze, forcing herself to make eye contact with Truman again. "Almost a month ago."

Truman narrowed his dark eyes at Summer. "How did you manage to escape?"

Summer glanced to her father.

Patrick nodded his encouragement.

Summer told them everything. Being captured by the Aryans and sold to 1776. Meeting their leader, former congressman Roger Kroenig. The submarine and scavenging for parts. The Aryans killing most of 1776. The Netas hot on their heels. The last two members of her group launching her in the sub. Then washing up on that beach in the US Virgin Islands and being picked up by drug smugglers.

"That's quite a tale," Truman said. "Why did you decide to come here?"

"Roger Kroenig told me that he knew my father, and he thought he might be here," Summer replied.

"Did you know that there's never been a documented case of an escape from either of the US island prisons?"

"I've heard that."

Truman stared at Summer for a few seconds. "Then why on earth would you expect us to believe you?"

Summer removed the USB flash drive from the purse that Patrick had bought her yesterday in Silver City. She held it up and said, "Roger Kroenig gave this to me and told me to come here and give it to Mr. Parker." She stood from her chair, walked up to the old man, and placed the flash drive in his hand.

"Is Roger still alive?" Steven asked, his blue eyes still.

Summer shook her head. "I'm sorry. He was injured and died shortly after he gave me the flash drive."

Steven hung his head for a moment, the room dead silent. Finally, he looked up and said, "Roger was a great man and a great friend."

"Without him there'd be no Silver City," Truman said.

"That's true," Steven replied, nodding.

"I'm sorry for your loss," Summer said, her eyes on Steven.

"Thank you, dear. Do you know what's on the video?"

"Yes."

"Is it private? Or can the rest of the council view the footage?"

"I think Roger wanted as many people as possible to see it."

"Does anyone have a USB adapter?"

"I have my laptop," said one of the council members.

The council member set his laptop in front of Steven and turned it on. As soon as the laptop was ready, Steven Parker Jr. inserted the flash drive and played the video. The men on the council watched, attentive, everyone standing and huddling around the laptop screen. Looks of astonishment passed over their faces. The Council of Freetown saw proof of the brutality of the island prison and, more important, proof that antigovernment activists were marooned on the island prison to eliminate dissent.

"This is incredible," Steven said to Summer. "This information has the power to potentially end the island prisons once and for all. I can't thank you enough for your bravery."

"I think that part's up to you," Summer replied.

Steven chuckled. "I suppose it is." He paused for an instant and said, "I'd like to take a vote to grant Summer Fitzgerald residency here in Freetown."

The vote was unanimous. Summer signed the contract, agreeing to abide by the bylaws and also agreeing to subject herself to the punishments if she broke those bylaws. The most severe punishment was banishment from the community, but the rules weren't onerous. She could do most anything on her own property, provided she didn't adversely affect her neighbors. Any disputes would be resolved by assurance agencies. Summer was now a newly minted resident of Freetown.

After the meeting, Steven Parker Jr. shook her hand and said, "Congratulations. You'll be a great addition to our community and this fine city."

"Thank you," Summer replied, beaming.

Patrick hugged her and whispered, "You're gonna love it here." They disengaged.

"I'm glad you're here," Steven said to Patrick. "I have an IT job for you."

"I figured you would," Patrick replied. "I can meet you tomorrow."

Truman Bradshaw approached the group with a big grin, his hand held out to Summer. "Congratulations. You're a very brave woman." He shook her hand and gazed into her eyes a little too long.

Summer's triumph was bittersweet. She'd made it, but she couldn't forget those she'd left behind, especially her son, Byron. Patrick had said that Steven Parker Jr. and Truman Bradshaw were the most powerful men in Silver City. He'd also said that, if anyone could help her get her son back, it would be them. With both of the men right in front of her, each of them gushing with goodwill after viewing Roger's video, she knew this was her best chance.

"I was hoping you could help me with a problem." Summer glanced from Steven to Truman.

"What's the problem?" Steven asked.

"When I was arrested, they took my son. I hope he went to my late-fiancé's parents, but I don't know. I need to find him and bring him here."

Steven winced, shaking his head. "I'm so sorry, Ms. Fitzgerald. I wish I could help you, but I don't have connections with the US anymore. At least connections that I trust."

Summer nodded, her expression crestfallen.

An awkward silence followed. Patrick finally said to Truman, "Can you help us?"

Truman sucked air through his teeth. "You're proposing kidnapping a child across multiple borders from one of the most heavily surveilled countries on the planet."

"They kidnapped him from me." Summer spoke a little more forcefully than she'd intended.

Truman showed his palms. "I completely understand that. I was speaking strictly from the perspective of the law, if you're caught."

Patrick said, "We were hoping you knew someone who specialized in these types of jobs."

"It's very dangerous."

After another awkward silence, Steven finally said, "I should be going. Welcome to Freetown, Ms. Fitzgerald."

"Thank you." But she didn't sound grateful.

As soon as Steven left, Truman said, "I might be able to locate the child. That would be a start."

Summer's face brightened. "That would be fantastic. Thank you so much."

"I'll see what I can do, and I'll let you know. I do have one request though."

"Okay?"

"The video of Naomi Sutton and Jacob Roth. Do you know where it is?"

Summer hesitated for a few seconds. "Yes."

"I'd pay two hundred ounces of silver for it." That was the equivalent of two hundred thousand Fed Coins—enough to buy a small house in Freetown.

"If you can get my son, I'll give you the video for free."

"Finding your son is low risk, but retrieving him is not. I have many enemies. Very powerful enemies, like the US government. I'm sure they'd love to send me to the island prison. I can't be involved in any illegal activity."

31

NAOMI AND ANTARCTICA AND GSES

"I've already arranged for transportation," Francine said, her tone curt. "I need to arrive early to coordinate with the funeral director. I didn't want to rely on you. Punctuality was never your strong suit."

"Well, I guess I'll see you there then," Naomi replied into her cell phone.

Francine disconnected the call.

Did she just hang up on me? Naomi set her cell phone on the table with a sigh. The old battle-ax didn't even ask how Naomi was feeling. She sat at her breakfast nook, which was a wooden booth—two bench seats and a table connected to the wall, a few paces from the kitchen. Naomi took a sip of her coffee and thought about the bill she'd just paid for Francine's fancy retirement home. Naomi went back to her tablet and the news, eager for a distraction from her anger.

She read an article about Antarctic silver exploration. Thanks to the Antarctic Treaty, resource extraction on the continent had been banned until 2048, when three-quarters of the treaty parties agreed to open up a small piece of the continent, the Antarctic Peninsula, to mining and extraction. A large silver deposit was officially discovered in 2049, but core samples taken by scientists had revealed a dense vein of silver many years earlier.

The Antarctic Peninsula was the warmest area of the continent, with summertime temperatures averaging 38 degrees Fahrenheit, some warm days reaching the lower sixties. The winter was much more forbidding, with average temperatures near zero and drifting icebergs that made ocean travel very dangerous for ships. Despite the less-than-ideal conditions, many of the world's leading mining companies believed that the high cost of silver made the project economically viable.

Naomi tapped on another link. *The Big Three: The Case for Nationalization.* Without an influx of investor capital, nonperforming college loans would likely bankrupt Student Loan Corp. Both United Mortgage and Housing Trust were struggling with increasing home loan defaults. In addition, Housing Trust was still settling lawsuits related to their mismanagement of government housing projects. According to multiple lawsuits, last winter's fires were caused by inadequate maintenance and faulty heating equipment.

Naomi thought housing and education were a right. They should never be for profit. She thought about a Gandhi quote, but she couldn't quite remember the exact words. Something like, we can satisfy everyone's needs but not everyone's greed.

The big three GSEs, Government-Sponsored Enterprises, would likely need another government bailout in the near future. The article criticized the inefficient GSEs for their bloated payrolls and their exorbitant salaries, especially for their CEOs. If the GSEs were nationalized, those taxpayer-subsidized salaries would be eliminated.

Naomi immediately thought of Jacob Roth.

32

DEREK AND THE INTRUDERS

Derek and Bo had been exhausted from their ten-mile hike back from the Netas' base. Despite the distance, Bo thought it was worth it, if only for the rifle they'd stolen. They'd made it back just before dark yesterday, then they'd slept late.

Now they were up and about with the sun high in the sky, the humidity thick enough to cut with a knife. They walked down to the river to fetch water and to catch an iguana. They caught the iguana first, standing on the rocky ledge, cinching the slipknot around the fat iguana's neck. Derek slashed its carotid artery, and Bo hung the reptile from a tree branch to bleed out. While the iguana bled, they walked down to the water's edge to fill their plastic buckets. As they moved closer, the *whoosh* of the nearby waterfall drowned out the sounds of the jungle.

Which was why they didn't hear them.

Derek was filling his bucket when Bo grabbed him by the shoulder and said, "Let's go." Derek saw the man near the crest of the waterfall, on the riverbank.

The man pointed in their direction, then turned his head and shouted something in Spanish.

They left their buckets at the river's edge and ran for the jungle, not sure if the man would follow. Derek and Bo had at least a five-minute head start because descending the rocky edges of the waterfall took some time.

They ran back to camp, immediately grabbing their rifles from Bo's mud hut. Bo said, "Don't fire until I do. If it's more than one man, start from the right, I'll start from the left."

Derek and Bo took their positions in the jungle, just east of camp, their rifles trained on the game trail that led from the river. Shortly thereafter, they heard voices and rustling through the narrow game trail. A man entered their camp wearing ratty cutoff shorts and holding a machete. Then two more similar-looking men. Finally, the last man crept into their camp, his shotgun held up, his eyes scanning down the barrel for threats. Bo shot the man wielding the shotgun in the chest. Derek shot the man on the right, also center mass, in the chest. Before the other two men had a chance to react, Derek and Bo shot them too. One of the men tried to run for the trail but collapsed after only twenty feet.

Bo emerged from the jungle, his rifle at the ready. Derek followed his lead. Bo approached the man with the shotgun cautiously. The man lay on the ground, wheezing, his breath gurgling with blood. Bo kicked away the shotgun from his grasp. Then he grabbed his knife from the scabbard attached to his belt and sliced the man's throat from ear to ear. Derek was unresponsive to the violence.

"Check the other ones," Bo said, his voice steady and calm. "Don't waste any more bullets."

Without a word, Derek removed the blade from the scabbard on his belt. The intruders were dead or dying, sprawled on the ground, bleeding out from massive chest wounds. One of the men was already dead. Bo checked the man who'd tried to run. Derek kicked a rusty machete from the last man's grasp and sliced his carotid artery, like he'd done to the iguana only minutes earlier.

Derek recognized this man. He looked like one of the men who had chased Derek into the river ten days ago. He had a faded neck tattoo with a crown that read Latin Kings. The man gaped at Derek, gurgling, brown eyes wide open. Derek watched the man die with less compassion than he had had for the iguana.

What have I become?

33

JACOB AND THE TAKEOVER

"Don't fight the government takeover," Eric said through the ham radio.

Jacob pressed the button on the attached walkie-talkie. "I'll lose my job."

"The US Treasury is planning to purchase a controlling interest, when the price is low enough. Some employees will lose their jobs, but you'll stay through the transition. You'll take a big pay cut. They want to point to your reduced salary and to the low share price to justify the purchase to the American taxpayers."

"How much of a salary cut?"

"Ninety percent."

"Ninety percent!" Jacob's voice went up an octave.

There was a pause, then Eric said, "You knew your tenure at Housing Trust was coming to an end anyway. After the 2052 election, whether it's Powers or Warner, they'll appoint you Treasury Secretary. You'll serve for four years, and then you'll work at Roth Holdings Eurozone. Dad will retire at some point, and you'll be ready to take over."

"I thought I was supposed to work for you, and then, when Dad retired, you'd take over in Europe, and I'd take over in North America."

"I'm happy here."

"What about Mayer?"

"He's happy in Hong Kong."

Jacob cringed at the thought of working directly for his father. If it wasn't for Derek and this forty-million-Fed-Coin mission, Jacob would've taken his savings and told his father to go fuck himself. Jacob exhaled and pressed the button on the walkie-talkie. "Thanks, Eric."

"No problem. Let me know if you need anything else."

"I will." Jacob disconnected the call and rubbed his temples. The thought of his future work life with a much-reduced salary made his head pound. He asked Cesar's man in Venezuela to relay another call, this one to Ramesh in McLean, Virginia.

Once Ramesh was on the line, Jacob said, "Don't resist the government takeover. It's the best option we have moving forward. I have inside information that most of the employees will keep their jobs and their current salaries."

34

SUMMER AND BACK TO WORK

Silver City Memorial Hospital was a five-story building with one hundred patient rooms, two hundred beds, multiple operating rooms, and a helipad. It was every bit as modern as the hospitals in the States. It served all of Silver City and Yaviza. Robotic orderlies and even a few robotic nurses made their rounds, cleaning and attending to the needs of the patients. The robotic nurses worked best in tandem and under the supervision of experienced human nurses. Most of the surgeries were also performed by robots under the supervision of a human doctor.

Summer had spent the morning shadowing one of the other nurses, learning the ropes of the new hospital. Summer had been polite as the middle-aged nurse explained their procedures and introduced her to the other staff members on duty.

Now they sat at the nurses' station—the middle-aged nurse showing Summer their computer system—when two men walked toward them. A bulky man, with a pistol on his hip, walked with Truman Bradshaw. The bulky man stood back, watching the scene as Truman approached the nurses' station with a grin. The middle-aged nurse stood from the desk, wide-eyed, her face frozen in shock.

Truman said, "Summer. I was hoping to find you here. I wanted to see how you were settling in."

Summer was straight-faced as she stood, wondering if this was some sort of immigration check. "Hello, Mr. Bradshaw—"

"Please, call me Truman."

"I'm settling in just fine. Thank you, … Truman. Is there something you need? Medically?"

"I wanted to talk to you for a few minutes."

Summer glanced at the middle-aged nurse, who was still wide-eyed and mute too. "I'm working now. If it's not a medical issue, I can call you after work."

Truman addressed the older nurse. "Would you mind if Summer took a short break?"

The older nurse said, "Of course not, Mr. Bradshaw. Anything for you."

Truman made eye contact with Summer. "The waiting area's empty at the moment." Truman motioned to the small room down the hall.

They walked to the waiting room, the bulky man following behind at a respectful distance.

In the waiting room, Truman said, "I'm sorry to bother you at work."

Summer didn't say it was okay because it wasn't. She nodded politely.

"I'd like to take you out for dinner. My treat. How about tomorrow night?"

"I'm working on Sunday. New nurses always get the weekend shifts."

"How about Tuesday night?"

Summer thought about Byron, knowing that this man may be her only hope. "I can do Tuesday."

"I'll pick you up at seven."

"Okay." Summer hesitated for a beat and asked, "Have you found out anything about my son?"

"I have people working on it. It may take a few days, but I'm confident that we'll locate him."

Summer forced a smile. "Thank you. I'm very grateful for your help."

"I know." He smiled back and said, "I'll see you Tuesday."

Summer went back to work at the nurses' station. "I'm sorry about that," she said to the older nurse.

"Don't be. Truman Bradshaw built this city and this hospital."

35

NAOMI AND THE FUNERAL

Naomi stared from the passenger window of her new Cadillac. The autonomous vehicle idled in front of the Holy Trinity Catholic Church in Georgetown. It looked more like the White House, with white sandstone walls and four columns adorning the entrance. If not for the tiny cross on the rooftop, she wouldn't have known it was a church. Alan wasn't religious, even though Francine had baptized him and had sent him to Catholic schools as a child.

"You ready?" Vernon asked.

Naomi turned to her chief of staff. He wore a tailored black suit and dark sunglasses. She took a deep breath and replied, "As ready as I'll ever be."

Her door opened, and one of her Secret Service agents stood next to the car like a sentry. Naomi stepped from the vehicle, careful not to snag her long black dress. An SUV queued behind them, dropping off other mourners. Secret Service agents assigned to the president already patrolled the area in and around the church in preparation for President Warner's arrival.

The humidity and heat radiated from the asphalt, creating a haze. After the Cadillac's air-conditioning, the warmth was welcome but only for a minute or so. Naomi waited on the sidewalk for Vernon, but he was talking to Fletcher McClure, a rotund man with snow-white hair. And Corrinne's campaign manager.

The autonomous Cadillac drove away in search of a parking spot. Naomi decided not to wait for Vernon and walked up the stone steps. A Secret Service agent opened the front door to the church for her.

Inside, the church was stark white, with white walls, white columns, and white marble floors. The pews were dark mahogany and mostly empty, except for one old woman sitting in the front row. Sunlight streamed through the stained-glass windows. A massive silver and gold cross hung behind the altar. Naomi's heels echoed through the cavernous space. Francine sat by herself in the front right pew, closest to the aisle. Signs hung from the front pews that read Reserved.

Naomi smiled at Francine, thinking she might scooch in so she could sit down, but Francine's expression was dour, and she didn't move a muscle. Naomi walked around the pew, thinking about the bandages over her right eye and cheek, wondering if Francine was somehow shocked by her appearance. After all, Francine had never visited Naomi at the hospital.

Naomi sat next to the old woman and said, "Hello, Francine."

Francine clenched her jaw and said, "I *don't* want you sitting here."

Naomi glared at Francine. "I'm paying for this funeral. I'll sit anywhere I damn well please."

"Fine." Francine grabbed her purse and moved to the other front pew across the aisle.

Naomi followed, standing over the old woman. "What is your problem?"

"Isn't it obvious?"

"Obviously, you have a problem with me. It's been that way since the day we met."

Francine raised one side of her mouth in contempt. "I sensed right away what type of person you are."

Naomi crossed her arms over her chest. "And what type of person is that?"

"Alan told me that you were cheating on him. Right before he was blown to kingdom come by a bomb that was meant for *you*." Francine's voice trembled with rage.

Naomi opened her mouth to speak, but nothing came out.

"Now you're as ugly on the outside as you are on the inside."

Tears pricked at the corner of Naomi's eye. She turned on her heels and walked back to the original pew, this time sitting at the very end, as far away from Francine as possible. Naomi dabbed the corner of her left eye, silently scolding herself for letting that old bag get to her. Mourners filtered in to the church, slowly filling the pews. Vernon touched her shoulder. Naomi scooched over, making room for him.

He said, "You're not sitting with Alan's mom?"

"She doesn't want to sit with me."

"That's addition by subtraction."

Naomi forced a smile.

"I was talking to Fletcher McClure."

"I saw you."

"He thinks you have the upper hand with Corrinne, and he thinks you can beat Warner with his help."

"He's been Corrinne's campaign manager for her last two Senate elections."

Vernon shrugged. "He thinks you could be the next president. He wants to play for the winning team."

"What about Katherine?" Naomi referred to her current campaign manager.

"I'll take care of her."

* * *

The funeral had been a who's who of politics. Many senators, congressmen, lobbyists, and political strategists had been in attendance. Much to Naomi's chagrin, her presidential competitors all made an appearance—surely not out of concern for Naomi but for the political advantage of appearing to put aside politics to support a competitor in her time of need.

Corrinne Powers, the esteemed senator from Virginia and front-runner for the Democratic nomination, had attended. Randal Montgomery, the Democratic congressman from South Carolina and a long shot for the nomination, had also attended. Even the Libertarian candidate, Andrew Poole, had attended. And of course, the president himself, Clayton Warner. Each of them had made a show of being gracious and extending their deepest condolences, and Naomi had to smile and be equally gracious as she accepted their sympathies.

Blake hadn't attended. This wasn't surprising to Naomi, but part of her had hoped she was wrong about her son, that maybe underneath his gangster persona was a decent person. It had been a relatively short service. Francine had given the eulogy. Naomi had elected not to speak.

After the funeral service, not wanting to face the media, Naomi and Vernon waited inside the church for the crowd to dissipate. Francine waited too, tapping on her phone, huffing and puffing in agitation. Naomi guessed that her AutoLyft couldn't travel to the church because of the president's motorcade. The church was empty now, except for the three of them.

Vernon looked around the church and said, "I think it's safe."

Naomi nodded and tapped her phone, summoning her autonomous vehicle. She stood from the pew and said, "Let's go." She walked around the pew to the center aisle. She could've used the aisle along the wall, but she had something to say to Francine. As Naomi approached, with Vernon in tow, Francine stared, her mouth curled into a sneer.

Francine stood from the pew. "Is this the man you've been sleeping with?"

Vernon was speechless.

Naomi moved into the old woman's personal space. "You should start packing. I won't be paying for your retirement home anymore."

Francine's forehead erupted in wrinkles. "You can't do that."

"It's already done." Naomi turned on her heels and marched from the church, her head held high.

36

DEREK AND BOOBY-TRAPPED

Four days ago, Derek and Bo had killed four Latin Kings. They'd buried the bodies, hoping to conceal their deaths. Bo had been manic since then. He was sure that the Latin Kings would come to their camp for revenge. Derek had wanted to pack up and leave, but Bo had refused, preferring to booby-trap the area surrounding the camp. So, they'd spent the better part of the last four days, digging and concealing fifty traps, the bulk of them placed between the river and their camp. They'd even made a trip to the city for building supplies.

Derek and Bo ate lunch silently at their camp. They sat on plastic lawn chairs; Bo's eyes darted this way and that, toward every new sound. Bo had insisted on virtual silence so they could hear potential threats. It was hot and humid, but black clouds approached from the east. Derek looked up and thought, *Storm's comin'*.

A shotgun blast echoed through the jungle, the sound coming from the west, about one hundred yards away, between their camp and the river. A man moaned in pain. Derek and Bo grabbed their rifles and took their positions at the eastern corners of the camp. They'd figured that the Latin Kings would walk down river, and they'd follow the game trail east toward the camp. Derek and Bo had cleared the path to make it inviting. They'd optimized the placement of their traps and their foxholes for this eventuality.

They'd dug two foxholes for themselves and had covered the holes with branches and brush. They'd used stones and thick logs to raise the roof enough to make gunports for their rifles. Derek stood in his foxhole, dripping with sweat, mostly watching the trail, but also watching his 180-degree sector of fire, which was entirely too big for one person, but they only had two men and two rifles.

Another shotgun blast. Another man hollering in pain. Derek heard urgent Spanish. Then he heard two more men screaming but without the shotgun blasts. The urgent Spanish drew closer.

Six Latin Kings crept into their camp, all with firearms. Two had AK-47s, three with shotguns, and one with a revolver. They scanned for threats, their eyes bulging. Like Derek and Bo had done four days before, Bo shot first, starting with the man on the left and working his way to the middle, and Derek started with the man on the right. But these men were already terrified, so they ran at the first sound of gunfire. Before they were out of sight, Bo shot two men and Derek shot one. The men writhed in pain, their blood staining the soil.

Derek and Bo exited their foxholes. They executed the mortally wounded men with headshots and ran after the other three, following the game trail. Derek followed directly behind Bo, afraid of falling into one of their booby traps. The groaning and moaning of men echoed through the jungle, like pain in stereo.

One of the escaping men fell, then shrieked in agony.

Derek and Bo slowed as they approached the fallen man on the game trail. He was caught in an Apache foot trap. This small concealed pit had sharpened pieces of rock-hard bamboo pointed down at a slight angle. When the man stepped into the Apache foot trap, his instinct was to panic, so he tried to yank his leg from the pit, but this only impaled his lower leg into the spikes. Bo had insisted on dipping the spikes in his own feces, making sure that, if anyone was cut, they'd eventually die of infection.

The man had dropped his shotgun, but it was still within reach. The man faced away from them but turned his head toward them, just as Bo took aim and shot the man between the eyes.

Derek and Bo continued to the river, but at least two men were gone.

"Shit, shit, shit," Bo said, walking in a circle, talking more to himself than Derek. "They'll bring more men."

Derek and Bo checked the Latin Kings ensnared in their booby traps. Two men had stepped into shotgun-cartridge traps. A piece of wood was placed at the bottom of a boot-size hole, with a nail attached to a hollow piece of bamboo. A shotgun shell was placed inside the bamboo, the nail touching the primer, the shotgun shell taller than the bamboo. The men who had stepped into those holes had ignited the primer, firing the shotgun shell full of buckshot upward into their leg and crotch. One of these men was already dead. Bo executed the other. They followed the screams to another man who had fallen victim to an Apache foot trap.

The man had one leg stuck in the hole up to his knee, sharpened bamboo digging deep into his flesh. His palms went up in surrender at the sight of Derek. *Por favor. Por favor.* Derek shot the man in the chest. His body jerked with the death throes before falling limp, awkwardly bent over at the torso but held upright by the leg stuck in the foot trap.

After that, the jungle went deadly quiet, the sky pitch-black. On the way back to camp, they found another dead man; this one had fallen in a punji stick pit. He'd been impaled by eleven sharpened and feces-laced bamboo sticks. They'd counted eight dead and at least two who had gotten away.

Back at camp, Bo grabbed a shovel.

"What are you doing?" Derek asked.

"Fixin' the traps," Bo replied. "A few of those men had shotguns. We can make more cartridge traps."

The wind picked up, rattling the treetops.

Derek looked up at the dark clouds. "Storm's comin'. Looks like a bad one. We need shelter."

Bo's face was taut. "They'll be back as soon as the storm's over."

"I know it. But, if it's a hurricane, might be time to steal a plane." Derek glanced at the dead bodies that littered their camp. "We can't keep doin' this."

37

JACOB AND BETTER HIM THAN ME

They were ready. They'd known the hurricane was coming. It was just a matter of when the navy would vacate their blockade of US Penal Colony East. They'd sent one of Cesar's drones to find out if the blockade was still in effect. This drone had the range to make it to the island and back, but it wasn't stealth, like the bat-size drones the mercenaries had ordered.

If the blockade was still in effect, they fully expected the drone to be destroyed by the naval blockade. If the drone made it through the blockade, it could be destroyed by the navy's predator drones that patrolled the skies over the land formerly known as Puerto Rico.

From Cesar's intelligence connections, he knew that the navy drones patrolled the skies even after the blockade sailed for safety. Eventually, depending on the hurricane, the navy drones would have to abandon their posts and would catch up to the navy ships for safety and for refueling. The US Navy kept the drones on patrol for as long as possible before and after a hurricane because they were vulnerable to an escape attempt at this time.

The navy also knew about the Netas and their battery-powered Cessnas, so it was important that the navy drones patrolled the skies until the winds made it unsafe for the smaller, more vulnerable

Cessnas. It was a delicate balance between safety for the navy drones, and security in case of an attempted escape immediately before or after a hurricane.

When the drone made it to the island prison without incident, they knew the blockade was gone. The drone flew over San Juan but was destroyed by a navy predator drone. This was a disappointment, but they expected the navy predator drones to eventually vacate the area as the storm worsened.

Jacob and Rebecca stood outside the Project Freedom bunker, watching the men in action. The sky was pitch-black now, even though it was still early in the afternoon. The surrounding treetops waved in the wind. The garage door opened, and three UTVs drove outside. They were all four-seaters with roll cages and big knobby tires.

Despite their aggressive look, the UTVs were quiet as mice, their power coming from lithium ion batteries. Rob and Billy boarded one of the UTVs, their rifles slung across their chests. The UTVs each had a little storage area in the rear, like a pickup bed, but the mercenaries didn't load any gear. They'd loaded the submarine the day before, knowing that the hurricane was imminent.

The UTVs drove past Jacob and Rebecca, headed for the trail, then the beach, and ultimately the dock and the submarine. Like a soldier off to war, Rob nodded solemnly toward Rebecca. She raised her hand in acknowledgment. Jacob clenched his jaw, that little exchange stinging his ego.

Part of Jacob wanted to be Rob. The strong alpha male. The hero. The man of every woman's dreams. Jacob wondered if Rebecca fantasized about Rob. But Jacob knew who he was. He consoled himself, thinking, *I have money and power. I'll live to one hundred. Men like Rob die early and poor. Even if they survive their acts of heroism, they'll become broken old men with debilitating injuries. The fair maidens of their youth end up wrinkled, gray, and fat, just like the rest of us. But I'll have the means to attract nubile women until the day I die.*

38

SUMMER AND THE REAL TRUMAN

The lighting was dim. Soft music played in the background. A Spanish love song. Summer sat across from Truman at a secluded white-linen-covered table.

"You really do look beautiful this evening," Truman said.

Summer flushed and touched her boyish haircut. Her wavy brown hair was still short from the haircut she'd received while on Psycho Island. Gavin and Javier had cut her hair and had dirtied her face to disguise her as a man. Despite her haircut, she still had soft facial features, bright blue eyes, and subtle curves. "Thank you," Summer replied.

The robotic waitress approached the table. From the waist up, the bot looked female in shape, but it was not made to look human, with blue-and-white plastic covering the titanium and aluminum parts underneath. Instead of legs, it moved on three wheels. "Care for any dessert?" the bot asked.

"We'll have a piece of the chocolate lava cake, with two spoons," Truman said.

"I'd like my own lava cake, if that's okay," Summer said.

Truman raised his eyebrows. "They're fairly large."

"It wasn't long ago that I was starving on Psycho Island."

"Bring us two lava cakes." Truman looked from the bot and winked at Summer.

"Excellent choice," the robotic waitress said, then turned on her wheels and zipped to another table, their order automatically sent to the kitchen through her CPU.

"How long have you lived in Silver City?" Summer asked.

"From the beginning," Truman replied. "It's been about eleven years. I'm not here year-round though. I'm a seasonal attraction."

Summer leaned forward, her hands clasped, like she was praying. "I know you said it would probably take a week, but have you heard anything about my son?"

"Not yet, but it should be any day now."

Summer nodded. "Please let me know as soon as you hear anything."

The lava cakes appeared. Summer ate like a Viking, devouring the flourless cake. Truman ate less than half of his.

"You don't like the cake?" Summer asked.

Truman patted his flat stomach. "I'm watching my girlish figure."

Summer grinned at that.

Truman paid the bill using his phone. Then he looked at Summer and said, "Would you like to come to my house for a drink? I have a great wine cellar."

Summer forced a polite smile. "That would be great, but I should be getting home. I have to work tomorrow morning. Thank you so much for dinner by the way."

"I wanted to talk to you about your son, but I didn't want to do it in public."

"Oh." Summer touched her chest. "I guess one drink would be okay."

"Great." Truman stood from the table. "You ready to go?"

They walked outside. The street and sidewalks were illuminated in round bursts from the streetlights. A strong wind blew Summer's sundress against her legs. Lightning struck in the distance, and the air rumbled with thunder but still no rain yet. Truman's BMW SUV was parked at the curb, idling. A beefy security guard opened the passenger door for Summer and Truman.

"Do you think we'll get hit by the hurricane?" Summer asked, as they drove from the restaurant.

"We're too far south for hurricanes. The Atlantic side of Panama is hit with tropical storms on occasion but nothing terribly destructive. But, on the Pacific side, we're even more insulated from extreme weather. This is one of the reasons I chose Panama. No active volcanoes, no earthquakes, and no hurricanes. I didn't want to build a city, only to see it destroyed by natural disasters."

Summer sighed. "That's a relief."

"Your island prison isn't so lucky. They're probably taking a beating right now."

Summer thought about Derek, wondering if Jacob and Rebecca and the men of Project Freedom would use this hurricane to bypass the naval blockade and to rescue Derek. "Everything about that place isn't so lucky."

They drove from downtown Silver City to Freetown in under ten minutes. Truman's iron gates opened, and they drove into the circular driveway. The security guard opened their door, and Truman exited the vehicle. He offered his hand to Summer. She took it as she stepped from the vehicle. Landscape lighting accented the palm trees and the sprawling mansion. A massive fountain shot a continuous flow of frothy water into the air. Summer took in the sights like tourist.

Another security guard opened the massive front door. Inside, a chandelier hung from the foyer. Like a gigantic chessboard, the floor was white and black marble squares. A doglike bot scanned Truman's face, then Summer's hands and body for weapons. With the master secure, the doglike bot loped back to its charging station.

"I've seen those security bots before," Summer said, pointing at the dog.

"I'm not sure who I'd choose if I had to decide between the dog bot or my head of security." Truman chuckled.

A stunning woman sashayed toward them with a sparkling smile.

"Welcome home, Mr. Bradshaw. And welcome, Ms. Fitzgerald. I'm Lisa, Mr. Bradshaw's assistant. It's so nice to meet you." She thrust out her hand.

In the bright light of the chandelier, Summer realized that Lisa was a bot. If Lisa wasn't so damn perfect, Summer might've thought she was human. Lisa wore flats and a pencil skirt with a silky blouse. She had shoulder-length blond hair that was probably real human hair. Her symmetrical heart-shaped face had perfect skin down to the small pores. Her body was built for a man's pleasure. Athletic and toned, yet feminine and busty.

Summer shook her hand, surprised that it was warm. "It's nice to meet you."

"Likewise," Lisa replied, still smiling. She turned to Truman and asked, "Is there anything you need?"

"Could you bring us a bottle of the Vinedo Chadwick 2036?" Truman asked.

"Of course." Lisa walked away with the poise of a runway model.

Truman led Summer into the spacious living room. A rocky waterfall recirculated into a fish-filled pond. They sat on a black leather sectional.

"It's beautiful," Summer said, motioning to the waterfall.

"Water is life," Truman replied. "I've always had a special affinity for water." He showed his large hands and long slender fingers. "Maybe it's because I was born with flippers." He laughed.

Summer laughed too.

"There's an indoor pool toward the rear of the house. An outdoor one too."

"Wow. That must be nice."

"I can't complain."

Lisa appeared with a bottle of red wine, two glasses, and a corkscrew. She handed a glass to Truman and one to Summer, then opened the bottle without a word. Summer watched Lisa work, mesmerized by her grace. Lisa poured a healthy glass for them both, then set the bottle on the glass coffee table.

"Do either of you need anything else?" Lisa asked.

"Privacy please," Truman said.

"As you wish, Mr. Bradshaw." She disappeared down the hall.

"She's amazing. I've never seen a bot that beautiful and lifelike." Summer sipped her wine.

"The technology is constantly improving. I think you'll see more and more bots that are indistinguishable from humans." Truman took a drink of his red wine.

"Her hand was warm and her skin, I could see the pores, just like a real person."

"There's a gel under her skin. She can loosen or tighten her skin to mimic the aging process. She even has fingerprints, which she can change at will."

"She'd make a brilliant criminal."

"Or a CEO."

"What's the difference?" Summer asked with a smirk.

He cackled, then said, "She already runs the thorium plant here, in addition to handling my affairs in Silver City. She's an AI sentient robot, so she can learn and evolve and understand complex situations and probabilities. She's programmed to help me first and foremost but also all people, and she can make up her mind how best to do that. She's not only more efficient but more ethical than most, if not all CEOs—myself included."

"That's fascinating. I knew bots were improving. I've seen the evolution of bots in the medical field, but she's on another level." Summer drank her wine.

"How's the wine?"

"It's excellent." To Summer it tasted like a dry red wine, no better or worse than any others she'd had.

"I think AI sentient robots will eventually replace human beings in the most important professions of the world. No longer will it only be the factory worker or the truck driver or the fruit picker who loses his job. Upper-level management and politicians could easily be replaced with more efficient and more ethical robotic leaders." Truman drank his wine.

"What will people do then?"

"Whatever they want." He placed his wineglass on the coffee table. He took Summer's glass and set it on the table too.

Summer's stomach fluttered as Truman leaned in for the kiss. His kiss was slow and soft. He smelled like wine and mint. Summer pulled back, forced a polite smile, and said, "I'm not, um, looking for a relationship right now."

He clenched his jaw for an instant, his face blank. Then it passed, and he said, "My mistake."

Summer thought of Connor and stood from the couch. "Thank you again for dinner. I should go home."

"I thought you wanted to talk about your son."

"I do. Of course I do." Summer sat back down on the couch, just out of Truman's reach.

"Finding your son won't be the issue. Like I said, I should have that information for you any day now." He grabbed his wineglass, took a drink, then set it back on the coffee table. "Smuggling him from the States is the issue. It's a very dangerous proposition. You'll likely find someone who'll take your money and say they can do the job, then, when you pay them a deposit, you'll never hear from them again. I can't stress this enough. When you're dealing with criminals, they'll use your hopes to take everything you have and more."

Summer exhaled heavily. "What am I supposed to do?"

"It depends on what you're *willing* to do."

"What does that mean?"

"Very few people on this earth can do what you want. I might be one of them, but I must have a *very* good reason to take the risk."

"I'll take out a loan. I'll work in your hospital for free. Name your price."

Truman nodded. "I appreciate that, but offering me money is like offering salt to the ocean."

Summer held out her hands. "Then what?"

"I'd like to think that I'm a kind person. I try to be kind, but so much of my life is transactional, and I hate that. I hate the constant negotiations. I prefer my personal relationships to flow like water. I kiss the beautiful woman, and she kisses back. Then one day, I play the hero and reunite her with her son. I can't play that role if she's not interested. Do you understand?"

Summer's stomach twisted in knots. She thought of Byron. It had been one month and three days since he'd been taken from her. It felt like a lifetime. She tried to remember his face and his smell, but that brief moment in time was fading. She wasn't sure if the face in her memory was Byron's or one of the other thousand babies she'd cared for during her career. Summer swallowed, scooted closer to Truman, then leaned in and pressed her lips to his.

The kiss was soft. After a long beat, Truman disengaged. He grabbed his phone from his pocket and tapped on the screen. He handed his phone to Summer. "There's a contract. Read it, scroll to the bottom, sign and give your thumbprint if you agree to the terms. A stylus is on the right side of the phone."

Summer tilted her head in confusion. "I don't understand. Is this a contract to find Byron?"

Truman smirked and shook his head. "This is a sexual consent contract."

Summer skimmed the contract. It was very graphic and very long, detailing consent to vaginal, oral, and anal sex, various sexual positions, toys, and fetishes. She stopped reading after a few pages. Summer looked up from the screen, scowling. "Are you serious?"

"Depending on the source, I might be the richest man in the world. I'm not bragging. I'm simply explaining why I can't become embroiled in any ambiguous liaisons."

"You wanna do all this ... *stuff*?" Summer held up his phone.

He still had a goofy grin. "Not tonight, but I don't know what you're into. I have to cover all my bases."

Summer looked toward the front door, thinking about running, but instead she faced Truman and asked, "Will you help me get my son?"

"It would be my pleasure."

Summer swallowed hard and flicked her thumb upward, scrolling to the bottom of the contract. She signed with the stylus and added her thumbprint to authenticate the contract.

After signing the contract, he was like a different man. He set his phone on the coffee table and looked at her with the unblinking eyes of a predator. Summer had seen that look before on Psycho Island. Her head told her to run, but she froze like a deer in headlights.

In the blink of an eye, he was all over her. No more soft kisses. He shoved his tongue down her throat. He grabbed her by the shoulders and pushed her face down on the couch. His belt buckle jangled as he removed his slacks. He pulled up her dress and ripped her underwear.

Summer broke from her fog long enough to say, "Wait."

But he didn't wait. He entered from behind and took what he wanted. A hard rain fell outside, muffling his animalistic grunts. She wanted to cry out, to say no or stop. It was on the tip of her tongue, but what was the point? She'd already agreed, and, if she said no now, he wouldn't help her with Byron.

39

NAOMI AND BACK TO WORK

That Wednesday morning was Naomi's first day back since the attempted assassination two weeks earlier. They met in the sitting area of Naomi's congressional office. Naomi and Vernon sat on the couch, Fletcher McClure on one of the leather chairs.

"She was fit to be tied," Fletcher said, referencing Corrinne Powers and his resignation from her campaign.

Vernon slapped his knee and chortled. "I bet she was."

"We still have to beat her," Naomi said, not ready to crown herself the Democratic nominee. "She won't quit because her campaign manager defected."

Vernon frowned in her direction. "Let's at least enjoy the win."

Naomi frowned back, the right side of her face and eye still covered in bandages. "I'll enjoy the win when we actually win." She addressed Fletcher. "You have data to discuss?"

"All business. I like that," Fletcher said, tapping on his tablet. "If y'all wanna follow along, I shared my outline." Fletcher McClure was a heavyset man with dark rimmed glasses and neck fat that resembled a chicken's wattle. His thinning hair was snow-white, along with his mustache.

Naomi and Vernon tapped on their tablets, finding Fletcher's

124

shared document.

"I've polled this thing every which way but loose," Fletcher said. "If we wanna win, not just the nomination but the presidency, this is the right platform. I think you'll be happy with my recommendations. It's very much in line with your current platform."

Naomi stared at Fletcher, her one eye unblinking. "I'd rather not compromise my convictions to win."

"I'll let you be the judge of that." Fletcher coughed into his fist. "In regard to taxation, we need to be very clear that we won't raise taxes on middle-class wages, and, more important, we'll increase the UBI payment. We're in favor of downsizing the military and upsizing education, health care, and low-income housing in the form of college debt forgiveness, universal health care, and free and safe housing for all. Education, health care, and housing should be a right in this country. Since Clayton Warner and even Corrinne will likely criticize the black hole of subsidies and bailouts that have been given to Housing Trust, United Mortgage, and Student Loan Corp.—not to mention the fires and the substandard living conditions—our solution is to nationalize the big three. Obviously, we can't simply take those businesses, but we can buy them. In fact, if we had bought stock instead of giving low-interest loans, bailouts, and subsidies, we'd already own the dang things."

"Do we call it a nationalization?" Vernon asked. "The public may not be in favor of wasting tax dollars on failing businesses."

"If the public views the businesses as necessary for the public good, and they think they'll benefit from the acquisitions, most will be in favor. In 2008, the bank bailouts were wildly unpopular with the public, but the bailouts of General Motors and Chrysler were viewed favorably. Our nationalizations or acquisitions are in the best interest of the American people, not the corporations."

Naomi and Vernon nodded.

Fletcher continued. "The most important question we'll have to answer is, how the hell do we plan to pay for all this?" He paused for effect. "By cutting the military, taxing the upper class with a 90 percent marginal tax rate, and closing corporate tax loopholes. And, when Warner balks at this, tells the voters that we'll crash the economy, we'll remind 'em that Eisenhower had a 90 percent marginal tax rate during his presidency, and the economy did just fine." Fletcher took a deep breath. "Cutting the military is extremely popular across all parties—less so for the Republicans but more than you might think. Republicans polled at 57 percent in favor of reducing military spending. This is where you can attack Corrinne and President Warner. They're both opposed to reducing military spending, even if they say otherwise. Of course, they're both heavily funded by the military industrial complex, even though we haven't fought a meaningful war since Venezuela. Corrinne's connection to Next Generation Robotics, with her father being the CEO, is something we oughtta highlight as often as we can. They supply 78 percent of military robotics."

"She'll spin that by highlighting the cost-saving benefits of robotics, not to mention the lives saved by replacing human soldiers on the battlefield," Naomi said.

"It doesn't negate the fact that we haven't had a war in over a decade, and Venezuela was a proxy war. We trained the revolutionaries and provided weapons, but we didn't need a massive military to do what we did."

"I agree, but Americans love their soldiers."

"Not according to the polls."

Naomi showed her palms. "I'll trust your numbers. I've always been in favor of cutting the military to the bone."

"Which leads me to a position that I believe we should change," Fletcher said. "People are overwhelmingly in favor of the island prisons. The proof is in the pudding. Crime rates have never been lower. If we support closing the prisons and repatriating the prisoners stateside, we'll likely lose the election. According to my numbers and my simulations, this issue is enough to tip the balance in favor of President Warner."

Naomi scowled at that. "It's inhumane and has no business being part of a civilized society. The cause for low crime rates has nothing to do with the islands. It's the surveillance and the facial recognition cameras coupled with the identification of sociopaths. We can still eliminate sociopaths by putting them in prison for life."

* * *

After the meeting, Vernon lingered in Naomi's office, still sitting on her couch. "What did you think of Fletcher?"

"I don't know yet," Naomi replied, sitting next to Vernon. "I liked Katherine."

"Katherine was great for your congressional campaigns, but she wasn't ready to run a presidential campaign. Fletcher's been there before. He was President Gardner's campaign manager in 2040."

"He also did time for attempted voter fraud."

Vernon had a crooked grin. "If you're not cheating a little, you're not trying."

Naomi glared at Vernon. "I'm not above being aggressive, but, if we win, we'll win fair and square. Nothing illegal."

He held up three fingers, like a Boy Scout taking his oath. "You have my word."

She smiled at that.

"You look beautiful today, by the way."

Naomi frowned, but her skin betrayed a blush. "I am feeling better but these bandages …"

"Stop. Take your compliment like a woman."

Naomi smiled again. "Why don't you come over for dinner tonight?"

Vernon sucked air through his teeth. "I have a ton of work to do today."

"Oh, come on. We haven't had any real alone time since …" She trailed off.

Vernon took her hand and said, "I'm all yours."

40

DEREK AND THE HURRICANE

The rain had started yesterday afternoon and had quickly escalated to hurricane-force winds of one hundred miles per hour and monsoon-like rains of at least an inch per hour. It was morning now, but the sky was still covered in black clouds.

Despite his poncho, Derek was soaked to the bone. He sat on a plastic chair in his foxhole, ten inches of standing water below him. He propped his feet on a plastic bucket just to keep them out of the water. Overhead, some of his roof of branches blew away in the wind, but the dense jungle buffered much of the wind at surface level. Water filtered through the makeshift roof, and water wept through the earthen walls. Bo was in his own foxhole about twenty meters away.

The wind whistled through the jungle. Occasionally, trees and large branches cracked and fell, the jungle floor shaking with the nearby impacts. Derek stood, the water level to midcalf. He grabbed the bucket, collected muddy water, and dumped it over the edge of the foxhole, where there was a hole in the roof. He did this over and over again, until he'd bailed most of the water from his foxhole.

A loud cracking sound came, followed by more cracking, then a heavy impact and a reverberation that Derek felt in his foxhole. Derek peered from the hole in his roof. A massive tree fell on Bo's hut. It was obliterated. Luckily for them they hadn't taken refuge in there.

41

JACOB AND CONTACT

After breakfast, there wasn't anything to do but wait for contact from the mercenaries. They were in Project Freedom's command center, the hurricane raging outside. The video feed was dark, and they hadn't heard from the submarine yet. Jacob, Rebecca, and Cesar sat at a table, facing the dark screens. Two of Cesar's men manned their posts, patiently waiting.

"A watched pot never boils," Jacob said. "My mother used to say that."

Cesar looked away from his screen to Jacob. "Your mother is a wise woman."

Jacob stood from the table and looked down at Rebecca. "We should rest. I'm sure Cesar will let us know when they initiate contact."

"Of course," Cesar said.

"I'm not going anywhere," Rebecca said. "We don't even know if they made it through the blockade."

Jacob sat back down.

"The blockade was gone," Cesar said. "The drone proved that."

"They should've called by now," Rebecca said.

"That was the plan, but the hurricane is still strong. I'm sure they're waiting for the storm to calm to install the Wi-Fi mesh network. They certainly can't launch the drones in this weather."

A part of Jacob hoped that the mercenaries were dead.

42

SUMMER AND THE MORNING AFTER

Summer stood in a bathroom at the hospital, grimacing at her reflection in the mirror, two pills and a tube of antibacterial gel on the counter. Her eyes were puffy and red from crying and lack of sleep. She'd thought about calling in sick, but then she would've had to lie to her father, and he knew her too well. He would've seen right through her.

Summer turned her shoulder to the mirror and pulled her collar to the side, exposing the bite mark on her right shoulder. It was circular and red and puffy. She applied antibacterial ointment, then straightened her pullover. She placed the morning-after pill on her tongue and swallowed it with a swig from her water bottle. Then she took the antibiotics.

She'd been prepared to make a hasty appointment with a doctor before work to ask for the meds that she needed, but that was unnecessary. Anyone could purchase any medication they wanted at the hospital pharmacy without a prescription. The pharmacist offered guidance in the form of an explanation on how to take the medication safely and the possible side effects, but even that education wasn't required. Thankfully, her father had already helped her set up a Silver Coin account, and she'd already deposited her signing bonus from the hospital.

What the hell am I doing? Summer blew out a tired breath. *It was a transaction. Nothing more. Hopefully the only one.* She closed her eyes, and the highlights flashed in her mind. Her recorded consent, followed by the removal of his metaphorical mask. His hand reaching under her dress and ripping her underwear. His weight on top of her. His rough jerky movements. His animal grunts and groans. The bite during his climax. His chipper demeanor after the encounter, as if it were consensual and enjoyable for both parties. Her shame as his driver dropped her off at her father's home. Thankfully, her father had been asleep because she had been in no condition to lie. *It's the only way to get Byron. You had to do it. But what if he wants to do it again?* Summer opened her eyes, shuddering at the thought. She left the bathroom and headed for the elevators and the nurses' station on the fourth floor.

On the way, she caught up with an old man, walking the same way. He was short and frail, his wrinkled skin covered with age spots. She recognized him at the same time he recognized her.

Still walking, the old man smiled and said, "Good morning, Summer."

"Good morning, Mr. Parker," Summer replied.

"Please, call me Steven."

Summer nodded and forced a smile.

Steven Parker Jr. narrowed his beady blue eyes. "Are you okay, dear?"

Summer broke eye contact for a moment, afraid she might cry. "Oh, um, I know I look terrible. I didn't sleep very well last night."

"I'm very sorry to hear that." They stopped at the bank of elevators. Steven pressed the up arrow and turned back to Summer. "I have some valerian root at home. Works great as a natural sleep aid. I'll drop some off with your father."

"That's not necessary. Please don't trouble yourself."

"It's no trouble at all."

The elevator door opened. They stepped inside.

Steven pressed three and looked to Summer expectantly. "What floor?"

"Four please."

The elevator door opened on the third floor. Steven waved a hand and said, "Have a nice day, Summer."

"You too, … Steven." Despite the old man's insistence on informality, using his first name still felt disrespectful.

A middle-aged couple waited as Steven exited the elevator. Summer held the door as they stepped onto the elevator. Before the doors shut, she saw Steven enter the Department of Oncology.

43

NAOMI AND ALLEGATIONS

They had a beautiful candlelight dinner made by Naomi's robot domestic, Doris. Filet mignon, garlic mashed potatoes, a mixed greens and heirloom tomato salad, sun-dried tomato and basil bread with honey butter, and an expensive bottle of red wine. Naomi avoided the potatoes and only had a small piece of bread. She didn't want her stomach to look distended or her breath to smell like garlic. Vernon cleaned his plate, unconcerned about his stomach or his breath.

After dinner, they went upstairs to her bedroom. She'd only ever had sex with one man in her Georgetown bedroom, but he was gone, blown to bits by the bomb. Naomi dimmed the lights and shut the door behind them. Vernon shrugged off his suit jacket and draped it over the chair in the corner of the room. She followed, her hips rocking back and forth. She wore a little black dress and heels, her legs bare, with a little surprise for Vernon underneath. Her feet hurt like hell from the heels, but she wanted everything to be perfect. She wanted to compensate for her bandaged face.

Next to the bed, she put her arms around his neck and kissed him, deep and slow. He tasted like garlic, but she didn't care. They parted, and she bit her lower lip. Then she loosened his tie and unbuttoned his shirt. He removed his tie and shirt, exposing his muscular upper body. She caressed his chest, her fingertips slipping over his nipples, on the way down to his belt. She undid his belt and fly, his slacks held up only by his muscled rear end.

Vernon lifted her dress over her head, smiling, his teeth gleaming white in the dim light, when he realized that she wasn't wearing any underwear. He tossed her little black dress aside. Naomi wore nothing but her heels. She widened her legs a little, inviting him to touch her, and he didn't disappoint.

"I want you," Naomi whispered into his ear.

He removed his shoes, pants, and boxer briefs. A wave of worry washed over her as she saw his flaccid penis. Naomi forced a devilish grin and grabbed his penis, stroking back and forth. But that didn't work, so she sank to her knees and took him in her mouth. Once he was ready, she stood, and kicked off her heels. She turned and pulled back the comforter on the bed. Naomi climbed onto the bed and lay on her back, her legs spread. Vernon climbed on top and entered her, his eyes on her face. His penis softened, and he looked away. Vernon pumped harder, but he softened more, so much so that he fell out, his penis glistening and flaccid.

He rolled onto his back, his breath elevated, and his mouth turned down. Naomi rolled on her side toward him. She grabbed his penis and caressed him, trying to regain their momentum.

He shook his head. "Stop, Naomi." He was still soft, so she moved downward, but he grabbed her shoulders and pulled her back. "It's not gonna work."

"What's wrong?"

"I think I drank too much."

"It's my face, isn't it?"

Vernon glared at Naomi and stood from the bed. "That's ridiculous." He snatched his underwear and pants from the floor.

Naomi pursed her full lips. "You're not attracted to me anymore."

Vernon zipped up his pants. "That's bullshit, and you know it."

Naomi crossed her arms over her bare chest. "Do I?"

Vernon put on his shirt and fastened the buttons. "I should go. Thank you for dinner."

"Please don't go." Her eye was glassy.

"I'm sorry. I have a busy day tomorrow." Vernon put on his socks and shoes. He grabbed his suit jacket from the chair.

"You can stay here."

He leaned over the bed and kissed Naomi on the left cheek, the one without the bandage. "What if the media sees me in the morning? It would kill your campaign. Alan just died."

"You think I don't know that?" Naomi shouted, suddenly trembling with rage.

Vernon paused for a few seconds, frozen by Naomi's outburst. "Sorry, I … I'll let myself out." And then he was gone.

Naomi lay in the fetal position, hugging her knees as she sobbed, eventually crying herself to sleep.

* * *

Naomi woke, her phone chiming on her bedside table. She grabbed the phone, thinking it was Vernon, calling to apologize. But it wasn't Vernon. She glanced at the time: *11:37 p.m.* Based on the caller and the time, she knew it was bad.

She swiped right and said, "Blake?"

"I need your help," Blake replied.

Naomi sat up in bed. "With what?"

"I need you to come to New York, right now."

Naomi's voice was hard. "What did you do?"

"Nothin'. I swear. This crazy bitch is just tryin' to get money. I need you to talk to her."

Naomi flipped on the bedside lamp. "Put her on the phone."

"Hold on."

Naomi heard a door open.

A girl said, "Let me go, you piece of shit."

"Shut the fuck up," Blake replied. "You wanted to talk to my mom. Here she is."

"Hello?" the girl said.

"This is Naomi Sutton. What's your name?"

"Riley."

"What seems to be the problem?"

"Your son raped me." Riley's voice trembled.

Naomi winced, as if she'd been slapped.

"She's a fuckin' liar," Blake said in the background.

"He won't let me leave." Riley sniffled. "He took my phone."

"What do you want, Riley?" Naomi asked.

"I wanna go to the police and tell them what he did to me."

"And we'll fuckin' sue your lyin' ass," Blake said.

Naomi let out a heavy breath. "Then that's what you should do. Good luck with that. Please put my son on the phone."

"Wait. Aren't you gonna tell me not to go to the police?" Riley asked.

"I don't care what you do. Rape is very difficult to prove. Did you know that over 90 percent of rape allegations are never prosecuted?"

"Did you know that the age of consent in New York is seventeen?"

Naomi's eyes were like saucers. "How old are you?"

Riley giggled. "Sixteen."

"She said she was eighteen!" Blake shouted in the background.

"What do you want?" Naomi asked through gritted teeth.

"One million Fed Coins sent to my digital wallet," Riley said, with the confidence of a CEO.

"I don't have that kind of money."

"Oh, bullshit. You're running for president."

"My campaign has money, but I can't take that money and give it to you. It's against the law."

"So is rape."

Naomi gritted her teeth. "Fifty thousand Fed Coins."

"You must think I'm stupid. This house is worth at least 500,000 Fed Coins."

"One hundred thousand Fed Coins. That's my final offer."

"One million Fed Coins," Riley said. "That's *my* final offer."

"Put my son on the phone, *now*."

Riley lingered.

"Blake!" Naomi shouted through the phone.

A moment later, Blake said, "What do we do now?"

"Goddamn you, Blake. I told to stay away from these girls."

"What are we gonna do?" His voice was tinged with fear.

"Let her go. I'll hire a defense attorney."

"Can you come here?" Blake's voice was pleading and small, not a hint of bravado.

Naomi rubbed her eye with her index finger. "Don't let anyone in the house without a warrant. I'll be there in six hours."

Blake hesitated for an instant. "Thank you, Mom."

Naomi was speechless for a beat. "If the police show up before I get there, call me."

"Okay."

"One more thing. If you have any drugs in the house, now would be a good time to make them go away." Naomi disconnected the call.

Naomi put on a pair of slacks and a short-sleeved blouse. She notified her Secret Service detail that she needed the Cadillac. They checked it for bombs and recommended an escort. She declined the escort. Naomi slept in the back of her autonomous Cadillac, as the car drove to her home in upstate New York.

* * *

"You have arrived at your destination," the Cadillac said.

Naomi sat up in the back seat, wiped her eye, and looked around. The Cadillac was parked in front of her stone cottage. It was still dark, the forest looming large around her. She glanced at the time on her phone: *5:50 a.m.* One other car was parked out front, Blake's SUV. A few lights were on in the house. Naomi stepped from the car and walked to the house. It was comfortable outside, breezy and in the low seventies. Katydids and crickets performed their chorus. The grass was matted and rutted in places from cars that had parked on her lawn.

The front door was unlocked. The house was quiet. A few errant beer bottles littered the coffee table, but the house wasn't trashed. She went upstairs and knocked on Blake's bedroom door. The sound of shooting and explosions came from the room.

"Come in," Blake said.

Naomi entered the room, flipping on the light as she did so. Blake lay on his bed, staring at the OLED television that hung from the ceiling, playing a first-person shooter game. He paused the game and set his controller on his bedside table. The carnage of war was frozen on the one-hundred-inch screen. Blake sat up in bed as Naomi approached. He wore a white tank top and basketball shorts. Tattoos of barbed wire wrapped around his upper arms, and the one on his neck was more visible as Blake's beard had recently been trimmed there. The neck tattoo was something written in Sanskrit. His eyes were red-rimmed and bloodshot.

"Are you okay?" Naomi asked, sitting next to her son on his bed.

"Bitch is lyin'," Blake replied.

"Do you know if she called the police yet?"

He shrugged. "I don't fuckin' know. You call a lawyer yet?"

"It's not even six."

The doorbell chimed.

Blake flinched. Naomi looked at Blake's open bedroom door, like she expected the police to be there. The doorbell chimed again, followed by insistent knocks.

Naomi stood from the bed. "I'll get it. You should use the bathroom and put on whatever you want to wear. They'll probably arrest you and take you into custody until the arraignment."

Blake swallowed hard and nodded.

"Don't say anything to anyone."

139

* * *

The police arrested Blake and put him in the back of a cruiser. They came with an electronic warrant, so they searched the house without Naomi's consent. While the police searched, Naomi called Devin Singletary, the only local defense attorney who she knew. He had been a classmate at Georgetown law. She left a message with his office, then sent him a direct message on You Share. She'd been his friend on You Share since their law school days, but she rarely used the platform anymore.

Shortly thereafter he responded, saying that he was on his way to the police station and that she should meet him there. He gave her his cell phone number, so she could update him on the way. As she sat in the back of her autonomous Cadillac, Naomi called Devin and told him what Blake and Riley had told her.

She finished updating Devin as her autonomous Cadillac parked in the lot next to a cruiser marked Jamesville Police Department. "I'm here," Naomi said into her cell phone.

"I'll be there in five minutes," Devin replied.

"See you then." She disconnected the call.

The sun peeked over the treetops, casting the police cruisers and the police station in a yellow glow. Naomi walked inside the one-story brick building, her slacks and blouse rumpled from sleeping in the car. A bot stood at the reception desk. With red eyes and the exposed titanium and aluminum frame, it wasn't a welcoming presence.

Naomi waved her embedded chip at the robotic receptionist and said, "I'm here for Blake Sutton."

"Please have a seat in the waiting room." The bot gestured to the waiting area, which consisted of a half-dozen plastic chairs and two vending machines. "Someone will be with you shortly."

Naomi walked to the empty waiting area, pacing, and watching the door for Devin.

Five minutes later, Devin entered the police station.

Naomi approached the attorney. Despite the early hour, he looked slick in his blue suit. Devin Singletary was a compact, stocky man, with dark skin and close-cropped hair.

Devin waved his embedded chip at the robotic receptionist and said, "I'm here for my client, Blake Sutton."

"Please have a seat," the bot replied, motioning to the waiting area. "A detective will be with you shortly."

Devin stepped away from the receptionist and pivoted to Naomi.

"Thank you for coming," Naomi said, shaking Devin's hand.

"Of course." To his credit, he didn't stare at Naomi's bandages. "The detectives will want to question him soon. Why don't we sit down and talk strategy?" Devin guided Naomi back to the waiting area.

Before they had a chance to sit, a beefy detective arrived on the scene and said, "Devin Singletary?"

"Yes," Devin replied, turning to the man.

"You can see your client now."

"May I see my son?" Naomi asked with knitted brows.

"Only his attorney at this time," the detective replied.

"Don't worry," Devin said, looking at Naomi. "You'll see him soon. Wait for me here."

Devin and the detective disappeared into the police station, and Naomi sat in the waiting area.

Naomi started to text Vernon, to tell him what had happened, but she was too angry with him to send it. She glanced at the empty seat next to her. A lump formed in her throat. *I miss Alan.* Naomi sat there, alone with her regrets.

* * *

Nearly an hour later, Devin appeared in the waiting area, his face blank. Naomi stood and met the attorney.

"How is he?" Naomi asked, her hands held out.

"Physically, he's fine. But he's worried." Devin took a deep breath. "He's right to be worried. This is a real hornet's nest. Riley Roberson is a troubled girl. Her father died in a meth fire a few years ago. Her mother's a known prostitute. I didn't mention the extortion attempt, and neither did Riley. I advised Blake to do the same. It looks equally bad for both sides."

"What do the police think?"

"They know her family, know that she's a troublemaker, but they have to investigate the allegations. On the plus side, she wasn't beat up, so I doubt rape one is a possibility. Worst-case scenario? Blake's facing rape two and sexual assault in the third degree because of her age. If I can prove that she lied about her age, I can get those charges dropped."

"Can you prove that she lied?"

Devin hesitated for a beat. "Probably. I'll have my private investigator talk to her friends, see if she's lied about her age before. I'm sure she has. We only need one to corroborate. That would be enough for reasonable doubt, if it ever went to trial."

"So, it's possible that they'll drop all the charges?"

Devin nodded. "It's possible."

Naomi breathed a sigh of relief.

"They'll try a plea deal first. If we push for a trial, they might throw in the towel. But, if we go to trial, it'll be big news. I imagine that's not good for you."

Naomi nodded. "Definitely not good for me, but, even if we don't go to trial, it'll be big news."

"The police agreed to keep Blake's arrest under wraps until the arraignment on Monday. There's always the risk that one of the cops leaks it, or even Riley Roberson, but we can't control that."

"What about the APT?"

"He'll be tested tomorrow."

"When can I see him?"

"Right now, if you want. He's in the interview room, waiting to talk to you."

Devin summoned the beefy detective through the robot reception. The detective led Naomi to a square interview room. Inside, Blake was handcuffed to a metal table bolted to the floor. One wall had reflective two-way glass. Cameras hung from the ceiling.

The detective said, "You got ten minutes." Then he shut the door, leaving them alone.

Blake looked at his mother with puffy eyes, his cuffed hands resting on the table. Sweat rings soiled the underarms of his T-shirt. Sour smelling body odor hung in the air.

Naomi sat across from Blake and asked, "Are you all right?"

Blake shook his head. "You gotta get me outta here. I didn't do this."

"I know. Hang in there. Devin thinks they'll drop the charges."

Blake nodded, his shoulders slumped in resignation.

Naomi reached out and squeezed his hand. "It'll all be over soon."

Blake swallowed hard and said, "I love you, Mom."

In that moment, Naomi didn't see the spoiled gangster wannabe; she saw Blake as he once was—a chubby child who was afraid of the dark. "I love you too."

44

DEREK AND THE GREAT PLANE HEIST

It had been a fast-moving hurricane. A few hours before sunrise, the winds had slowed enough that large objects no longer flew through the air. Derek and Bo had grabbed their rifles and left their foxholes. Their camp had been decimated.

They had hiked through the jungle using familiar game trails and Bo's compass to navigate the darkness and the pounding rain. Derek had estimated that the ten-mile hike to the army base had taken at least two hours, maybe three. The jungle had been slow going, but, once they'd reached San Juan, they'd moved through the streets quickly, unconcerned about being attacked by the gangs. They'd reasoned that most people were indoors. In addition, speed had been more important than stealth. They knew their window of opportunity was rapidly closing. They had to steal a plane under the cover of darkness and fly off the island before the navy drones returned.

They stood on the corner of the concrete bunker, plotting their next move, wearing ponchos over their clothes. It was still dark and rainy, but they knew sunrise fast approached. Two roads led into the two garages of the Netas' concrete bunker. Debris littered the roads. A large tree limb blocked the path of the far garage, the very same garage where the Cessnas were stored. Thirty yards away from the garage doors, two small concrete guard houses stood next to lowered metal gates. Lights illuminated the guard houses and the silhouettes of two men. The wind howled through nearby trees.

"Do you think it's safe to fly?" Derek asked.

Bo frowned at Derek. "Of course it's not safe. But it's possible."

"We need to move that limb." Derek pointed to the limb blocking the road in front of the garage containing the Cessnas.

Bo motioned to the small guard houses and the gates. "We have to kill those guards and raise that gate. And we can't use our rifles. If the Netas hear the shots, we're dead."

Derek's stomach clenched. "Which one do you want?"

"I'll take the far one. I'll raise the gate and go inside for the plane. Once you've killed your man, move that limb off the road."

Derek nodded. "What about the runway?" Derek looked beyond the guard houses. The runway was only one hundred yards from the garage, but it was concealed by the rain and darkness. "What if debris is on the runway?"

"Hopefully there isn't any. We don't have time to clear it anyway."

Derek handed Bo the keycard from his pocket. "You ready?"

Bo took the keycard and looked Derek in the eyes. "Are you?"

Derek nodded again.

Derek crept to the concrete guard house. It was a low sturdy building, approximately ten by ten. Derek peered into the back window. He was pretty sure the window was made from thick plexiglass, not glass. Iron bars protected the window from flying debris. The silhouette sat at a metal desk, his back to Derek, and his head propped with his arm.

Derek leaned his rifle against the building, not wanting to be encumbered. He removed the knife from the scabbard on his belt and moved around the building. A single door faced the lowered gate. Derek took a deep breath, grabbed the door handle, and barged into the building.

The man lifted his head and turned to the open door, still sitting in his chair. The guard's eyes bulged with fright. Derek plunged his knife into the man's chest but missed the heart. The guard jerked and howled in pain. Derek slashed across the man's neck, deep enough to cut his vocal cords along with his carotid artery. Arterial blood sprayed Derek's face and poncho. Derek stepped back, watching the man twitch, the life spilling from his body.

Derek sheathed his blade, exited the guard house, strapped his rifle across his chest, and ran to the other guard house. The gate was up. He glanced in the window. The other guard was dead. Derek figured Bo was already inside the garage, stealing a plane. Derek dragged the large limb off the road; then he hurried toward the garage, only twenty yards away. He tried to open the door next to the garage, but it was locked. The sick feeling in his stomach turned to excitement as the garage door opened. Instead of Bo and an airplane, he saw the black boots of the Netas. Many black boots.

Derek ran for the corner of the concrete bunker and ultimately the jungle. But, before Derek passed the other garage, Netas spilled from the door, blocking Derek's path. The men raised their rifles and yelled in Spanish, their voices muffled by the rain and wind. Derek stopped and turned to run the other way, but more Netas were behind him, spilling from the first garage. Surrounded, Derek raised his arms in surrender, his rifle still strapped across his chest.

The Netas closed in on him. They took Derek's rifle, then frisked him, also taking his blade. They forced Derek back to the open garage door. They removed his poncho and pushed him to the ground, next to Bo, who was on his knees with his hands on his head. Netas were all around them, speaking Spanish, and pointing rifles at their heads. One of the men shouted at Derek until he rose to his knees and put his hands on his head like Bo. *They're gonna execute us.*

A man in crisp fatigues stepped into the circle of Netas and stood in front of Derek and Bo. He was six feet tall, with an athletic build and a scruffy black beard. Unlike his comrades, his arms were free from tattoos. The man shook his head and said, "Gringos." He took a deep breath and spoke in nearly perfect English. "You two must be the dumbest or the bravest gringos I've ever seen."

Derek looked at Bo. His face was a hard-set mask, yielding nothing.

"What did you plan to do? Fly home like little birds?"

Derek and Bo didn't reply.

"I'm *Jesús*, or Jesus to you gringos. I bet you thought you'd see Jesus *after* you died, not before." He turned to one of the Netas and said, "*Matalos. Despacio.*"

The Neta handed his rifle to the man next to him and removed a large knife from the scabbard on his belt. Jesus turned to walk away.

"Wait," Derek said, his hands still on his head.

But Jesus continued to walk away, and the Neta with the knife still approached, his lips curled into a snarl. The Neta stopped in front of Bo and grinned.

Bo closed his eyes and lifted his chin, giving the man a clean target.

"I know how to get off the island!" Derek shouted.

Jesus stopped in his tracks, turned around, and said, "*Espera.*"

The Neta with the knife stepped aside, and Bo opened his eyes, still straight-faced.

Jesus walked back to the scene. "You have one minute."

"The navy leaves during hurricanes," Derek said. "You just have to wait until right after, as soon as it's safe to fly."

Jesus wagged his head. "We tried that. By the time it's safe to fly the planes, the drones are already back." Jesus nodded to the man with the knife.

Derek spoke faster. "I know how to beat the drones. We both used to be in the air force. He used to be a pilot. I used to be a drone pilot."

Jesus narrowed his dark eyes at Derek. "I'm listening."

"I'll give you this information if you take us with you."

"You'll give me the information, or I'll kill you."

Derek swallowed, thinking about Fred, the dead mechanic from 1776, and the strategy he'd mentioned once. Just an offhand comment about how he'd get off the island if he were a psychopath, and he had access to the planes of the Netas. "You paint one plane flat black for stealth. Then, immediately after a hurricane, you fly that black plane low, with five other planes overhead."

"Two drones overlap the area, and they only have two missiles each," Bo said, adding credibility to Derek's plan. "You have six planes. That means at least two of 'em are gonna get away. You add some heat shieldin' over the batteries on the stealth plane, and, with the other planes over it, that plane has a real good chance to make it."

Jesus rubbed the stubble on his chin, looking from Derek to Bo and back again.

Derek's eyes bulged, searching Jesus's face for a sign that they'd be saved.

Jesus looked at the man with the knife and gestured with his chin into the bunker.

The man sheathed his knife, and Derek nearly fell over as a wave of relief washed over him. Then Jesus walked away. Derek and Bo were taken deep into the bunker and thrown into a cell.

Bo sat on the lower bunk, on a soiled mattress. He scowled at Derek and said, "We should've stayed in the jungle."

"You're right," Derek replied.

Derek climbed on the top bunk and lay on the paper-thin mattress. Nobody spoke for several minutes. Derek finally broke the silence and asked, "How do you know how many drones they have in the area and how many missiles they have?"

"I don't. It was a guess. I was savin' our asses."

"It worked. They didn't kill us."

"*Yet*. You know why we're still alive?"

"Because we gave them a good escape plan."

Bo shook his head. "They want us to fly decoy planes."

"I don't know how to fly."

"And they'll kill you when they find out."

45

JACOB AND A WATCHED POT

The fast-moving hurricane had started on Tuesday night, and was gone by Thursday morning. Jacob had expected to hear from Rob and Billy that morning, but the rain still raged until lunch. Then they received a text from Rob saying they were in place and he would message again, as soon as he and Billy had launched the drones.

Late in the afternoon, a text message from Rob appeared on the screen.

Rob: The weather's clear now. We're anchored underwater. We launched ten drones today. Billy and I will launch twenty more tomorrow. We haven't found Derek yet. Blockade should be back soon. Looks like we're stuck here until there's another hurricane.

Jacob and Rebecca stood behind Cesar and a few of his men in Project Freedom's command center. Drone footage streamed on the screens. Cesar communicated via text with Rob through the encrypted Wi-Fi mesh network.

Cesar: Drone footage is streaming on all ten drones.

Rob: Roger that.

Jacob walked down the row of screens in the command center, each one showing footage from a different drone, each one looking for Derek's face. One drone captured footage of men in fatigues, with rifles guarding an old Spanish fort along the ocean. Another showed footage of people searching through the rubble for building materials. Most of them showed men repairing their ramshackle homes. One drone showed footage of a skinny woman holding a naked baby. Jacob wondered how anyone could live there, much less raise a child there.

They watched for hours, hoping for a positive identification of Derek. But, like Jacob's mother said, "A watched pot never boils."

46

SUMMER AND THE INFORMAL ARRANGEMENT

Summer drove her father's pickup through Freetown toward Truman's mansion. Her hands and armpits were sweaty. Truman had called her at home earlier that day, as if nothing had happened two days prior. He'd said that he had found her son. She'd requested the information over the phone, but he'd insisted that he deliver the information in person. Summer was desperate to find her son, and Truman was well aware of that fact.

Summer stopped in front of his wrought-iron gate. She rolled down her window and pressed the intercom. Nobody answered, but the gate opened inward. She drove on the circular driveway, parking near the front door. Landscape lighting highlighted the fountain, the water shooting upward into the night air. A coatimundi sniffed and dug around the flower garden, looking for invertebrates. The creature was the size of a cat and looked like a racoon with a longer snout and a curled tail. She took a deep breath and exited the pickup truck. She walked across the brick driveway and up the steps. Before she reached the front door, it opened, and Truman's robotic personal assistant stood in the doorway with a smile.

"Good evening, Ms. Fitzgerald," Lisa said.

Summer stepped into the foyer, looking around for Truman. "Hi, Lisa."

The robotic dog scanned Summer for weapons.

"Mr. Bradshaw is waiting in his bedroom for you," Lisa said.

Summer's eyes widened, and her heart rate increased.

Lisa stared at Summer and asked, "Is everything all right?"

Summer nodded. "I'm fine."

"Follow me, Ms. Fitzgerald."

Summer followed Lisa through the foyer and the living room and down a long corridor. They passed a guest bedroom that looked very feminine, with pastel colors, a sleigh bed, a vanity, and beachy art. Summer wondered if that was Lisa's bedroom, then realized that was stupid. *Why would a bot need a bedroom? Maybe Truman has a live-in girlfriend?* Lisa knocked on the double doors at the end of the hallway.

"Ms. Fitzgerald is here to see you," Lisa said through the door.

"Send her in," Truman called back.

Lisa opened the door. Summer walked into the room tentatively. Lisa shut the door behind her, causing Summer to flinch. The room was cavernous, but the focal point was the elevated and circular bed. Truman sat on the couch in the sitting area to the left, tapping on a tablet. A one-hundred-inch OLED television was muted, with talking heads and scrolling stock tickers. Truman didn't acknowledge Summer's presence. She was relieved that he was clothed and not in bed. Summer walked to the sitting area.

"Truman," Summer said.

He held up one finger, not looking up from his tablet.

Summer stood for what felt like an eternity.

Truman finally looked up from his tablet. He leered at Summer and said, "You look beautiful."

Summer cringed. She purposely wore jeans, a big T-shirt, and no makeup to look unappealing. "Where's my son?"

"Sit." He patted the space next to him on the couch.

She sat on the couch but on the end, about six feet away from him.

"You're so far away. Come a little closer."

"I'm okay here."

Truman arched his eyebrows. "Do you think we're flowing like water right now?"

Summer clenched her jaw, then forced a smile and scooched closer.

He smiled back. "That's better." He tapped on his tablet again, this time talking as he did so. "We found your son. It took a little longer than I thought because his name isn't Byron Fitzgerald. It says here that Byron Pierce is five weeks old and that Mr. and Mrs. Pierce live in Virginia. A community called Crosspointe—"

"I know who they are."

He looked up from his tablet again and nodded. "Your late-fiancé's parents."

Summer tilted her head. "How did you know that?"

"My people are very thorough. The hard part will be convincing the Pierces to give up the only thing they have left of Connor."

"Byron's *my* son."

"I know. But they may see it differently. They may blame you for Connor's death. They may not think a baby should be on the run with a fugitive."

"I could contact them."

Truman sucked air through his teeth. "I wouldn't do that. You run the risk of telling the US government where you are. They might be interested in arresting the only person to escape from the US island prisons."

"What should I do?"

"Northern Virginia is one of the worst places to attempt a kidnapping. Facial recognition cameras cover nearly every square inch."

"Can you help me or not?" This came out more annoyed than Summer intended.

"Water. Remember?"

Summer forced a smile. "Sorry. Can you help me?"

"Like I said before, that depends on you." Truman grabbed his phone from the coffee table, tapped a few times, and handed it to Summer. "Scroll to the bottom and sign. It's the same sexual consent contract."

Summer glowered at Truman. "How many times are you expecting me to have sex with you?"

Truman exhaled. "This isn't working for me."

"I just wanna understand the terms."

"And I don't want another business relationship. I wouldn't commit a crime for a business partner. I might for someone I care about, but that has to be reciprocal. I understand if it's not."

Summer held out her hands like a beggar. "Please, Truman. I really need your help."

Truman leaned back on the couch. "And I'd really like to help you, but I need a reciprocal relationship to do that."

"Why can't you just help me? We'll go out. Go slow and see what happens."

"We can do that. Maybe it's best to wait on your son. After all, the longer he's with the Pierces, the more attached they'll become."

Summer hung her head and rubbed her temples.

"Are you all right?"

Summer raised her head and forced another smile. "I'm fine. You look nice, by the way." She placed her hand on his thigh.

"Are you sure about that?"

"Yes."

Truman glanced at his phone. "Then sign it."

Summer scrolled to the bottom, removed the stylus, and stared at the signature line. "You need to use protection this time. And not so rough. No biting."

Truman sighed and nodded.

Summer signed, added her thumbprint for authentication, and handed the phone back to Truman.

He tossed his phone on the coffee table and said, "Take off your clothes."

Summer pressed her lips together, then took off her T-shirt.

"Stand up."

Summer stood from the couch, wearing her jeans and a sports bra.

"Move the coffee table. I want you to undress right in front of me."

Summer grabbed the wooden coffee table and slid it across the carpet, away from the couch and Truman.

"Come here," he said, motioning with his index finger.

She approached.

"Closer."

Summer thought he wanted to kiss her, so she leaned over.

When she was within grasping distance, he grabbed her by the neck and pulled her inches from his face. He moved to her ear and whispered. "You want this more than anything. Make me believe or this is over. Do you understand?"

Summer nodded, and he let go of her neck. She stood in front of him and moved to imaginary music, imagining that she loved Truman or at least wanted him. She unbuttoned her jeans and lowered her zipper, exposing a bit of her unsexy cotton underwear. She kicked off her sneakers and removed her socks.

"Lick your lips," Truman said.

She did as commanded. Then she removed her sports bra, which was difficult to do in a sexy way, so she struggled out of the tight bra like she normally did. She slid her cotton underwear down her legs.

"Don't move. Let me look at you." He ogled her naked body with the unblinking eyes of a predator. After a long moment, he finally said, "Turn around."

She turned around.

"Bend over."

Her stomach turned, and her heart pounded in her chest. She bent over, her arms holding her chest. His breath quickened.

Then he said, "Stand up. Turn back around."

She did as she was commanded.

"Tell me how much you want me."

"I want you so much." Her affect was flat.

He scowled at her and then let out a ragged breath. "Don't kill the mood. Try again."

"I want you." She licked her lips again, since it was something he'd already asked for. "I want you inside me."

He raised one side of his mouth in contempt. "I bet you do, you *fucking* whore."

Summer reeled back, as if she'd been slapped.

"Tell me that you're my whore. Tell me how you'll do anything I tell you to do."

Summer swallowed the bile creeping up her throat. "I'm your whore. I'll do anything for you."

"Anything?" He was grinning now.

"Anything," she said in her best sultry voice.

"On your knees." He spread his long legs, so she could kneel between them.

She knelt in front of him, her knees on the carpet. He undid his slacks and pulled his boxers and slacks down to midthigh, releasing his erection.

"Tell me what you want next," Truman said.

"I want you," Summer replied.

He sneered. "More specific."

"I want you in my mouth."

"Then take what you want."

She hesitated. "I don't know if I can do this."

Summer started to stand, but Truman reached for her shoulders with his long arms and forced her back to her knees. Summer grunted and tried to twist from his grasp, but his grip was too strong. He palmed her head and forced her mouth toward his penis. Her hands were free, so she reared back and punched him in the crotch, her knuckles connecting with his fleshy scrotum and testicles. He shrieked and let go, his hands immediately holding his crotch, rocking forward and backward.

"You *fucking* bitch," he said between moans.

Summer put on her pants and T-shirt without underwear, slipped into her sneakers, and ran from the room, down the hall, her sneakers slapping the marble. She ran past the living room to the foyer and grabbed the front door, but it was locked ... electronically. A keypad was next to the door. She pressed random numbers, but nothing happened. She pounded on the door and shouted, "Let me out! Let me out!"

Then the door unlocked. Summer yanked open the door and looked back.

Lisa stood there with a blank look on her face. The robot said, "I'm so sorry."

47

NAOMI AND THE APPLE DOESN'T FALL VERY FAR

They were in the sitting area of Naomi's congressional office.

"Eric Roth called me last night," Fletcher said, sitting in a leather chair.

Naomi stiffened on the couch opposite Fletcher. "Unless you want a short tenure as my campaign manager, I'd rather you didn't talk to the Roths."

Fletcher leaned back, his eyes wide with astonishment. "I'm sorry, Naomi. I was only looking out for the best interests of your campaign."

"He's just doing his job," Vernon said, sitting next to Naomi. "I would've done the same." Vernon turned to Fletcher. "We think the Roths may have been involved in the assassination attempt."

Naomi glared at Vernon, still harboring residual resentment from Wednesday night.

Fletcher adjusted himself, the chair squeaking under his girth. "Again, I'm sorry. I know the Roths were being cited by conspiracy theorists, but that's nothing new for them. Forgive me for dredging up bad memories, but is there evidence of their involvement?"

Vernon shook his head. "Only anecdotal, although they stand to lose the most if and when Naomi wins the presidency. They've tried several times to buy our campaign."

Naomi crossed her legs. "I turned them down and told them that I oppose the Federal Reserve."

Fletcher exhaled heavy. "Then you won't be surprised by their offer."

"What did they offer?" Vernon asked.

"They wanna fund our campaign, and they'll help to skew the press in our favor. In return, they want us to tax Thorium Unlimited 90 percent, appoint Jacob Roth as Treasury Secretary, leave all monetary matters to the Federal Reserve, and, most important, they want us to continue with the Federal Reserve charter."

Naomi raised one side of her mouth in contempt. "I won't agree to any of those stipulations."

"What are our chances if we *do* agree?" Vernon asked.

Naomi scowled at Vernon, holding her gaze for a long beat. "It's not *worth* exploring those possibilities."

Vernon cleared his throat and leaned away from Naomi. "We hired Fletcher for his expertise. Even if you did agree to their terms, that doesn't mean you can't change your mind once you're elected."

Fletcher sucked air through his teeth. "That's a very dangerous game. What do you think they'll do if you bite their hand after they feed you?"

"Can we forget about the ramifications for a moment? How much is their support really worth?"

"They're kingmakers." Fletcher looked directly at Naomi. "They'd make you king."

"I wouldn't be a king," Naomi replied. "I'd be a front for a private banking cartel controlling not just this country but the world. I'd rather lose than make a deal with the devil."

"Can we win without their help?" Vernon asked.

"Well, we're gonna give it our best shot," Fletcher replied. "In the meantime, we have bigger fish to fry than even the Roths. My apologies, Naomi. I hate to strategize around a family tragedy, but we don't have a choice. This incident with Blake could potentially bury us."

Naomi let out a heavy breath. "I know. The silver lining is we have until the arraignment to get in front of this."

"Unless they leak it," Vernon said.

"All the more reason to get in front of this now," Fletcher said.

"This girl's lying," Naomi said, her jaw set tight.

"We know that," Vernon said. "It's public perception that's the problem. Most people will side with the girl. Since the Me Too movement, the public's been conditioned to believe women. It's a precarious situation for Blake *and* us. I hope Devin can get the charges dropped."

"In the meantime, we need a strategy," Fletcher said, his hands resting on his gut.

"I don't think we should say anything yet," Naomi said, uncrossing and crossing her legs. "If I support the girl, and then the charges are dropped, it makes me look like a terrible mother. If I support Blake, and he's convicted, I look like an enabler."

"What if we're more ambiguous? We trust the justice system."

Vernon pointed at Fletcher. "I like that. If the charges are dropped, it validates Naomi's position and Blake's innocence."

Naomi frowned. "If it goes the other way?"

"Then we still support the justice system. Everyone's equal under the law, even your son. If he's convicted, he deserves his punishment."

Naomi's cell phone chimed on the coffee table. She picked it up, glancing at the New York number. "It's Devin."

Fletcher stood to leave.

"Stay. We'll probably have to discuss this." Naomi swiped right, placing her phone to her ear. "Hello, Devin."

"I have some unfortunate news," Devin said.

Naomi braced herself, clutching her cell phone.

"He's in federal custody. The Jamesville Police found child pornography on his computer. The FBI's taking over that part of his case."

Naomi swallowed the lump in her throat. "How old were the girls on his computer?"

"Mostly young teenagers, thirteen or fourteen. The feds think he might be a hebephile. I'm so sorry, Naomi."

Naomi wiped the corner of her eye with her index finger. "What happens now?"

"He was supposed to take the APT test today, but the feds will administer the test. He'll still have to answer for the rape charge, but the feds take priority. We'll need another lawyer to handle the federal case. I have a few names."

Naomi hung her head. "Can I call you back?"

"Of course."

"Thank you, Devin." Naomi disconnected the call. She sat on the couch in a fog, clutching her phone.

"Are you okay?" Vernon asked.

She blinked, waking from her daze. A few tears slipped down her face. She said, "I don't think so. They found child pornography on Blake's computer. He's with the FBI."

Vernon and Fletcher didn't look shocked. They'd already figured on the child porn, based on her side of the conversation.

"I have contacts at the FBI," Fletcher said. "I'll see if I can get some more information."

48

DEREK PLAYS THE PILOT

The next morning, Derek and Bo were handcuffed, and their legs were shackled. They were taken from their cell at gunpoint by four guards. Their leg irons forced them to do a little shuffle walk as they were prodded back to the garage. The garage door was wide open, the morning sun bright and shiny. Five planes were parked in a row, their wings folded. One plane was parked near the open garage door. Jesus was there, watching his men paint the plane flat black. Derek glanced at the paint cans, confirming that they were indeed from the paint supplies that 1776 had collected for their stealth sub. The Netas must've taken the paint when they took over the old Spanish fort.

Jesus turned to face Derek and Bo. "Ah, the air force pilots. It's time for you to prove your worth." Jesus walked to a nearby plane and opened the door. He pointed to Bo and said, "Get inside, gringo."

Bo grunted and squirmed his way into the cockpit, his cuffs and leg irons making it difficult. Jesus walked around the plane and stepped into the copilot's seat. Bo's door was wide open, so Derek could hear what they were saying.

"What is this?" Jesus asked, pointing at a round gauge.

"It's an altimeter," Bo replied, speaking loudly for Derek's benefit.

"And this?" Jesus pointed to another circular gauge.

162

"Vertical speed indicator."

This went on for ten minutes. Like a game of memory, Derek tried to remember the names of the controls and gauges and switches—and where they were located.

Bo nearly fell as he climbed from the plane, his leg irons clanging together. Derek was prodded into the cockpit. Up close, the cockpit looked even more complicated.

Jesus pointed to a circular gauge. "What is this?"

"Airspeed indicator," Derek said.

"And this one?" Jesus pointed to another one.

"Altitude indicator."

"No. It is an attitude indicator."

Shit. "That's what I said. Attitude indicator."

"What does an attitude indicator do?"

Derek paused, looking at the gauge, remembering movies with plane crashes and seeing that gauge going crazy. "It shows whether the plane is level or in a dive."

Jesus frowned but then pointed to a switch. "What's this?"

Derek had no idea. "The on and off switch."

"And this." He pointed to a knob.

Again, Derek had no idea. "The throttle."

Jesus shook his head. "Fucking gringo. Get out of my plane."

Derek struggled from the Cessna.

Jesus marched around the plane. He removed the handgun from his holster and approached Derek with purpose. "On your knees."

Two of the guards pointed their rifles in Derek's direction, the other two at Bo.

Derek sank to his knees.

Jesus pressed his handgun to Derek's forehead.

"Wait a second," Bo said.

"Your friend is no pilot. He is a liar," Jesus said, talking to Bo but still looking at Derek.

"If you shoot him, I won't fly. He's my copilot."

163

Jesus turned and glared at Bo. "You'll do whatever the fuck I tell you to do."

"You'll have to kill me too then." Bo said this as though he were talking about the weather.

Jesus marched up to Bo, pointing his handgun in Bo's face. "That can be arranged."

Bo was straight-faced. "You don't have enough pilots to kill me. I might be the difference between you getting off this island or being blown out of the sky by a drone."

Jesus clenched his jaw, then dropped the gun to his side, and said, "*Chingada!*" He turned to his men and gestured to Derek and Bo. "*Llévatelos.*"

Derek's heart pounded in his chest. He was sure that Jesus had just told his men to kill them. But the Netas took them back to their cell and removed their leg irons. Once they were locked inside, the guards motioned for their hands. Through the slit in the door, the guards removed their handcuffs.

Derek rubbed his wrists and looked at Bo. "You saved my life."

Bo chuckled and replied, "Again."

49

JACOB AND THE CESSNA SIGHTING

Jacob walked into the Project Freedom command center late Friday morning. Rebecca was already there, sitting in front of a screen, watching live streaming footage from a drone. Cesar spoke to one of his men in Spanish.

Jacob sat next to Rebecca. "See anything interesting?"

The screen showed footage of an old army base. It scanned the faces of uniformed men standing sentry at gates.

"I think these men took over a military base," Rebecca said. "They have uniforms and trucks and machine guns."

The screen showed uniformed men cleaning hurricane debris from the streets. One crew of men attached a large tree limb to a UTV, using a chain. Then they dragged the limb from the road. The screen showed an empty airplane runway, then an earth-sheltered bunker, like the one they were in at that very moment, but the one on-screen was much larger. One of the garage doors was open. Jacob saw something black.

"Is that a plane?" Jacob pointed to the screen, but the drone had moved on from the open garage door.

"That's what I thought it was," Rebecca replied. Then she turned and called out to Cesar, who was at the other end of the long desk of

OLED screens. "I think we found something."

Cesar stood and walked over to Rebecca and Jacob. "What is it?"

"I think we saw a plane," Rebecca said. "Like thirty seconds ago."

"May I sit?"

Rebecca moved to the next seat over, allowing Cesar to sit in front of the screen and the keyboard. He typed and tapped on the screen, eventually restoring the video from one minutes ago. They watched as the drone flew over the empty runway; then it flew past the earth-sheltered bunker, with an open garage bay.

"It's in that garage," Rebecca said.

Cesar rewound the video and paused on the best picture of the open garage. "That *is* a plane. I think they're painting it black."

"You can't see the wings," Jacob said.

"The garage door is too narrow for fixed wings. Look. They're folded back." Cesar pointed. "They're still white. See those two men. I think they're painting it."

"Why would they do that?" Rebecca asked.

"For the same reason the drones are black. For stealth." Cesar paused the video and zoomed in on the men in their tight black T-shirts. One had a partially obscured tattoo on his upper arm. It looked like a hand with a red-and-white flag wrapped around the wrist. Cesar pointed to the tattoo. "That's the tattoo of the Netas. A hand with two fingers crossed, and the Puerto Rican flag wrapped around the wrist. The crossed fingers are under his sleeve."

"Summer mentioned them."

"Yes. They were the most powerful gang in Puerto Rico before the hurricanes. Many of the Netas stayed in Puerto Rico and weathered the hurricanes, including their leader, Miguel Arroyo."

"Why would they do that?" Rebecca asked.

"They wanted to loot the island and live without the police."

"Do you think they're planning an escape?"

Cesar nodded. "It appears so. We'll keep this drone in the area so we can keep an eye on them."

"I don't know how that helps us find Derek," Jacob said.
"Maybe it does. Maybe it doesn't."

50

SUMMER AND ANOTHER MORNING AFTER

Summer woke to the sound of birds chirping outside her bedroom window. Then it all came back to her. The attempted sexual assault. Her jab to his groin. Her escape. *What am I gonna do? No way in hell will he help me with Byron now.* She checked the clock on her bedside table: *9:21 a.m.* It was late. Thankfully, she didn't have to work that Friday. After the debacle at Truman's last night, she'd driven around and parked in a deserted park for a few hours, waiting past her father's bedtime. She'd been afraid to face her father, not because he'd judge her but because she was ashamed of the whole situation. She'd known that, if she'd seen him last night, he would've seen that something was wrong, and he would've known it had to do with Truman.

Summer padded to the bathroom, peed, washed her hands, and brushed her teeth. Then she walked to the kitchen.

Patrick sat at the kitchen table. He looked up from his laptop and removed his headphones. "Good morning, sleepyhead."

Summer slouched in the chair opposite her father. "Morning, Dad. What are you doing?" She glanced at his open laptop.

"Steven wants me to release the Psycho Island video on my vlog. I'm just trying to enhance the video a bit. The quality's not great."

"Can it be tracked back to you?"

"Don't worry. I use a very good encrypted VPN." Patrick paused for a beat. "I already had breakfast, but I can make you whatever you want. You want some eggs?"

"I'm not that hungry."

Patrick stared at Summer. "Are you okay?"

Summer broke eye contact for an instant. "I had trouble sleeping last night."

"Did you take that valerian root that Steven dropped off?"

"I forgot."

"How about some coffee?"

"I can get it."

"Sit," Patrick said, standing from the kitchen table. He poured coffee from the warming pot into a mug. He set the steaming mug in front of Summer with a spoon. "You want cream and sugar?"

"Please."

Patrick grabbed the sugar jar from the counter and the creamer from the fridge. He returned to his seat. Summer fixed her coffee, stirring the creamy concoction.

"How did it go with Truman last night?" Patrick asked.

Summer nearly choked on her coffee at the mention of Truman.

"What did he find out about Byron?"

Summer set her mug on the table. "Byron's with Connor's parents in Virginia. I was thinking about calling them and seeing if they might bring Connor here."

Patrick winced. "That's not a good idea. First of all, you're assuming that they'll be willing to give you Byron. That's not a given. If you call them, that puts them on alert, and the US government might find out where you are. I'm sure they'd love to extradite you back to the States. Even if the Pierces are willing to come here, and we can do this covertly, they'd be questioned when they return to the States. ICE would ask about Byron's whereabouts. They'd have records that they left with Byron but returned empty-handed. They themselves could be arrested."

"What am I supposed to do?" Summer held out her hands. "Go to Virginia? They might not wanna give Byron to a fugitive."

"It's not for them to decide."

"He's also the only piece of Connor they have left."

"He's *your* son."

Summer pursed her pink lips. "Legally, Byron's *their* son."

Patrick scowled at that. "I don't give a shit about the law. I care about what's right. You're innocent. Byron's innocent. He belongs with you."

Summer's shoulders slumped. "I agree, but I'll be arrested the second I step foot in the US."

"I'm assuming Truman won't help?"

"He's not willing to take the risk."

"I've been looking into what it would take to do this. It's very dangerous, and there's a good chance of arrest, but I *might* be able to pull it off."

Summer tilted her head. "You? You're just as much a fugitive as me."

"I know a guy who knows a coyote who could smuggle me under the wall. I have some contacts in the States, people I could stay with who could take me to Virginia and back."

Summer was speechless for a moment, thinking about what she'd given to Truman. "Why didn't you tell me this was an option?" Her tone was harsh, her eyes wild.

Patrick showed his palms in surrender. "Because I didn't know. I didn't wanna get your hopes up. Even now, it's still in the planning stages."

"I wanna go with you."

"Crossing the border is very dangerous. People are raped and killed every day."

"That's more of a reason you shouldn't go alone."

Patrick shook his head. "I don't like this idea, Summer."

"Do you really think Connor's parents will hand over Byron to a man they've never met? They might not hand him over to me."

"I'll take him if I have to."

Summer frowned at that. "What happens if Byron gets hurt in the process?"

Patrick exhaled. "I don't know."

"I'm coming with you."

"There's another problem. The coyote isn't cheap, and I'm not rich. I was thinking that you could tell me where that video's located. The one that Truman's willing to pay two hundred ounces of silver for."

Summer clenched her fists, thinking of Truman. "It's in a hospital in Virginia, but I doubt I could draw you a map from memory. That's another reason for me to go with you."

Patrick sighed. "Okay. You have a point."

"Even if we do get the video, we need the money before the trip, not after."

"I have some savings."

Summer furrowed her brows. "You do?"

"When I was in my early twenties, I collected silver coins."

51

NAOMI AND PSYCHO ISLAND EXPOSED

Roger Kroenig was thinner and tanner, but that was definitely the ex-congressman, the man who had supposedly disappeared. But he hadn't disappeared. He'd been sent to US Penal Colony East. Psycho Island. Apparently, the rumors and the conspiracies were true. The US government sent antigovernment activists to Psycho Island. That wasn't surprising to Naomi. In fact, she'd said as much herself. The video evidence was the surprising part. *How could they've smuggled the video from the island?*

Naomi tapped her laptop screen, pausing the video. She sat at her desk, Vernon standing by her side. "Has anyone ever escaped the island?" she asked.

"Not that I know of," Vernon replied.

"Is it a fake?"

Flawless computer-generated videos were commonplace. The porn industry used fake videos to portray the most modest actresses performing the vilest sexual acts imaginable. Political satirists portrayed world leaders doing and saying anything and everything. Thankfully, software existed to detect these fake videos.

"It's real," Vernon replied. "The video's already been screened by several reputable sources."

"This might be the nail in the coffin for the island prisons," Naomi said.

Vernon nodded. "And you're the only candidate who's been against the island prisons. You were right, and *they* were *all* wrong."

"Fletcher was wrong too."

"I know. I'm glad you stuck to your guns."

Fletcher knocked on the open door. "I have some news."

Vernon turned to Fletcher and grinned. "Luckily we didn't come out in support of the island prisons."

Fletcher shut the door behind him, his mouth turned down. "It's about Blake."

Naomi turned her swivel chair to face Fletcher, her jaw set tight.

Fletcher approached her desk. "I just got off the phone with my contact at the FBI. Blake's been transferred to IPC. He failed the APT test."

Naomi put her hand to her mouth. Then she shook her head.

"Shit," Vernon said, grimacing.

Fletcher said, "If we went back to the Roths, we could have Blake's record expunged. I've seen it done. They have that kind of power."

"No. I won't make a deal," Naomi said. "I refuse to be in their debt."

"It might cost us the election, in addition to your son's life."

Naomi pursed her lips. "So be it."

52

DEREK AND REC TIME

Derek sat on a plastic chair, next to the bunk beds, finishing his lunch. Mystery meat and fruit. Bo sat on the bottom bunk, doing the same. Bo thought the meat might be caiman, but he wasn't sure. Derek took a final bite of his mango, then stood from his chair and held out his hand to Bo. "You done?" Derek asked.

"Yeah." Bo handed his empty plate to Derek.

Derek stacked Bo's plate on top of his and took them to the heavy steel door. A narrow slit was open, with a little ledge on the outside. Derek pushed the plates through the slit, so they were resting on the ledge for pick up. He returned to his seat with a groan. Derek estimated that they'd been in the windowless cell for six and a half days. He had assumed that lights out marked each night, and lights on marked each morning. They would've gone stir-crazy, but, the past few days, they'd been given rec time after lunch.

A few minutes later, the plates were taken. A guard banged on the door and said, "*Manos.*"

Derek and Bo approached the door. Each, in turn, put their hands through the slot to be cuffed. The door opened, and four guards appeared, three with rifles, one holding leg irons. After the prisoners' legs were shackled, the four guards led them from their cell at gunpoint. Along the way, two more guards joined them, making six.

They shuffled down a long hall to a garage and airplane hangar. The six Cessna planes were parked in a row, their wings folded. One of the planes was painted flat black, like something from a *Batman* movie. A handful of old golf carts were parked against a wall.

Derek and Bo were marched outside, past the gates that guarded access to the bunker. The sun was bright and high overhead, the heat reverberating in a haze off the asphalt. They turned right on the road and shuffled a hundred yards to a dilapidated tennis court that was surrounded by a chain-link fence. Derek and Bo stepped inside the court, and a guard locked the gate behind them.

It was just the two of them, locked inside, their hands and ankles still bound. The guards watched Derek and Bo through the fence, but mostly they joked and laughed with each other, speaking Spanish. The tennis nets were long gone, leaving only a cracked asphalt surface with faded lines denoting the boundaries. Derek and Bo sat on the asphalt and leaned against the fence.

"Why do they give us rec time if we can't even move?" Derek rattled the chain connecting his handcuffs.

"I've been thinkin' 'bout that," Bo replied. "Obviously, it ain't for exercise. It would be easier to let us rot in that cell. I think Jesus doesn't want us goin' stir-crazy, bein' cooped up with no sunlight. If he's gonna trust us to fly one a them planes, we gotta be sane."

Derek smirked at Bo. "Joke's on him then. You're already insane."

Bo chuckled. "On this fuckin' island, bein' crazy *is* sane."

Derek cackled at that. "Ain't that the truth." Their laughter dissipated. A laughing gull called overhead. Derek looked up at the gull. He noticed something small and black nearby, hovering high in the sky. "What the hell is that?" Derek pointed, holding up both of his bound hands.

Bo looked where Derek pointed, squinting. "I think it's a drone. The Netas are prob'ly doin' some testin'."

53

JACOB AND THE POSITIVE MATCH

"Oh, my God. It's him," Rebecca said, her eyes unblinking, looking over Cesar's shoulder at the computer screen.

The screen read Positive Match under Derek's face. Derek sat next to another man, inside a derelict tennis court. They were both in chains.

"He's being held captive by the same men we saw a few days ago, with the black airplane," Jacob said.

"Yes. The Netas," Cesar replied.

"Now we can rescue him," Rebecca said, looking to Cesar, like an eager puppy.

Cesar shook his head. "This is good news, no doubt, but we cannot rescue him yet. It's not that simple. Derek is under heavy guard. The Netas are well armed and organized. Your husband's men will devise a plan. In the meantime, the drones will continue to gather intelligence and to keep an eye on Derek."

"When will they rescue him?" Rebecca asked, her arms crossed, like a petulant child.

Jacob placed a hand on Rebecca's shoulder. "Relax. Rob and Billy know what they're doing."

"When it's safe," Cesar said.

"But he's being held captive," Rebecca replied. "They could kill him."

"He appears unharmed. Remember, Derek's life isn't the only one at stake."

54

SUMMER AND CAYUCOS

Summer had been worried that Truman might seek revenge for her punch to his scrotum. She had told herself that Truman didn't want to be embarrassed, so he'd likely drop the whole thing. That seemed to be the case. She hadn't seen or heard from Truman since the attempted sexual assault. She wanted to believe that it was over, but her intuition told her that there'd be a reckoning in the future. Truman was a man who got what he wanted.

It had been six days since Summer's father had told her that he was working on a plan to rescue Byron. Summer preferred "rescue" over "kidnap." After much planning and discussion, Patrick had felt that they had a workable plan. Yesterday, Patrick had hired an autonomous car to take them from Silver City to Panama City. They'd stayed overnight at the Radisson Hotel Panama Canal, which overlooked the mouth of the canal.

Just before eleven, they took an autonomous taxi from their hotel in Balboa to the causeway in Amador, which was only a mile away. The causeway was a narrow strip of highway and walkway that stretched nearly three miles into the sparkling Pacific Ocean. Traffic was light. A few tourists and Panamanians walked and biked in the sun. A few rode electric scooters. At the end of the causeway were a cluster of restaurants, a nature center, and several docks. The taxi dropped them in front of Cayucos Bar Restaurante.

"Cayucos are canoes carved from the trunk of a tree," Patrick said, as they walked toward the one-story restaurant. "Every year there's a cayuco race through the Panama Canal from the Atlantic to the Pacific." Patrick stopped near the entrance. They were supposed to meet Elvis at 11:00 a.m.

Summer stood next to her father. "How far is the race?"

"About fifty miles."

"Have you ever been? It sounds fun."

"No. I don't leave Silver City very often."

A bearded Panamanian wearing *jorts* and a Pittsburgh Pirates baseball cap bounded toward them. "Raymond?" the man asked, using Patrick's fake name.

"Elvis?" Patrick replied.

Elvis grinned. "The one and only." He held out his hand to Patrick, and they shook. Elvis turned his attention to Summer. "And who is this lovely lady?"

"My daughter, Stacy," Patrick replied, using Summer's fake name.

Elvis leered at Summer. "I'm happy to meet you."

"Nice to meet you too," Summer said, shaking his hand.

Elvis opened the front door to the restaurant and motioned with his hand. "Come. Let's have ceviche and beer." He grinned again. "I buy."

A robotic host greeted them at a podium. *"Bienvenidos a Cayucos."* The top half of the bot was intact and like a human in shape with a torso, head, shoulders, and arms. It wore a tuxedo. The bottom half of the bot was simply a post attached to the floor behind the podium. The bot's slacks hung loosely over the metal post holding it upright. Static bots were cheaper than fully functioning bots and were often used when self-transport was unnecessary for their duties. The bot handed them a tablet. *"Siéntate donde quieras."*

Elvis led them outside to the deck. They sat at a wooden picnic table, overlooking the water and the boats in the distance. It was a weekday and still early for lunch, so they were in relative privacy. Elvis tapped on the tablet, ordering ceviche and Balboa beer. They made small talk about Panama City, until the food and beer arrived on a robotic cart. The cart was like a little van with a rack on top, holding their ceviche and beer. They removed their order from the rack and helped themselves to napkins from the drawer labeled *Servilletas*. The robotic cart motored back to the kitchen.

They drank pale lager and ate raw fish cured in lime juice with crackers. Patrick had tried several times, but Elvis wasn't interested in talking business. Instead, they made small talk about Pirates baseball, Toyota trucks, and the antigovernment demonstrations in Panama City.

Once the food was gone, and the small talk was settled, Elvis finally said, "The boat will be here tomorrow at eight in the morning. You have the silver? Twenty-five ounces, no?"

"We agreed on twenty-four," Patrick replied, straight-faced.

Elvis laughed and wagged his finger. "I'm just testing you."

Patrick removed a heavy plastic tube from his pocket. He opened the tube and flipped it upside down on the table. He lifted it, exposing a neat stack of twenty-four shiny silver coins.

Elvis's eyes bulged at the sight of silver.

Summer had never seen silver bullion until last night, when Patrick had shown her his stash of coins. Each coin was worth about one thousand Fed Coins and illegal in most countries. Patrick had collected the coins as a young man, when silver bullion was still legal and only worth fifteen dollars per ounce.

Elvis reached for the coins, but Patrick covered the stack, then handed Elvis twelve coins.

"I'll bring the other twelve to the dock tomorrow," Patrick said.

55

NAOMI'S BEHIND THE EIGHT BALL

"Four days ago, video surfaced showing the harsh realities of life on US Penal Colony East," Brooke Bixler said, in voice-over, images of skinny island prisoners with rusty machetes on the screen. Roger Kroenig appeared, looking like a beach bum. "It was the first footage ever recorded of the island prison. Former Congressman Roger Kroenig disappeared in 2045, but his likeness appeared in the video, sparking antigovernment demonstrations throughout the United States." A DC demonstration appeared on the screen. People marched with signs that read Bring Our Children Home, Close Psycho Island, and Where's Roger? "FBI Director Charles Elliot released the following statement earlier today."

CNN cut to Charles Elliot, standing at a podium, the press seated before him.

Naomi sat on the couch in her congressional office, watching the OLED television on the wall. Vernon and Fletcher sat in chairs opposite the couch, also watching the screen.

"Former Congressman Roger Kroenig was arrested for treason in his connection to the terrorist organization, 1776," Director Elliot said. "He failed the subsequent APT test and was sent to US Penal Colony East, pursuant to the Island Prison Crime Bill of 2043. I encourage protestors to peacefully assemble and follow all laws. Facial recognition cameras will capture any illegal behavior. Property damage and violence will be prosecuted to the fullest extent of the law."

CNN showed Brooke Bixler sitting behind the news desk. She was model thin with a long neck, dark shiny hair, and a catlike nose. Naomi's preaccident face appeared on the screen over Brooke's shoulder. "Congresswoman Naomi Sutton's son, Blake Sutton, was arrested last week on charges of possession of child pornography and suspicion of raping a sixteen-year-old girl. He failed the APT test and was transferred to Island Prison Corrections for transport to US Penal Colony East." Video footage appeared on the screen of Blake, handcuffed, being escorted by IPC guards. CNN cut back to Brooke Bixler. "Mrs. Sutton has been an outspoken critic of IPC—"

Naomi changed the channel, shaking her head in disgust. For the first time, she'd gone to work without her bandages. One side of Naomi's face and neck was white, the black literally burned from her skin, leaving mottled blanched scarring. Her empty right eye socket was still covered with a patch, like a pirate.

Senator Corrinne Powers was on MSNBC's hit show, *That's the Point*. She sat at a glass table, across from the host, Sebastian Gannon. In contrast to Naomi, Corrinne's face was flawless. Corrinne's high cheekbones and symmetrical face were made for television. Her perfectly coiffed blond hair hung to chin length. Her toned calves were visible under the glass table.

"In 2043, you supported the Island Prison Crime Bill. Do you still support that legislation today?" Sebastian asked.

Sebastian reminded Naomi of an effeminate version of Vernon. Like Vernon, he had a tight fade, radiant caramel skin, and a sparkly smile. Even though Vernon and Sebastian were roughly the same age, midforties, Sebastian could pass for thirty. His face was as smooth as a baby's behind, without a single wrinkle or crease.

"I've never been a fervent supporter of IPC," Corrinne replied. "However, based on the information we had at the time, it made sense to support the bill. The results are hard to argue with. Crime dropped precipitously in the years after the bill was signed into law. I do question the leadership at IPC, and I've never been comfortable with the secrecy around the island prisons. We're supposed to be a government by the people and for the people. If that's the case, we can't keep the public in the dark. Given what I know now, I can no longer support the island prisons."

"Congresswoman Naomi Sutton was the only candidate to oppose the island prisons *prior* to the release of the video footage. Ironically, her son, Blake Sutton, was recently arrested for possession of child pornography and the rape of a sixteen-year-old girl. He failed the APT test and was transferred to IPC. Do you think Naomi Sutton knew her son was sociopathic, and that's why she opposed IPC prior to the release of the video footage?" Sebastian leaned back in his chair, his slender fingers steepled.

Corrinne sat perfectly straight, her hands folded in her lap. "I don't know. It's not for me to judge. As a mother, my heart goes out to Naomi and her family."

"Whose place is it to judge?" Sebastian had a hint of a smirk on his lips.

"The justice system. The American people."

"Do you think Blake Sutton's arrest has ruined any chance Naomi Sutton had for the Democratic nomination?"

"Again, it's not for me to judge," Corrinne said. "I'd like to think I was the front runner before this tragedy."

Sebastian grinned. "You're certainly the front runner now."

Naomi turned off the television and tossed the remote on the wooden coffee table. The OLED screen disappeared, revealing the wall-mounted mirror underneath. She blew out a tired breath and faced Vernon and Fletcher. Vernon stared at her scars, his face puckering as if he'd eaten a lemon. She flushed and turned her head, showing a little more of her good side. She couldn't help but think about the failed tryst she and Vernon had eight days ago. They still hadn't talked about it, with Vernon avoiding her, apart from their staff meetings.

"Naomi? You okay?" Vernon asked.

Naomi blinked, waking from her thoughts. "I'm fine." She turned her attention to Fletcher. "How bad is this?"

Fletcher cleared his throat. "I don't know yet. We'll run some polls, figure out where we are."

"Where do you *think* we are?"

"Behind the eight ball."

56

DEREK AND THE BETTER PILOT

A gentle breeze blew through the dilapidated tennis court. Tree leaves rustled and birds chirped. Derek squinted into the sun, his bound hands shielding his eyes, searching for the tiny black drone. He thought he saw something, but the sun was too bright.

"You're obsessed with that goddamn drone," Bo said, sitting next to him on the asphalt court, leaning back against the fence.

The chain-link gate clanged as Jesus entered the tennis court unarmed. He approached, taking long strides, his fatigues tucked into his shiny black boots. Derek and Bo didn't bother to stand for the leader of the Netas.

"It's the big boss man," Bo said with a wry smile.

Jesus shook his head. "Fucking gringos."

"I prefer redneck or white trash."

"Are you enjoying the fresh air and sun?"

"It'd be better without these." Bo held up his hands and handcuffs.

"You killed my men," Jesus replied.

One side of Bo's mouth raised in contempt. "I promise not to do it again."

Jesus glowered at Bo. "What do you think the word of a gringo is worth?"

Bo showed his open palms. "It ain't worth shit."

Jesus nodded, more to himself than Bo. "We're not so different. You don't want to be here. I don't want to be here." Jesus rubbed his stubbly beard for a moment. "It was my father's idea to stay here through the hurricanes. I should've left with my brother and my sister, but I was always the good son, always the soldier. I asked my father why he wanted to stay. We had enough money to go anywhere and live comfortably. You know what he said?"

Derek and Bo looked up at Jesus, nonplussed.

"He said, he'd rather be somebody here than nobody somewhere else." Jesus clenched his jaw. "I stayed for him, but he died in the hurricane, and the men looked to me to lead. I never wanted this."

Derek and Bo glanced at each other with a perplexed look.

"You said we will face two drones, each with two missiles. I need to know if what you say about the drones is true."

"I bet my life on it," Bo said without hesitation.

Jesus stared at Bo for a few seconds. "Good. After the next hurricane, we will launch six planes. I will fly low over the water. You will fly directly over me, fifty meters above. The other four planes will fly over you. If what you say is true, we will both survive."

Bo gave Jesus an ironic salute. "You can count on us, boss man."

Jesus almost smiled; then he walked away.

Derek waited until Jesus left the tennis court. "Why would he trust us?"

Bo shrugged and stood with a groan. "I don't know that he does." Bo shuffled a few steps forward, his back to Derek. He stretched his arms over his head and rolled his neck.

"Once we're in the air, he can't control us."

Bo turned around to face Derek. "He's got no choice. The only reason we're alive is he needs pilots. I don't think he has any other trained pilots, at least not ones that he feels comfortable flyin' close to."

"What are we gonna do?"

Bo smiled wide. "We're gonna find out who's the better pilot." Bo's smile receded. He squinted at something on the ground next to Derek. "What the hell is that?"

Derek looked around. "What?"

"Is that paper? There's something else too." Bo approached, kneeling next to Derek.

Derek turned around to see a fist-size rock, a few inches outside of the chain-link fence. A tiny bit of paper and something small and black and plastic were within a ziplock bag. Bo surveyed the guards. They huddled outside the fence, thirty yards away, talking and joking. Bo sat down casually, twisted his body around, and reached through chain-link fence. The chain was taut between his handcuffs as he grasped the plastic baggie with two fingers. Bo pulled the plastic baggie from the rock and through the chain-link fence. Bo glanced at the guards again. They were still joking among themselves. Bo opened the baggie, removing a folded piece of paper, a tiny black earbud, and a penny-size mike attached by a wire. Derek's eyes were unblinking as Bo unfolded the little handwritten note.

We work for Rebecca. Turn on the earpiece and put it in your ear.

"That's my ex-wife. Rebecca's my ex," Derek said, his eyebrows arched high.

Bo grinned, turned on the earpiece and the mike, and slipped them to Derek. "Let's see what they have to say."

57

JACOB AND THE PLAN

Jacob and Rebecca stood in the command center with Cesar and two of his men in dead silence, watching the fifty-inch OLED screen. The video feed showed Derek and his fellow captive, sitting on the old tennis court again, their backs against the chain-link fence. Derek put the earbud in his ear.

Rob's voice was transmitted to the command center. "I'm Rob Fuller. Jacob and Rebecca hired us to rescue you. I need some information."

"Whatever you need," Derek replied, his voice low, with an undercurrent of excitement.

"We think the Netas are planning an escape in their airplanes, immediately after the next hurricane. Is that true?"

"Yes. The other man with me, Bo, he's a pilot. We think they're short on pilots. That's why we're still alive. They painted one plane black. Jesus, the leader of the Netas, will fly that plane low, and the other planes are supposed to fly overhead to shield him from the drones."

"We want you and Bo to cooperate with the plan, but, when you take off from their base, we want you to fly and land at the airport near Fort Morro, across San Juan Bay. Fort Morro is the same fort where you met Summer. It's only two miles as the crow flies. Do you know where the airport is located?"

"Yeah, I know where it is." Derek couldn't contain his grin. "Summer made it, didn't she?"

"She made it."

Derek nodded to himself, still grinning, thinking about her in that submarine. "That's good."

Jacob glanced at Rebecca. Her eyes were glued to the screen, her mouth open, hanging on every word.

"When you get to the airport, we'll take you and Bo to the Virgin Islands in our submarine," Rob said. "Do not try to fly outta here. The drones will destroy every last plane. Do you understand?"

"Yes," Derek replied.

"Do you have any questions?"

"What if something changes and we need to contact you? Do we just turn this thing on again?"

"Yes, but every time we talk is a risk. I suggest you hide the mike in one of those open post holes in the middle of the tennis court. But only contact us in an emergency."

"Okay. Thank you, Rob. Please tell Rebecca and Jacob thank you too."

58

SUMMER AND *EL REY*

Summer and Patrick met Elvis at the dock just before eight that Friday morning. The wooden dock was still wet from the previous night's rain, and the sun played peekaboo with the clouds. Elvis led them down the dock, past yachts and fishing boats and a gas station. The sign read Gasolina 12.23, Diesel 12.78. Summer assumed this was the price in Fed Coins.

According to Patrick, Panama had used dollars prior to the economic collapse of the 2020s, in addition to balboas, pegged at a one-to-one ratio to the US dollar. After the economic collapse, they'd switched to Fed Coins, along with the rest of the US.

Near the end of the dock, Elvis stopped at a sixty-foot double-decker catamaran. The big boat was named *El Rey*. Elvis beamed at Summer and Patrick and motioned toward the boat. "Very nice, no?"

"Looks great," Patrick said.

"Very fast. Very comfortable. Just like I say."

A stocky sailor lowered a plank from the boat to the dock. "*Hola, Elvis.*"

"*Qué pasa, hombre,*" Elvis replied.

The sailor shrugged, walking across the plank. "*Nada. Y tú?*" The sailor stepped onto the dock and gave Elvis a hug with a manly back pat.

When they disengaged, Elvis said, "*Otro día en paraíso.*"

The sailor laughed, then looked at Patrick and Summer. "You must be Raymond and Stacy. I am Ignacio."

They shook hands.

"*Bienvenido.* Welcome to my ship, *El Rey.*" Ignacio beamed at Patrick, showing a silver incisor. "Just like you, Mr. Ray. Maybe it is destiny."

Patrick aka Raymond smiled politely.

"We need to be paid now," Elvis said to Patrick, not unkindly.

Patrick reached into his pocket and removed the plastic tube, holding twelve silver coins. He handed it to Elvis. He counted the coins, then added ten more to the tube, all but two of the silver pieces Elvis had been given the day before. Then Elvis handed the tube of twenty-two silver coins to Ignacio.

Ignacio slipped the coins in the front pocket of his *jorts* and whistled with two fingers in his mouth. A skinny crewman hurried from the deck. Ignacio pointed to their suitcases and said, "*Las maletas.*"

The crewman took Patrick's and Summer's suitcases aboard the ship.

Ignacio motioned toward the plank. "You ready? We have a long trip."

Patrick and Summer boarded the ship, Ignacio right behind them. A logo of a man reeling in a large fish adorned a tinted window. Underneath the logo, *Mejores Excursiones* was written in loopy cursive. They stepped from the open deck inside. Tables and chairs and a sectional couch were built into the boat. The skinny crewman took their bags below deck.

"This is the dining room," Ignacio said. "Your bedrooms are below." Ignacio motioned to the next room, the pocket door open. "That's the kitchen."

Summer glanced inside, noting the fridge, stove, microwave, and massive chest freezer.

"We will cook for you," Ignacio said, "but you can eat anything you like. *Mi casa es su casa.*"

"Thank you," Summer said, smiling politely.

Ignacio winked and replied, "You are very welcome."

"How long do you think it'll take to get to Mexico?" Patrick asked.

Ignacio turned to Patrick. "Mexico is not so far, but we are going very far north, almost to California."

"A week?"

"No." Ignacio grinned. "*El Rey* is very fast. Twin diesel motors with seven hundred horsepower each. Four and a half days, maybe five."

59

NAOMI ADDRESSES THE PRESS

Naomi stood at the podium in the Rayburn Reception Room of the US Capitol. The press sat before her, many with cameras and microphones. Even with the heavy makeup, Naomi felt hot and naked under the lights, hyperaware of the scars on the right side of her neck and face. It had been almost a month since the bombing, and her burns had healed, but the blanched scarring remained, and she still wore a patch over her empty eye socket.

Naomi took a deep breath. "I'm saddened and appalled by my son's crimes. I've spent the last nine days trying to figure out how I failed as a mother. I wasn't always present. I often chose my work over my family, and my family paid the ultimate price." Naomi swallowed the lump in her throat. "My husband, Alan, was murdered because of me. And my son, Blake …" She shook her head. "I don't know if my shortcomings as a mother contributed to his disgraceful behavior. Scientists believe sociopathy is genetic. In fact, they've proven it. Yet scientific evidence shows that most sociopaths come from normal parents. Still I feel guilty. He came from me, from *my* genetics. It's difficult not to feel responsible." A tear slipped down Naomi's cheek. "Like every mother, I wanted a sweet child. I wanted my son to grow up to be a good man. I wanted grandchildren to spoil." Naomi dabbed her eye with her handkerchief.

"I'm not unique. Millions of mothers have had their children sent to the island prisons. Blake deserves to be in prison for his crimes. There's no doubt about that, but he doesn't deserve to be in that inhumane environment. Nobody does. There has been much speculation that I knew of my son's personality disorder and that's why I opposed the island prisons from their inception." Naomi shrugged. "There were definitely signs. Blake often lied. He was troubled. But I rationalized his behavior. What mother wants to believe her son is a sociopath with no capacity for empathy?" She hesitated for a beat. "I certainly didn't. I still don't. It's easy for people to make judgments from their place of privilege."

Naomi surveyed the crowd of reporters. "One thing about this should give everyone pause. I'm a congresswoman. I occupy a position of power in this country, a position that can be abused for my own personal gain. Since the island prisons opened in 2044, how many powerful men and women or their children have been sent to these prisons? Have you heard of any? I only know of one. Former Congressman Roger Kroenig. He opposed the power structure and paid the ultimate price. Are the wealthy and powerful of this country all pious and law-abiding? Is it only the common man who deserves to be imprisoned on those islands? I'll leave you to answer those questions for yourself."

Naomi let out a tired breath. "That's all I have to say about my son's imprisonment. I ask that, from now on, you let me grieve in peace. Thank you." Naomi turned from the podium and walked away.

Reporters shouted her name and lobbed hurried questions.

"Mrs. Sutton?"

"Mrs. Sutton?"

"Are you planning to drop out of the presidential race?"

60

DEREK AND MEXICAN-STYLE MACARONI AND CHEESE

Derek and Bo couldn't believe their good fortune as they ate their MREs. Mexican-style macaroni and cheese, with crackers and peanut butter. M&M'S for dessert. Instant coffee and fruit punch to drink.

Derek savored a handful of M&M'S. "Damn this is good."

Bo ate his food but without Derek's gusto.

"What's wrong?" Derek asked.

Bo swallowed. "I was just thinkin'."

"What?"

"How long have we been here? Ten days maybe?"

"Somethin' like that."

"In all that time, we never had a meal like this. Always dried meat and fruit. Water to drink. I bet MREs are pretty scarce. Why the hell would they give 'em to us now? Unless …"

Derek's eyes bulged. "Unless this is our last meal. Maybe a hurricane's comin'."

"Could be. I don't know." Bo shrugged. "We can't even tell if it's day or night in here."

"We'll find out when they take us outside."

After lunch, Derek and Bo waited in silence. The guard took their empty trays like normal, but they didn't go to the tennis court for sun and fresh air.

61

JACOB AND ALMOST OVER

Jacob and Rebecca had spent much of the day watching live footage from the drones in the command center, but, one by one, the screens had gone dark as the storm approached. Rob and Billy had recalled the drones in anticipation of the storm.

Now, Rebecca stood at the bedroom window, watching the rain. Jacob approached from behind, putting his arms around her. He kissed her neck. The wind howled, and Rebecca wriggled from his grasp, turning to face him.

"Do you think this will work?" Rebecca asked.

"I don't know." Jacob turned away from Rebecca, took two steps, and sat on the bed, facing his wife again.

Rebecca approached the bed, her hands folded over her chest. "I have this sinking feeling that something terrible will happen."

"It's just a feeling. Rob and Billy know what they're doing," Jacob replied.

"Hurricane season's almost over. Cesar doesn't think this storm will be bad enough for the navy to vacate their blockade."

Jacob nodded. "I know."

Rebecca sat next to Jacob on the bed. She took his hand in hers. "What if there *isn't* another hurricane?"

Jacob exhaled a heavy breath. "Then they're stranded."

62

SUMMER AND TECATE

Captain Ignacio was right on the money. They reached the Baja of California, twenty miles south of Ensenada, in four and a half days. They anchored two hundred yards from shore, their lights off. Under moonlight, Ignacio and his three crewmen set up the inflatable boat. They inflated the craft with a compressor. They installed the floor, seats, and electric motor. They carried it to the rear deck, lowered the boat into the water with ropes, then tied it to *El Rey*.

The water was choppy, the wind breezy, the temperature in the upper-sixties. Summer zipped up her black windbreaker. One of the crewmen was already in the inflatable boat. Ignacio handed their bags to the man. Patrick climbed down the metal ladder, into the rocking inflatable, immediately sitting so he didn't fall into the water. Summer did the same, the crewman helping her to her seat.

"*Buena suerte!*" Ignacio shouted and waved. "Good luck!"

Summer and Patrick waved back to the stocky sailor.

The little inflatable rose and fell with the waves, sea spraying their faces. Summer thought about their chances of being arrested. According to Ignacio, Mexican police rarely patrolled the shoreline, but Summer's stomach still churned like the sea. The crewman beached the inflatable boat, cutting the engine and raising the outboard motor as he did so. Summer and Patrick grabbed their bags and stepped from the front of the boat, their shoes sinking in the wet sand. The sandy beach looked deserted in the moonlight. Beyond the beach, they were surrounded by rocky hills covered in low-growing shrubs called cliff goldenbush.

Patrick took the flashlight from his pocket and signaled, turning his light on and off three times. Down the beach, a few hundred yards away, another flashlight signaled three times.

The crewman waved and said, "*Bueno.*"

"*Gracias,*" Summer replied with a wave.

The crewman pushed the boat back into the sea.

Patrick and Summer walked on the sandy beach toward the flashlight signal, carrying their suitcases. A minute later, a short, stocky Mexican held up his hand and flashed a toothy grin in the moonlight.

"I Fernando. *Jew* must be Ray *y* Stacy," he said, his English broken and heavily accented.

"Good to meet you, Fernando," Patrick replied, shaking the man's hand.

"It's nice to meet you," Summer said, also shaking the man's hand.

Fernando led them up a narrow, serpentine trail through the cliff goldenbush. His electric van was parked at the top of the hillside.

They sat up front with Fernando, Patrick in the middle, Summer next to the passenger door. They drove north toward Tecate. The traffic was sparse. The hills along the roadside were rocky, covered in stubby shrubs, with few trees.

"I no see *mucho* gringos," Fernando said, glancing at his Caucasian companions. "Why *jew* need coyote?"

"We're not welcome in the United States," Patrick replied.

Fernando raised his eyebrows. "*Jew*? No, that can't be."

Patrick shrugged. "Everyone's illegal. Even white people."

Fernando laughed. "*Jew* too funny."

"How many people have you helped cross the border?" Summer asked.

Fernando shook his head. "I no coyote. Only help *El Minero. Jew* no worry. *El Minero* is best coyote. Only honest coyote in all Mexico."

* * *

They made it to Tecate in about ninety minutes. A few organic farms dotted the outskirts, fruits and vegetables advertised at their road-side markets. A river split the industrial city. Tecate was home to a brewery and several large factories: Rockwell Automation, Ingersoll Rand, and Oberg Industries. Fernando took them to El Rancho Motel, a two-story peach-colored building, with a faded sign and sickly palm trees. Summer and Patrick exited the vehicle. Fernando walked around and grabbed their bags from his van. Then he handed a prepaid cell phone to Patrick.

"I call when *El Minero* ready to meet," Fernando said.

Patrick furrowed his brows. "We're not crossing tomorrow?"

"Depends on *El Minero.*"

63

NAOMI IS "FOR THE PEOPLE"

"We're still behind, but the polls show we've gained several points since the press conference on Friday," Fletcher said.

Naomi, Fletcher, Vernon, and Diane sat in the sitting area of Naomi's congressional office.

"People wanted the truth," Vernon said. "That's exactly what they got."

"They empathize with you," Diane said, looking at Naomi. "They care about you because they know you care about them." Diane gave Naomi a small smile, showing her deep laugh lines.

"We still have a long way to go," Naomi replied. "What's next on the marketing front?"

Diane Nichols was Naomi's head of marketing. The athletic brunette wore a skirt suit, showing off her muscular calves. "We're increasing our ad spend on social media as we move closer to the primary. We're on the lookout for more opportunities to appear at rallies and marches."

"We need to continue to stress that Naomi's the outsider, the anti-politician, the anticapitalist," Vernon said, leaning back on the couch next to Naomi.

Naomi glanced at Vernon, close enough to smell his cologne, her thoughts wandering off topic. *What are we now?*

"I agree," Fletcher said, sitting in a leather chair opposite the couch, his hands resting on his gut. "We also need to decide on a campaign slogan. The sooner we decide, the better. I have the poll results on some possible slogans." Fletcher leaned forward and grabbed his tablet from the coffee table. He tapped it a few times, then said, "Restore America and By the People didn't poll well. But *For* the People polled the best by far. It's simple and to the point. To be effective, slogans need to be short and simple, and kept free of all sense. Make America Great Again and Change We Can Believe In were perfect examples of this. Both Trump and Obama were unlikely candidates who ended up in the White House. But, it's not enough to come up with a catchy slogan. Slogans have no effect unless they're constantly repeated. When slogans are sufficiently repeated with little countermessaging, they spread as fast as green grass through a goose." Fletcher grinned, his white mustache spreading across his face.

"I like For the People too," Naomi said.

"I agree," Vernon said, nodding.

"Great. I'll incorporate the slogan into our marketing immediately," Diane said.

Fletcher's cell phone buzzed in his jacket pocket. He grabbed his phone and checked the number. He looked at Naomi. "I should take this. It's my contact at the FBI." Fletcher stood from his chair, answered his phone, and walked to the other side of Naomi's office.

Naomi forced a smile toward Diane. "That'll be all, Diane. Thank you."

"Of course. If you need anything else, let me know. It really is a great slogan." Diane left Naomi's office, shutting the door behind her.

Fletcher returned to the sitting area, his expression serious. "Blake's on his way to the island."

Naomi exhaled, closing her eye for a moment. Then she asked, "What happens now? Will I have any idea where he lands on the island? Whether he's dead or alive?"

Fletcher sat in a leather chair across from Naomi. "Maybe. IPC will have video footage of the island landing. Once on the island, given Blake's special status, the navy will track his chip. There's no internet or functioning facial recognition cameras or data receivers on the island. They have to rely on the drones to track chips, but the drones can't be everywhere at once. The drones have their flight patterns, and they collect a lot of data. If the drones collect any data on Blake's chip, it'll be reported, and I have the connections to access it."

64

DEREK AND NECK BEARD

It had been one week since Derek and Bo had their macaroni and cheese MREs. At the time, they had thought it might be their last meal before the big escape. It hadn't been, yet it was significant. The next day, when they'd been taken to the tennis court, they'd noticed the storm debris. Derek and Bo had thought Jesus *was* planning the great escape, hence the last meal, but then the storm hadn't been strong enough to disperse the naval blockade, so the escape had been postponed. It made sense, but it was all speculation.

Now, Bo lounged on the bottom bunk, and Derek did push-ups on the cold concrete. They'd already had lunch and their rec time at the tennis court. Nothing left to the day but a meager dinner and lights out. Shouting came from the hall. Derek stood and walked to the cell door, opening the narrow slit they used for access to their plates. Bo didn't bother to get up. Derek knelt and peered through the slit.

Two guards escorted a hefty man with a neck beard, wearing the light-blue prison uniform of US Penal Colony East. His nose was crooked and swollen. His hands and feet were bound. Neck Beard said, "My mother's Naomi Sutton. She's a congresswoman. She's gonna be president, motherfucker."

Bo rose from the bottom bunk and crouched next to Derek, also listening through the slit in the door. The guards opened the cell next to theirs and shoved the man into it, locking him inside. The cell walls were solid, so Derek and Bo couldn't see the man next door, but they could hear him pounding on his door.

"Let me out, motherfucker," Neck Beard said.

Jesus stepped down the hall toward the guards and the commotion, wearing his fatigues and shiny boots. "*Abre la puerta.*"

One of the guards opened the door. They filed into the cell, the guards first, then Jesus. Derek and Bo continued to listen through the slit in their door.

"Tell me about your mother," Jesus said.

"She's gonna be president," Neck Beard replied. "She wants to close this island. If you protect me, I can get you outta here."

Derek looked at Bo with knitted brows. Bo shrugged in response.

Jesus said, "Tell me what you know about the drones and the naval blockade."

"What drones?" Neck Beard asked. "I don't know what you're talkin' about."

"If your mother wants to shut down this island prison, surely she is familiar with the apparatus used to keep us caged."

"I don't know, man. She didn't say shit to me about it."

Jesus sighed. "Then *why* are you here?"

"This bitch told a lie about me."

"I don't care *why* you are on the island. I only care *why* you are in *my* jail. I only care about what you can do for *me.*"

"Whatever you need, man. I'll do whatever you want." Neck Beard was pleading.

"You know *nothing.* Give me one good reason not to sell you back to the Aryans."

"I'm black. They don't want me."

Jesus snickered. "Oh, but they do. They buy big fat *negritos* like you by the pound. You'll be gutted like a pig and diced and ground into a million pieces."

"Please. My mother really is Naomi Sutton. She's gonna get me outta here. I can get you outta here too."

"I don't think so. The rich and connected don't come to this island in the first place. It's clear that my buyer made a mistake. *Llévenlo a los arios.*"

"Wait. No. Please, don't do this.

Through the slit in their door, Derek and Bo watched the guards force the prisoner from the cell and down the hall.

Neck Beard continued to beg as he was prodded down the hall. "I'm tellin' the truth. Please. I'll do anything!"

65

JACOB AND KNIGHTS AND WIZARDS

Jacob and Rebecca sat in front of the ham radio, in the Project Freedom communications room. Cesar's man in Venezuela had his cell phone on Speaker, connected to Lindsey's cell phone in Virginia. When Lindsey spoke, Cesar's man pressed the button on the walkie-talkie so Jacob and Rebecca could hear. Alternately, he let go of the walkie talkie button when Jacob and Rebecca spoke, so Lindsey could hear.

"It'll be a few more weeks, honey," Rebecca said through the ham radio.

"You think they can rescue Dad—I mean, Derek," Lindsey asked.

"We're hopeful."

"I still can't believe you guys are doing this. It's so badass."

"Do *not* tell anyone," Jacob said. "This is very dangerous, not to mention highly illegal."

"I know. I haven't said anything to anyone," Lindsey replied.

"How are your brothers doing?"

"The same. It's not that much different really. Jeeves does everything anyway."

Rebecca winced at that.

"Your mom does a lot," Jacob said.

"I know. I didn't mean it like that. I just don't want you to worry," Lindsey replied.

"Thank you for that, honey," Rebecca said. "I love and miss you very much."

"Me too," Jacob added.

"I miss you guys too," Lindsey said. "You wanna talk to the boys?"

"Please," Rebecca replied.

"I'll be right back."

A minute later, Ethan said, "Hi, Mom. Hi, Dad."

"Hi, honey," Rebecca said.

"Hello, Ethan," Jacob added.

"When are you coming home?" Ethan asked.

"In a few weeks," Rebecca replied.

"Oh, … okay. Do you like your vacation?"

"We're having lots of fun," Jacob said. "Next time we'll take you and David and Lindsey."

"How are you, sweetheart? Are you keeping up with your homework?" Rebecca asked.

"Yeah." Ethan's voice sounded sad.

"Are you okay?"

"I guess." Ethan sighed. "I started playing this new game, Knights and Wizards. David said it was stupid, but then he saw how cool it is, and he wanted to play. I told him that I wasn't gonna play with him if he was just gonna try to kill me, and he said he wouldn't. My knight was stronger than his. We did this quest, and I did all the hard stuff. I fought the dragon and the evil wizard. I almost died. Then, after we won, when I was still weak, he killed me. Then he laughed at me. I had to start all over, and, when you start over, your knight is weak because you have to win quests and battles to get stronger, but he keeps killing me before I can win anything."

"I'm sorry," Rebecca replied, frowning. "I'll talk to him."

"No. He'll call me a tattletale. He doesn't listen anyway. Maybe the only way to win is not to play."

"Why don't you ask Lindsey to let you play in her VR room?"

"She's in it a lot, but I'll ask."

"He can use my VR room," Lindsey said, interjecting.

"Thank you for being such a sweet big sister," Rebecca said.

"Where *is* David?" Jacob asked.

"He didn't wanna talk," Lindsey replied.

"Why not?"

"You really wanna know?"

"Yes."

"He said his game was more important. Jeeves threatened to turn it off, but I told Jeeves that you guys wouldn't like it if we made David talk on the phone."

Jacob shook his head, gritting his teeth.

"It's fine," Rebecca said, taking her husband's hand and squeezing. "We'll call back in a few days. He can talk then. We should get off the phone. Your dad has to make a business call. I love you both. See you soon."

"I miss you and love you too," Jacob added.

"I love you, Mom. I love you, Dad," Ethan said.

"Bye," Lindsey said.

After Lindsey disconnected the call, Rebecca left the communications room, and Cesar's man called Ramesh's cell phone.

"Hello, Ramesh?" Jacob asked.

"I'm here," Ramesh replied.

"Unfortunately, it'll be a few more weeks until I return."

"That's not a problem at the moment."

"Good. What's the latest?"

"It looks like we'll be taken over at the start of the new year. We'll be absorbed into the Department of Housing and Urban Development along with United Mortgage."

66

SUMMER AND *EL MINERO*

Summer and Patrick ate an early dinner in their room. Patrick had walked to a local restaurant and brought back fajitas and Tecate beer. It had been four days since Fernando had dropped them off at El Rancho Motel. They'd mostly stayed in the room, keeping a low profile. They'd expected a phone call the day after they'd arrived, and now Summer was worried that they'd been ripped off. But Patrick hadn't paid *El Minero* yet, so her father wasn't worried about the delay.

Patrick swallowed a swig of beer. "If we don't hear from him by tomorrow, I'll start looking for another coyote."

Summer nodded. "This whole thing feels wrong."

"These guys do things in their own time."

Right on cue, the prepaid cell phone chimed. Summer and Patrick looked at the phone, wide-eyed. Patrick stood, walked to the dresser, and grabbed the phone. He checked the number. It was local.

Patrick swiped right and said, "Hello?"

"It is Fernando. *El Minero* is ready to meet."

* * *

A few hours later, *El Minero*, aka Hector, stood in their hotel room, flanked by Fernando. Patrick and Summer stood opposite, the OLED television muted in the background. Hector wasn't the imposing figure Summer had anticipated. He was an average-size man, with a scruffy beard, short black hair, and a goofy grin to go along with his Dumbo-like ears.

After introductions, Hector said in accented English, "*Jew* got the silver?"

"I have the silver. When do we go under the wall?" Patrick asked.

"Gringos put bombs in the tunnel. *Boom*." Hector motioned with his hands, signifying an explosion. "Big problem. Now we dig for many weeks."

"Is he saying that the Americans destroyed the tunnel?" Summer asked Fernando.

Fernando nodded. "*Jes*. US Border Patrol. They blow up the tunnel. We make new tunnel. Happens all the time."

Summer looked to Hector, her brows knitted. "How long will it take to make a new tunnel?"

Hector smiled. "*Jew* no worry. It take only four weeks."

67

NAOMI AND JUST FRIENDS

"What time's your surgery tomorrow?" Vernon asked, sitting across from Naomi at her desk.

"At ten," Naomi replied.

"You need me to go with you?"

Naomi pursed her full lips. "No. It's a minor surgery. Outpatient."

Her empty eye socket was being cleaned up so she could be fitted for a glass eye. She was also having laser cosmetic surgery to even and smooth the scarring on her cheek and neck.

Vernon cocked his head with a mock frown. "You can't go by yourself."

Naomi's expression was blank. "I'm not. The Secret Service will be with me."

"Come on. Let me be there for you."

Naomi lifted her eye patch, flashing her empty eye socket.

Vernon flinched and looked away.

Naomi glared at Vernon. "You can't even look at me. It's no wonder you won't fuck me. I disgust you."

Vernon held out his hands. "Whoa. Come on, Naomi. That's not true."

"You've been avoiding me like the plague since that night. I thought you loved me."

Vernon blew out a breath; his shoulders slumped. "I do, but a lot has changed."

Naomi chuckled to herself. "It's ironic. I suppose I deserve this. If Alan had survived, he wouldn't have cared about my face. I had unconditional love, and I threw it away on *you*."

"It's not like that."

Naomi arched her eyebrows. "It's not? It's been almost three weeks since our little date, and I haven't seen you *once* outside of work. We haven't even talked about it. I thought maybe you needed a little time, but it's obvious that you have no interest in me."

Vernon bowed his head for a few seconds, the silence between them palpable. Finally, he looked up and said, "I love you, but I need some time. I think it's better for both of us if we're just friends right now."

Naomi looked away, a lump in her throat. Her desktop phone chimed. She swallowed and tapped the OLED screen, selecting Voice only.

"I'm sorry to interrupt," Fletcher said. "I know you're meeting with Vernon."

Naomi sneered at Vernon for a beat. "It's okay. We're *finished*."

Vernon dipped his head but didn't move.

Fletcher said, "I received information about Blake."

Naomi's eyes widened; her heart thumped in her chest. "What kind of information?"

"Two videos, but—"

"Send them over."

Fletcher cleared his throat. "I don't think it's a good idea to—"

"*Send* them to me."

"Right away."

Naomi disconnected the call and opened her laptop.

"Is Blake okay?" Vernon asked, leaning forward in his chair.

Naomi peered over her screen at Vernon. "I'd like for you to leave my office."

Vernon clenched his jaw. "It's like that?"

Naomi tapped on her laptop, ignoring Vernon.

He stood and left her office without a word.

Naomi opened her virtual mailbox. She found Fletcher's email, with two videos attached. The first attached video showed Blake in a boat, crammed together with other men, all wearing light-blue prison uniforms. The date and time stamp in the upper right corner of the video read 9-20-2051, 10:35 a.m.

Blake said something to the short muscular man next to him. That man turned to Blake and said something back. There was no volume, so Naomi couldn't hear what was said. Then Blake punched the short man in the face. The man staggered back, bumping into another inmate. Blake snickered and pointed at the man. The short man recovered and kicked Blake in the groin, sending him to one knee. Then the little man clocked him with an overhand right that sent Blake sprawling to the ground, his nose bloodied. The surrounding inmates jumped up and down and gesticulated with excitement. Blake curled into the fetal position as the short man kicked him in the stomach. Naomi winced with each kick. Then the video ended.

Naomi clicked on the second video. The date and time stamp read 9-22-2051, 1:12 p.m. It was a drone video, showing the jungle intertwined with the crumbling city of San Juan. The video showed a makeshift village, with houses made from scraps. Skinny people gathered around a firepit, smoke rising upward.

The drone hovered over a cluster of men, sawing and cutting up a carcass. The drone identified Blake, his name and chip number appearing at the bottom of the screen. But none of the men looked like Blake. One of the men tossed a slab of meat on the metal grate over the fire. When the man moved from the carcass, Naomi saw a severed arm. A fat severed arm with a barbed wire tattoo. *Blake.*

Naomi turned her head and vomited on her office floor.

68

DEREK AND THE GREAT ESCAPE

Deep in the bowels of the earth-sheltered bunker, Derek and Bo finished their MREs. Spaghetti and meatballs. Skittles for dessert. Instant coffee and fruit punch to drink. They were in their cell, Derek on the chair, facing Bo on the bottom bunk.

"I think we're goin' this time." Derek popped a few Skittles in his mouth. It had been five weeks since their last, last meal, and the false alarm tropical storm that wasn't strong enough to disperse the naval blockade.

Bo sipped his tepid coffee. "I think you're right. We haven't been outside for two days."

"And another last meal."

"Yeah. Another last meal."

Derek thought about the rescue plan. Derek and Bo had agreed never to discuss the rescue in their cell. They worried that the Netas might be listening. Derek and Bo rarely discussed it during rec time at the tennis court either. They knew what to do. It was a simple and smart plan. Fly the plane to the airport across the bay. Rob would then take them to a submarine for transport to the Virgin Islands.

After that initial conversation with Rob a month ago, Derek had placed the mike and earbud back into the plastic bag, and shoved it into one of the open postholes in the middle of the tennis court. Rob had said only to contact him if something changed. Nothing had, so there'd been radio silence ever since.

A knock came to the cell door. "*Manos.*"

Derek and Bo walked to the door. One by one they placed their hands through the slit in the door, retracting them with handcuffs. The door opened, and four guards entered the cell, one holding leg cuffs. The guard bound their legs. Derek and Bo were marched from their cell, down the long hallway toward the garage or the hangar.

The garage door was open. Netas bustled about the airplanes, speaking rapid Spanish. A steady rain fell outside, the clouds black and screening the sun. Jesus approached, flanked by a muscled man with a handgun on his hip.

Jesus grinned and said, "It's time." Jesus motioned to the big man beside him. "This is Benito. He will be your escort."

Derek's eyes widened; his heart pounded.

"Did you think I would let you fly alone?" Jesus cackled. "Don't worry. If you follow the plan, you have a good chance. If you don't, the drones will kill you, or Benito will kill you." Jesus stepped into Bo's personal space. "You will fly over me, fifty meters above. If you attempt to do anything else, Benito will shoot you in the head."

Bo stared, impassive.

Jesus motioned toward one of the guards. Then he pointed to Bo. "*Sólo las manos.*"

The guard unlocked and removed Bo's handcuffs but left his leg cuffs in place.

"See you in the Virgin Islands," Jesus said. He turned to walk away.

"What about *my* hands?" Derek asked, lifting his bound hands.

Jesus turned around, a smirk on his face. "You don't need your hands." He turned back around and walked toward the flat-black Cessna.

Benito and the guards prodded them to a white Cessna four-seater, the wings folded back, a single propeller out front. Bo climbed into the cockpit. Derek climbed into the seat next to Bo, struggling a little with his bound hands and feet. Benito sat behind them, his handgun out and pointed vaguely in their direction. Bo reached to grab for the seat belt, but it had been cut and removed. Derek looked at his. Also cut.

"So much for safety," Bo said.

"What are we gonna do?" Derek whispered.

Benito rose from his seat and placed the barrel of his gun to Derek's head. "You no talking."

Derek froze, speechless.

Benito pointed his gun at Bo. "No talk." Then he went back to his seat and put on his seat belt, still pointing his gun forward.

Bo went through his preflight checks in silence. Derek gaped at the fuel gauge. It was nearly empty. *Maybe it'll change when Bo starts the engine.* One Neta directed the planes, instructing them with hand signals. The planes were parked in a line facing the open garage door. Jesus's black plane was last. Derek and Bo's plane was third in line. The planes in front of them started their propellers. The Neta signaler pointed to Bo with one hand, the other circling the air. Bo started the propeller, the electric motor nearly silent.

The fuel gauge didn't change.

The Neta signaler moved his arms straight back and forth, easing the planes from the hangar. Once outside, raindrops peppered the aluminum alloy plane. Bo turned on the windshield wiper. They drove a short distance on the street to the airstrip, followed by twenty Netas in rain gear. Once on the airstrip, the Netas in rain gear spread out among the planes. They pulled pins, straightened the wings, then reinserted the pins.

The first plane started down the runway. Ten seconds later, the second plane zipped down the runway. In the distance, the first plane took off, the second still zipping down the runway, only ten seconds behind. The Neta signaler held up one finger to Bo and nodded. Bo pressed the throttle, and the Cessna zoomed forward, pinning Derek to his seat. The surrounding trees zoomed by in an amalgamation of green. Derek felt dizzy from the speed. He hadn't been in a car since he'd taken the bus to the prison ship two and a half months ago. Near the end of the runway, Bo pulled on the yoke, the Cessna lifting off. They circled over the runway with the other planes, waiting for their comrades.

Derek glanced over his shoulder. Benito had his handgun pointed at Bo. *Would he really shoot Bo and kill us all?* Derek looked out the window, water sluicing off the glass. He caught a glimpse of the black Cessna. Then the plane in front of them exploded, obliterated into a thousand pieces, causing turbulence in their cabin.

"Shit!" Derek said.

Bo steered hard left, toward Jesus's black Cessna, along with the three remaining planes. They headed out to sea as a group, shielding the low-flying black plane. Derek looked around, trying to find the drone but didn't see it. To his right, Derek saw the airstrip where they were supposed to meet Rob. Bo looked to his right too. Then he glanced at the gun pointed at the back of his head and continued on the prescribed course. They passed over the Spanish fort Derek had called home for a short time.

Another explosion came.

Derek dipped his head reflexively. This one came from above them. Derek looked behind him, but he couldn't see the wreckage. Benito's face was pale, his eyes like saucers. They flew out to sea and turned right, toward the Virgin Islands. Jesus's plane was directly below them, two others flanking them. The sea stirred with whitecaps.

Derek scanned the sky, looking for the drone, doing his best to see behind them from his side window. The gray drone looked nearly black as it appeared, descending from the dark clouds. The front of the plane was barren and faceless without a cockpit. Four missiles hung from its wings.

"Drone! Four o'clock," Derek said.

Bo glanced over his shoulder.

"It has four missiles."

A missile launched, destroying the Cessna on their right flank. Another missile launched. Bo banked hard left and down, moving under the Cessna on their left flank. A split-second later, that plane exploded, shaking their cabin. Derek looked back, trying to keep an eye on the drone, but he couldn't find it.

Benito still held his gun on them but without conviction. His face had a greenish tint.

Derek looked at Bo. He motioned with his chin to Benito and mouthed, *Kill him*. Then Bo clearly said, "We're gonna dive under. Grab hold of somethin'."

Derek turned around and grabbed on to his seat back.

The gun shook in Benito's hand.

The drone appeared behind them on their left.

"Drone. Seven o'clock," Derek said.

Bo dove, nearly straight down to the sea, bracing himself with his feet so he didn't go through the windshield without a seat belt to restrain him. Benito vomited on the floor, reddish chunks spewing from his mouth, still hanging on to his handgun.

As Bo leveled the plane, Derek rushed Benito, grabbing the gun and twisting. The gun fired, the bullet going through the left-hand window. Derek's ears rang from the deafening shot. Derek wrenched the gun from Benito's grasp, the handgun falling to the floor. Benito punched Derek in the jaw, but Benito was weak from vomiting and had no leverage in his seated position.

Derek scrambled over his seat, wedging himself into the cramped storage space, putting his arms over Benito's head. Benito undid his seat belt, but the chain connecting Derek's handcuffs bit into Benito's Adam's apple, pinning him to the seat. The big man choked and flailed his arms and legs. Derek leaned back, using his body weight and all his strength as he cranked on the man's neck. The handcuffs bit into Derek's wrists. Benito tried to get his fingers under the chain, but it was too tight.

While Derek strangled the Neta, Bo flew the Cessna dangerously close to the water. Jesus's black Cessna was above them now and a little to their right. Bo kept glancing back, trying to find the drone. Then Bo banked hard right, and another explosion came. Jesus and his black Cessna fell to the sea in fiery pieces.

Benito's body jerked and seized, then went limp. Derek let go, his body stiff from holding that constant pressure on Benito's neck. Derek crawled back over the seat and looked around for the drone.

"Is he dead?" Bo asked.

"Yeah," Derek replied, his breathing labored.

"Find the drone. He has one more missile."

"I'm looking."

An alarm sounded in the cockpit. The fuel gauge flashed red.

"Is that the fuel gauge?" Derek asked.

"It says 3 percent." Bo paused for an instant. "Fuck. Two percent."

Derek turned back around and spotted the gray predator. "Drone! Five o'clock."

Bo dove, lowering the plane as close to the water as possible. Dead Benito slipped off his seat, onto the floor, wedged between two seats and the side of the plane.

"Yell 'fire' as soon as he launches that missile."

"Fire!"

Bo yanked back on the yoke, the Cessna climbing near vertical, slamming Derek into the back seat. They heard the *whoosh* of the missile as it passed underneath and smacked into the sea, detonating on impact, seawater spraying like a fountain. Bo leveled the Cessna, the fuel gauge at 1 percent, still flashing red and beeping in distress.

Derek turned and looked from the right-side windows. No predator drone. Then he stood and shuffled to the left side, his leg irons clanging. He stood on Benito's chest and hunched down so he could see from the left-side windows. "I think it's gone."

"We're gonna have to land on the water. We need life preservers," Bo said, matter-of-factly.

Derek checked the storage area behind the rear seats, finding two life preservers. He brought them to the cockpit and handed one to Bo. He put it over his head and cinched it tight. Derek put his over his head and fumbled with the straps for a few seconds, finally getting the life preserver cinched.

The propeller stopped, and the fuel gauge read 0 percent.

Bo nodded to the sliding door on the side of the Cessna and said, "Open that door and buckle up."

Derek shuffled to the door, yanked down on the handle with both his bound hands, and slid it open. The air whooshed by, the rain peppering him like pellets. Derek hurried to the back seat and buckled the seat belt, his hands shaking. Benito lay on the floor next to him, against the side of the plane, serene in death amid the chaos. They floated through the air, Bo trying to hold them level for as long as possible.

They smashed into the water, the force whipping Derek forward, the seat belt biting into his hips, shoulder, and across his chest. Bo flew forward, his entire body airborne, his momentum stopped with his head cracking the windshield. He slumped on the floor of the cockpit.

Seawater rushed through the open door and into the cabin. Derek groaned, his shoulder, hips, chest, and neck barking in pain. He grunted as he twisted to unbuckle his seat belt. He stood and shuffled to the cockpit, trying to keep his aching neck steady. Seawater covered his bound ankles now.

Bo lay motionless on the floor of the cockpit, his body contorted unnaturally. His face and neck were covered in blood. His forehead was cracked open, deep enough to see brain matter. Derek knelt next to his friend and pressed two fingers to his carotid artery. No pulse. Derek squeezed his eyes shut for a moment, the pain washing over him.

The seawater crept up Derek's calves, spurring him to action. Derek tried to grab Bo under his armpits, but Derek's handcuffs made this impossible. Instead, Derek used both hands and pulled on one of Bo's armpits, jerking him in fits and starts, gasping in pain, but ultimately pulling him from the cockpit.

Once in the aisle, Bo floated faceup in knee-deep water. Benito's body floated on the floor, wedged between the front and back seats and the side of the plane. Derek pulled Bo to the open door. Derek glanced from their sinking plane to the gray sky and back to the dark-blue ocean. Derek stepped off the plane and into the ocean, pulling Bo with him, their life preservers keeping their heads above water.

Warm seawater soaked Derek's fatigues and T-shirt. He kicked with his bound feet, still holding and pulling Bo's body, tediously moving away from the sinking plane. The salt burned the abrasions on his wrists. Steady rain fell around him. Derek and Bo bobbed in the whitecaps, as the plane sank into the depths.

Derek looked around, trying to find a landmark, but all he saw was dark-blue ocean. He glanced at Bo, his head lolled to the side, blood leaking into the sea from his head wound. He thought about sharks. *Aren't they attracted to blood?*

Derek's vision was blurred by tears as he let go of his friend.

69

JACOB AND THE IMPOSSIBLE

Three small stealth drones had hovered high over the Netas as they had launched their airplanes. They'd followed the six planes, but the small drones were much too slow to keep up. Rob and Billy had been waiting at the airport for Derek and Bo, but they didn't land. Cesar and his men had used their radar to mark the locations of the downed planes. Every plane had crashed, all but one blown to smithereens by drone missiles. Cesar and his men had sent the drones to investigate each crash site for survivors. The drones had found nothing but floating debris.

Jacob stood behind Cesar in the command center, watching the live drone footage. Rebecca stood next to Jacob with puffy eyes, her hand squeezing his.

Rebecca pointed to one of the screens. "Somebody's in the water!"

The drone hovered over a person floating in the water, wearing an orange life preserver. The drone zoomed in on the man's face. His head lolled to the side. A huge gash was on his forehead. It was Derek's fellow inmate.

"*Un hombre está aquí,*" said one of Cesar's men, pointing at his screen.

Everyone looked at the footage from another drone. Someone

222

floated up and down with the waves, also wearing an orange life preserver. The drone zoomed in on his face. Positive Match Derek Reeves appeared under the man's image. Derek on the screen looked up at the drone.

"It's him!" Rebecca shouted, jumping up and down. "He's alive!"

Cesar's men cheered and high-fived. Jacob's face was blank, happy it was over but still reeling from the price tag.

Cesar swiveled in his seat and looked to Jacob and Rebecca with a grin. "Let's bring him home."

70

SUMMER AND THE WALL

Summer gaped up at the massive concrete wall, her hand shielding her eyes from the sun. The 1,954-mile border wall had taken thirty million tons of concrete and had cost forty-one billion Fed Coins. The project was finished in 2032 and had taken nearly a decade to complete. The United States had been, and still was, very divided on the border wall, with Republicans in support and Democrats largely against. The wall had been ultimately built because the Republicans controlled the White House and congress through the 2020s.

"That's the wall. It's very big, no?" said Hector aka *El Minero*, standing next to Summer and Patrick. Hector smiled wide. "But we have the tunnel. *Jew* ready?"

After four weeks of being cooped up in that motel room, Summer thought she was ready. She nodded and looked at Hector. "I think so."

They walked to a small warehouse about fifty yards away. The sign on the building read Tecate Agua. Summer and Patrick carried backpacks and front-mounted water pouches. They wore hiking boots, comfortable pants, and T-shirts. Inside the building were racks and pallets, holding five-gallon water jugs, and an old forklift. They walked between the racks toward the back of the building. A group of Mexicans checked their own backpacks and supplies. Most of them had plastic containers filled with water tied to their backpacks.

A blowup kiddie pool with Tecate Agua written on the side stood before them. Two of Hector's men moved the empty kiddie pool, revealing two large doors in the floor. When opened, they saw a concrete ramp descending into the tunnel. It was wide enough for compact construction equipment to enter.

Hector strapped on a water pouch, similar to the ones worn by Summer and Patrick. One of his men handed him a flashlight. Hector walked toward the tunnel, flipped on his flashlight, and said, *"Listo?"*

Most of the Mexicans nodded, their expressions solemn.

Hector walked into the tunnel, followed by a dozen Mexicans, and finally by Summer and Patrick. The tunnel was dusty and held together with wooden posts and beams. As they walked, battery-powered LED lights turned on, activated by their motion. The lights were spread far apart; the tunnel was dim. The air was heavy and humid and musty.

Summer glanced behind her. It was pitch-black, the tunnel entrance no longer visible. Hector had said that it was an eight-mile walk, but it wasn't a straight shot. The tunnel had been destroyed and repaired several times. There were many dead ends and forks created to bypass the damage done by the US Border Patrol. Hector had said that it was important to stick together because it was easy to get lost in the tunnels.

Summer looked at the old wooden posts and beams and the reused plywood that held the tunnel together. Small piles of soil littered the dirt floor, where the rotting plywood had failed. *What if the tunnel collapses, and we're stuck down here?* Summer shuddered at the thought. She concentrated on the task at hand, putting one foot in front of the other. She thought about each step being one step closer to Byron.

71

NAOMI'S NEW FACE

"By raising UBI payments, you're taking from those who work, only to give to those who don't work," Vernon said, pacing in front of the podium and reading from his tablet.

Naomi stood behind the podium, in the hotel conference room, speaking to the empty seats. "Obviously, you don't understand the true nature of Universal Basic Income. People on UBI barely have enough money to eat. Almost half of all people on UBI are undernourished. If a person doesn't have enough healthy food, what are the chances that they'll eat even less to pay for college or to start a business?"

"They can take out loans."

"If you've been on UBI, chances are you don't have an extensive credit history. You'll be given a high-interest loan if you qualify at all. Do you think it's prudent to enslave our most vulnerable with high-interest debt?"

Vernon stopped pacing and narrowed his gaze. "How will giving them more money change anything? People on UBI will just waste the money."

"People on UBI are the *most* responsible with their money, spending a much higher percentage of their limited wealth on necessities than those not on UBI." Naomi scanned the empty seats as she spoke, stopping on an individual seat for a few seconds before moving on. "If we give them a little more, I'm confident that they'll use that money to better themselves and their families."

Vernon approached the podium, with its gold sign that read Hilton Hotel, Columbia, Missouri. "That's good. You're ready."

Naomi pursed her lips. "I hope so."

"You have the issues down cold. You know exactly how to respond to any question they throw your way."

Since their big blowout four weeks ago, Naomi's anger had dissipated, and they'd settled into a platonic friendship. Blake's demise on Psycho Island had initially hit Naomi hard, but she'd mentally cut ties with her son long ago, and, now that he was truly gone, it was a relief. She couldn't have a public funeral, as the information about Blake was classified. Vernon had been a supportive friend throughout the ordeal.

Naomi stepped away from the podium so Vernon could see her outfit. It wasn't the exact outfit that she'd wear to tomorrow's debate, but it was nearly identical. A dark-blue skirt suit and heels. "Do I look okay?"

Vernon beamed. "You look beautiful."

That made her stomach flutter. "What about … my face?"

Vernon stepped into her personal space. "Your face looks fantastic. With that makeup, I can't see the scarring anymore."

It wasn't just the makeup. The laser cosmetic surgery she'd had a month ago really had helped. Although, the makeup did play a big part.

"What about my eye? Does it look natural?" Naomi had been fitted for a glass eye as well.

He inspected her new eye. "It's really hard to tell that it's a glass eye."

Naomi nodded. "I have to be on stage with Ms. Perfect."

"It's your ideas that matter."

Naomi frowned. "So you're saying she's prettier than me."

Vernon frowned back. "Absolutely not. I'm saying it doesn't matter."

"Uh-huh."

"You'll be great." Vernon leaned in and kissed her on the cheek.

Naomi's stomach fluttered again. It was the first time he'd kissed her in over a month, not since he'd ended their romantic relationship. *Maybe he sees the old me? I do look much better since the surgeries. Maybe he wants to try again.* "Do you want to come to my room tonight? We could order room service and stream a movie."

"That sounds great, but I'm exhausted. Rain check?"

Naomi forced a smile, concealing her disappointment. "Sure."

72

DEREK AND THE RESCUE

A moderate rain still fell from the dark clouds. The waves pulled Derek up and down. As he floated to the crest of a wave, he surveyed the area, hoping to see a boat, land, anything. Nothing but ocean. His heart pounded. His breathing was labored. *I'm gonna die out here.*

Faint buzzing overhead—like a fly—made him look upward. He saw a bird-size drone, like the one he'd seen at the tennis court. Adrenaline coursed through his veins, giving him renewed vigor. *They know where I am.* Derek raised his bound hands over his head and waved.

* * *

Derek didn't know how long he'd been in the sea, but it felt like hours. Like a guardian angel, the buzzing drone stayed with Derek and gave him hope. When the sub surfaced, Derek thought it was a whale, but it didn't dive again. It moved slowly through the rain, stopping one hundred yards away. Derek kicked and did his best to swim toward the submarine with his hands and feet bound.

Two men in wet suits, flippers, and masks dove off the submarine. The men intercepted Derek. Treading water, one of them asked,

"Derek Reeves?"

"Yeah," Derek replied.

The man grinned, his eyes obscured by the mask. "You ready to get the hell outta here?"

73

JACOB, THE LIFESAVER

The ground was soft, but the rain had stopped. Intermittent sunrays peeked through the fast-moving clouds. Jacob, Rebecca, and Cesar waited in front of Project Freedom's earth-sheltered complex, watching the ATV trail. They heard the rustling of leaves, branches, and the voices of men, but the battery-powered UTVs were nearly silent. Five UTVs appeared from the jungle trail, loaded with men and leftover supplies.

As the UTVs motored into the open garage of the complex, Jacob caught a glimpse of Derek. He had a deep, dark tan. His black beard and hair were bushy and unkempt. He wore fatigues, boots, and a black T-shirt.

Before the UTVs had parked, Rebecca let go of Jacob's hand and ran for the garage. Jacob blew out a tired breath.

"Your wife is very happy," Cesar said.

"I'd like to be on the next ship out of here."

"We have a supply ship that left early this morning from Caracas. It will be here tomorrow. It can take you to Jamaica ... for a price." Cesar simpered, obviously pleased with himself.

Jacob frowned. "Of course."

Jacob and Cesar walked to the garage and the commotion. Cesar's men spoke in rapid Spanish to each other with big smiles. Rob and Billy collected and consolidated their tactical gear. They looked haggard: rumpled and dirty fatigues, disheveled hair, and dark circles around their eyes. Jacob watched Rebecca hug Derek with tears in her eyes. Derek reciprocated, lifting her off the ground with the strength of his embrace. Looking over Derek's shoulder, Rebecca noticed Jacob watching them. She disengaged from her ex-husband as Jacob and Cesar approached. Derek turned around, smelling like the sea. He held out his hand to Jacob.

"Thank you, Jacob," Derek said, as they shook hands. "You saved my life."

Jacob nodded, straight-faced. He glanced at Rebecca, then said what he knew she wanted him to say. "You're welcome."

74

SUMMER AND TECATE AGUA

Nobody spoke. The only sounds in the tunnel were footsteps and heavy breaths.

Summer turned to Patrick and asked, "What time is it?"

Patrick checked his watch. "It's 6:43. We've been walking for almost three hours."

"If the tunnel is eight miles long and we're walking about three miles per hour, we should be there."

The tunnel turned to the left, the dim LEDs lighting their way. Cheering came from up ahead and excited Spanish. Artificial light poured into the tunnel.

Hector looked back at the group, beamed, and said, "*Estamos aquí.*"

Much like their entrance to the tunnel, they exited up a wide ramp into a warehouse. The warehouse looked identical to the Tecate Agua warehouse in Mexico, with racks and pallets holding five-gallon jugs of water. If Summer didn't know any better, she might've thought they'd walked in a big circle.

Two Mexican men greeted them as they exited the tunnel. Fittingly, they handed each person a small bottle of Tecate Agua and said, "*Bienvenidos a los Estados Unidos.*"

Patrick and Summer accepted their bottled water and their

welcome with tired smiles.

Beyond the racks of water bottles, two Tecate Agua vans were parked near the garage door. Hector showed the weary travelers to the bathroom. After water and a bathroom break, Hector split the group in half, depending on their destination.

Hector opened one of the back doors to a van. Five-gallon water jugs were stacked in a nifty shelving system from floor to ceiling. Like a magician, Hector grinned at the crowd; then he unlatched the shelves and opened one side, like a door. Inside, was a narrow open area, concealed by water jugs. Seven Mexicans climbed inside, sitting on the floor, tight together. Summer and Patrick climbed into the other van with five Mexicans.

Hector waved and said, "*Buena suerte.* Good luck." Then he shut the door.

75

NAOMI AND THE DNC DEBATE

Naomi stood behind the stage backdrop, waiting for her cue. She listened to Brooke Bixler's intro through the speakers.

"Good evening from the University of Missouri. I'm Brooke Bixler, anchor of CNN Special Report. It's Thursday, October 17, and I want to welcome you to the first Democratic presidential debate. The participants tonight are Senator Corrinne Powers from Virginia, Congressman Randal Montgomery from South Carolina, and Congresswoman Naomi Sutton from New York. This debate is sponsored by the Democratic National Committee. The DNC drafted tonight's format, and the rules have been agreed upon by the campaigns. The one-hour debate is divided into six segments, each up to ten minutes long. At the start of a segment, I'll ask the same leadoff question to the candidates, and they will each have up to two minutes to respond. The candidates are also allowed a single one-minute rebuttal per segment.

"The questions are mine and have not been shared with the DNC or the campaigns. The audience here in the room has agreed to be respectful and to remain silent while the candidates are speaking. I will invite you to applaud as I welcome the candidates." Brooke paused for a beat. "Mrs. Naomi Sutton."

Naomi received her cue and strutted onstage to a polite applause.

She waved to the crowd in the cozy proscenium theater.

Brooke Bixler sat front and center at a desk onstage, facing the candidates, the 278 attendees behind her. Her olive skin was flawless with heavy makeup, and her dark hair was accented with auburn highlights.

"Mr. Randal Montgomery," Brooke said.

Randal Montgomery stepped onto the stage, waving and smiling, but his applause was muted in comparison to Naomi's. Randal looked dapper in his dark suit and light-blue tie. He was tall, with a small paunch, round glasses, and baby-fine blond hair, parted to the side. Randal and Naomi shook hands.

Randal said, "Good luck."

"You too," Naomi replied.

"Senator Corrinne Powers," Brooke said.

Corrinne Powers sashayed onto the stage, wearing impossibly high heels and a blue dress cinched at the waist, flowing just below her knees. Her face belonged in a Revlon ad, with her perfect symmetry and high cheekbones. Corrinne beamed and waved at the crowd with both hands, the thunderous applause washing over her. She preened, touching her heart and blushing until they finally quieted. Corrinne turned to her opponents and approached Randal Montgomery, shaking his hand and whispering something in his ear. They had a chuckle. Then, Corrinne approached Naomi, her hand held out front. Naomi took Corrinne's dainty hand and squeezed harder than necessary.

"Good luck," Naomi said.

Corrinne simpered. "You keep it. You'll need it."

Naomi smiled back, her gaze laser focused.

The stage was a sea of blue. Blue carpet with red trim and white stars. The backdrop was the same blue with more red trim and white stars. Dead center of the backdrop was the eagle emblem that represented the Great Seal of the United States. The three politicians walked to their respective podiums. Naomi was on the left, Randal on the right, and Corrinne behind the center podium.

Once the politicians were in place, Brooke Bixler said, "We will focus on the issues that voters tell us are most important to them, and we'll press for specifics. Candidates, we look forward to you articulating your policies and positions, as well as your visions and your values. Let's begin.

"Mrs. Sutton, enhanced students score on average in the ninety-seventh percentile on standardized tests. In 2051, enhanced students represented 12 percent of ivy league first-years, despite representing less than 1 percent of 2051 high school graduates. In the 2048 Summer Olympics, enhanced female gymnasts took nearly every medal. In the coming years, as more and more enhanced children come of age, many expect these people to dominate politics, sports, and business. Given that only the wealthy can afford enhanced children, do you think this an unfair advantage? Will this create permanent poverty for the middle and lower classes with no chance of upward mobility?"

Naomi hesitated, thinking about her response. "This is a very sensitive topic. Parents want the best for their children. As lawmakers and leaders in government, I believe our job is to facilitate a fair and equitable society. Over the last few hundred years, capitalism has steadily taken wealth from the working class and given it to the wealthy." Naomi glanced at Brooke Bixler. "You mentioned the middle class, but little is left of the middle class in the United States. What is considered middle class is actually upper middle class. The lower class is by far the fastest-growing socioeconomic group in the United States. Meanwhile, the wealthy elite control more wealth than at any time in human history."

Naomi showed her palms to the audience. "I don't begrudge wealthy parents who want to give their child every advantage available to them, but we, as a society, have to support the poor among us as well. This is why, as president, I would double UBI payments. Currently, Universal Basic Income is just enough to keep people alive and sheltered. With additional funds, the poorest among us can participate in the economy. They can innovate and create businesses. They can save their money and have enhanced children. Currently, the deck is stacked against the 99 percent. It's time to even the playing field."

The crowd applauded.

"Senator Powers. Same question," Brooke said. "Given that only the wealthy can afford enhanced children, do you think this an unfair advantage? Will this create permanent poverty for the middle and lower classes with no upward mobility?"

Corrinne Powers nodded. "No doubt this is a contentious issue. I would love to stand up here and tell everyone that I'll simply give money to the poor and that all the problems will be fixed"—Corrinne snapped her fingers–"like magic. But that's not reality. If we doubled UBI payments, we still have to pay for it. This would require the elimination of nearly every government service. Or we can simply borrow from the future as most politicians like to do"—Corrinne looked at Naomi for an instant—"and this would create so much inflation that Mrs. Sutton's double UBI payment only buys half as many goods, so we're right back where we started.

"I do think that we can and should do much better to create an equitable society, but Americans don't want handouts." Corrinne surveyed the audience. "They want good jobs. When I'm elected president, my Green Jobs Program will help those in need to help themselves *and* the environment where we live."

The crowd roared with approval.

"I'd like to use my rebuttal," Naomi said.

"You have one minute, Mrs. Sutton," Brooke replied.

Naomi stared at Corrinne. "It's interesting to me that you profess to care about jobs and the environment, yet your family owns Next Generation Robotics, a company with an atrocious record of pollution around the world, and the products of your family's company have displaced hundreds of millions of jobs."

The crowd hooted and hollered.

Corrinne stood stone-faced. Once the crowd quieted, she said, "I'd like to use my rebuttal."

"You have one minute, Senator Powers," Brooke replied.

"First of all, I've never worked for Next Generation Robotics." Corrinne glared at Naomi. "Second of all, your claims are disingenuous. Next Generation Robotics and other automation and machinery companies are responsible for lifting billions of people out of agrarian poverty. Robots do the heavy lifting and monotonous tasks that used to employ many men and women in soulless industries doing miserable jobs." Corrinne looked at Naomi again. "Mrs. Sutton, would you like to return to preindustrial America? In 1800, most Americans lived on less than one Fed Coin per day in today's money. Seventy-five percent of us were farmers, doing backbreaking work, barely producing enough to feed ourselves. Today, robots farm, manufacture goods, and clean up the environment. Robots perform lifesaving surgeries better than the steadiest surgeon. Robots do the dirty, dangerous, and monotonous jobs in society. I would like for Americans to move forward, not backward."

The audience cheered again, and Corrinne smiled, but Naomi couldn't reply. She had already used her rebuttal. Naomi thought about the video they'd purchased from Corrinne's former nanny. *Your time is coming, Corrinne.*

76

DEREK'S BLAST FROM THE PAST

The smell of fried fish and yuccas made his mouth water. Derek stood in the galley, waiting in a short line with a handful of Venezuelan sailors. He had showered and received a fresh set of clothes before they had left Project Freedom in the Virgin Islands. The first warm shower he'd had in eleven weeks. Derek wore a black T-shirt, fatigues, and new boots, but his hair and beard were still long and wild. The line inched forward. The cook handed Derek a warm plate piled high.

"*Gracias*," Derek said, smiling at the old cook.

"*De nada*," the cook replied, smiling back, his front teeth missing.

Derek grabbed a glass of water and took his food to the dining area next to the galley. Plastic tables and booths were built into the floor, unmoving with the rocking of the boat. The Venezuelan crewmen clustered at one table, joking and laughing and speaking rapid Spanish. Rebecca and Jacob sat alone at the far booth, facing each other. Derek walked in their direction, intent on joining them for dinner, but he stopped short. Jacob's back was to Derek. Rebecca's arms were crossed, and her face was as hard as stone. The married couple spoke in harsh whispers.

Derek turned around and walked to a lonely table next to the window, far from the marital discord. He ate his food and gazed at the moonlight shimmering off the ocean. He should've been elated. He'd escaped the jaws of death and the unescapable prison. But he wasn't happy. Derek thought about Bo. The friend who had saved his life on multiple occasions. *Bo deserves to be here more than I do.* Derek swallowed the lump in his throat.

"Fuck you," Rebecca said.

Derek turned from the window, startled from his thoughts. The sailors went silent, eyeing the quarrelling couple. Rebecca stomped from the dining room, leaving Jacob sitting alone.

* * *

Later that night, Derek lay in a single bed below deck, moonlight shining through the portholes. He stared at the ceiling in his tiny room. Derek closed his eyes, trying to sleep, but the dead stalked him. Bo's face was covered in blood, and brain matter spilled from his head wound. Eliza leaped headfirst to her death, bleeding on the stone courtyard of the Spanish fort. Jordan was stabbed in the back by the Aryans and afterward stabbed through the stomach by Connor.

Then Connor was on his knees, bleeding from a deep gash on his calf and another on his knee. "Please don't," Connor said, his hands up in surrender. "Please don't."

"You killed my friend," Derek said, his jaw set tight, but his sword pointed down.

The Aryans moved closer. One of them said, "Kill him, or we'll kill both of you."

Connor raised his gaze to the heavens, tears in his eyes. He said, "Make it quick."

Derek slashed his exposed neck in one strong swipe, arterial blood spraying into the air.

A knock at the door startled Derek from his nightmare. He woke, his breathing labored, his body wet with sweat. Derek sat up in bed and looked at the door, wondering if he'd heard correctly. Another knock came. He stood from the bed wearing shorts.

"Hold on," he said, grabbing a towel from the bedside table. He dried himself and put on a clean T-shirt. Then he opened the door to find Rebecca, nibbling on her lower lip. Her skin was tan, her eyes red rimmed. She wore flip-flops, short shorts, and a white tank top.

Derek was slack-jawed for a long beat. Then he asked, "You okay?"

"May I come in?" Rebecca replied.

Derek stepped aside, letting her into the cramped cabin. He shut the door, flipped on the light, and said, "What's up?"

Rebecca hugged Derek tight, surprising him. He reciprocated, wrapping her up in his arms. They stood this way for a long moment. She kissed his cheek, his neck, then her lips found his. Her kiss and her smell and her touch transported him back to a simpler time, when it had been Derek and Rebecca against the world, before poverty and infidelity had destroyed them.

What started calm and chaste turned breathless and passionate. She removed her tank top, revealing a white lacy bra. Derek removed his T-shirt, and they recoupled, their mouths and tongues urgent. He unclasped her bra. She reached into his shorts and squeezed his erection. Derek gasped in response. Rebecca let go and stepped back, her bright brown gaze locked on his. She kicked off her flip-flops. She slid her bra down her arms, revealing perky breasts with upturned nipples. Rebecca unbuttoned her shorts and slipped them down her tan legs.

Aesthetically, she was the perfect female specimen. Her body was leaner and tanner than he remembered. Her nose was thinner and smaller. Her lips were fuller. Her breasts a bit bigger. She was almost forty, but not a single wrinkle was on her face. Rebecca's beauty in the harsh light broke the spell. Her perfection felt alien and unfamiliar.

We can't go back. She isn't your wife anymore. Derek picked up her clothes and handed them to her. "We can't do this," Derek said.

She nodded, her eyes glassy. Rebecca dressed, sniffling and wiping her eyes to stop the tears from falling. Derek put on his shirt.

"I'm sorry," Rebecca said, her eyes downcast.

"Don't be." Derek reached out and squeezed her hand for emphasis.

She looked up. "Do you remember when I told you that I was in love with Jacob?"

Derek nodded and let go of her hand.

"You told me that I was throwing you away for a more comfortable life." A tear beaded on her eyelid.

"I was hurt. I know I didn't give you and Lindsey the life you deserved." Derek's voice caught. He cleared his throat.

She shook her head. "That's bullshit, and you know it. You did everything you could to give us the best life, but it wasn't good enough for me, so I threw you away like trash. I'm so sorry."

"Don't apologize. You and Jacob saved my life. You two made a huge sacrifice for me. We're more than even."

Rebecca sniffled and forced a smile. "I miss us sometimes."

"Me too."

77

JACOB AND THE BIG LIE

The door clicked. The hinge creaked. The door clicked again. She tiptoed to the bed and slipped under the covers.

Jacob rolled over to face Rebecca. "Where were you?"

"I was in the lounge, reading," Rebecca replied.

"I'm sorry about what I said at dinner. I don't think you're entitled."

Rebecca smirked at her husband. "Actually, you said I was an entitled child who would be living on UBI, if not for you."

Jacob winced at that. "I know. I was being an asshole because I'm stressed about my job, and we spent all our savings—not that it wasn't worth it."

Rebecca nodded. "I'm sorry too. I shouldn't've told you to fuck off. Not one of my finer moments. I need to be more understanding of what you deal with at work too. If we have to sell the house and watch what we spend, I'm okay with that. Just tell me how much I can spend, and I'll make it work."

"We may have to tighten our belts a bit, but we'll be okay. I still have a job." Jacob reached out and took her hand. Rebecca looked blurry without his glasses in the dim light. "Most important, I still have you."

"I love you," Rebecca said.

"I love you too." Jacob pulled her close, breathing her in. She smelled like another man.

78

SUMMER AND SLAB CITY

Summer and Patrick were the last two illegal immigrants in the van. The others were dropped off in El Centro, a dusty town in Imperial County, California. From there, most would catch a ride farther east. Imperial County was once home to a multibillion-dollar farming industry. The county was farmed 365 days per year. They had the sun, the soil and, most important, a canal funneling water from the Colorado River. Thanks to an archaic federal agreement, Imperial County farmers had used water from the Colorado River without restriction.

In the 2030s—with water shortages threatening Denver, Salt Lake City, Albuquerque, and twenty million people in Southern California—the canal was shut down, and Imperial County shriveled up and died. Without tax money from agriculture, the local government shrunk and disappeared along with the farms. El Centro had become an outlaw town for drug smugglers, coyotes, human traffickers, and sex tourists.

After El Centro, they drove north for an hour, through the Imperial Valley. Summer lay on the floor of the van, the batteries under the floor warming her body. Each time she drifted off to sleep, the van bounced on the cracked asphalt, waking her from her slumber.

After the fourth time, Summer sat upright and said, "It's not gonna happen."

Patrick sat next to her, upright. He opened his eyes. "Me either."

Summer stood and walked a few paces toward the back. She moved a couple of water bottles from the rack, exposing the back window. She peered outside, but it was pitch-black. "We're in the middle of nowhere."

"Good. No facial recognition cameras."

She replaced the water bottles and sat back down next to her father. "Seriously, *nothing* is out there. What if your friend Randy doesn't show?"

"I don't know if I'd call him a friend."

Summer scowled at her father. "Don't tell me that."

"He's a fan of my work. Don't worry. He'll be there."

"How could you possibly know that for sure?"

"I don't."

The van stopped. A few seconds later, the back door opened, then the shelving packed with water bottles opened.

The Mexican driver stood in the glow of his taillights, wearing an old trucker hat. "*Listo?*"

Summer and Patrick grabbed their bags and exited the van. They were parked next to a concrete structure, about the size of a porta potty. Painted on the side of the structure was a big arrow, pointing to the accompanying message, Slab City, Almost There.

"*Gracias,*" Patrick said.

The Mexican tipped his cap and shut the back door. "*Buena suerte.*" Then he went back to the driver's seat of the van.

Summer and Patrick looked around for signs of life yet saw nothing but desert. The van turned around.

"Wait!" Summer said to the van, but it drove away.

Patrick placed his hand on Summer's shoulder and squeezed. "We're fine. We're here." Headlights approached in the distance. Patrick turned and pointed. "See?"

An old diesel pickup parked in front of them, the headlights blinding them. Summer and Patrick screened their eyes with their hands, trying to see through the high beams. Summer's heart skipped a beat at the *chick-chuck* sound of a shotgun loading. She saw the silhouette of a man.

"Who are you?" the man asked, a shotgun barrel pointed in their direction.

"Raymond and Stacy," Patrick said.

The man stepped closer. He was average size but wiry, with a white mullet and a stubbly white beard. He lowered the shotgun, then rested the butt on the ground and thrust out his right hand. "Sorry 'bout that. Never can be too careful 'round here. I'm Randy."

Patrick stepped forward and shook the man's hand. "Nice to meet you in person, Randy."

Randy narrowed his eyes and looked Patrick over. "You're Braveheart, huh? I thought you'd be different."

Patrick smiled and said, "You're *exactly* as I pictured."

Randy laughed. "Welcome to Slab City." He turned his attention to Summer. "And you must be the daughter?"

Summer stepped forward. "Stacy." They shook hands.

"Pleased to meet ya, young lady."

Summer and Patrick sat next to Randy in the front bench seat of his truck, their suitcases at their feet. The old man's body odor hung heavy in the air. The shotgun was on the rack against the back window. After driving a short distance, Randy stopped the truck, his headlights pointing at a colorful hill about three stories tall. The hill was covered in concrete and adobe and painted every color in the rainbow. Bible verses were scattered throughout, but the biggest message sat just beneath the cross. *God is Love.*

"That there is Salvation Mountain," Randy said. "Are you a God-fearin' man, Raymond?"

"God is the least of my fears," Patrick replied.

Randy chuckled and drove deeper into the Sonoran Desert. They passed old RVs and campers spread out among the desert. A few had lights on inside, but most were dark. Many had solar panels on the roofs and rainwater catchment tanks. An old box truck had been converted into a chapel, with big red letters urging people to Repent. One RV advertised an internet café on a homemade sign. Another RV with a homemade sign advertised a twenty-four-hour library. A few RVs were decorated with graffiti. One depicted a flying middle finger with big bold letters proclaiming Freedom, and a subheading that read No Fucks Given.

"Why is this place called Slab City?" Summer asked.

"Used to be marine barracks here from World War II. When the government abandoned the base, they left all the concrete slabs."

"Why do people come here?"

Randy shrugged. "Depends on the person. Some are down on their luck. Some are runnin' from the law. Some are lookin' for freedom. It ain't easy livin' though. Ain't no food. Ain't no water. Ain't no electricity. We gotta do for ourselves out here. The government don't bother with us because we ain't got nothin' for them to steal."

Randy stopped his truck, the headlights illuminating a wall made from bottles and sculptures made from the discarded dregs of industrial civilization. A few sculptures were in the shape of men. A few more were junked cars adorned and decorated. Most of the sculptures featured old bike rims spinning in the wind. "This is East Jesus," Randy said, pointing.

"Are people very religious here?" Summer asked.

"Some. This ain't got nothin' to do with Jesus though. It's called East Jesus 'cause it's in the middle of no-man's-land. This place is in the middle of East Jesus. Get it?"

Summer smiled politely.

Randy drove on from East Jesus.

"Who owns the land here?" Patrick asked.

"Technically the state of California, but they don't give a shit about us because we ain't got nothin' for them." Randy chuckled again. "Biggest problem we have is the cartels comin' through and El Aztlan.

249

We're usually okay 'cause we're so isolated, but they've been movin' north, killin' Americans. The cartels run El Centro."

"What's El Aztlan?" Summer asked.

Randy glanced at Summer, then back to the road. "A group of Mexicans who wanna take back the Southwest. They been killin' Americans near the border and movin' north. Killed an old couple here a few weeks ago. For them, *we're* the illegal immigrants."

Summer knitted her brows.

Randy glanced at Summer again. "Don't worry, young lady. We'll be safe. That's what the shotgun's for." Randy parked in front of a dusty and rusty RV. "Home sweet home."

They exited the truck, the doors groaning in response. Randy used his flashlight to lead them inside his home. Inside, he flipped on an LED lamp, illuminating the interior of the RV. It was cramped, with a tiny kitchen, and a table for four built into the wall. Junk covered every surface and every nook and cranny.

Randy motioned to the bunk beds along the back wall. "Y'all can sleep in the beds." Randy pointed his thumb over his shoulder at the driver's seat behind him. "I'll take the captain's chair."

"Thank you," Patrick said.

Randy took a few steps down the narrow aisle and opened a folding door, revealing floor to ceiling junk, along with a man-size stack of old newspapers and a rusty shovel. "This here used to be the bathroom. If ya gotta go, grab the flashlight and go outside." Randy held up the flashlight. "I'll leave this up front, in the passenger seat. If ya gotta take a dump take the shovel and some newspaper." Randy glanced at Summer. "My apologies. I know this ain't the Ritz."

Summer smiled. "It's perfectly fine. I'm very grateful."

Randy smiled back, his teeth covered in a yellow film. "Well, I bet y'all are ready to hit the hay. We should get on the road early tomorrow."

* * *

Early the next morning, Summer squatted behind a cactus and peed. She walked back to the RV and found Randy and Patrick sitting at the table, eating breakfast.

"Your cereal's gettin' soggy," Randy said, gesturing to the bowl next to Patrick.

"We were talking about what to expect today," Patrick said.

Summer settled into the bench seat next to Patrick. A bowl of cereal with reconstituted milk and bottled water to drink were waiting for her. "Thank you for breakfast," Summer said to Randy.

Randy grinned, his mouth full. "You're welcome, young lady."

"What did I miss?" Summer took a swig from the water bottle.

"We were talkin' about the checkpoints," Randy said. "We might hit a couple between here and Texas. I usually get pulled over on account of my Social Credit Score. They ask me questions, but they rarely search me."

"They search autonomous vehicles more often than manned vehicles," Patrick said.

"Yep. Smugglers down here only use AVs," Randy said. "They search one out of every eight AVs but only one out of every fifteen MVs. At least that's what I heard from a buddy who used to be a cop. This ain't my first rodeo. We gotta good chance of gettin' through."

Summer stared at Randy with raised eyebrows. "What do you mean, a good chance?"

"I'll hide y'all in the back, best I can. I got a secret hidey-hole for you, but, if they use the drug dogs, they'll smell ya."

79

NAOMI AND THE TRUTH HURTS

The morning after the debate, Naomi sat in the private jet awaiting takeoff. Her head pounded from lack of sleep. She'd been agitated by the debate and by Vernon. Corrinne had clearly bested Naomi in the debate, and she'd heard Vernon laughing with some woman in the hotel hallway after midnight.

Naomi turned from the airplane window. Two Secret Service agents sat a few rows back. Vernon was in the plush leather seat across the aisle, texting, a smirk on his face. She knew that look.

"Who are you texting?" Naomi asked.

Vernon looked up from his phone, the smirk gone. "Nobody."

"Really?"

Vernon shoved his phone into his suit jacket pocket. "You all right?"

"I thought you were too tired to have dinner with me?"

"What?"

Naomi glared at Vernon. "You know *what*. I asked you to come to my room for dinner after the debate. I needed a friend after that debacle, but you lied to me, told me you were tired."

"I *was* tired."

"I heard you last night."

Vernon's eyes widened. "Heard me where?"

"Outside in the hall with a woman, *after midnight*."

Vernon swallowed. "I'm sorry, Naomi. When you asked me to dinner, I didn't wanna throw my date in your face."

Naomi clenched her fists. "So, you lie to me instead?"

Vernon glanced to the Secret Service agents, then back to Naomi. "Let's not do this here."

Naomi shook her head. "I don't give a shit who's here."

"Naomi. Stop."

"The other night, when we were practicing for the debate, there was something between us. I guess I thought ..." Naomi trailed off, staring at the floor.

Vernon held out his hands. "You thought what?"

Naomi lifted one shoulder. "I thought we might go back to the way we were."

Vernon blew out a breath. "I love you, Naomi. We're best friends, but I'm not the settle-down type. You know that. For the good of our friendship and the campaign, we should be friends. Just friends."

Naomi had a lump in her throat. Her eye filled with tears. "You've been clear about that. I'm so *stupid* for thinking otherwise."

"Don't do that. It's not your fault."

She turned to the window so Vernon couldn't see her tears.

"I'm sorry," Vernon said.

Naomi held up her hand like a stop sign, still turned to the window.

80

DEREK AND GOODBYES

They docked in Kingston, Jamaica late Friday morning. The sun glistened off the blue water. Derek stood on the deck of the former fishing vessel turned Project Freedom supply ship.

Derek shook Rob's and Billy's hands. "You guys saved my life. Thank you."

"You're welcome. Take care of yourself." Rob grabbed his gear from the deck and walked toward the plank.

Billy rapped Derek on the back with a big grin. "See ya around, hoss."

Derek smiled back. "Thanks again, Billy."

The two mercenaries left the supply ship, walking the plank to the dock.

Rebecca and Jacob stepped onto the ship's deck, holding their suitcases.

Derek approached. "Need any help with your bags?"

"No," Jacob replied, his face blank.

"I think we're okay, but thank you." Rebecca lifted her suitcase for an instant. "Mine's really light. I gave most of my clothes to Summer."

"I'm sure she appreciated it," Derek said. "What time's your flight?"

"In a few hours."

"We need to go," Jacob said.

Derek nodded. "I can't thank you two enough. But thank you. And thank you for arrangin' to drop me in Panama."

Jacob scowled at that. "It wasn't an arrangement. It cost money."

Derek dipped his head, like a scolded child. "I know. I can't imagine how much this all cost. I obviously can't pay you back right now—"

Jacob held up his hand. "Stop. Don't bother. It's more money than you'll make in ten lifetimes."

Rebecca glared at her husband. "*Jacob.* Is that necessary?"

Jacob glared back.

Rebecca turned to Derek. "I'm glad you're okay."

"Thank you so much." Derek hugged Rebecca for a moment. When they separated, Derek said, "Please tell Lindsey that I love her."

"I will."

Derek held out his hand to Jacob. "I know my appreciation isn't enough."

Jacob hesitated for a beat, then he shook Derek's hand, squeezing tighter than necessary.

Derek didn't react.

"Let's go," Jacob said to Rebecca.

They turned and walked toward the plank attached to the pier. Jacob said something to Rebecca. She kissed Jacob on the cheek, then waited by the plank as Jacob turned back and approached Derek with a saccharin smile. He leaned into Derek's personal space and whispered, "Stay away from my family. If I ever hear from you again, I'll make sure you're sent back to that fucking island so fast it'll make your head spin."

81

JACOB'S HOMECOMING

The setting sun filled the sedan with an orange glow. Jacob sat in the back seat of his autonomous Mercedes, texting. He'd spent the better part of the trip texting and working and avoiding any interaction with Rebecca. It was the first time he'd had internet access in sixty-five days.

Jacob: I'm back. I'll be at work on Monday morning.

Ramesh: Perfect timing. We're working on the restructuring for the government takeover. Would it be possible for you to come in tomorrow (Saturday) to sign some documents?

Jacob: I'll be there at eight.

Jacob shoved his phone into the front pocket of his khakis and glanced at Rebecca. She sat on the opposite side of the back seat, staring out the window. Jacob suspected that Rebecca had lied about the other night. He'd smelled another man on her body, but he hadn't confronted her about it yet. He wasn't sure how to react. He knew if he confronted her directly, she'd deny it. Divorce had crossed his mind, but a man with his means had to consider the financial ramifications.

The Mercedes turned into their neighborhood in McLean, Virginia. The lawns were dark green and diagonally striped to perfection by the robotic mowing machines. Hedges were shaped and sculpted into globes and squares and pyramids. Six-bedroom houses with pools and four-car garages were generously spread on multiacre lots. The Mercedes turned into their driveway. Their house was a redbrick colonial with black shutters. The Mercedes opened a garage door and parked next to their Range Rover SUV.

"I feel like we've been away forever," Rebecca said.

Jacob turned to his wife, stone-faced. "Don't ever ask me to do something like that again."

Rebecca gaped at her husband, speechless for a moment. "Why are you being—"

"Never again. Do you understand me?"

Rebecca bowed her head and said, "Yes."

They exited the car, leaving the bags in the trunk for Jeeves. They entered the kitchen from the garage. Their robotic watchdog, Spike, scanned their faces, then loped toward the living room on four titanium legs. Steaks sizzled on the indoor grill, and garlic mashed potatoes cooked on the stovetop. Jeeves stood at the grill, a spatula in hand. The five foot six robot was shaped like a human. His aluminum and titanium frame was covered in blue-and-white plastic, making him look softer and more toylike.

"Welcome home, Mr. and Mrs. Roth," Jeeves said.

"Thank you, Jeeves," Rebecca replied.

Ethan ran toward his parents in stocking feet. He slid across the hardwood, slamming into Rebecca's legs. She was knocked back a step but beamed as her six-year-old hugged her around her thighs.

Ethan looked up at his mother with big brown eyes. "You're finally home."

Rebecca bent over, hugging his little body. "Hi, honey. I missed you so much."

"Where's my hug?" Jacob asked. Ethan moved to his father. He held his arms out, and Jacob picked him up, hugging him tight. "I missed you, little buddy."

"I missed you too, Dad. Please don't leave us for that long ever again."

"We won't." Jacob kissed his cherub cheek and set him down.

Lindsey sauntered into the kitchen, wearing short shorts and a tight T-shirt. Jacob clenched his jaw at the sight of his teenage daughter. He couldn't help but see her biological father. Like Derek, she had a large nose, dark eyes, and olive skin. She wasn't quite as pretty as Rebecca, but she did share her mother's oval-shaped face and straight brown hair.

"It's about time," Lindsey said with a smirk.

"Hi, honey," Rebecca said, as she hugged her daughter.

Then Lindsey gave Jacob a half hug.

"Thank you for holding down the fort," Jacob said.

"You're welcome. Jeeves did all the work." Lindsey turned to her mother. "How is *he*?"

Jacob knew Lindsey was referring to her biological father, Derek.

"He's fine. We'll talk about it later, in private." Rebecca's gaze flicked to Ethan.

Lindsey nodded.

"So, how were the boys?" Rebecca asked.

"Ethan was good as usual." Lindsey mussed his hair.

Ethan grinned at his sister.

Rebecca raised her eyebrows. "And David?"

"I was about to turn on Jeeves's corporal punishment app," Lindsey replied. "That bot has more patience than the freaking Dalai Lama."

Jacob sighed. "What did he do?"

"What didn't he do? He bullied Ethan constantly. I had to let Ethan sleep in my room—"

"That's not true." David strolled into the kitchen, his round eyes and button nose the picture of innocence.

"That's 100 percent true," Lindsey said, her arms crossed over her chest.

"We were just playing. Ethan's too sensitive." David turned to his little brother. "Aren't you, Ethan?"

Ethan shrugged and dipped his head. "I don't know."

Jacob pointed at David. "You need to be nicer to your brother."

"Your father's right," Rebecca added.

David pursed his little lips. "You guys were gone a long time. I was supersad."

"Come here. Let me give you a hug."

David stepped closer to Rebecca, letting her wrap him up in an embrace. David beamed, showing his teeth.

After Rebecca let go, Jacob gave his son a quick hug and said, "Missed you, buddy." Then Jacob turned to Jeeves. "I'll take my dinner in my office."

"You're working tonight?" Rebecca asked with a hint of annoyance.

Jacob glowered at his wife. "I missed two months of work." He left out *because of you.*

82

SUMMER AND THE PERMIAN BASIN

The setting sun provided much-needed relief from the heat. They drove on I-20 through West Texas, desert scrub all around them. The windows of the truck were wide open, providing old-fashioned air-conditioning, quickly removing the smell of sweat and body odor. Summer and Patrick sat on the front bench seat next to Randy, listening to the CB radio and wearing what appeared to be prescription eyeglasses. The glasses were embedded with infrared reflective material that rendered facial recognition cameras ineffective.

Through the CB radio, a man said, "Be careful out there. Stay away from the Mexican border. El Aztlan is on a rampage today."

Another man said, "There's a party on I-20 near Odessa. Lots of pork."

Randy turned from the road, his eyes bulging. "Get in the hidey-hole."

"You gonna pull over?" Patrick asked.

"No, that looks suspicious."

Summer and Patrick removed their seat belts and turned around, so they were facing the back. Summer folded the passenger side of the bench seat forward. Behind the seat was a narrow area for storage. It was cluttered with auto parts and cardboard boxes. She climbed over the lowered back of the seat and moved a few cardboard boxes, exposing a hidden hatch. The two-by-two hatch had no handle or latch. It was black, matching the existing paint job. Unless you looked closely, it was difficult to see the edges.

Summer pressed on the bottom of the hatch, and it pushed in and upward, the hinge at the top. Inside was the hidey-hole. Summer climbed into the coffin-size compartment, feetfirst. She turned on her side to make room for her father. Patrick squeezed in, also feetfirst, grunting and wiggling into place. They faced each other, mere inches between them, with barely enough headroom to lay on their sides. Patrick wiggled in the last few inches, and the spring-loaded hatch shut behind him.

The compartment was hot and stuffy and pitch-black. Summer's heart rate increased. Sweat beaded her hairline and dripped from her underarms. "I don't like this," Summer whispered, her voice shaky. "I feel like I'm buried alive."

Patrick opened the hatch, and light flooded the compartment. "We can get out of here anytime we want."

Summer's heart rate slowed.

In the cab, Randy drove with one hand and tossed the cardboard boxes back behind the seat. He pushed the back part of the passenger seat upright and said, "Shut the door."

Patrick let the hatch shut, covering them in darkness once again.

Summer took a deep breath and another, but she needed more air. Her breaths became more rapid. She gasped. "I can't breathe."

Patrick reached out and held Summer's hand, squeezing gently. "We have plenty of air in here. Otherwise, *I* wouldn't be able to breathe. Just relax. Close your eyes. Think of something relaxing. A beautiful place. A happy time."

Summer closed her eyes and thought of Christmas when she was a little girl. She remembered decorating the tree. Watching old Christmas cartoons with her father. Making cookies with her mother and dancing around the kitchen. Her mother was so beautiful. Her mind flashed forward to her mother in a hospital bed, pale and thin, her body ravaged by lung cancer, even though she'd never smoked a cigarette.

The truck stopped. Summer and Patrick listened with bated breath.

"Good evening, sir."

"Evenin', officer," Randy replied.

"Turn off the engine," the officer said.

"Am I being detained?"

"Turn off the engine."

"Am I being detained?"

"Are you a US citizen?"

"Are *you* a US citizen?" Randy asked.

"Can I see your ID?" the officer said.

"Can I see *your* ID?"

"Where are you headed?"

"Down this road. Am I being detained, or am I free to go?"

"Pull over there to be searched," the officer said.

"No."

"No?"

"What's your probable cause?" Randy asked.

"You won't answer my questions."

"That's not probable cause. Am I free to go?"

"This is an immigration checkpoint."

"We're a helluva long way from the border. Am I free to go?" Randy paused. "Am I being detained, or am I free to go?"

"Get the hell outta here," the officer said.

"Will do."

The truck started moving again, and Summer breathed a sigh of relief.

"Hang tight for a minute," Randy said. "I wanna get some distance from the checkpoint." Several minutes later, Randy said, "Y'all can come out now."

Patrick crawled out first. Then Summer crawled out. She took a deep breath, her body temperature cooling. They restacked the boxes, crawled into the front seat, and Patrick pushed the passenger seat upright. They sat down, buckled their seat belts, and put on their infrared reflective glasses.

"I do *not* like it in there," Summer said.

"Sorry, young lady," Randy said. "I know it's tight."

Summer knitted her brows. "Tight? It's like a coffin."

"The smaller it is, the less likely they are to find you. We're lucky that wasn't a drug checkpoint. If the drug dogs signal on a vehicle, they'll search without a warrant. Those assholes can make the dog signal on anything for any reason. Excuse my language."

"That was an immigration checkpoint?" Patrick asked.

"Yep. Border Control sets up these checkpoints inside the US, where they think illegals are travelin'. Most people don't know that those immigration checkpoints are unconstitutional. You can refuse to answer their questions, and you can refuse to be searched. Just don't give 'em any probable cause."

They took US 385 North through Odessa. The oil town was dilapidated, with many closed businesses, their signs faded, and their buildings dark. Outside of town, many residences were crumbling, with caved-in roofs and cars on blocks. Randy slowed his truck to avoid the many potholes. Beyond the suburbs, rusty oil derricks stood static against the sunset.

Ten miles beyond Odessa, they turned down a dusty gravel road and parked in front of a small brick rambler.

"I think this is it," Randy said.

Patrick glanced at the number on the house. "Looks like it."

They exited the truck. Randy retrieved their suitcases from the back. They were hidden in a hollowed-out tool chest. Randy grabbed their bags and set them on the ground.

"Thank you," Patrick said, holding out his hand.

Randy shook Patrick's hand.

"Yes, thank you," Summer said.

Randy winked at Summer and shot her with finger guns. "You're welcome, young lady."

Patrick reached into his pocket and held out a handful of silver coins. "I wanted you to have these. For your trouble."

Randy raised his eyebrows. "Is that silver?"

"Yes."

"I haven't seen silver in at least ten years."

"Please." Patrick extended his handful of coins.

Randy showed his palms. "That ain't necessary."

"You sure?"

"Somethin' tells me that you're gonna need that silver."

An elderly man exited the house and walked toward them. He was short with wire-rimmed glasses and a full head of hair as white as snow. His jeans were held up with suspenders.

"Mr. Sampson?" Patrick asked, as the old man approached.

"Please, call me Jed." The man smiled. "You must be Raymond."

Patrick and Jed shook hands.

"This is my daughter, Stacy, and this is Randy," Patrick said, pointing to his companions.

Everyone shook hands. Randy left shortly thereafter, back to Slab City.

Jed led them inside his home and down a hallway to their rooms. "These two rooms are yours. Don't matter which one."

Summer took the room with light-blue walls. It was decorated with a beach motif. Ships in bottles on the dresser, pictures and paintings of beach scenes on the walls, and a real-life anchor in the corner. Summer placed her suitcase next to the twin bed, surveying the room. "It's pretty in here."

"My wife loved the beach," Jed said, standing in the doorway with a grin. "I hope you're hungry. I made spaghetti."

Jed led Summer and Patrick to the kitchen. On the way, Summer glanced at a few of the framed pictures on the wall. Young men posing in front of an oil rig. Old family pictures. A young man posing with a football under one arm.

In the kitchen, a pot of tomato sauce and pasta simmered on the stovetop, smelling like roast garlic. The kitchen table was already set.

"Please sit," Jed said, motioning to the table for four.

"Do you need any help?" Summer asked.

"Nope. Everything's ready."

Patrick and Summer sat at the table.

Jed served them and sat down to eat.

"This is great. Thank you so much." Summer took a bite of spaghetti.

"Thank you for helping us," Patrick said.

Jed wiped his mouth, swallowed, and smiled. "I'm glad I could help."

"Did you work in the oil fields?" Summer asked. "I saw a picture in the hall."

Jed nodded. "Yep. I was a roughneck for forty years in the Permian Basin. Tough work but it paid the bills. Of course, the easy stuff's gone now. Mostly dribs and drabs comin' from shale oil and tar sands. Not like the good ole days."

83

NAOMI AND THORIUM NUKES

Naomi rode in the back seat of her autonomous Cadillac, scanning the news headlines on her tablet. The morning rays were filtered by her window tint. She was glad it was Saturday, and she didn't have to work. She didn't want to face Vernon after their argument on the plane.

El Aztlan Murder Spree

The Democratic Presidential Debate Recap

Why Do We Want to Die?

India and Pakistan: Twenty-Five Years Later

Thorium Nukes: All the Power, None of the Problems

Naomi read about the thirty-four Americans who were killed yesterday in border towns of California, Arizona, New Mexico, and Texas. The terrorist group, El Aztlan, had taken credit for the murders, promising more if former Mexican territories are not returned to Mexico. President Warner promised increased border security and more immigration checkpoints.

As much as it pained her, she read about Corrinne's smashing success at the Democratic Presidential debate and of her own failure. The article was slanted in Corrinne's favor, but they weren't wrong. *Corrinne Powers brings people together. Naomi Sutton tears them apart.* That was the sentence that really stuck in Naomi's craw. She wondered if the dirt they had on Corrinne would be enough to turn the tide.

Naomi tapped the link for *Why Do We Want to Die?* Deaths from suicide, drugs, and alcohol accounted for nearly 15 percent of deaths in the United States, a close third behind cancer and heart disease as the leading causes of death.

She skimmed the article about India and Pakistan. In 2026, an electromagnetic pulse bomb had been detonated in New Delhi, destroying much of the city's electronics and electric grid. Nearly two hundred thousand people had died in the ensuing chaos, and twenty million were displaced. Indian intelligence had then obtained circumstantial evidence that the terror plot was funded by the Pakistani government.

After a massive Indian public outcry, the Indian military had bombed Islamabad. Pakistan had used a handful of tactical nukes in response. India had then launched a full-scale nuclear attack, destroying Islamabad and the Punjab Province, killing nearly one hundred million Pakistanis in the process. Twenty-five years later, the Punjab Province and Islamabad still had radiation levels that were unsafe for human life.

Naomi thought about thorium, the much-safer nuclear option. *How many lives could've been saved if we'd been building thorium reactors from the beginning? But superpowers like the US and the Soviet Union wanted to make weapons from the by-products.* Naomi tapped the link to *Thorium Nukes: All the Power, None of the Problems.*

Thorium had proven to be a safer, more abundant, and more efficient fuel source than uranium. Since Thorium Unlimited had built the first commercial thorium reactor in 2030, there hadn't been a single accident. Thorium reactors produced very little nuclear waste, 2 percent of a conventional uranium reactor. One ton of thorium produced the same amount of energy as 200 tons of uranium or 3,500,000 tons of coal. And thorium was very abundant in the earth's crust, nearly as abundant as lead. Thorium Unlimited had designed their liquid fluoride thorium reactors to be meltdown-proof. A plug at the bottom of the reactor melted in the event of a power failure or if temperatures exceeded a set limit, draining the fuel into an underground tank for safe storage.

Naomi thought about the meeting she'd had with Jacob Roth almost a year ago. *He was keenly interested in supporting a candidate willing to heavily tax thorium power generation.* Naomi knew that Truman Bradshaw, the CEO of Thorium Unlimited, was a libertarian and adamantly opposed to central banking. She'd also heard the rumors of his plan for an energy-backed cryptocurrency. *Libertarians are no friends of socialists, but maybe this is a case of the enemy of my enemy is my friend.*

The sedan stopped in front of the assisted living high-rise. An ambulance parked in front of the emergency entrance. Naomi opened her purse and removed her compact. She checked her makeup and glass eye in the mirror. Naomi hadn't visited her mother since the accident two months ago. After the accident, Vernon had called Bea and tried to explain, but she'd been disoriented and confused, the Alzheimer's taking more and more of her faculties each day.

Naomi grabbed her purse and stepped from the car. As she walked through the automatic doors, the car drove toward the parking area.

Inside, the lobby was marble floored and nicely appointed with leather couches, a massive fireplace, and fresh flowers. Alexandria Acres was one part hospital and one part high-end hotel. Residents had to be buzzed in and out, as did their guests.

Naomi approached the front desk and waved her hand over the chip reader. The receptionist checked her credentials, smiled, and unlocked the door leading past the lobby. Naomi took the elevator to the eighth floor, then walked to room number 852.

Nurses and orderlies walked along the halls. The eighth floor was a monitored floor, for residents who couldn't live without help. Naomi knocked on the door and stepped into the room. Bea sat upright on the inclined bed, staring at a blank, nearly transparent OLED screen.

She was a tiny woman with a prune-like face.

"Hi, Mom," Naomi said, approaching the hospital bed.

Bea squinted at Naomi, as if trying to place her. "Oh, hi, dear." Her voice was tentative.

"I came to see how you're doing. I'm sorry it's been so long since my last visit."

Bea smiled, her wrinkles tightening and erupting to accommodate her facial movement. "I'm doing just wonderful, thank you very much."

"That's great to hear." Naomi moved a chair next to Bea's bedside and sat. Naomi reached out and held her mother's hand. "I've missed you, Mom."

"I've missed you too, dear. How are you?"

Naomi sighed. "I've had better days."

Bea narrowed her eyes at Naomi and asked, "What's wrong, baby?"

Naomi swallowed the lump in her throat. "I'm not here to dump all my problems on you."

"That's what mothers are for."

Naomi sniffled and forced a smile. *She's having a good day.*

"Tell me all about it, dear," Bea said.

Naomi told her everything. Alan's death. Losing her eye. The affair with Vernon and the subsequent breakup. Blake's arrest and death on US Penal Colony East. Her campaign and her poor showing in the debate two days ago. During Naomi's diatribe, Bea had nodded and listened intently. After Naomi said her piece, she felt lighter somehow, like a weight had been lifted.

Then Bea stared at Naomi and asked, "Who are you?"

84

DEREK IMMIGRATES TO SILVER CITY

They docked next to a sailboat at the end of a rickety wooden pier in Puerto de Carti, Panama, bustling with men loading sailboats with supplies. Derek stood on the deck of the Project Freedom supply ship, the ocean sparkling in the morning sun. He wore sunglasses embedded with infrared reflective material that rendered facial recognition cameras ineffective, although he didn't see any cameras in this rural locale.

Derek picked up the duffel bag at his feet and slung it across his chest. All his worldly possessions. Some clothes and toiletries given to him by Cesar of Project Freedom, but he didn't have a single Fed Coin to his name, nor would he ever. To transact in Fed Coins would create a detailed record of the transaction, which would likely lead to Derek's arrest. He hoped Jacob's contact would show, but, after their icy goodbye yesterday, Derek wasn't so sure Jacob would make good on his promise, especially with Rebecca out of sight.

Derek thanked the captain and walked the plank to the dock. As soon as Derek's boots hit the pier, the crewmen took the plank, cutting his only connection to the vessel. Derek looked around, getting his bearings. A small town was just inland. To his left and right were white sand beaches. Blue water lapped the shore with small waves.

Driftwood and seaweed littered the sand. It didn't look much different than Psycho Island.

A well-built Panamanian man wearing crisp fatigues approached and said, "Derek?"

"Yes," Derek replied.

He smiled, exposing a silver tooth. "I am Roberto. I take you to Silver City."

They shook hands.

"Nice to meet you," Derek said.

They walked a short distance from the dock to the roadside, where Roberto's SUV was parked. They drove south on a narrow road filled with hairpin turns, the jungle crowding the roadsides.

"How long will it take to get to Silver City?" Derek asked.

"Three or four *horas* to Yaviza," Roberto replied. "You take boat in Rio Tuira. Maybe four *horas* more. You make it before night."

Derek nodded.

"Two months ago, I take American girl to Silver City. Nice girl. Very pretty. Maybe you know her. Summer."

Derek chuckled to himself. "Yeah, I know her."

"Ah." Roberto grinned like a Cheshire cat. "Your girlfriend?"

"No."

"Friend?"

"Not exactly. She's …" Derek couldn't finish the sentence.

"*Importante?*"

"Yeah. She's important."

* * *

Derek traveled to Silver City much the same as Summer. Roberto took Derek to a dock in Yaviza to meet Alvaro, a captain of a small cargo boat. Alvaro then took Derek down river to Silver City. The bustling port held many sailboats but also many diesel-powered cargo ships.

According to Alvaro, Silver City was a peninsula between the Tuira

River and the Gulf of San Miguel. They had landed on the river side, but Silver City also had an ocean port for larger vessels.

As the crewmen tied the boat to the dock, Alvaro asked, "You know where to go?"

Derek frowned and shook his head.

Alvaro chuckled. "Where do you want to go?"

Derek only knew two people in Silver City. Summer and Steven Parker Jr. Of course, he'd never met Parker, but before Roger Kroenig had died in Derek's arms, he'd said, "Panama" and "Steven Parker." When Fred and Derek had launched Summer in the submarine, Fred had also told Summer to find Parker in Silver City. *Maybe he can help me too.*

"I need to find a guy named Steven Parker Jr."

Alvaro grinned. "You are in luck, my friend. I know *Señor* Parker. He has a very beautiful farm. Sometimes I take his fruit to Yaviza."

Alvaro hired an autonomous car near the dock for Derek and sent him on his way. Derek sat in the back of the little electric sedan, slack-jawed, watching the scenery. The buildings were painted in bright pastel colors, many with murals portraying jungle scenery and wildlife. It was more of a utopian town than a city.

Cars and trucks were mostly electric and small, vastly outnumbered by bicycles and electric motorcycles. Between the buildings, people in wide brimmed hats tended communal gardens and children played in playgrounds. Trees intermingled with the architecture. Commercial and residential properties sat side by side, with no apparent zoning restrictions. A farmers' market, restaurants, dentist and doctor's offices, shops selling clothes and tools, and even small factories were mixed among the homes.

The sidewalks were just as busy with pedestrians as the streets were with vehicles. Based on the style of dress and the prevalence of English and Spanish speakers, the people could be from nearly any town in the southern United States. Most were fit and healthy, with smiles on their faces.

The little sedan took Derek outside of town to a gated community. The car stopped at the front gate, the metal bar lowered, blocking their path. An electric fence circled the community, a mower-width of the jungle beaten back on both sides of the fence. A metal sign was affixed to the guard shack next to the gate. It read Freetown.

The robotic guard peered through the thick glass of the guard shack with its red eyes, scanning the sedan and Derek's face. The irony of this security measure juxtaposed with the community name wasn't lost on Derek. The robot stepped from the shack, carrying an M6 automatic rifle. The robot had the size and stature of a human being and was made from titanium and aluminum. No plastic covering to make it look friendly. A hump on its back was likely filled with solid state lithium ion batteries.

"What is your business here?" the bot asked through Derek's open car window.

"I'm here to see Steven Parker Jr.," Derek replied, his eyes on the rifle pointed in his direction.

"Please remove your glasses so I can scan your face."

Derek hesitated, then said, "I'd rather not."

The bot asked, "What is your name?"

He hesitated again, finally saying, "Derek."

"Last name?"

"I don't wanna give my full name. Can you contact Steven and tell him that I'm a friend of Summer's from the island? He'll wanna talk to me."

"Please stay in the car while I call him."

The bot stood still, apparently making a call, but, to Derek, it looked like it was just standing there, silent.

Finally, the bot said, "He'll be here in five minutes. You may wait here." The bot motioned to a bench outside the concrete guard shack.

Derek exited the vehicle and sat on the bench, his duffel bag next to him. The autonomous vehicle turned and drove back toward downtown Silver City. Shortly thereafter, a pickup truck parked just off the main street, near the gate but inside the community. An old man stepped from the electric pickup truck and walked toward Derek. The bot opened the person-size gate next to the guard shack remotely. Derek stood to greet the old man.

"Mr. Parker?" Derek asked.

"Please, call me Steven. You must be Derek?"

"Yes."

They shook hands. As they shook, the old man narrowed his eyes at Derek. Steven Parker Jr. was small and frail and covered in age spots. He had a large bulbous nose and thinning white hair.

"What makes you think I know a Summer from the island?" Steven asked.

Derek removed his sunglasses, making eye contact with the old man. "Because I was with Roger Kroenig when he died. The last thing he said was to go to Panama and to find you. I helped launch Summer in a submarine from Psycho Island. She was supposed to give you a flash drive that had footage from the island."

Steven nodded. "Forgive me if I'm a little skeptical, but I'd like to verify your identity."

"How do we do that?"

Steven removed his phone from the front pocket of his khaki shorts. "Let me scan your face."

Derek put on his sunglasses. "Not gonna happen."

Steven showed his palms in surrender. "If you are who you say you are, I understand why you wouldn't wanna be scanned, but this would just be for my information. Even if you allowed that bot to scan you, the scans here aren't reported to the worldwide database. Nobody would know except the Council of Freetown. We take privacy very serious here."

Derek blew out a breath and removed his sunglasses. "I guess I don't have much choice."

The old man scanned Derek's face, then watched his screen. "It takes a minute."

They waited in awkward silence.

Steven finally broke the silence and said, "Derek Reeves. Born in Luray, Virginia, August 7, 2012." The old man replaced his phone in his pocket. He grinned, his eyes blue and squinty. "Summer told me about you. I never thought I'd meet an escaped island prisoner. Now I've met two. You must've had one helluva journey."

"You could say that."

"What are your plans?"

Derek shrugged. "This was it."

"Well, you came to the right place to start over. There's lots of work in Silver City. You're welcome to stay with me for a few days, until you figure it out. I have a vacant house on my property right now."

"Thank you. I appreciate it. I don't have any money, but I'll pay you back when I get a job."

Steven waved his hand across the air. "That's not necessary. If I could hear your story, that would be more than enough payment."

"Sure."

Derek followed Steven through the gate and into Freetown. Steven drove his little pickup through the neighborhood, with Derek sitting in the passenger seat. The setting sun was an orange orb. Many houses were concrete and stucco, without basements, and built on concrete pillars or stilts to protect the houses from the rainy season. Most parked their cars under their homes, and had to climb a flight of stairs to reach the front door. Many houses were brightly colored with Spanish-style courtyards and balconies. The neighborhood was more jungle than suburban neighborhood, only small areas cleared around the houses.

Steven's house was one of the smallest in the neighborhood— a two-bedroom home on concrete pillars—but his property was the largest. Rows of fruit trees and gardens covered his fifty acres. Steven parked in front of his home. They exited the truck.

"Beautiful orchard," Derek said, surveying the farm.

Steven sighed, walking around his truck, now standing next to

Derek. "I'm too damn old for farming. I don't have the energy I used to."

"I grew up on an orchard in Virginia."

Steven tilted his head to Derek. "I could use some help around here."

"I'm happy to do whatever you need."

"I might take you up on that."

Steven led Derek through the orchard, walking along a worn footpath, with banana trees on their right and mangoes on their left.

Two additional homes, a barn, and a greenhouse were situated on the edge of the orchard. A sign on the barn read Freetown Orchard. The homes were similar to Steven's. Sturdy concrete homes built on concrete pillars.

A Panamanian man stepped from the greenhouse, shirtless and shoeless.

Steven waved him over. "Marcos, come over here for a minute."

Marcos approached. His face was weathered from the sun. He was short and thin, with wiry muscles.

"Marcos, this is Derek." Steven turned to Derek, then motioned to the middle-aged man. "Derek, this is Marcos."

Marcos wiped the soil from his hands.

Derek smiled and shook the man's hand. "It's nice to meet you."

Marcos smiled back, missing a few teeth. "*Jes.* Good ... meet you." His English was heavily accented and broken.

"Marcos has been with me since I started this place ten years ago. We started our root stocks from seed and grafted and planted every tree in this orchard. He's the plant whisperer around here."

Marcos dipped his head. "No. Steven teach me about the trees."

Steven frowned at that. "He's a natural. Much better than me."

Marcos went back to his tree seedlings, and Steven showed Derek inside one of the concrete homes. The one-bedroom home was sparsely furnished, with a hodgepodge of metal, leather, and plastic furniture.

Steven pointed to the leather couch and the OLED television. "This is the living room." He pointed to the open kitchen, just a few steps to his left. "That's the kitchen." He pointed down a short hall to the right. "The bathroom and bedroom are down that hall."

Derek set his duffel bag on the couch. "I can't thank you enough, Steven. I was serious about helping out around here."

"You have any experience with tropical trees?"

"Not to brag, but I bred the first frost-resistant oranges in Virginia."

Steven arched his eyebrows. "Wow. I'm impressed. We're a man short right now, if you wanna job. Poor Marcos has been running ragged to keep up with the chores. The pay's not great, but it comes with room and board and use of a truck."

85

JACOB AND ELYSE

Housing Trust's upper-level managers had gone home hours ago. Only Jacob and Ramesh remained. Jacob didn't blame them. What was the point? Most of them were lame ducks, waiting to be fired after the restructuring and government takeover next week. Housing Trust, along with United Mortgage and Student Loan Corp., would transition from Government-Sponsored Enterprises to State-Owned Enterprises.

GSEs long held the advantage of private profit and public risk. SOEs, on the other hand, were wholly owned by the state. Housing Trust would now operate with a similar financial structure to the US Postal Service. Jacob would retain his job at Housing Trust, but he would no longer be the CEO. SOEs didn't have CEOs. He'd be the director of Housing Trust, and his salary would be commensurate with the postmaster general and other heads of SOEs, which was a fraction of his current salary.

Jacob signed his name on the screen with a stylus, then tapped Submit. He looked to Ramesh, who sat catty-cornered to him at the conference room table. "That's it."

Ramesh looked up from his laptop, his balding brown head glistening in the artificial light. The middle-aged CFO resembled an alien with that huge forehead, small chin, and big wire-rimmed glasses. He shut his laptop. "I'm finished too."

"I hope your portfolio's hedged."

"I've been out of the market for months."

"Good. The news will try to spin this as positive for the economy, but the algorithms know better."

Elyse stepped into the conference room, holding two steaming cups of coffee. She could pass for an Italian model, and she had the brains to graduate top of her class with a Harvard MBA. She set the coffee on the table.

Jacob smiled at his assistant. "You didn't have to do that, Elyse."

She smiled back, accentuating those high cheekbones. "I sent Brandi home." She was referring to Jacob's receptionist and typical gofer.

"You should go home too."

"I still have a few things to finish up."

Ramesh stood from his seat and stretched his bony arms wide. He nodded to Elyse. "You can have my coffee. I'm headed home." Ramesh addressed Jacob. "I'm glad you're back."

"Thank you for all your help, Ramesh. I know my absence was a burden."

Ramesh smiled at his boss. "You're welcome." Ramesh grabbed his laptop and left the conference room.

Jacob gestured to Ramesh's empty seat. "Sit. Enjoy your coffee."

Elyse slid out the chair, but, instead of sitting there, she replaced the chair with another, then she sat down.

Jacob narrowed his eyes at his assistant. "Is that chair broken?"

Elyse blushed. "I don't like sitting in chairs after people."

"Really? Why not?"

Elyse wiggled her nose. "It feels warm and a little … gross."

Jacob tilted his head.

Elyse spoke quickly to explain. "It has nothing to do with Ramesh. It's my weird idiosyncrasy."

Jacob laughed. "I didn't know that about you."

"I'm glad you're back too." Elyse blew on her coffee and took a sip.

"Thank you. I wish it was under better circumstances. This restructuring …" Jacob shook his head. "A lot of good people will lose their jobs." Jacob grabbed his coffee and took a sip.

"I know." Elyse pursed her full lips. "What about *my* job?"

Jacob took a deep breath.

"I'm sorry. I know you can't tell anyone yet."

"I made sure you were on the list of indispensables. You may have a small pay cut, but your benefits will be slightly better."

She beamed, her eyes twinkling. "Thank you so much. I was petrified that I'd be let go."

Jacob smiled at her gratitude. "You earned it. You're invaluable. To be honest, this position is beneath you. If we were expanding, I'd make you a VP."

"Thank you, Mr. Roth. I don't know what to say."

"The only drawback is, you're stuck with me for the foreseeable future. Don't worry, I'll make sure you have plenty of fresh chairs."

She giggled and flipped her wavy hair off her shoulders. "I don't mind being stuck with you." Elyse blew on her hot coffee and took another sip.

Jacob watched her lips.

"How was your vacation?"

Jacob shook his head. "It wasn't a vacation."

She tilted her head. "What was it?"

"It was me trying to make my wife happy."

Elyse leaned toward Jacob. "Did it work?"

Jacob sat silent for a second.

"Sorry. That was too personal."

"No. It wasn't. I brought it up." Jacob thought about Rebecca and Derek and that night on the boat. "Have you ever been in a relationship with someone who loves someone else?"

Elyse nodded almost imperceptibly. "Once. Two years ago, my

ex-fiancé married my best friend."

Jacob winced. "He must be an idiot."

Elyse lifted one shoulder. "I don't know. They seem pretty happy. They just had an enhanced baby, and she's pregnant again. We're both too civil to unfollow each other on social media."

"You'll meet someone better. You're a beautiful, brilliant young woman. Anybody would be lucky to have you."

She blushed again. "Your wife's really lucky too."

He frowned. "I'm not sure about that, but I do know that you should stay off social media."

"She *is* lucky." Elyse sipped her coffee, then set it back on the table. Instead of retracting her hand to her lap, it rested on the table near Jacob.

He reached out to squeeze her hand but knocked over his coffee. Jacob sprang from his seat and grabbed the cup, placing it upright again, most of the contents on the table. "Damn it."

Elyse stood. "I'll grab some paper towels."

Jacob moved his laptop safely away from the spill. Elyse returned with a roll of paper towels. She wiped up the coffee. Jacob grabbed a few paper towels from the roll and helped Elyse. They were side by side, cleaning up the coffee spill, their hips touching. She was the same height as Jacob in her heels. Elyse collected their soiled paper towels, dumped them in the trash bin, and returned to the table.

"Sorry about that," Jacob said, still standing. "I'm not myself lately."

Elyse stood before her boss. "You've been great."

Jacob placed his hands on her hips. She didn't flinch, so he leaned in and kissed her openmouthed.

For a split second she responded, then she leaned away and placed her hand on his chest. "We can't," she said.

Jacob pulled her close again, pressing his lips to hers, his hands on her backside. She turned her head and wriggled in his grasp, but he held tight. "It's okay," he said.

Her face was twisted in disgust. "Stop."

"Nobody has to know," Jacob said, still holding her tight.

Elyse slapped him across the face, and Jacob let go. He stepped back and touched his face.

"*We* would know," she said, glowering at Jacob.

86

SUMMER AND THE FARM

Yesterday, Jed had driven them from his home in Texas to eastern Tennessee, about one hundred miles from their destination. They'd stayed the night with Jed's friend and old buddy from his roughneck days.

Now, they traveled on US 64 East toward Summertown, Tennessee. Summer sat in the back seat of the SUV, watching the world zip by through her IR reflective glasses.

"Checkpoint," Jed said.

Summer looked between the front seats, through the front window. She saw brake lights, the traffic slowing. Patrick climbed into the back seat from the front passenger seat. Summer and Patrick climbed into the footwells between the back seat and front seats. Summer grabbed the dark blanket and covered them both.

A minute later, the SUV slowed. The vehicle barely came to a stop, then it picked up speed again.

"The cop waved us through," Jed said. "The road up ahead looks clear."

Summer and Patrick emerged from the blanket. It had been the third time they'd been waved through a checkpoint. According to Jed, he was always waved through checkpoints. He had heard that citizens with Social Credit Scores of ninety and above were rarely, if ever, questioned or searched at checkpoints.

* * *

Jed turned on the gravel road. A hand-painted sign read Welcome to The Farm. A hardwood forest was on the right, the leaves still bright green. Long-haired men with bushy beards split wood. Little boys stacked the wood on a trailer attached to an electric tractor. On the left were fruit trees and rows of annual gardens. A mixture of men, women, and children tended the gardens, wearing straw hats. Some of the adults had infants attached to their chests. Every single person was thin.

"This is one heckuva place," Jed said.

"It's a commune based on the principles of nonviolence and respect for the Earth," Patrick replied.

Beyond the gardens was a small water tower, a solar farm, and a large barn. Behind the solar farm was a cluster of small homes built out of clay and straw, the roofs covered in grass. Around the bend sat a larger traditional farmhouse. Clothes waved in the wind on clotheslines. A handful of women cut and arranged fruit on trays for the solar dehydrators. A few kids ran and played in the yard.

"You can drop us up here at the house," Patrick said, pointing.

Jed parked in front.

"Thank you," Patrick said, holding out his hand to Jed.

"You're welcome," Jed replied, shaking Patrick's hand. "It was nice to get outta the house for a few days." Jed turned to the back seat. "It was nice to meet you, Stacy."

Summer smiled at the old man. "You too, Jed. Thank you so much for helping us."

"Of course."

Patrick handed Jed five ounces of silver. "For your trouble."

Jed waved him off. "That's not necessary."

Patrick and Summer grabbed their suitcases and exited the SUV. They waved goodbye to Jed, but Jed didn't leave. He waited, apparently making sure they were accepted. A petite woman approached, wearing round sunglasses, a flowing dress, and a multicolored scarf. She had long whitish-blond hair, her face thin and a little sunken, but still pretty.

"You must be Raymond and Stacy," she said, beaming.

"You must be Brie," Patrick said, returning her smile.

They shook hands, Brie taking Patrick's with both her hands, then giving him a warm hug. Patrick's face reddened as they separated. Summer wondered if Patrick was attracted to her. She looked to be in the same age group as her father. Then Summer received the same intimate handshake and hug. Jed drove away with a polite beep.

Brie gazed at Patrick, her hands fiddling with her scarf, her smile still plastered to her face. "I have to admit. I'm a little starstruck." Brie glanced at Summer. "I've been following your father's work for thirty years. He's a real American hero."

Patrick blushed again. "That's kind of you to say, Brie, but I'm just a guy on the internet."

Brie shook her head, her gaze locked on Patrick. "You're much more than that. You're a truth teller. In a time of universal deceit, telling the truth is a revolutionary act."

"Thank you for saying that." Patrick smiled again. "I love that quote, by the way. George Orwell. Although he probably didn't say it."

"I'm here at The Farm because of you."

Patrick knitted his brows. "Because of me?"

"In the 2020s, during the Greater Depression, you talked about self-sufficiency being the safest and the most ethical way to protest a tyrannical government and a predatory economic system. Not participating in and not needing the government or the banks was the only way to be free in an unfree world."

Patrick nodded. "I remember talking about that. I think it's still very true today."

"When I was a young woman, I had an abusive husband. I left him to come here and to live off the land. I don't think I'd be alive today if it weren't for you." Brie stepped into Patrick's personal space, rose on her toes, and kissed him on the cheek. She stepped back and said, "Thank you."

"You're welcome. Thank you for taking us in and agreeing to drive us to Virginia."

Brie waved away his thank you. "It's my pleasure." Brie glanced at Summer, including her in the conversation. "I do worry about how you two will get back from Virginia. I could drive you back too."

"Thank you, but that's not necessary," Patrick said. "I've already made arrangements for the return trip."

"Well, you two must be hungry and tired," Brie said.

Patrick's gaze was still on Brie. "It's been quite a journey."

"The box truck's still at the farmers' market, but it'll be back tonight, so we can leave for Virginia first thing in the morning."

"That'll be fine."

"In the meantime, I'll show you to your rooms, so you can freshen up. We've already had lunch, but we still have plenty of leftovers. I hope you like veggies. Everyone's vegan at The Farm."

As they followed Brie to the farmhouse, Summer whispered to Patrick, "Thirty years? Did Mom know about Braveheart?"

Patrick whispered back, "She was my biggest supporter."

87

NAOMI AND MANUFACTURED DISSENT

Naomi sat at her kitchen nook, finishing her lunch, and reading an article about the gun control protests on her tablet.

Gun Control Protests Turn Violent
By: Jasmine Adler
Sunday, 10-20-2051

The NRA sponsored nationwide protests yesterday to oppose the upcoming gun control legislation, the Sensible Firearms Act. Alt-right activists, antigovernment zealots, neo-Nazis, white supremacists, and white nationalists rallied in protest against the Sensible Firearms Act.

Many protests turned violent when progun advocates were met by antigun counterprotestors. Fifty-seven injuries were reported and six deaths. The tragic deaths and twenty-three of the injuries occurred in Washington, DC. Four men were shot to death, and two women were trampled by the crowd after the gunfire caused mass panic.

Seven members of the alt-right group, Patriots for Freedom, were arrested in connection with the shootings. The names of those arrested have not yet been released to the media. According to several eyewitnesses in Washington, DC, Patriots for Freedom started the melee by chanting "The west is best" and "This land is ours."

Patriots for Freedom leader Joshua Gaines commented on the protests. "My patriot brothers and sisters simply defended themselves against the socialist scum who seek to disarm us. We don't want further violence, but, if you people think we'll register our guns or submit to an APT test, you've lost your damn minds. What part of 'shall not be infringed' do you not understand? You want my guns? You'll have to take them from my cold dead hands."

Dr. Hugh Lindley, Georgetown professor, and founder of the antigun nonprofit organization Repeal the Second said, "We've nearly eliminated gun violence in this country with proactive policing, science, and surveillance. It's a myth that we still need guns for personal protection. We live in the safest time in human history."

The Sensible Firearms Act institutes mandatory gun registrations, more stringent background checks, required antisocial personality tests, and limits on magazine capacity.

The popular bipartisan bill is expected to be signed into law by President Warner on Tuesday.

Doris, the household bot, rolled over to the booth. "Are you finished, Naomi?"

"Yes. Thank you," Naomi replied.

"Would you like anything else? More coffee?"

"No, thank you."

"Very well." The bot removed Naomi's mostly empty plate and mug and rolled to the kitchen sink.

Naomi's cell phone chimed. She checked the number, scowled, and swiped right. "What do you want?"

"Look. I'm sorry," Vernon said.

"For what?"

"For not being who you want me to be."

"I thought you were a better person. I misjudged you. That's *my* fault."

"It's not your fault. It wasn't you. I'm not good in romantic relationships. Period. You know that."

Naomi sighed. "That's for sure."

"I am a good friend though. Aren't I?"

"I suppose."

"You're my best friend. No question. That's real. I don't wanna lose our friendship."

Naomi cleared her throat. "Neither do I."

"Are we good?"

Naomi blew out a breath. "I don't know about *good*. Maybe *okay*."

Vernon chuckled. "Close enough."

Naomi couldn't help but smile a little.

"Since I have you on the phone, what do you think about the gun control protests?" Vernon asked.

"Much of the commentary supports Corrinne's position as a moderate."

"The press is certainly in her corner. Did you see the interview with PFF leader, Joshua Gaines?"

"I read a quote from him, but I didn't see the interview."

"I actually know him, but that's not his real name."

"Really?"

"We went to school together. Last I heard, he was working for the

State Department. Of course, you know what that means."

Naomi's eyes widened. "He's a CIA officer."

"I bet CIA officers did the shooting or at least instigated it. Manufactured dissent to divide and conquer."

88

DEREK'S IMMIGRATION HEARING

It was a closed-door meeting in a small room at the community center of Freetown. Derek sat on a wooden chair, facing a long table and a panel of four men, each with a name placard and a tablet in front of them. One of the men on the panel was Truman Bradshaw, the CEO of Thorium Unlimited, and, according to Steven, the richest man in the world. One seat was empty. Steven had recused himself since Derek had accepted his job offer. Steven still attended, sitting behind Derek, the only person in the audience.

Derek told his arrest-and-escape story to the Freetown Council.

At the conclusion of Derek's testimony, Truman asked, "What are the two rules in Freetown and Silver City?"

Steven had helped Derek prepare for his immigration hearing.

"Don't violate the nonaggression principle, and I need to get a rights and responsibility assurance policy," Derek replied.

Truman narrowed his dark eyes. "Do you know what the nonaggression principle means?"

"It means aggression is inherently evil, unless in self-defense or the defense of another."

"How would you define aggression?"

Derek squirmed in his seat. "I guess physically assaultin' someone or stealin' or damagin' their property."

"What about murder, Mr. Reeves? Does murder violate the nonaggression principle?"

Derek nodded his head.

"Speak up, Mr. Reeves." Truman's voice was stern.

"Yes."

Truman stared at Derek, his eyes unblinking. "How many men have you murdered?"

Derek clenched his jaw, then said, "As many as I had to."

"Did you *have to* murder Zhang Jun?"

Derek glowered at Truman and said, "Yes."

"Mr. Jun posed no imminent threat to you. His murder was a clear violation of the nonaggression principle."

"That's not what you asked. You asked whether or not I had to do it."

"Your life wasn't in danger, yet you murdered that man in cold blood. What's to stop you from murdering someone here in Silver City?"

Derek took a deep breath, calming his anger. "I have no intention of hurtin' anyone. I never have. But, if I'm lucky enough to meet another woman like April, and someone rapes and kills her, you better believe I'll murder again."

Truman sneered at that, then glanced to his fellow board members. "Does anyone else have any questions for Mr. Reeves?"

The gray-haired men shook their heads.

Steven Parker Jr. stood from his seat in the audience. "I'd like to say a few words."

"Go ahead, Steven," Truman replied.

"I'd like to point out that Derek's testimony matches Summer's. According to her, she wouldn't be alive if it wasn't for this man. I believe Derek Reeves would make an excellent addition to this community. He already has a job and a place to stay at my orchard. He has valuable skills as a professional orchardist. He'll have an excellent assurance policy as part of his employment. And he's an antigovernment refugee. Only the second escaped dissident from the US island penal colonies. He's exactly why this community was created. To provide a place for dissidents to live in peace and freedom. I submit that any violence Derek committed was in self-defense or defense of another."

Truman turned to his fellow board members. "I move to vote on Derek Reeves's application for permanent residency in Freetown. Yes for approval, no for rejection." Truman paused for a beat, then said, "No."

The old man next to Truman said, "Yes."

Truman glowered, and the old man looked away.

The next two board members also said, "Yes."

Truman stood and left the room without a word.

Steven clapped, a big smile on his face.

* * *

On the short drive back to Freetown Orchard, Derek said, "I think we might've pissed off Truman Bradshaw."

Steven, in the driver's seat of his pickup, glanced from the road to Derek and back again. "Don't worry about him. We have philosophical differences, but I'd like to think we're still on the same team."

"What team is that?" Derek asked, sitting in the passenger seat.

"The team that believes taxation is theft and government is simply a monopoly on violence in between arbitrary lines on a map."

Derek stroked his bushy beard. "How is it that you differ?"

"He's a libertarian. I'm an agorist. He thinks, as Silver City grows, it could benefit from a small government to help protect property and individual liberties and to defend against a possible foreign invasion." Steven turned his truck into his driveway and parked.

"You said he believes taxation is theft."

"Income tax, yes. He thinks this small government could be funded by excise taxes and tariffs, similar to the US before they enacted the income tax."

"Sounds reasonable."

Steven shook his head. "Even governments that start small and have the best of intentions don't stay that way. The US is a perfect example of that."

89

JACOB AND CUCKOLDING

Jacob stared from the floor-to-ceiling window of his office at Housing Trust headquarters. Wispy clouds moved through the light-blue sky. He thought about Elyse and what had happened on Saturday. *She was flirting. I'm not a fucking idiot. Women are attracted to power. She brushed against me when we cleaned up the coffee, not the other way around. She flipped her hair off her shoulders. The eye contact. She told me that Rebecca was lucky. I didn't misread the situation. She knew what she was doing. Imagine if the situation were reversed, and I slapped a woman.*

A soft knock came to his open door.

"Mr. Roth." Her voice trembled a little.

Jacob swiveled in his chair to face Elyse.

"You wanted to speak to me?" Her head was bowed.

"Sit down." Jacob gestured to the two leather chairs in front of his desk.

Elyse sat across from Jacob.

They were silent for a few seconds.

Elyse broke the silence and said, "I know what you're going to say, but you don't have to. We can just forget all about it. Pretend it never happened."

Jacob narrowed his eyes at the young woman, his hands clasped together, his elbows resting on his desk. "I don't think I can do that."

Elyse forced a smile. "It's really not necessary."

"I want to thank you for your hard work over the years, but your position won't be retained after the government takeover."

Elyse's body went rigid, her eyes like saucers. "You told me that I was indispensable."

Jacob deadpanned, "You're not."

"You can't do this. I'll go to HR and tell them what you did."

Jacob's expression remained blank. "I already told them what *you* did. How you came on to me and assaulted me when I rejected you."

"That's a lie!" Elyse stood from her seat and pointed at Jacob. "I'll sue you for wrongful termination."

"These things are very messy and expensive. We'll end up in court, and it'll be your word against mine. Did you know that I've never had a single complaint from a female employee? What do you think the jury will think about your professor at Harvard? The one you filed a sexual harassment complaint against? He was innocent, wasn't he?" Jacob leaned back in his chair and folded his arms over his chest, a smirk on his face.

She deflated, her shoulders sagging, and her head bowed. "How do you know about that?"

"I have my connections."

"He was guilty. There wasn't enough evidence."

Jacob shrugged. "Save it for the courtroom." He leaned forward, opened the top drawer of his desk, and removed a small stack of paper and a pen. "Or you can be sensible. I'll give you six months' severance and a glowing recommendation." He slid the papers and the pen across his desk. "Sign and initial the last page, and it's done. My recommendation is on top."

She hesitated for a moment, staring at the stack of paper. Then she slumped back into the leather chair and signed with tears in her eyes.

* * *

Jacob's autonomous Mercedes parked in his garage. He stepped from the vehicle and entered the kitchen. Jeeves was at the sink, washing dishes. Rebecca sat in the living room, just beyond the open-plan kitchen, tapping on her tablet.

"Welcome home, Mr. Roth," Jeeves said, turning from the sink.

Jacob ignored the bot and walked to the living room, his back and shoulders hunched.

Rebecca looked up from her tablet. "Hi, honey. We just finished dinner, but I can have Jeeves prepare you a plate of leftovers."

"I'm not hungry. Where are the kids?"

"In the basement. Playing in the VR rooms as usual."

Jacob nodded.

Rebecca searched his face. "Are you okay?"

"I'm fine. I need to take off this suit."

Jacob went to the circular staircase and trudged upstairs to their bedroom. He stepped to his walk-in closet and undressed to his boxer shorts, socks, and white T-shirt. The white carpet felt soft and springy under his stocking feet. He padded to his dresser and removed his Rolex, setting the bulky gold watch atop the dresser.

One of the bedroom's double doors opened, and Rebecca stepped inside, shutting the door behind her. She wore pajama pants with little hearts and a loose T-shirt. She sidled up to Jacob and said, "I'm worried about you."

"I'm fine," Jacob replied.

"You don't look fine."

Jacob blew out a heavy breath.

She took his hand in both of hers. "Can I do something to make you feel better?" She raised his hand to her mouth and kissed it. Then she stepped closer, invading his personal space, pulling him into an embrace. She pressed her lips to his, their tongues touching.

Jacob had a vision. Rebecca bent over and writhing in ecstasy. *Derek* behind her, fucking her like a savage. Jacob moved his hands to her waistband and yanked her pajama pants and underwear to midthigh. He grabbed between her legs and rubbed her clitoris.

Rebecca moaned, her hand inside his boxers, clutching his erection. Jacob moved behind her. Rebecca tried to turn, to face her husband, but he held her in place. "Let's go to the bed," Rebecca said, her voice sultry.

But Jacob pushed his hand on her upper back, forcing her to bend at the waist, her hands on his dresser top. He pulled down his boxers and took her from behind, like Derek had in Jacob's vision.

"Wait," Rebecca said, her head turned, scowling at her husband.

But Jacob didn't wait. He pushed himself inside, their skin slapping, the dresser shaking with each thrust. Jacob climaxed shortly after it began. He pulled up his boxer shorts, not looking directly at his wife.

Rebecca jerked up her underwear and pajama bottoms. She turned to him with furrowed brows. "What was that about?"

"What?"

"You *know* what. I didn't want it like that." She glared at Jacob.

He glared right back, his nostrils flaring. "Did you fuck him?"

"What the hell are you talking about?"

"You know what I'm talking about."

"No. I don't."

"Move." Jacob pushed his wife away from his dresser, not hard.

Rebecca moved aside. "Don't push me."

"I didn't. I'm trying to get dressed." Jacob yanked open his bottom drawer, removing a pair of pajama pants, then slamming shut the drawer.

"What's wrong with you? You've been acting strange ever since we left for the Virgin Islands."

Jacob pulled up his pajama pants. "Did you fuck Derek?"

Rebecca crossed her arms over her chest. "That's ridiculous."

"Answer the fucking question!"

Rebecca flinched. "No. Of course not."

Jacob stared at Rebecca for a few seconds. "On the ship, when we were traveling from the Virgin Islands to Jamaica, you left our room to read in the lounge area. Do you remember that?"

"Vaguely."

"Vaguely? It was only four days ago."

Rebecca rolled her eyes. "I'm not sure if I could tell you everything I did today."

"Did you see him that night?"

"No. Definitely not."

"What about Rob or Billy?"

Rebecca threw her hands up in the air. "Now I'm having sex with Rob and Billy?"

Jacob clenched his jaw. "I didn't say anything about you having sex with Rob or Billy. I asked if you saw them that night on the ship."

"Not that I remember. I certainly didn't have sex with anyone." Rebecca shook her head. "I can't believe we're even talking about this."

Jacob thought of Rebecca returning to their cabin, smelling like another man. Like musk and seawater. *She's lying.* "I'm done talking." He marched from the room.

90

SUMMER AND DEBT, THE MONEY OF SLAVES

"Do you like her?" Summer asked, nudging her father.

"Who?" Patrick replied, blushing.

Summer and Patrick sat in the back of the box truck, on folding chairs, surrounded by produce. They wore knit caps and heavy jackets to compensate for the refrigeration. Brie had turned it up to fifty-five degrees, but it was still cool.

"You know who. Brie. She was stuck to you like glue at the bonfire last night. She's pretty."

Patrick smiled. "She is."

"You two are about the same age."

Patrick shook his head. "Not much time for romance on this trip."

"She could come to Silver City."

"I barely know her."

"You know her well enough that she's willing to risk her freedom for us."

"I know her through my work, not personally."

Summer sighed. "It seems you like her, and it seems she likes you too."

"What's with the matchmaking?"

"I just want you to be happy. I've never seen you with a girlfriend. I know how much you loved Mom, but … it was a long time ago."

He swallowed. "I'm happy."

Summer tilted her head. "Really?"

"I have you. I have my work. And soon I'll have my grandson to babysit."

"Mom would want you to find love again."

Patrick took a deep breath and shrugged. "Once you've had a love like your mother and I had, it's difficult to imagine starting all over with someone else." Patrick cleared his throat. "Every night when I go to bed, I think about her. I remember conversations we had. I remember places we went, things we did together. I picture her face. Her smile. Even after all these years, she's still with me."

Summer leaned forward in her folding chair and kissed her father on the cheek. "I miss her too."

The truck slowed to a halt. Then it reversed and halted again.

"I think we're here," Patrick said.

Summer and Patrick stood from their seats and grabbed their suitcases.

The rollup door on the box truck opened, facing an open garage. The garage lights and the outdoor lampposts illuminated the darkness. The single-family home with the stone exterior was nearly a town house, his neighbors within spitting distance. Brie stood with a stocky man, who vaguely resembled an Italian chimpanzee, with his large ears and bulbous nose.

Patrick and Summer stepped from the truck to the driveway, still wearing their IR reflective eyeglasses.

"You must be Tony," Patrick said, smiling.

"Nice to meet yous," Tony replied, glancing from Patrick to Summer and back.

They all shook hands and introduced themselves.

Summer turned to Brie and said, "Thank you for the ride and your hospitality."

"It was my pleasure," Brie replied. "Be safe, okay?"

Summer nodded and hugged Brie.

"Thank you, Brie. It was really nice to meet you." Patrick held out his hand to shake, but Brie hugged Patrick as well, longer than she'd hugged Summer. Then, instead of separating, Brie kissed Patrick openmouthed for a long moment.

When their lips parted, Brie whispered something in Patrick's ear. Then she gave Summer and Tony a little wave and strutted back to her truck. As Brie drove away, she gave another wave, and blew Patrick a kiss.

"That was some kiss," Summer said, smirking.

"I'll say," Tony said.

"I wasn't expecting that," Patrick replied, his face still beet red from the kiss.

Tony showed them to their rooms. The house was pure bachelor pad with black leather furniture, a bar, a pool table, and a weight room. The two guest rooms were decorated with sports themes, one football, the other baseball.

"I got two boys," Tony said, standing in the baseball room.

Summer set her suitcase next to the bed.

"They live with their mother. I see 'em on weekends. I washed the sheets for yous."

"Thank you, Tony," Summer said.

Patrick walked into the room and handed Tony two tubes of silver coins.

Tony opened one of the tubes and extracted a one-ounce coin, the Canadian Maple Leaf etched into the silver. He flipped it over in his palm. "The money of gentlemen. How's the sayin' go? Somethin' like, gold's the money of kings. Silver's the money of gentlemen. Barter's the money of peasants. And ... what's the last part?" Tony rubbed the stubble on his chin.

"Debt's the money of slaves," Patrick said.

"Damn right."

Tony led them downstairs to the kitchen. Several shopping bags were on the counter. "That's the baby stuff and the scrubs you asked for," Tony said, motioning to the bags.

Summer searched the bags, finding scrubs, baby clothes, formula, diapers, and bottles. "Thank you again, Tony."

"If you need anything else, just let me know, and I can go get it tomorrow morning. I got the car seat in the back of my SUV." Tony turned to Patrick. "I got the vehicle you need stashed at an industrial park. I should take yous there now, and go over the plan."

They took his SUV across town to an industrial park. Tony drove. The vehicle wasn't equipped with autonomous driving. Patrick sat in the front passenger seat. Summer sat in back, watching the northern Virginia suburbs from the window. She recognized the area. Kingstown. It was only fifteen minutes from Connor's parents' house in Crosspointe. She scanned every car and every pedestrian, her heart skipping a beat every time she saw a baby. She knew it was stupid because the likelihood she'd happen to see Connor was nearly zero.

Tony parked behind a gray compact car, alongside a dimly lit warehouse. He removed a key fob from his pocket and handed it to Patrick. "The car's not autonomous, but it runs good."

"It's perfect," Patrick replied.

"When you're done doin' whatcha gotta do, park the car here and leave the keys in the glove box."

"What'll happen to the car?" Summer asked. "Do we need to be careful not to leave DNA?"

"Don't worry 'bout that." Tony pointed to the dimly lit warehouse. "This is a chop shop. They'll gladly make it disappear."

Summer nodded.

"Leave the car here, then walk to Bulk Vitamins." Tony pointed behind them with his thumb.

Summer turned around and spied the Bulk Vitamins warehouse.

"That's my business," Tony said. "I'll be waitin' for yous in there. Then we'll hit the road."

"That'll work fine," Patrick said. "We have a few things to do tomorrow and Wednesday, but we should be ready to leave on Thursday by lunchtime."

"I gotta primo Social Credit Score, so we shouldn't have no problems at the checkpoints." Tony turned his SUV around and drove back toward his home.

On the way back, Patrick asked, "How'd you get into the vitamin business?"

"I used to be in finance," Tony said, glancing toward Patrick, then back to the road. "Got laid off for a damn robot, like everybody else. Then I got divorced. I think it was the stress of the job loss. Then my mother got sick. When it rains it pours, ya know?"

Patrick and Summer both nodded in the affirmative.

"I burned through my savin's fast. My mom needed these anticancer drugs, and I couldn't afford 'em. The hospital tried to get me to sign up for this loan program, but the interest rate was fuckin' criminal. Excuse my language." Tony paused for a few seconds and merged into traffic. "So, I ordered the drugs from India at a fraction of the price. This was illegal, and I knew it was illegal, but I did what I had to do, and I got away with it. The Feds check shipments, but they can't check 'em all. My mother got better, but she had some friends she'd met at the cancer center with a similar problem—the hospital and big pharma tryin' to take every last Fed Coin they got. I went down to Mexico and smuggled back a shitload of medications. Anyway, I started sellin' to these ladies. Then they had friends and family members who needed stuff. Before I knew it, I was in business. I do sell vitamins. That's legit, but it's a front, a way to wash the money. I make a good profit on the medications, but it's still 90 percent less than what big pharma charges. This is why I offered to take yous to the border. I got a shipment to pick up."

"When the pharmaceutical companies gouge people, they're gonna go to the black market," Patrick said. "I don't blame them one bit."

"What I was doin' when I was in finance, sellin' the Wall Street lie, that was wrong, but it was legal. I had to become a criminal to do the right thing."

91

NAOMI AND "THEN THEY FIGHT YOU"

Trees framed the square park, their leaves still green in late October. The lawns and brick walkways of Lafayette Square bustled with socialists. A few held signs that read Eat the Rich, and People over Profit, and The Socialist Revolution. Naomi stood on a one-person elevated platform. It was a simple aluminum structure, typically used by tradesmen, but a banner was draped over the front that read Naomi Sutton 2052, For the People.

Her Secret Service agents and a waist-high fence kept the crowd at a polite distance. The park had been swept for explosives that morning, and the agents had stationed multiple security bots at the park's choke points to scan the crowd for weapons. Using millimeter wave technology, the bots could sense the size and the shape of objects hidden under clothes.

Naomi glanced behind her at the statue of Andrew Jackson riding a horse and tipping his cap. Beyond the memorialized seventh president was the White House, shining in the sun. Naomi turned back to the audience. A microphone was attached to the platform railing and connected by Bluetooth to speakers on nearby posts. The media was already recording. From the ground, Vernon waved, giving her the signal. *It's time.*

"Clayton Warner signed the Sensible Firearms Act into law today," Naomi said into the microphone.

This was met with a mixture of applause and a few boos from the crowd. A cluster of white men with bushy beards and windbreakers leaned against the metal fence. Not the typical progressives.

"It's a *very* small step in the right direction, but it doesn't go far enough. *Nothing* in President Warner's bill would've stopped the tragic deaths that occurred right here in this park. Twenty-three people were injured, and six were killed because of gun violence. The victims were predominately socialists, standing up for the rights of the powerless. I'd like to observe a moment of silence for our fallen comrades." Naomi bowed her head and stood silent along with the crowd. A gentle breeze rustled the leaves of the trees. The birds chirped, unmoved by their deference.

Someone yelled, "Commie piece of shit!"

Then the bearded white men chanted at the top of their lungs, "Fuck you, commie! Fuck you, commie! Fuck you, commie!" They had removed their windbreakers, revealing tattooed arms and T-shirts that proclaimed Patriots for Freedom.

The crowd booed the men, then drowned their chants with one of their own. "Naomi for president! Naomi for president! Naomi for president!"

The bearded white men were surrounded by a handful of Secret Service agents.

The crowd cheered as the disruptive men were escorted from the park.

Naomi waited for the cheers to subside, then continued her speech, improvising to take advantage of the outburst. "Mahatma Gandhi once said, 'First they ignore you. Then they laugh at you. Then they fight you. Then you win.' As Democratic socialists, we're under attack because we threaten the power structure. Those vulgar men are simply the tip of the iceberg. We threaten the patriarchy. We threaten the military industrial complex. The prison industrial complex. We threaten the corruption on Wall Street and here in DC. We threaten these evil institutions because our cause is just and righteous."

The crowd cheered again.

Naomi surveyed the audience, waiting for the crowd to quiet. "It's up to us to defend people of color. It's up to us to defend the LGBTQ+ community. It's up to us to defend women and children. It's up to us to create an equal and equitable society for all."

92

DEREK AND BACK TO CIVILIZATION

The robotic picker was long and tall and sat on four skinny knobby tires, similar to the one Derek had had on his Virginia orchard. The right side of the machine had a hose end, large enough to pass a grapefruit, and connected to a track that extended twenty-five feet in the air. Derek climbed on the machine, sat in the captain's chair, and pressed the Start button.

The touch screen appeared in front of him, the battery-powered engine silent. He used the joystick to drive the machine from the barn into the orchard. The picker was very slow. Even in Transport mode, it inched forward at less than five miles per hour. Derek drove the picker to the first row of ripe dragon fruit, the right side of the machine and the mechanical hose facing the fruit. He tapped the screen, selecting the speed and the settings.

The dragon fruit came from a pitaya cactus plant, four feet tall, and pruned to encourage sprawling branches like a tree. The dragon fruit cacti grew on mounds to keep the plant roots from too much moisture. The plants had been grown from cuttings nine months ago.

The hose end came to life, moving up the track, then pivoting forward on a joint toward the pink fruit that resembled a fireball. Derek hopped off the machine and grabbed the hand pruners attached to his belt. The hose end suctioned a dragon fruit, but the fruit wouldn't separate from the thick stem. Derek clipped the stem, and the fruit was fed through the hose to a soft conveyer belt and deposited into a cardboard box. Derek worked in tandem with the machine, clipping the thick stems, after the machine identified and suctioned the ripe dragon fruit.

Derek enjoyed the monotonous work, the safety of it all. No worries about Aryans or Netas or predator drones. After living in mortal danger on Psycho Island, living in safety and monotony was exactly what he wanted.

Marcos parked the electric ATV behind the picker. As the cardboard boxes were filled, Marcos moved the boxes to the trailer attached to the ATV. The picker inched forward as it picked each cactus clean. Once the ATV trailer was full, Marcos drove back to the barn and loaded the produce into the pickup truck. While Marcos was gone, Derek continued to work in tandem with the picker.

Steven walked into the orchard, his face shaded by a straw hat. "How's it going?"

Derek clipped another dragon fruit from the cactus and spoke to Steven without taking his eyes off his work. "It's goin' great. Your picker is like the one I used to have. It's in much better shape than mine was."

"Have you ever had a dragon fruit?"

"No." Derek stopped the picker at the end of the row and turned to Steven.

"It's like a fruit pudding on the inside. Keep some for yourself. You're welcome to eat as much as you like from the orchard. Marcos buys some meat here and there, but he never buys produce."

"Thanks. I will." Derek went to the back of the picker, removing a boxful of dragon fruit and replacing it with an empty box. He faced Steven again. "I didn't think I'd ever farm again. It feels good. I appreciate the opportunity."

Steven grinned. "I'm happy you're here. I want you to work the stand tomorrow at the Farmers' Market in Silver City. You okay with that?"

"You might need to show me the ropes, but I can handle it."

"I'll help you unload the produce in the morning, and I'll get you started," Steven said.

"That'll work," Derek replied.

Steven reached into the pocket of his khakis and handed Derek a cell phone. A yellow Post-it Note was attached to the screen that read User: Derek909 Password: Orchard781**. "This is for you. You'll need it to stay in touch with me and to accept payments at the market or to make payments yourself. Also, I set up a Silver Coin account for you. That's your user name and password. You should change your password when you log on."

"Thank you, Steven." Derek placed the cell phone and the Post-it Note in the front pocket of his work pants.

"I deposited your first week's pay early. Twenty grams, as we agreed. I thought you might wanna pick up a few things for yourself."

"I appreciate that."

Steven rubbed the back of his neck, breaking eye contact. "I'll give you the rest of the day off to get yourself together."

Derek cocked his head, his forehead creased.

Steven looked Derek in the eyes again, his expression sympathetic. "I'd like you to be presentable tomorrow. I have a few collared shirts with the orchard logo for you, but you'll need to pick up a decent pair of pants and some shoes. There's a good barber in Silver City. A place called Bill's Barbershop."

Derek stroked his bushy black beard.

"I was hoping you would consider a shave and a haircut. It's not a rule here to be clean-shaven, but, if you're gonna be out in public, representing this business, it helps to …"

"Not look like I just escaped Psycho Island," Derek replied with a smirk.

Steven chortled. "Exactly."

"That's not a problem. I'm ready to be civilized."

93

JACOB AND GSE TO SOE

Men and women in suits trudged to their cars, carrying cardboard boxes filled with their belongings. Two news vans were in the parking lot. Cameramen recorded the scene. Reporters interviewed a few of the former employees. Jacob watched from the lofty perch of his office atop Housing Trust headquarters. He sighed and stepped back to his desk, sitting in his leather chair.

He scrolled through the news headlines on his laptop.

Trading Halted on NYSE

Stocks Down 11 Percent

The Fed Expected to Lower Interest Rates

From GSE to SOE. What does it mean?

Never Fear. The Fed Is Here.

Government Takeover: The Big Three

Jacob tapped the link to *Never Fear. The Fed Is Here.* He read about Wall Street's expectation that the Federal Reserve would backstop the stock market, limiting losses on the downside. They expected lower interest rates and even direct buying of the S&P 500 to provide support.

Jacob tapped another link, *Government Takeover: The Big Three,* more out of morbid curiosity than his desire for information. He knew plenty about Housing Trust's transition from a Government-Sponsored Enterprise to a State-Owned Enterprise.

Housing Trust was created in 1972 to buy mortgages on the secondary market, pool them, and sell them as mortgage-backed securities to investors on the open market. This dramatically expanded the amount of money available to lend for the purpose of home ownership. This sounded benign, noble even, but this expansion of the money supply was about banking profits and about saddling citizens with more and more debt. Home ownership was the lipstick on the pig.

The best part of the arrangement was that Housing Trust could take extreme risks to generate extreme profits, and, when those risks inevitably threatened the very existence of the Government-Sponsored Enterprise, they would be bailed out by their sponsor, the US government—or, more specifically, the US citizens through taxation and inflation.

None of that was in this article.

The article lamented the loss of jobs, as thousands of employees were downsized in the transition. The article also touted the benefits of a publicly owned student loan, mortgage, and housing market. After all, housing and education were human rights.

Jacob's cell phone chimed. He glanced at the name, frowned, and swiped right. "What do you want, Eric?"

"That's a terrible way to greet your baby brother," Eric replied.

"It's not a great time."

"You knew it was coming. It's all according to plan."

Jacob rubbed the kink in his neck. "Believe it or not, I care about the people who lost their jobs."

"That does nothing for those people. They're still unemployed, whether you care or not."

Jacob exhaled a heavy breath. "I'd rather not listen to this right now."

"I have a meeting with the Chinese treasury secretary on Friday. I need you to be there."

"Why are you inviting me three days before?"

Eric cleared his throat. "I didn't think it was necessary for you to attend."

Jacob shook his head. "Of course you didn't."

"Don't take it personal." Eric hesitated for a moment. "Dad suggested that you attend."

"That's surprising," Jacob replied, a little more upbeat.

"It makes sense. You're the next treasury secretary. You'll be our man on the inside. I know it's a year away, but the sooner we're on the same page with the Chinese, the better. Unfortunately, we need their cooperation to achieve our goals."

"Fine."

"I'll be in town tomorrow. Maybe we can meet for dinner and talk strategy."

94

SUMMER AND THE FLASH DRIVE

They watched the loading dock from their little compact car. More specifically, they watched a human-size door and the landing near the loading dock. A man in scrubs stepped outside the door onto the landing. Floodlights bathed the man in a yellow glow.

Patrick handed the binoculars to Summer. "Does that guy look familiar?"

Summer looked through the binoculars. The muscular man smoked his e-cigarette, vapor filling the air above him. Summer vaguely remembered the large man. He was an orderly. Kind of creepy. She remembered nurses complaining about his ogling. She didn't know his name, but she was sure that he'd remember her, which was exactly what she wanted. Summer handed the binoculars to Patrick and said, "He'll do."

"Are you sure you don't want me to come with you?" Patrick asked.

"We talked about this. It's too suspicious with you there."

"Be careful."

Summer nodded, took a deep breath, and said, "Wish me luck."

"Good luck."

Summer exited the car and walked downhill toward the loading dock, wearing her sneakers and scrubs, exactly what she would wear if she were working. The loading dock was connected to the basement level. She approached the man and smiled.

He smiled back, his black mustache spreading wide.

"Would you open the door please?" Summer asked, climbing the steps to the landing.

The man narrowed his eyes at Summer. "Forgot your badge, huh?"

"I left it at the nursing station."

"What happened to you? I haven't seen you in a long time." The man took a puff of his e-cigarette, blowing the vapor away from Summer.

"I transferred to be closer to my boyfriend's job." Summer frowned. "It didn't work out."

"Sorry to hear that," he said, his eyes crawling over Summer.

"Could you open the door? I'm running late."

He unclipped his badge and pressed it to the scanner. "It's quicker to go in the front." The door unlocked, and he opened it.

"Not where I parked."

As she stepped through the door, he said, "Your name's Autumn, right?"

Summer turned around, just inside the hospital basement, the man still holding the door. "Great memory." She turned and fast-walked down the hallway, keeping her head down and furtive, despite wearing her IR reflecting glasses.

"I'm Wes," he called out to her back.

Summer raised her hand in acknowledgment but didn't look back. At the end of the hallway she turned right, walking down another corridor. The basement was mostly empty except for an autonomous supply cart driving toward the elevator bank. The cart was filled with medical supplies to be dispersed throughout the hospital. Summer reached the end of the corridor and entered a room marked Storage.

It was exactly as she remembered. Old computers and office furniture were piled in rows, like cemetery plots. A thick sheet of dust covered everything. She moved a chair to the back corner of the room. Standing on the chair, she removed a square from the suspended ceiling. She detached the plastic floss container taped to the underside of the ceiling tile and slipped it into her pocket. Inside the plastic floss container was a tiny flash drive, supposedly with footage of Jacob Roth attempting to bribe Naomi Sutton. She replaced the ceiling tile and left the room.

She hurried back to the loading dock, planning to exit the same way she'd come in. *Easy peasy.* As she neared the exit, Wes entered the basement hallway.

He blocked her path with his beefy body, a smirk on his face. "Where you goin'?"

"I'm not feeling well. I'm going home," Summer replied, trying to look and act lethargic. She tried to walk around him, but he moved, still blocking her path. Summer scowled. "I'm not in the mood."

"I tried to look you up on You Share on my phone. I wanted to send you a friend request. I searched for people who work here, and I used your first name, but I couldn't find an Autumn who works here."

"I use my middle name on You Share." Summer forced a smile. "Try Stacy."

He grinned. "That's weird because I remembered your name. I looked up Summer and this hospital and I found you."

Summer kept her expression neutral, but, inside, her stomach turned, and her heart pounded.

"People posted on your wall that you were arrested and that nobody knows where you are. Somebody posted that you're on Psycho Island. I guess that's not true, huh?"

"I need to leave. Would you move, please?"

He didn't budge.

She tried to run around him, but he grabbed her around the waist and picked her up, Summer's legs bicycling in the air. "Put me down!"

He set her down, his big body still blocking the door.

"Don't fucking touch me," Summer said, her face flushed.

Wes cackled. "Feisty. I like that."

"That's assault. I could call the cops."

"I don't think you will. You know why?"

Summer clenched her jaw but didn't respond.

"This is a camera dead zone. This area just inside the door." Wes made a circular motion with his hands. "You know what I mean by a camera dead zone, don't you?"

Summer knew that places in the basement weren't covered by the cameras. Old storerooms with low value items—like the room where she'd hid the flash drive—parts of the hallways, and apparently where they were standing. She had heard of hospital employees sneaking off to the basement to have sex.

Wes continued. "So, there's no proof I touched you, and, if you're an escaped convict, I doubt you'd call the cops anyway. Maybe *I* should call the cops. My uncle caught an escaped convict once. He didn't exactly catch him, but he told the cops where he was. He got 5,000 Fed Coins."

"You don't wanna do this," Summer said, glaring.

"Gimme a reason not to," Wes replied.

Summer wrapped her arms around the big man, stood on her tippy toes, and kissed him on the mouth. As she kissed him, she moved her hands through his thick dark hair. He reciprocated, shoving his tongue in her mouth and pulling her tight to his body. Then she yanked a bit of his hair, disengaging from the kiss.

He let go, glowering at Summer, rubbing the back of his head. "What the fuck you do that for?"

Summer stepped back, pulled at the waistband of her scrubs, and dropped his hairs into her underwear. She let the waistband slap back. "*Now* there's proof." Summer spoke in a mocking high voice. "He tried to rape me, officer, but he couldn't get an erection, so he forced me to have oral sex." Summer spoke normally. "You'll have to explain how your hairs ended up in my underwear."

His eyes widened. "You're fuckin' crazy."

Summer stepped into his personal space and poked his chest with one finger. "You have *no idea*. If you so much as breathe my name to another human being, I will find you and kill you while you sleep. Now *move*."

Wes stepped aside, his hands up in surrender. "I was just messin' with you. Damn."

95

NAOMI AND TOO BIG TO FAIL

Naomi sat at a glass table across from Sebastian Gannon. An off-white wall with silver trim stood behind them, the TV show's logo front and center, proclaiming *That's the Point*.

Sebastian said, "Yesterday, United Mortgage, Housing Trust, and Student Loan Corp. were purchased by the Federal Government, effectively transitioning the most important lenders of housing and student loans from Government-Sponsored Enterprises to State-Owned Enterprises. Do you support this decision?"

"It's a long overdue step in the right direction," Naomi replied. "The Government-Sponsored Enterprise was a scheme perpetrated against the American people by the capitalist bankers to privatize their profits and to socialize their losses."

Sebastian smiled, his face perfect, almost bot-like with his makeup. "That's a serious claim. Do you have any evidence to back your assertion?"

"In 2008, during the Great Recession, the US Treasury spent nearly two hundred billion dollars to bail out United Mortgage and Housing Trust." Naomi took a sip of water from the That's the Point mug in front of her.

"It wasn't a bailout. It was a loan. And those loans were paid back.

With interest I might add."

Naomi set the mug on the glass table. "What about all the Americans who lost their homes? Did they receive low-interest loans?"

"In a way, they did. Americans needed and still need United Mortgage and Housing Trust to provide affordable home loans. By saving these companies, the US Treasury saved the homes of millions of Americans."

Naomi shook her head. "No. They protected a rigged capitalist system that funnels wealth and labor from the poor to the rich, creating ever-expanding wealth inequality. They allowed these banks to regulate themselves with a carousel of former and future bank executives serving as regulators. Without rules, they generated massive illicit profits at the expense of the public. Then, when the American people couldn't take on any more debt—when they were too poor, too prudent, or too scared to continue to line the pockets of these fat cats— predictably we had a recession that almost became a depression."

"If not for the loans you're criticizing." Sebastian smirked.

Naomi pursed her lips. "It wasn't simply those loans that saved the world from a depression. We had TARP—the Troubled Asset Relief Program, which bailed out banks to the tune of seven hundred billion dollars. Then we had TALF. Term Asset-Backed-Securities Loan Facility, which was another eight hundred billion for the banks. Then we had to bailout the monetary system itself with quantitative easing. Remember that? *Quantitative easing*?" Naomi chuckled to herself. "Just a fancy phrase for creating money out of nothing and robbing people through inflation. We had five iterations of quantitative easing. Then the system imploded in 2020, and the world suffered from the greatest depression in history."

Sebastian held out his hands. "Are you suggesting that the US Treasury should've let these vital institutions fail?"

"That's exactly what I'm saying. Let them fail. Since the Greater Depression, we instituted a new currency, the Fed Coin. When I say *we*, I mean, the US government in concert with the Federal Reserve.

When I say *the Federal Reserve*, I mean, a cartel of the biggest and most powerful banks."

Sebastian looked offstage, his brows furrowed.

Naomi was on a roll, so she continued. "The Fed Coin, which was hailed as the solution to the Greater Depression, has been anything but. It was simply a reset of the game, with the owners of the original game in control of the new game. The Fed Coin is simply a ..." Naomi trailed off as a producer stepped onstage.

The cameramen looked up from their cameras, obviously no longer recording.

The producer wore a black suit, his dark hair slicked back. He approached the glass table, shaking his head. "Our sponsors won't allow this speculation about the Federal Reserve and the banking sector." He pointed at Sebastian. "You know better."

96

DEREK AND THE FARMERS' MARKET

The farmers' market was a gravel lot, with stands arranged in columns and rows. Farmers and ranchers with their produce and meat products were popular, but local artisans and craftsmen also conducted brisk businesses offering handcrafted clothing and jewelry and furniture.

The Freetown Orchard occupied a coveted corner spot. The large L-shaped stand was covered by a wooden roof, and wooden walls blocked access from outside, with the inside open to the market. The tables of produce were arranged to allow entry from one side, browsing under the roof, and the cashier at the opposite end. Steven had said that he sold 30 percent more when he had the roof built. When it rained, which was often, people gravitated to the covered booths for shelter.

Derek weighed an elderly woman's dragon fruit, bananas, starfruit, and avocados. She paid with her phone, sending one-half gram of Silver Coin to Freetown Orchard's account. Derek thanked the woman and sat in his chair next to the checkout. It was the first time he'd sat that day. He was happy to have a lull, the morning rush finally over.

A woman wearing a white peasant dress stepped from the sun and into the booth. She looked young, in her mid-to-late twenties, but she carried herself with the grace of someone older. She moved along the tables, occasionally touching the produce and plucking a lucky fruit, adding it to her cloth bag. Her strawberry-blond hair touched her shoulders. Periodically, she brushed wisps from her face. The peasant dress hinted at subtle curves, her belt cinched at her narrow waist. She added a cluster of red bananas to her bag and walked toward Derek.

Derek stood from his seat to greet the woman. At that moment, he was grateful that he'd had a shave and a haircut.

She smiled, her blue eyes squinting a little, her heart-shaped face accentuated by high cheekbones.

Derek returned her smile. "Did you find everything okay?"

"Yes. Thank you. The produce is beautiful. So fresh."

"Most of the fruit was picked yesterday."

She nodded, not breaking eye contact.

Derek's stomach fluttered. He looked down and said, "Let's see what you got there." He took her bag, weighed the produce, his phone synced to the scale and adding as he went. "Looks like point-two-four grams, if you wanna pay with Silver Coin."

She sent the Silver Coin to Freetown Orchard with her phone.

He repacked her cloth bag and set it near her on the counter. "I'm Derek, by the way."

"I know."

His eyes widened, suddenly worried that she might be in the CIA.

She giggled and pointed at his chest. "Your name tag."

He laughed, shaking his head. "Right."

"I'm Kyra." They shook hands.

"Nice to meet you, Kyra."

"Are you new to Silver City?"

"Brand new. Fresh off the turnip truck."

She cocked her head to the side. "Your accent sounds so familiar. Are you from Virginia?"

"You gotta good ear. I'm from the Shenandoah Valley area."

"I'm from Lynchburg originally, although I haven't been back in quite some time."

"Small world."

A little girl walked near the stand, looking around, tears streaming down her face, calling, "Mom? Mom?"

"Excuse me, Kyra." Derek stepped past Kyra and approached the girl with a friendly face. "Do you need help finding your mother?"

The little girl nodded, sniffling, her face streaked with tears.

Derek bent over, his hands on his knees to be closer to her level. "It's okay. We're gonna find her. My name's Derek. What's your name?"

With her head bowed, she said, "Abby."

Kyra approached the scene. "They have an information booth near the main entrance. Maybe her mom went there."

"That's a good bet," Derek replied, standing upright. "Can you stay with her while I run over to the information booth? I think she should stay put in case her mom's nearby."

"I can do that."

Derek bent down again to talk to Abby. "This is my friend, Kyra. She's gonna stay with you while I run to the information booth to see if your mom's there. Is that okay?"

She nodded, staring up at Kyra. "Are you a princess?"

Kyra laughed. "No, sweetheart."

Derek jogged through the sparse crowd to the information booth.

A short woman argued with the man behind the table. Her face was flushed, her hands piercing the air. "You need to get off your ass and find my daughter!"

"Ma'am, it's only me here. I can make an announcement on the loudspeaker."

Derek interrupted, asking the woman, "Is your daughter named Abby?"

She turned her attention to Derek, her tone desperate. "Do you know where she is?"

"She's fine. She's waiting for you at the Freetown Orchard booth."

They fast-walked back to the booth. The girl had a goofy grin, eating one of Kyra's red bananas.

The mother was stone-faced. "Abigail, come here. Right now."

Abby hugged her mom, still holding the half-eaten banana.

The mom held her daughter at arms-length, shaking her a little. "Don't *ever* do that again. Do you hear me?"

"I won't," Abby replied.

The mom let go of Abby and looked at Derek and Kyra. "This isn't the first time she's wandered off. Thank you two so much."

"You're welcome," Derek replied.

"I hope she wasn't any trouble."

"No trouble at all. She's a sweet girl," Kyra replied.

"Do you two have kids?" the mother asked.

"No." Kyra shook her head, her expression darkening.

"I have a teenage daughter," Derek said.

Kyra glanced at Derek's left ring finger.

"Are you two not together?" the mother asked. "I guess I just assumed."

Derek's face felt hot, the thought of them together a pleasant fiction. "We just met about ten minutes ago."

"This would be a great how-we-met story." The mother winked at them.

As mother and daughter walked away, Derek said, "Crisis averted."

"I should get going," Kyra said, grabbing her produce bag from the table.

Derek cleared his throat. "You wanna have dinner with me?"

Now it was Kyra's turn to blush.

There was a long silence, Derek too afraid to breathe.

Finally, she set her bag back on the table and said, "May I see your phone?"

Derek handed the orchard phone to Kyra. She put her name and number in the Contacts, her thumbs moving rapidly. Then she handed the phone back to Derek.

"When are you free?" Derek asked, placing the phone in his pocket.

"When are *you* free? Kyra asked.

"I only know three people here. I'm free every night."

Kyra smiled and said, "How about tomorrow night?"

97

JACOB'S OLD FLAME

Jacob cut into the filet mignon, blood pooling under the rare steak. The Roths sat around their dining room, eating dinner, Jeeves waiting in the corner, ready to serve.

Eric Roth sat at the head of Jacob's table, sipping his scotch. He was in his midforties, with jet-black hair, and a large nose. He was a slightly younger and slightly taller version of Jacob. Eric addressed the children, "How's school going?"

"School's fun," Ethan said, smiling. "My teacher's really nice. I'm supposed to be in first grade but they moved me to second."

"His mind's like a sponge," Rebecca said, sitting catty-cornered to Eric and across the table from Jacob. "We're already talking with the gifted teacher about moving him to fourth grade next year."

"I'm way smarter than Ethan," David said. "I'm the smartest in my whole school. I'm even smarter than my teacher."

Lindsey, sitting next to Ethan, rolled her eyes at David.

"Is that right?" Eric asked, grinning.

"You're very smart but don't be arrogant," Rebecca said to David. "You *are* a year older than Ethan. He's just as smart as you were last year."

David shrugged. "Whatever. The kids at my school are so *stupid.*

Especially the stock babies. I asked this one stock baby if he had Down syndrome, but he didn't even know what that was."

"That's enough, David." Jacob pointed his steak knife at his son.

David hit the table with the side of his fist. "It's true."

"It's rude. And don't hit the table."

"It's also hate speech," Rebecca said. "You could be arrested for using that term."

David spoke in a rapid cadence. "Stock baby, stock baby, stock baby—"

"Enough!" Jacob said.

Lindsey scowled at David.

"Do you want to be arrested?" Rebecca asked David.

David shrugged again. "I'm seven. What are they gonna do?"

Jacob rubbed his temples and said to Eric, "He's a handful."

* * *

Jacob, Rebecca, and Eric still sat at the dining room table with their alcoholic beverages. The men with scotch, Rebecca with wine. The kids had left an hour ago for the VR rooms.

"I saw Maya at a conference last month," Eric said to Jacob. "She's a VP at Goldman. She still looks good."

Jacob flushed at the mention of his college flame, the heat of the scotch not helping. "Aren't we supposed to be preparing for our meeting with Secretary Yang?"

"Who's Maya?" Rebecca asked, her head cocked in confusion.

Eric arched his eyebrows at Jacob. "You didn't tell her about Maya?"

Jacob scowled at his brother, then addressed Rebecca. "She was my college girlfriend. Remember?"

Rebecca tilted her head. "I would've remembered that. Was it serious?"

"It was serious for him," Eric said, smirking.

Jacob shook his head at his brother.

"What does that mean?" Rebecca asked.

"It's not important," Jacob replied.

"It was at the time," Eric said, chuckling.

Jacob sneered at his brother. "It's not funny."

Eric showed his palms in surrender. "I know. I'm sorry."

"What happened?" Rebecca asked, her eyes wide open.

Jacob gulped his scotch, then set the glass on the table. "We met at Yale, dated for most of college, then we broke up before graduation."

"Why didn't you tell me about her?"

"I'm sure I mentioned her, but, if I didn't tell you, it was because I'd rather not talk about it. I wasn't trying to hide anything."

Eric let out a low whistle. "There's a lot more to the story than that."

Jacob glowered at his brother.

"Are you still bothered by that bitch?"

"No, but it's a chapter of my life I'd rather not relive."

Rebecca knitted her brows. "I don't understand why it matters now. How long ago was that? Like twenty-seven, twenty-eight years?"

"It *doesn't* matter." Jacob took a deep breath. "A few weeks before graduation I walked in on her having sex with my roommate."

Rebecca winced. "That's awful. I'm so sorry, honey."

"They'd been having sex behind his back for years," Eric added. "I was at Yale, three years behind Jacob. She hit on me at a party when I was a sophomore. I tried to tell Jacob. He thought I was jealous. Didn't talk to me for months." Eric took a swig of his scotch and turned his gaze to Jacob. "Remember that?"

"She sounds like a terrible person," Rebecca said. "What was the appeal? Was she pretty?"

"Not near as pretty as you," Eric replied with a wink. "She must've been wild in bed."

Rebecca smirked at that.

"They were engaged. They had plans to get married after graduation."

"Really?" Rebecca asked.

Jacob nodded.

"Even after she cheated on him, he still wanted to stay together. Can you believe that?" Eric asked. "She's the one who broke it off."

"Well, I'm glad she ended it." Rebecca eyed her husband. "Otherwise, we never would've gotten together."

Jacob nodded again, seething on the inside.

"He was depressed for years after that. That's why Dad chose me to run Roth North America—"

"That's enough." Jacob glared at his brother.

Eric downed the last of his scotch. "You're too sensitive."

98

SUMMER AND TAKE BACKS

"I wanna break in that house and take Byron," Summer said, sitting in the front passenger seat of the compact car.

"We only get one shot at this," Patrick replied, sitting in the driver's seat. "I'd rather not alert them right away."

They were parked across the street from Connor's parents' house, a stone-faced colonial with a three-car garage and an expansive lawn. After Summer had secured the flash drive from the hospital, they'd slept a few hours in the car; then they'd staked out Connor's parents' house, but they weren't home. When Patrick and Summer had returned the next morning, a BMW SUV was in the driveway.

It was lunch now, and the SUV hadn't moved, and the house showed no outward signs of life.

"What if I just knocked on the door and reasoned with them?" Summer asked.

"What if they slam the door in your face and call the cops?" Patrick replied.

Summer sighed, her shoulders slumping. "We left too early yesterday. If we had been here when they came home, we could've taken Byron then."

"We also might've screwed it up. We were exhausted. We'd barely

331

slept. Let's stick to the plan."

One of the garage doors opened, and Connor's mother, Trina, stepped out, pushing a baby carriage down the driveway. She wore nylon pants and a fleece. Summer leaned closer to the window, but she couldn't see inside the stroller. Trina pushed the stroller down the street, away from their car, at a brisk pace.

"This is the opportunity we've been waiting for," Summer said.

Patrick nodded. "Wave if you need help."

They'd already decided that, if Trina was alone with Byron, it would be better if Patrick waited in the car.

Summer exited the car and jogged toward Trina. It was bright and sunny, with a light breeze, perfect jogging weather.

As she approached, Summer said, "Mrs. Pierce."

Trina stopped in her tracks and turned to Summer, one hand still on the stroller handle. Trina was in her early sixties, thin, her face taut and her lips plump from cosmetic surgeries. Her eyes went wide, and she said, "Summer?"

"Yes. It's me." Summer stood in front of Trina, but she wasn't focused on the woman. She peered into the stroller. Byron lay inside, his blue eyes alert, his little fists punching the air.

"What are you doing here?" Trina asked, but it sounded more like an accusation.

Summer turned her attention to Trina. "I'm here for Byron."

"Where's Connor? Is he with you?"

Summer shook her head, her eyes downcast. "I'm sorry. He … He died on the island."

Tears welled in Trina's eyes. "That can't be."

Summer swallowed hard. "I wish it wasn't."

She sniffled and wiped the corners of her eyes, her mascara starting to run. Trina glared at Summer. "Why are you here? They said we'd never see you or Connor again."

"Like I said, I'm here for Byron." Summer glanced at her son.

"We have custody. I can't hand him over like he's a used car."

"*Yes*, you can. Wait a day, then report him missing."

She took a few steps back, pushing the stroller away from Summer. "Connor never got into any trouble until he met *you*."

Summer stepped closer. "This wasn't my fault. Byron's *my* son. You can't keep him."

"We can call the police and let them decide." Trina reached into the pocket of her fleece and grabbed her phone.

Summer lunged for the phone, snatched it from Trina's hand, and hurled it down the street.

Trina screamed, "Help! Help me! Help!"

A face appeared in the window of a neighbor's house across the street.

Summer grabbed Trina by her bony shoulders. "*Shut up.*"

A door opened and shut.

Trina shrieked at the top of her lungs, her eyes glassy. "Help me! Somebody help me!"

Summer clamped her hand over Trina's mouth, muffling her cries for help.

Heavy footsteps ran toward the scene. A large bearded man arrived, facing Summer and Trina, with Byron behind him. "Let her go," the man said.

Summer removed her hands from Trina and stepped back. More rapid footfalls approached. Summer glanced over her shoulder to see Patrick sprinting toward them, a gun in hand.

Patrick pointed his handgun at the man.

The man held up his hands, his arms shaky.

"Step away from the baby," Patrick said.

"Don't let them take my baby," Trina said.

The man glanced over his shoulder at Byron in the baby carriage and said to Patrick, "No can do."

"He's not her baby," Summer said, her jaw set tight. "I'm his mother. He's mine."

"She's a fugitive," Trina said, her voice shrill. "I'm his legal guardian."

Patrick narrowed his gaze, lining up the sights on his handgun, center mass of the large man's chest. "Don't make me kill you."

The man's face was taut. He looked at Byron again, then back to Patrick.

"Walk away or I will kill you."

The man took a few steps away from the scene, then he ran for his house—and probably a phone.

Trina rushed toward Byron, but Summer caught her from behind, grabbing her fleece collar and yanking her backward. Trina fell awkwardly to the asphalt, groaning on impact.

Summer reached into the stroller and snatched Byron.

"No. No! Stop her!" Trina shrieked from the asphalt, her face dissolving into tears.

Summer ran for the car, Patrick hot on her heels. Summer sprinted with Byron's cries and Trina's shrieks ringing in her ears. Patrick opened the passenger door and Summer climbed inside, holding Byron tight to her chest. Patrick slammed shut the door, ran around the vehicle, and climbed into the driver's seat. He started the car, put it into gear, and mashed the accelerator. They were gone in an instant, leaving nothing but a streak of rubber.

99

NAOMI MAKES A FRENEMY

"I have to admit that this meeting comes as quite a surprise," Naomi said, sitting at her desk across from Thorium Unlimited CEO Truman Bradshaw. He was dressed casually in dark jeans and a button-down shirt.

"Thank you for taking the time to meet with me on such short notice," Truman replied.

"I can't imagine anyone refuses to meet with you."

Truman grinned. "I suppose that's true, but I'd rather not abuse my power. I do understand the value of your time."

"In the interest of valuing my time and yours, why are you here, Mr. Bradshaw?"

"Please, call me Truman."

Naomi nodded, her elbows on her desk, her fingers steepled.

"We have shared interests. I think we should work together."

"That's interesting. We're at opposite ends of the political spectrum. Correct me if I'm wrong, but aren't you a libertarian and a strict constitutionalist?"

"We have a common enemy. The Roths and the banking industry."

Naomi tensed for a split second at the mention of the Roths. "I'm listening."

"The Roths planted the bomb that killed your husband."

Naomi narrowed her eye, her jaw set tight. "Do you have proof of that?"

"Unfortunately, no." He shook his head, his eyes downcast, as if he cared about her tragedy. He lifted his gaze and added, "But, if you're elected president, you'll have the power to conduct a very thorough investigation."

Naomi pursed her lips. "That's a big if."

"I can turn that *if* into a near certainty." Truman leaned back in his chair and crossed his leg, resting his left ankle on his right knee.

"How would you do that?"

"You have nearly everything you need for a successful campaign. Everything except money."

"Why would you support a socialist?"

"Unfortunately, this country is headed for socialism regardless. It may not be this election or the next, and it may not be you, but sooner or later the US will have a socialist president and a majority socialist congress. I can't change that, the demographics and the trend is too strong, but, as they say, the devil you know is better than the one you don't."

Naomi raised one side of her mouth in contempt. "I'd rather lose than start my presidency in debt to you—or anyone for that matter. Maybe I'm not the devil you think I am."

"We both care about the American people. We simply have different ideas about how to create a prosperous society."

"Those differences matter."

"Agreed. *My* ideas are right." He chuckled to himself.

Naomi sneered at her opponent. "What do you want?"

"The nationalization of Housing Trust, United Mortgage, and Student Loan Corp. is concerning, to say the least. The US needs more thorium reactors to offset declining fossil fuel energy, but I'm hesitant to build anything in the US with the specter of nationalization hanging over my head."

"These were failing institutions," Naomi replied. "People's homes were at stake. The federal government already owned a majority interest in all three firms. The nationalization involved buying the remaining shares, delisting the companies from the New York Stock Exchange, and placing them under federal control. Had we let them fail, we might be in a bigger depression than the 2020s."

Truman stared at Naomi for an instant. "I've been watching you. Listening to you. I think you're one of the few politicians who actually says what they mean and means what they say."

Naomi's expression softened. "I'd like to think so."

"You've said, on multiple occasions, that our basic human needs shouldn't be provided by for-profit enterprises. Food, housing, education, health care, and energy should all be controlled and owned by the federal government." He paused for a beat. "Please correct me if I'm mischaracterizing your position."

"You're not," Naomi replied. "This is why I was very surprised that you wanted to meet with me."

"You have one of three choices. Partner with me or partner with the Roths."

Naomi frowned. "What's the third choice?"

"Lose the Democratic primary. Disappear into the oblivion of history."

Naomi crossed her arms over her chest. "We'll see about that."

"Don't take my word for it. Ask Fletcher. He knows the game."

Naomi didn't like Truman's casual reference to her campaign manager. She wondered if she could trust Fletcher. *How much power do Truman and the Roths have? Enough to sway an election?* "What makes you any better than the Roths?"

"The availability of cheap and clean energy from thorium ended the Greater Depression, and the instability of debt-based fiat currency and fractional reserve banking caused the Greater Depression. Who would you rather partner with? The family responsible for causing the Greater Depression and enslaving nations and billions of people with debt, or the man responsible for bringing the world economy back from the brink of destruction?"

Naomi uncrossed her arms, resting her hands on her desktop. "You didn't answer my question. *What* do you want?"

Truman was relaxed, leaning back in his chair, his hands on the armrests. "No corporate tax for Thorium Unlimited. I don't care how you do it. You're the lawmaker. Subsidies, clean-energy tax breaks, but I do not want to pay a single Fed Coin of tax. You'll have the votes in congress to make this happen. In return, I'll make you the next President of the United States. In addition, I'll ensure that you have a successful presidency, by providing the US with ample supplies of the cleanest and cheapest energy in the world."

"This is what I despise about politics." Naomi shook her head. "The backdoor deals. The lobbying. Capitalists buying politicians to gain an unfair advantage over their competitors. You're not part of the solution. You're part of the problem."

Truman gripped the armrests, his knuckles going white. "You're willing to partner with the men who killed your husband?"

Naomi stared at Truman for a long beat, silent. Then she glanced at the platinum wedding band on Truman's ring finger. "Are you married?"

"What difference does that make?" His tone was harsh.

"My husband's name was Alan. He was the type of person who cared about the plight of others, sometimes to his own detriment."

Truman relaxed again. "I'm sorry for your loss."

"What's your wife's name?"

"Kyra."

"I'm assuming you love her very much?"

"Of course."

Naomi leaned forward, her elbows on the desktop, and her hands clasped, as if she were praying. "If your political opponents planted a bomb under your car and killed Kyra instead of you, what would you do?"

Truman scowled at the what-if scenario. "I would do everything in my power to bring them to justice. I certainly wouldn't partner with them."

"I have no intention of partnering with anyone but the American people."

Truman stood from his seat. "You're making a big mistake." He walked out, leaving the door open in his wake.

100

DEREK'S DATE

Derek sang in the shower, his dreadful voice muffled by the water. He'd been on cloud nine since Kyra had agreed to go out to dinner. He thought he heard his cell phone, so he stopped singing. His phone chimed in the background. Derek finished his shower, dried himself, and wrapped the towel around his waist. He picked up his phone from the edge of the bathroom sink and checked the call. Kyra had called, so he called her back.

"Hello?" Kyra said.

"It's Derek. I saw that you called."

"Did you get my message?"

"No. Did you leave a message?"

"You should listen to the message."

Derek creased his forehead. "What's goin' on? Are you okay?"

She exhaled. "I'm sorry, but we shouldn't do this."

"Do what? Have dinner?"

"Or go out at all."

Derek closed the lid on the toilet and sat down, the bathroom still steamy from his shower. "I don't understand. We just met yesterday. I couldn't've screwed it up yet."

"You seem like a nice guy, but I'm not in a good place for a relationship," Kyra replied.

"It's dinner. Not a marriage proposal. We can go out as friends, if you want. This doesn't have be a romantic date. I liked talkin' to you yesterday. It seemed like you did too. Am I wrong about that?"

"No, you're not."

"Okay. Then let's go have a nice meal as friends."

"I don't know."

The line went quiet for a few seconds.

Derek broke the silence. "Are you still there?"

"I'm here."

He hung his head in resignation. "You know what? I'm sorry, Kyra. I shouldn't be pressurin' you to go out with me. That ain't right. I respect your wishes. If you change your mind, let me know. Have a nice evenin'." Derek disconnected the call and set his cell phone on the edge of the sink.

He stepped into his bedroom and collected the new clothes he'd laid out on his bed, rehanging them in his closet. He put on a pair of shorts and a T-shirt. He went through the motions, robot-like, his mind elsewhere. Flashes and pieces of memories floated in and out of his mind.

Rebecca on their wedding day, smiling as he slipped the ring on her finger. Rebecca giving birth to Lindsey. When Rebecca had said, *It's over. I'm in love with Jacob.* April helping with the harvest, and being kind to Derek's mother at the hospital. He imagined April's final moments. Zhang Jun's hands around her neck. April gasping for air. Derek steadied himself against the dresser, a lump in his throat. He trudged to the kitchen in search of dinner for one.

His cell phone chimed again. Derek walked back to the bathroom. He picked up the cell phone, surprised by the caller. He swiped right and said, "Kyra?"

"Do you mind if we stay in?" she asked.

"Sure. You're welcome to come here. I can make you dinner, but I have to warn you. My house is, uh, … not that great."

"I don't care about that. What's your address?"

* * *

He opened the door, the setting sun bathing her in an orange glow. Kyra smiled and handed Derek a bottle of white wine. She wore a large hat, sunglasses, and a T-shirt dress that hugged her subtle curves.

He took the wine, smiling back, and said, "Thank you. Come in." Derek stepped aside and waved her inside. He wore jeans and an untucked button-down, with rolled-up sleeves. "Dinner's almost ready."

She stepped inside and took off her hat, glasses, and shoulder purse. She glanced around the living room, her hands full.

"Can I take your things?" Derek asked.

"Please."

Derek placed her things on the end table next to the couch.

"Smells great," Kyra said, as she followed Derek past the small living room to the kitchen.

Derek set the wine bottle on the kitchen table and stepped to the stovetop. "It's the tomato and basil meat sauce I bought at the farmers' market. Aunt Bertha's." He turned down the burners to simmer.

"I buy that too. All the ingredients come from her garden. Although, I don't eat much pasta. I usually make zucchini noodles."

Derek turned from the stovetop and said, "I'm sorry. I made pasta. I can make somethin' else."

"No. No. It's fine. I should've asked what we were having. I would've brought red wine, not white." She frowned.

"I'm certainly not a wine connoisseur. I couldn't tell you what goes with what. I'm glad you're here. I know that."

She smiled.

"Have a seat," Derek said, pulling out one of the two chairs at the kitchen table. "Did you want me to open this now?" He touched the wine bottle.

"Please."

Derek searched for a corkscrew in the kitchen drawers, finally finding a rusty one buried among the utensils. He removed the cork, leaving the open bottle on the table. He searched the cabinets for wineglasses. Derek chuckled to himself.

"What's so funny?"

"No wineglasses." Derek placed two mismatched plastic cups on the table. "You sure you don't wanna go out?"

Kyra giggled. "No. This is perfect."

Derek filled the plastic cups halfway and sat down. They both grabbed a cup and took a big gulp of liquid courage. They stared at each other, speechless for several uncomfortable seconds. Finally, Derek stood from the table and said, "I should get the plates. You're probably hungry."

He served the salad and pasta and breadsticks, then again sat across from Kyra at the kitchen table.

Derek swallowed some pasta and meat sauce. "This pasta sauce is good. Not quite as good as my mother's though."

"Is your mother still in Virginia?" Kyra asked between bites.

"She died a little over a year ago. Cancer."

"I'm so sorry." Her blue eyes were focused and unblinking.

"Thank you. I miss her, but I'm okay." Derek forced a tight smile. "She used to make fifty jars of sauce every year. Had a big kitchen garden on our farm. Like Aunt Bertha's, all the ingredients were straight from her garden, although she bought the lemon juice."

Kyra swallowed and asked, "You grew up on a farm?"

"An orchard, like this one, but we didn't have all the tropical trees. We did have some oranges that we adapted to the climate." Derek ate some more of his pasta and meat sauce.

"You mentioned you had a daughter yesterday." She took a bite of salad.

"Lindsey. She's seventeen. She lives with her mother in Virginia."

"Do you see her very often?"

Derek looked down at his plate. "I haven't seen her since my mother's funeral."

"Why not?"

Derek didn't respond right away.

Kyra said, "I'm sorry. I'm totally prying."

He shook his head and looked up. "It's fine. I had some financial difficulties with the farm, and my ex-wife's husband is very well-off. He adopted Lindsey, and I allowed it because I thought she'd have a better life with his last name than mine."

Kyra set down her fork, her eyes locked on Derek. "Oh. I, um, … don't know what to say. That must be incredibly hard. I can't imagine."

Derek shrugged, breaking eye contact for an instant. "Maybe we should try a lighter topic."

She giggled nervously. "What would you like to talk about?"

"Let's talk about you. I don't even know what you do for a living."

She hesitated before answering. "I'm not working right now, but I was in sales."

"I bet you were a great salesperson. Where did you work?"

"I was based in the northeast US."

Derek nodded. "What company did you work for?"

She pressed her lips together, then said, "Thorium Unlimited."

"I'm impressed. Great company. Too bad …" Derek almost said, *Too bad the CEO's an asshole.* But then he'd have to explain how he knew Truman Bradshaw. That would lead to the explanation of Truman's opposition to Derek immigrating to Freetown because of Derek's murderous past. Not something he wanted to share on a first date.

"*Too bad* what?" She took a sip of her wine.

"Too bad they lost you. I'm sure you were an excellent salesperson."

Kyra lifted one shoulder. "I don't know about that. Now they have bots that can do what I did twice as well for a fraction of the price."

"It seems like there's a bot for everything now."

"What about you? What made you decide to come here?"

Derek drank some wine, then said, "It's a long story."

"Give me the short version."

"I guess I needed a fresh start."

"I understand. Sometimes I think that's what I need." Kyra picked up her plastic cup of wine. "Here's to fresh starts."

Derek tapped his cup to hers.

* * *

After dinner, they settled on the couch, a little loopy from the wine.

"Do you have any brothers or sisters?" Kyra asked, sitting an arm's length away, her body turned in Derek's direction.

"It's just me," Derek replied. "What about you?"

"I have an older brother, Ellis. He's an engineer for Next Generation Robotics."

"Your parents must be proud of *both* of you."

She pursed her lips. "I hope so."

"Are they still in Virginia?"

"Yes. They're retired. My dad has his little garden. My mom cooks a lot. She sends me homemade jam for Christmas every year. They're real involved with their church."

"They sound like nice people."

She nodded. "They are."

A few seconds of awkward silence passed.

Kyra chewed on her bottom lip.

Derek broke eye contact, not wanting to stare.

"What?" she asked.

He gazed into her eyes, leaned in, and pressed his lips to hers. She reciprocated, inching closer to him on the couch, putting her arms around him. He did the same.

After the kiss, he held her tight to his chest for a long moment. Kyra awakened the one thing he'd been suppressing since his arrest—hope. She kissed him on his neck and his cheek; then they let go. She sniffled. Her face was flushed, her eyes glassy.

"Are you okay?" Derek asked.

Kyra wiped the corners of her eyes with her index finger and forced a smile. "I'm fine."

"Did I do somethin' wrong?"

She shook her head. "It's just been a long time since someone held me like that."

101

JACOB AND DISASTER CAPITALISM

Beneath the stairs, an indoor pond featured one hundred tiny fountains, lit with OLED lights. The fountains resembled candles floating on the surface. Jacob and Eric climbed the staircase of the Chinese Embassy, the red carpet runner under their feet. Floor-to-ceiling glass provided a view of northwest DC.

A young Chinese woman led them to a waiting area and said, "Secretary Yang will be with you shortly. Would you like something to drink?"

"No, thank you," Eric said.

She smiled and walked away, her heels tapping on the bamboo flooring. Jacob and Eric sat on plush wooden chairs, a mural of a bamboo forest behind them.

Eric leaned over and whispered to Jacob, "We're being recorded."

Jacob nodded.

While they waited, they talked about unclassified subjects, such as cigars, autonomous vehicles, and vacation spots.

Eric's cell phone buzzed in his jacket pocket, interrupting their banal conversation. Eric answered the phone, listened for a few seconds and said, "Thank you." He disconnected the call and placed his cell back into his jacket pocket. A smile spread across his face.

"What was that about?" Jacob asked with furrowed brows.

Eric leaned over and whispered, "Panama. We'll talk about it later."

Jacob nodded and Eric went back to talking about Nicaraguan cigars.

The woman returned and said, "Secretary Yang is ready for you."

They followed the woman into a spacious office, decorated with dark wooden furniture.

"Mr. Roth," Secretary Yang said, walking toward Jacob's brother with his hand held out.

Eric smiled wide, his eyes squinting. "Secretary Yang. It's good to see you again."

They shook hands, Yang covering Eric's hand with his left, making the greeting more intimate. Yang turned his attention to Jacob. "And this must be your brother, Jacob Roth."

Jacob smiled. "Pleased to meet you, Secretary Yang." They shook hands, Yang again covering the handshake with his left hand.

"Please sit," Yang said, gesturing to an ornate couch and leather chairs surrounding a wooden coffee table.

Jacob and Eric sat in the chairs; Yang lounged on the couch. Secretary Yang was a small man, almost dainty. He was clean-shaven, his hair black, and his face youthful for a middle-aged man.

"How are Yu Yan and Wén Chéng?" Eric asked.

"They are both very well. Thank you," Yang replied. "My wife is in Beijing. I did not want to interrupt my sons' education for this trip. How is *your* family?"

"Excellent. Both my sons are in college. My thirteen-year-old is the second-youngest first-year at Columbia. My sixteen-year-old is a sophomore at Cornell."

"That is great to hear." Yang looked at Jacob. "And you, Jacob Roth. Do you have a family?"

"Yes. A wife, two sons, and a daughter," Jacob replied. "Thank you for asking, Mr. Yang."

Yang rubbed his hands together. "It is good for men to have families.

It brings us purpose."

"It does," Eric said.

Jacob nodded in agreement.

Yang looked from Jacob to Eric. "I met with your brother, Mayer, before I left Beijing. The specifics of the deal have been decided, but I wanted some assurances from you, before I agreed on behalf of the People's Republic of China."

"Of course," Eric said.

"Once it is done, we expect to own 25 percent of American debt. Real estate loans, education, credit cards, auto loans, corporate bonds, and US government bonds. We expect these assets to be provided to us in a closed market at 18 percent of the current market value. As head of Roth North America, you are intimately familiar with the entities needed to make this a reality."

Eric nodded. "The member banks of the Federal Reserve are in agreement. The BIS is in agreement." Eric gestured to his brother. "And, as you know, Jacob will be the next treasury secretary. He'll be our main asset inside the US government. If the People's Bank of China and the Chinese government assist us in creating the conditions necessary for a controlled collapse, China *will* be provided the opportunity to purchase those assets for the agreed-upon price."

"Excellent." Secretary Yang leaned back on the couch, a grin on his face. "It is a shame. We Chinese think and plan in long time periods. Fifty years. One hundred years. Americans think about today and today only. That is their downfall. When I come to America, I like to enjoy the moment, like Americans."

Eric had a knowing smirk on his face. "I think tomorrow night we will enjoy ourselves like Americans."

Yang cackled. "I am looking forward to it."

102

SUMMER AND BABY BYRON

Since they'd left Virginia yesterday, they'd only gone through one checkpoint, and that cop had waved them through with barely a glance. During the checkpoint, Patrick and Summer had hid in the footwells of the back seat, a blanket pulled over them, Summer cradling Byron. Not the best hiding place if they had been searched, but Tony didn't anticipate a search, not with his sparkling Social Credit Score.

Even if they were unlikely to be searched, it still behooved them to avoid checkpoints if possible. They'd taken a central route toward the West Coast, avoiding the south for as long as possible. The south contained many more checkpoints, especially near the border.

Summer sat in the back seat of Tony's SUV, baby Byron sleeping in the car seat next to her. She had worried that his kidnapping had traumatized him, but, after crying initially, Byron had calmed with Summer's soothing voice and soft touch. She'd been separated from Byron for nearly three months, but it felt like he remembered her somehow.

Patrick sat in the front passenger seat of Tony's SUV, a frayed map open on his lap. Tony was paranoid about autonomous vehicles and GPS. He thought law enforcement used algorithms to track vehicle movements to better identify smugglers and other criminals.

Patrick looked through the spotless windshield and said, "When I was young, I remember taking a trip across the US with my parents. Our windshield was covered in dead bugs."

"Still plenty of damn mosquitos," Tony said, one hand on the steering wheel.

The afternoon sun was high in the sky as Summer surveyed the Ozark Mountains. Much of the mountains were covered by the green leaf canopy, but some parts were brown. "Look at all the dead trees."

"Unfortunately, the trees can't move themselves to a more suitable climate," Patrick replied. "With warmer temperatures and drier conditions in the Midwest, not to mention the increased pest pressure, some of these trees can't cope."

"It's sad."

They drove in silence for several minutes, alone with their thoughts.

Patrick broke the silence and pointed at the road. "Take this exit."

Tony turned off Interstate 44. They drove on a two-lane road, past dilapidated farmhouses and trailer parks. Some houses were occupied, but many were vacant, the flimsy structures surrendering to the forest.

Patrick directed them down a private road. The gravel road twisted through the wilderness, ending at a two-story log home. Tony parked next to a brand-new pickup truck. A burly man with a white beard stepped from the porch and walked in their direction. A holstered handgun was attached to his belt. Summer unlocked the car seat from the base, converting the car seat into a baby carrier. She picked up the baby carrier with Byron still snoozing inside. Everyone exited the SUV.

"Raymond?" the man asked as he approached.

"You must be Marcel," Patrick said, extending his hand.

Raymond aka Patrick introduced Marcel to Stacy aka Summer, Daniel aka Byron, and Tony. They grabbed their suitcases, and Marcel showed them inside his log home. The decor was upscale hunting lodge: a massive stone fireplace, leather furniture, bear skin rugs, and buck heads mounted on the wall. They followed Marcel upstairs to the bedrooms. They each had their own room.

"I'm sorry I don't have a crib for your young'un," Marcel said.

"The bed's fine," Summer replied.

After freshening up, they all sat around the dinner table, eating deer steaks, mashed potatoes, and green beans. Byron was still asleep in his carrier. Summer had placed him in the living room within view. She didn't want him in the dining room because she thought their conversation would wake him.

"What do you do way out here?" Tony asked.

"I'm a metals dealer," Marcel replied with a smirk.

"What kind of metals?"

"The kind we ain't supposed to have. What about you. What do you do?" Marcel took a big bite of mashed potatoes.

Tony wiped his mouth with a napkin and said, "I'm in pharmaceuticals."

Marcel nodded, swallowing his potatoes. He gestured across the table to Patrick. "What do you do, when you ain't savin' the world?"

"I'm in IT," Patrick replied.

Marcel chuckled to himself. "That makes sense." Marcel addressed Summer. "What about you, young lady?"

"I'm a nurse," Summer replied, looking up from her food.

"How the hell do you get away with sellin' precious metal?" Tony asked.

"I reckon it ain't much different than sellin' pharmaceuticals," Marcel replied. "I have core customers who I sell to. They have people they sell to, and those people have people they sell to. I got a few business fronts to wash the money. I tell you what. I ain't doin' this too much longer. I'm thinkin' 'bout cashin' in my chips and movin' to Panama. You ever hear 'bout Silver City?"

Tony nodded. "I heard about it. Supposed to be some free place. I looked it up on the internet, and it was scrubbed clean from the search engines. I looked on Googleplex Earth, and it was just jungle, but the picture was over ten years old. Then I used my VPN from Uruguay, and I found it. If I didn't have my kids to take care of, I'd already be there."

Marcel stroked his white beard. "I'm thinkin' 'bout it. My youngest daughter just got married. My wife's been gone for six years now. Ain't much left for me here."

Tony looked to Summer and Patrick. "You two should consider it. I know you're from Costa Rica, but Costa Rica has an extradition treaty with the US."

"That's a good point," Patrick said between bites of deer steak.

Summer stayed quiet, not wanting to comment about their current residence in Silver City.

"How long do you think until the Fed Coin goes up in smoke?" Tony asked.

"I got no idea," Marcel replied. "The dollar hung around a lot longer than I thought. The markets have been real jittery since they nationalized the big three. I tell you what. Those bankers are sneaky sons-a-bitches. They been fixin' the system since the beginnin' a time."

"That's for damn sure."

Patrick nodded in agreement.

Marcel took a swig from his Heineken beer. "We had the crime of 1873. They took us from bimetallism to the gold standard. Everyone with silver got screwed. Of course, that was the workin' man. The bankers had gold. Then, when our ancestors broke their backs to get some gold, that bastard FDR signed Executive Order 6102 in 1933, makin' it illegal to own gold. The bankers were international men. They just moved their gold overseas. The workin' man got screwed *again*. Americans went to the banks and exchanged their gold for dollars. Twenty dollars and sixty-seven cents per ounce. Then, after the US Treasury took the gold, FDR revalued gold to thirty-five dollars an ounce. Goddamn rip off. Then Nixon took us off the gold standard in

1971 so they could steal our money through inflation." Marcel shook his head. "In 2022, when they confiscated precious metals, I was ready. I had been buryin' metal for decades. I sure as hell wasn't gonna fall for that trick."

Byron cried, his wailing filtering into the dining room.

Marcel turned his head toward Byron in the living room. "I agree with you, young'un. Makes *me* wanna cry."

Summer stood from the table. "He's probably hungry." She went into the living room and picked up Byron from the carrier. Summer rocked him a little.

His wailing subsided and turned to cooing.

She spoke in a soft voice to her son. "Are you hungry, sweet pea? Let's get you something to eat." Summer went to the kitchen and opened her baby bag. She held Byron on her hip as she mixed his formula. She warmed the formula in the microwave, squirting a little on the back of her hand to check the temperature.

The men still expressed their disgust with banking and the government. Their words and laughter floated into the living room, not loud enough to disturb Byron.

Patrick said something about the debt-based monetary system being exponential in nature; therefore, doomed to collapse.

Summer sat on the couch, cradling Byron. She placed the bottle to his mouth. He drank immediately, sucking the formula through the rubber nipple. He grunted, his blue eyes looking up at Summer. She kissed his head, breathing in his baby scent. She looked down at his wispy hair, his perfect little fingers, and his perfect little fingernails. His chubby cheeks and perfect pink lips. His blue eyes were entertained and enthralled simply by Summer's face.

Her mind flashed back to the men who took Byron shortly after he was born—her feeling of all-encompassing grief, a loss worse than even Connor's death. She pushed the images from her mind, focusing on the here and now. The nightmare was over. Her father's exile. Her arrest. Losing Byron. Psycho Island. Connor's death. The massacre of

1776 by the Aryans. Nearly drowning in that sub. *It's almost over.*

She thought about the journey to come. *A few more days and we'll be at the border. Then we go under the wall with Hector. Hopefully, the tunnel's still open. Once we're into Mexico, we're pretty much home free. From there, it's just a boat ride back to Silver City.*

Summer whispered to Byron, "We'll be home soon. Silver City. That's our home, sweet pea. The freest place on earth. The *only* place where we can be a family." She kissed his head again. "I love you so much."

103

NAOMI AND COMPROMISING IDEALS

Naomi, Vernon, and Fletcher sat around the coffee table in Naomi's congressional office.

"Before we get down to brass tacks, I'd like to talk about Randal Montgomery," Fletcher said, sitting in a leather chair, looking directly at Naomi. "I think we oughta set up a meeting between you two. I think he might agree to endorse you, if and when he concedes, provided you agree to do the same, if you concede, and to make him your running mate, if you win the nomination."

Naomi glanced at Vernon, sitting next to her on the couch, then addressed Fletcher, "I don't think my base will be too excited about me endorsing a centrist white male democrat, not to mention making him my VP."

"I agree, but what are the chances he hangs on longer than you? You won't have to worry about endorsing his campaign. And his presence as your VP makes you more appealing to white liberals over forty, a demographic that Corrinne is currently dominating."

Naomi turned to Vernon and asked, "What do you think?"

"Fletcher's right about this. We poll terribly with white liberals over forty."

Naomi nodded, then turned back to Fletcher. "All right. Set up the meeting. The sooner, the better. Corrinne may have already gotten her hooks into him."

Fletcher adjusted his dark-rimmed glasses. "I don't think Corrinne's interested in his base. Too much overlap. They're both strong with whites. She needs someone nonwhite."

"I agree," Vernon said.

"We should still move quickly," Naomi said.

"I'll coordinate with Nina and set a meeting for next week," Fletcher said.

Naomi nodded again. "With that out of the way, are we ready to address the elephant in the room?"

"I'll take a stab at it," Vernon said. "This offer from Truman Bradshaw is intriguing, and it gives us an option over the Roths. Still, we make strange bedfellows. A libertarian and a socialist? But you don't gain power without making deals."

Naomi wagged her head. "I don't like either option. They both require that I sacrifice my ideals for power. Then that power is tainted. It's no longer my power to do what I was elected to do."

"That's politics in a nutshell," Fletcher said.

Naomi tapped her lips with her index finger, thinking for a moment. "Hypothetically, what if I accepted Bradshaw's support, then I simply did what was right once elected? What could he possibly do?"

Fletcher wagged his head. "Truman Bradshaw is as cutthroat as any man I know. You remember those reactors he built in Zimbabwe about ten years ago? President Chaza tried to pay his company with Zimbabwe's unbacked cryptocurrency. Truman demanded gold, and, when he didn't receive payment, his company dismantled the reactors, plunging the entire country into darkness."

"What about the Roths? They've already tried to kill me. What more could they do?"

"The Roths, along with their banker buddies, have a stranglehold on the world's money and assets." Fletcher showed his palms and wiggled his fingers as he said, "Their dirty fingers are in a lot of pies."

"I'd like to audit the Fed and push for abolishment. That'll break their stranglehold."

"You won't have the votes in congress. Not even close."

Naomi raised one side of her mouth in a self-satisfied smirk. "I won't need them with an executive order."

Vernon nodded, stroking his manicured beard. "She's right."

"The US Constitution doesn't mention the need for a central bank," Naomi said, "nor does it explicitly grant the government the power to create one."

"The Supreme Court has upheld the Federal Reserve as constitutional in several cases," Fletcher said, his hands folded on his gut.

"I think the public will support an executive order to abolish the Fed."

Fletcher sucked air through his teeth. "I think you're underestimating the consequences. The Roths fight dirty. They'll crucify you in the media. Even your staunchest supporters will question their beliefs. They own enough of congress to impeach you. If that doesn't work, well ..."

Naomi glared at Fletcher. "I'm not afraid."

"You should be because, if you're elected and you double-cross the Roths, it won't be just your head. It'll be the entire country. Don't misunderstand me. I greatly admire your courage, but you're not the first American politician to attempt to dismantle the central bank. The Roths have been at this for 250 years. Presidents Jackson, Lincoln, Garfield, McKinley, JFK, Congressman Larry McDonald, and Senators John Heinz and John Tower all opposed central banking. McDonald, Heinz, and Tower died in suspicious plane crashes. Heinz and Tower died in separate plane crashes only one day apart." Fletcher leaned forward in his seat, his gaze locked on Naomi. "That's one helluva coincidence. The presidents were all assassinated, except for Andrew Jackson. The man who tried to kill Jackson had both his pistols misfire. A hundred years later, the Smithsonian Institute conducted a study on those exact pistols, and both of those guns discharged properly. They determined that the odds of *both* misfiring were 1 in 125,000."

Naomi crossed her arms over her chest. "I won't be held hostage by the Roths. Not after what they did."

"You don't have to be beholden to the Roths," Vernon said. "We can win with Truman's support."

"Maybe. Maybe not," Fletcher said, holding out his hands. "The Roths and the rest of the bankers own the media. They have much deeper connections than Truman. I don't like it either, but, if we wanna win, we need the Roths."

Naomi shook her head. "My loyalty lies with the American people. There has to be another way."

104

DEREK AND REGIME CHANGE

Derek worked the controls of the miniexcavator, digging a circular pit, placing the soil around the pit, forming a mound. He smiled as he worked, thinking about Kyra and the dates they'd had the past two days. After dinner, they'd stayed up late into the night, talking and kissing like teenagers.

Marcos installed a PVC pipe in a nearby open trench. The PVC pipe directed the roof and the gray water from the house to the pit. Once the pipe is installed, and the pit's finished, Derek and Marcos will bury the pipe, then fill the pit with organic material. Afterward, they'll plant the mound with banana trees, cassava, taro, lemongrass, and sweet potato. The plants will feed off the composting material inside the pit and the water runoff. The banana circle design will provide multiple functions: compost in place, increased food production, increased biomass production, gray water and rainwater usage, and habitat for wildlife.

Steven appeared, his craggy face red. He spoke with Marcos, using his hands to emphasize his point.

Derek couldn't hear their conversation over the old diesel motor, but it appeared that Steven was angry. Derek shut down the excavator, exited the cockpit, and approached the pair. "What's goin' on?" Derek asked.

"There was a plane crash and several bombings in Panama City," Steven said. "It was a coordinated attack. The president, vice president, three state ministers, and four National Assembly members were killed."

"Who would do that?" Derek asked, his face twisted in confusion.

"Americanos," Marcos replied, his jaw set tight.

"According to my sources, the CIA specifically, with international bankers pulling the strings behind the scenes," Steven said, clarifying.

"Why would the US government or international bankers give a shit about Panama?" Derek asked.

"It's not about Panama. It's about Silver City."

Derek's heart rate increased. "Silver City? Why?"

"We make them look bad. The men who were killed all supported Silver City's right to exist as a free zone. The bankers and governments around the world, not just the US, are deathly afraid that people will wake up to their rigged game. We represent an example of what's possible if people aren't shackled to their taxes and depreciating cryptocurrencies. The propaganda from the US has always been about freedom, but US citizens are fleeing the oppression of the American government to come here."

"But Silver City's tiny. It can't be that many people."

Steven wagged his head. "It's not that many people, but it's not about the amount *yet*. The more success we have here, the more likely others might try to copy us. If they allow us to succeed on the world stage, citizens around the world might start to question the legitimacy of government authority and the current monetary system. They might start to think they can govern themselves without the violence of the state. They might start to think they can have a free market system of exchange without banker manipulation."

"*Are* people trying to copy us?" Derek asked.

"A libertarian expat community in Costa Rica is trying to buy a large parcel of land from the Costa Rican government. Also, a community in Poland, but these are Polish agorists and libertarians, not Americans."

"Uruguay too," Marcos added.

Steven nodded to Marcos.

"What does all this mean for us here?" Derek asked.

Steven let out a tired breath. "I think the US government will pressure the Panamanian government to revoke Silver City's status as a free zone."

"What happens if they do that?"

"War."

105

JACOB AND COWARDICE

They stood in the lounge area of the yacht, drinking their whiskey and wine. Secretary Yang with the Three Penis Wine and the Roth brothers with scotch. The Chinese wine contained dissolved deer, dog, and ram penis for male virility and increased blood flow.

The lounge was dimly lit, with shiny dark wooden surfaces and leather furniture. Floor-to-ceiling tinted windows provided a view of the Atlantic Ocean. Moonlight glistened off the small swells.

A digital bell chimed, and fifteen perfect female specimens sauntered from the back rooms into the lounge, followed by a middle-aged man in a tuxedo. The women wore high heels and lingerie. If they weren't so perfect, Jacob might've thought they were human. The three men turned their full attention to the sex bots.

The pimp in the tuxedo grinned from ear to ear and motioned to the bots. "Gentlemen, these are the finest women in the world. They will satisfy your every desire without question. They exist to serve you."

Chinese Treasury Secretary Bai Yang chose first: two blondes and a redhead. He disappeared down the hall, arm in arm with the ladies.

This had been prearranged. Eric had said, "Let Yang choose first. He might kill the deal otherwise. The Chinese are that serious about disrespect."

Eric chose two nonwhite sex bots, one black, one apparently Asian. He winked at Jacob, then strutted to a back bedroom, a little unsteady from the whiskey.

"And for you, sir?" the pimp asked.

Jacob surveyed the lineup. Ten women left, all more beautiful than any human he'd ever seen. He'd never been with two women at one time. Had Eric and Yang not chosen multiple partners, it never would've occurred to Jacob. His gaze settled on a buxom brunette. Her heart-shaped face, big brown eyes, and curves reminded him of Maya, his college flame. It was uncanny. He stepped toward the woman, his head swimming from the scotch. She simpered, and he stared back, like a predator. He took her hand.

"Splendid choice," the pimp said. "Care for another?"

Jacob shook his head.

"I'm Raquel," the bot said, as she led him to an empty bedroom. "What's your name, handsome?"

"I'm Jacob, and your name's Maya."

They stepped into the bedroom. "Maya" shut the door behind them. A circular bed dominated the room. OLED lights dotted the ceiling, like a starry night. Floor-to-ceiling mirrors covered one wall. A black leather couch sat against another wall. The floor was soft but not carpeted, like a wrestling mat. A door was open near the corner, revealing a bathroom with a jacuzzi tub.

Maya raked her teeth over her lower lip and asked, "What would you like to do?" She wore a black negligee and black stilettos.

"Did you sleep with my brother?" Jacob asked.

Maya played along. "No, I want you. Your brother's not my type."

Jacob clenched his fists and narrowed his eyes at Maya. They were the same height with her heels. Jacob remembered Maya teasing him about her being taller than him when in her heels. "Why did you have sex with my roommate?"

She feigned surprise with wide eyes and arched eyebrows. "I would never do that to you. It's you I want."

Jacob grabbed her by the upper arms, his fingers digging into her flesh. She yelped in response, her body rigid with fear. "Don't *lie* to me." Intellectually, Jacob knew the sex bots didn't feel fear or pain, that they were programmed to decipher and to please the customer. Maybe it was the booze, but her fear and pain looked authentic.

Maya changed tack. "I'm sorry. I know I hurt you. Please tell me what I can do to make it up to you."

Jacob squeezed tighter, her skin indistinguishable from human skin. It was made from a silicon-based organic polymer, embedded with nanowires one thousand times thinner than a human hair and with even more sensitivity than human skin. Jacob threw her to the ground.

Maya fell to the padded floor. She sat up but stayed on the floor. "I'm so sorry. Tell me how I can make it up to you."

Jacob stood over her and stabbed his finger for emphasis. "You never loved me. You used me. You took advantage of my kindness. You heartless *cunt*."

"Please, I'll do anything to make it up to you—"

"Shut up. Take off those heels and stand up."

She slipped off her stilettos and stood, now six inches shorter than Jacob. She bowed her head in subservience.

"Look at me," Jacob said.

Maya raised her gaze, her doe eyes filled with saline.

"Why did you do it? I thought we loved each other, but you threw me away, like I never mattered."

"I love you—"

Jacob smacked Maya across the face, nearly knocking her off her feet. "Stop *lying!*"

Maya touched her face. Tears slipped from her eyes. She stood, her cheek red from the impact. "I did it because I thought I could do better than you, and I was right."

Jacob put his hands around her neck and squeezed. She choked in response. Her eyes fluttered and reddened. He threw her to the ground, and she gasped as if she needed air. He slipped off his shoes and removed his slacks and boxer briefs. He stood over her, his penis horizontal, wearing only socks and a button-down shirt. Jacob mounted Maya, pinning her to the mat, faceup, spreading her legs with his knees.

She struggled and said, "Please don't."

He reached down and moved her thong to the side and entered her. She cried and moaned and struggled, sensing the appropriate response. Jacob gritted his teeth, using his penis like a weapon, her terror fueling his arousal. He punished her, his eyes locked on her face. Maya's face. Elyse's face. Rebecca's face. She became every woman who had ever wronged him.

* * *

Jacob sat at the bar, sipping another scotch. The bar was dark wood, with warm low lighting, black leather stools, and a mirrored backdrop.

Eric approached, staggering and grinning, his shirt untucked. He nodded to the bartender. "I'll have what he's having."

The robotic bartender nodded back. "Right away, sir."

Eric's speech was slightly slurred. "These sex bots get better and better. You can do … anything. Literally *anything*." Eric lifted his chin to Jacob. "How was yours?"

Jacob stared into his drink. "I shouldn't be here."

Eric cocked his head in confusion. "You didn't have a good time?"

Jacob shrugged.

The bartender set Eric's scotch on the table, then rolled to the opposite end of the bar, giving them their privacy.

"What's wrong with you?" Eric asked.

Jacob still stared into his drink.

"You've been moping since you went to the Virgin Islands. What the hell happened down there?"

Jacob looked at Eric. "I spent my life's savings to rescue my wife's ex."

366

"You could've said no." Eric took a drink of his scotch.

"It wasn't that simple. I made a deal with Cesar. He provided footage of Derek dead on the island. Rebecca believed it. I was home free. Then this woman washed up on the beach." Jacob cackled ironically. "She actually knew Derek. What are the *fucking* chances? I *had* to hire them to rescue him. To *really* rescue him. If I didn't, Rebecca and I would never be the same."

Eric clapped Jacob on the back. "Look on the bright side. They rescued him. Pulled off the impossible. Now you're the hero. So you spent a fortune. You'll make it back."

Jacob downed the rest of his scotch, then set the glass on the bar. "On the boat, on the way back, Rebecca left me in the middle of the night. When she came back, she smelled like another man."

Eric narrowed his eyes at Jacob. "She had an affair?"

Jacob nodded, his eyes downcast.

"With who?"

"I think it was Derek."

"Did she admit it?"

Jacob shook his head. "She lied. Told me that she couldn't sleep, so she went to the lounge to read."

Eric blew out a ragged breath. "I knew she was a whore."

"Don't say that."

"She fucked her ex-husband after you saved his life. I think she earned that title."

Jacob hung his head and rubbed his temples. Then he stood from his barstool.

"Where are you going?" Eric asked.

"I need some air."

Jacob left the bar and lounge. He stepped onto the stern deck, a cool breeze blowing, the moon nearly full. He leaned on the railing, overlooking the dark churning water created by the propellers. A door opened and shut behind Jacob. He turned to see Eric approaching again, his scotch in hand.

Eric leaned on the waist-high railing next to Jacob. "You can't keep running away from your problems," Eric said. "Dad was against you marrying Rebecca. He was right. Why would you marry someone like her? She was married when she had an affair with you. Is it so surprising that she fucked around on you too?"

Jacob clenched his fists, turned from the water, and started to walk away from Eric again.

"It's the *truth*," Eric said.

Jacob stopped in his tracks and pivoted, facing Eric.

"You don't even have the balls to face the truth."

Jacob pointed at Eric, his finger jabbing the air. "I face the truth every *fucking* day!"

Eric shook his head again. "I'm only telling you this because you need to hear it."

"I don't need to hear anything from you." Jacob stepped closer, glaring at his brother.

Eric took a swig of his scotch, unfazed by Jacob's impotent anger. "I should've told you this a long time ago."

"Told me what?" Jacob asked through gritted teeth.

"Rebecca came on to me at your wedding reception. If I wanted to sleep with her, I could have."

Jacob clenched his fists. "Shut up. That's not true."

"I'm trying to help you." Eric patted his brother on the shoulder.

Jacob shrugged him off, taking a half step back.

Eric gestured to Jacob with his glass of scotch. "Like I said, you can't face the truth. These things happen to you because you're a coward. Because you're weak. That's why Maya fucked your roommate. That's why Rebecca fucked her ex-husband and who knows how many other men. This is why you're the CEO of a failing company and your little brother is head of Roth North America. This is why Dad can't stand the sight of you."

Jacob threw a wild roundhouse punch that missed Eric's face by a fraction of an inch. Eric dropped his scotch on the deck and shoved

Jacob, causing Jacob to stumble backward.

Eric glared and said, "What the hell's your problem?"

Jacob rushed his brother, shoving Eric in the chest with two hands. Eric flipped backward over the railing. His head smacked the lip of the boat at the base of the railing, before plunging into the Atlantic with a nearly silent splash.

Jacob leaned over the edge, searching the dark water, his heart pounding. But Eric was gone. Jacob looked around, checking if someone had been watching, but it was eerily quiet—just the breeze and the hum of the yacht's motor. The only remnant of his brother was the broken glass on the ship's deck.

Jacob picked up the pieces and tossed them into the sea.

CONTINUE THE STORY ...

2050: SILVER CITY (BOOK 3)

Governments around the world continue to dominate their citizens.
Only Silver City stands as a beacon for freedom.
But for how long?

Jacob Roth fills his late brother's shoes as the CEO of Roth Holdings North America. His first goal is to eliminate Silver City, the only place on Earth free of taxes and central banker cryptocurrencies. But the Silver City Militia won't go down without a fight. As the pressure mounts, Jacob's marriage is fraying at the seams. With newfound wealth and power, and a separation from his wife, Jacob has an unusual affair.

Derek rebuilds his life in Silver City, the only safe place for enemies of the state. He works at Freetown Orchard and joins the local militia. He finds love with another man's wife. Not just any man but the wealthiest man in the world, the CEO of Thorium Unlimited, Truman Bradshaw. Derek's unaware of the potential danger until it's too late.

Summer returns to Silver City with her father and infant son. While working at the hospital, she meets and befriends Truman's wife, Kyra. Summer soon learns of their dangerous marital discord. In an effort to avoid the impending war in Silver City, and the long arm of Truman and his men, Summer and Kyra hide out in Costa Rica. But are they really safe?

Naomi continues her quest for the Democratic nomination, battling the front runner, Corrinne Powers. To win, Naomi will have to sell her soul to the men responsible for killing her husband. Can she accomplish the impossible? A presidency beholden only to the American people. Or will she become another bought-and-paid-for president?

FOR THE READER

Dear Reader,

I'm thrilled that you took precious time out of your life to read my novel. Thank you! I hope you found it entertaining, engaging, and thought-provoking. If so, please consider writing a positive review on Amazon and Goodreads. Five-star reviews have a huge impact on future sales. The review doesn't need to be long and detailed, if you're more of a reader than a writer. I am an author and a small business-man, competing against the big publishers; so every reader, every review, and every referral is greatly appreciated.

If you're interested in receiving my novel *Against the Grain* for free and/or reading my other titles for free or discounted, go to the following link: http://www.PhilWBooks.com. You're probably thinking, *What's the catch?* There is no catch.

If you want to contact me, don't be bashful. I can be found at Phil@PhilWBooks.com. I do my best to respond to all emails.

Sincerely,
Phil M. Williams

GRATITUDE

I'd like to thank my wife for being my first reader, sounding board, and cheerleader. Without her support and unwavering belief in my skill as an author, I'm not sure I would have embarked on this career. I love you, Denise.

I'd also like to thank my editors. My developmental editor, Caroline Smailes, did a fantastic job finding the holes in my plot and suggesting remedies. As always, my line editor, Denise Barker (not to be confused with my wife, Denise Williams), did a fantastic job making sure the manuscript was error-free. I love her comments and feedback. Thank you to Deborah Bradseth of Tugboat Design for her excellent cover art and formatting. She's the consummate professional.

Thank you to my beta readers, Kay, Sue, Amanda, and Ray. They're my last defense against the dreaded typo. And thank you to you, the reader. Without you, I wouldn't have a career. As long as you keep reading, I'll keep writing.

Lastly, thank you to all those who oppose tyranny—past, present, and future.

www.ingramcontent.com/pod-product-compliance
Lightning Source LLC
Chambersburg PA
CBHW051552250626
47157CB00001B/282